Mermaid Drowning

a novel by

Terry Jacobs and Tiffany Jacobs

Autumn Moon Books ~ Springfield

Copyright © 2013 Terry Jacobs and Tiffany Jacobs

This is a work of fiction. Names, characters, places, and incidents are products of the authors' imaginations or are used fictitiously. Any resemblance to actual events or locales or persons, living or dead, is entirely coincidental.

All rights reserved. Except as permitted under the U.S. Copyright Law, no part of this publication may be reproduced, distributed, or transmitted in any form or by any means, or stored in a database or retrieval system, without the prior written permission of the publisher or authors.

Published in the United States by Autumn Moon Books

Autumn Moon Books
P.O. Box 71254
Springfield, OR 97475-0191

First Printing, January 2013
10 9 8 7 6 5 4 3 2 1

ISBN-10: 0-988-64800-8
ISBN-13: 978-0-9886480-0-5

Library of Congress Control Number: 2012922946

Dedication

This book is dedicated to those who practice compassion, seek to understand, love unconditionally ... and chocolate.

Prologue
1986
Evelyn

The salty ocean water burned the long bloody scratches on my back as I pushed blindly for the horizon of the Pacific Ocean. In my sea, I was a nine-year-old mermaid in a magical world of possibilities and mystery. Here, I no longer had to fear my father's vicious words and hammering fists. I was safe.

My child's plan was simple: Find the grotto where the mermaids lived and be magically transformed into a real mermaid. In their home at the bottom of the sea, I would be safe and happy.

People said mermaids weren't real, but they had to be. They were my only hope.

As my strength abandoned me I stopped, sure that the South Pacific islands where the mermaids lived had to be near.

Thoughts of Mom still standing on the beach stole my hope for eternal happiness. I would never see her again. Pain welled up in me and I looked back hoping to see Mom but expecting only water. I stared wide-eyed. *But I had swum so long and so far. How could I not be across the ocean?*

Behind me stood Los Angeles wallowing in its stinging brown smog. *City of the Angels*, my teacher had called it, but I had found no angels there—only burning hate and burning eyes.

An ocean swell lifted me and for a brief moment I could see Mom watching from the soft white sand on the beach. She was the closest thing to an angel I had ever known. My heart cried for her. I couldn't get back.

Too tired to swim, my body became an anchor pulling me below the surface. I watched the world grow distant and dim above me. I looked down and saw nothing but sand and rock. No grotto. No mermaids.

I looked up. No Mom. I closed my eyes and struggled to hold back the tears my father forbade.

Something nudged me with the gentleness of a kiss so I opened my eyes. He didn't look like the pictures I had seen, but I instantly knew him. He didn't have a brilliant halo or feathery white wings. He did not even take the form of a man. He was long, a silky blue-gray, and spoke to me in clicking sounds.

I thought he would take me to my mermaid grotto, but through his clicks and whistles he said that I must go back. I would be with Mom again.

He then gently carried me to the surface and sped me to shore and the arms of my mother. People said I had been rescued by a dolphin, but Mom and I knew different. We had been blessed by an angel.

Chapter 1
Mermaid in the Deep
2009
Evelyn

My heart stumbled as the electrocardiogram's beep became a long plaintive whine ... then steadied as the beeping returned to its faltering cadence, once again keeping time with Mom's damaged heart. The taunting flatlines had filled our night. Death and angels drew close.

The doctors at UC San Francisco Medical Center had tried to be positive, but I could hear the doubt in their voices. The coronary blockage had done extensive damage to the left side of her heart. High levels of myoglobin from the dead tissue were already shutting down her kidneys. The doctors had done everything possible. We made her comfortable and prayed that she would heal.

I brushed a stray lock of hair from Mom's cheek. Lying in the hospital bed, she seemed so small and frail ... and somehow much older. Fifty-seven was young—too young for this.

Tears welled up in my eyes. She had left everything behind when we fled Los Angeles to hide in the shadow of the Golden Gate Bridge. In our new home, she had let my past become a secret. My rescues. My rebirth. My friends' deaths. All secrets. All carefully hidden away where no one could find them.

There had been so many changes since our move to Marin. The graduations, my marriage to Sam, births, and deaths. The one constant in my life had always been Mom. The idea that she could die was never a possibility in my mind. She was as much a part of me as my own hands. I needed her. She couldn't leave me. She wouldn't leave me.

Mom shifted and struggled to open her eyes. The warmth of her love comforted me. Even here and now, she was somehow my caretaker. She smiled up at me, her attempt to squeeze my hand little more than the caress of two hearts.

"I love you, and I am proud of you," she said in a whisper. "Be proud of your past, Eve. It is what made you the beautiful woman you are today. Embrace it. Sam loves you. He will stand by you."

"Hush, Mom. You need your rest—get back your strength."

I didn't want to be lectured. I wanted her to get well. She had to get well.

Our eyes lingered together as I denied what we both knew. The soft reverence in her voice drew me to her protective love. I bent close and kissed her forehead. Her eyes filled with sadness, and she struggled against weakness.

"'To live in hearts we leave behind is not to die,' my beloved daughter."

A chill ran icy and sharp through my body. She had used that quote at my brother and sister-in-law's memorial service.

"How can you expect your husband to be honest with you when you are not honest with him?" she asked.

"Shush, Mom. You need your rest." I kissed her forehead again.

Her smile wrapped me in love, and then her kind, infinite eyes closed for the last time.

My guardian, my pillar of strength, my wisdom—my mother—was gone.

I held my three children as they cried for their Grandma Louise. I helped with the funeral arrangements.

My husband, Sam, lived up to my admiration of him. Despite his aversion to a woman's tears, he had been perfect. He helped comfort our three children; he saw to the loose ends I missed while making arrangements; he knew when to hold me; and he knew when to step back and let me grieve in private.

After Mom's graveside service, we returned to our home and hosted a moving remembrance that celebrated Mom's life and our love for her. Long before the last guests had left, our son, Chris, and our two daughters, Angela and Grace, had retreated to their bedrooms to grieve in private.

My stepdad was the last to leave. I watched his normally confident strides falter with uncertainty. At his car, he fumbled with the keys, tried one that didn't work, wiped a tear from his cheek, found the right key, and got in.

Watching him, I mumbled, "We're alone now, Dad."

"I'm here," Sam said, pulling me close.

I had forgotten he was standing behind me. I looked up at him, wishing he could be there for me like Mom had been—but he didn't know me like she had.

She had shared my whole life and she knew all my secrets. She had accepted me when others condemned me. She had protected me. She understood me better than anyone else ever would. She had truly loved me unconditionally.

It was too late to share my secrets with Sam. Maybe Mom was right. Maybe he would stand by me. But I couldn't risk losing him, too.

I nodded and looked back to see Dad's car turn the corner and slip from sight.

On the Monday after the funeral, Sam returned to work, while the kids stayed home with me for a few more days. Even with Sam's care and the nearness of my children, Mom's death had ripped my soul from my body, leaving an anguished void that couldn't be filled.

By Thursday, Sam and the kids had returned to their normal routines. With them gone, I vacantly wandered the house looking at pictures of Mom and holding things that reminded me of her—a kitchen apron she had sewn, a blue ceramic mermaid she had given me, an unfinished needlepoint kitten she'd left at my house. Everywhere I looked, she had touched our lives.

On Friday morning, I hid in my bed beneath the quilted comforter Mom had made for me when I married.

"I miss you, Mom," I whispered.

I could hear Sam, my safe harbor, standing by the door. The comforting aroma of coffee was calling to me. It was time to buck up and get back to my life.

Determined to rejoin my family, I flopped the blankets and comforter onto Sam's side of the bed, rolled up into a sitting position, and stared at the floor. The carpet needed vacuuming and the pink polish on my toenails was chipped.

Fudge! I forgot my manicure appointment yesterday.

I had canceled my work appointments, or handed my clients off to another therapist, and taken two weeks off—though I felt like I would need a year.

"My sleepy mermaid is up," Sam said from the door with tender concern in every word.

His mermaid. My heart rose from an ocean of pain and beat with contentment. I loved that he had picked up that endearment from my mom. He said the name fit because of my obsessive love of mermaids and dolphins, although my fear of the water puzzled him.

"You'll be late," I said.

He shrugged and offered me my favorite cup—a heavy ceramic mug imprinted with a three-year-old picture of our kids.

"They'll wait," he said. "You up to taking the kids to school?"

I nodded, and his strong gentle hand caressed the hair from my face. We shared a quick kiss.

I saw Sam off to work and then went to the kitchen to get a slice of toast. I wasn't hungry but I needed to eat something.

My eight-year-old daughter, Grace, watched me, her eyes assessing the wisdom of approaching me with some as-yet-undisclosed plan.

"How you doing, sweetie?" I asked.

"Fine. Marla got a dog. Can I get a dog?"

"No, sweetie. Your dad is allergic to dogs. We're lucky to have a cat."

She pouted. "I close my window every morning," as if a dog would be an appropriate reward.

Her window had been a point of contention with us since she was old enough to open it. She said she couldn't breathe with it closed, but we were concerned about her safety. Sam put safety locks on it, but she learned to work them before I did. Eventually, Sam installed a window that opened enough to let air in but not enough to allow an adult to crawl through.

Now she closed her door and opened her window every night, no matter how cold the weather. In winter, we always closed it once she fell asleep, but half the time, chilly air was slipping under her door by morning.

I suspected her idiosyncrasy was related to the accident when she was two, but it was only a guess. I would probably never know for sure.

"Thank you, sweetie. That helps with the power bill, but we still can't get a dog."

My fourteen-year-old son, Christian, stormed into the kitchen.

"Mom! Angela's not ready, and I'm going to be late for first period again."

"Late for first period, or Kate … lyn?" Grace teased, in grade-school singsong.

"Shut up, twerp," Chris blurted.

"Chris," I snapped. "Don't call your sister names. And Grace, don't tease your brother." They scowled at each other. I knew they would settle it later, when Mom wasn't around.

Grandma Louise's death had hit them hard, too. Chris had become sullen and impatient. Angela was distant and argumentative—the unsettled hormones of puberty magnifying her mood swings by a factor of ten. And my baby Grace acted like nothing had happened, still teasing her brother with impish delight. I worried about her the most.

Though he still had a ways to go before reaching his dad's height, Chris now stood taller than his sisters and me, which delighted him immensely.

I started for Angela's room. "I'll hurry her along. If she's going to be too late, I'll take you and Grace and then come back for her. Alright?"

"We need to leave in five," he said curtly. Two weeks ago, I would have come down on him for being disrespectful, but I didn't have the energy to deal with him and Angela's mood swings at the moment. We'd talk later.

The lavender scent from Angela's candle greeted me in the hall. Angela and her grandmother had shared a love of scented candles, calligraphy, and poetry. Lavender was her blue-days candle, its scent chasing away troubles and infusing her room with tranquility.

Her face was buried in her pillow, muffling her tears. The zipper on her too-small burgundy-and-white Christmas dress was stuck at her waist. The dress had been a present from her Grandma Louise.

"You need to be getting ready for school, sweetheart."

A muffled and angry "I hate school" escaped the pillow.

I sat on the edge of the bed and rubbed her back.

"Are you having problems?"

She shook her head no, as her shoulders trembled.

"I miss Grandma," she said, her words flooded with grief.

"So do I, sweetheart." The room seemed dark and oppressive. I bit at my lower lip and struggled against tears. "Do you need to stay home?"

She tried to stifle her crying and nodded yes.

"It's alright to cry," I said, stroking her hair. "I've spent half my days crying, too."

She crawled into my lap and rested her head on my chest. At thirteen, she was nearly as tall as me—too big to hold like a child. But I held her and rocked her anyway. My tears dropped into her lavender-scented hair.

As punctual as his father, Chris appeared at the door four minutes later with backpack in hand.

When I returned home, Angela was dressed in holey blue jeans, a worn-out pink dolphin T-shirt she had inherited from me, and green tennis shoes with yellow socks. Her eyes were swollen and red and she looked worse than I felt—as if that were possible.

She suggested we go to the beach. It sounded like a wonderful idea to me.

Walking arm-in-arm along the still water of Heart's Desire Beach on Tomales Bay soothed my grief. This twelve-mile-long shallow estuary in the seaward end of a rift valley, under which lay the infamous San Andreas Fault, was my personal Garden of Eden. It was a magical area, bursting with aquatic life, forest animals, and a never-ending variety of birds that changed with the seasons.

We stopped and watched a mama and baby "reindeer" moving along the edge of the forest. Our reindeer are fallow deer, a non-native species. The males looked like the classical Santa's Reindeer, with their cute small size, distinctive scooped antlers, and Bambi spots. Because of their docile nature and the cute factor, they captivated both locals and tourists, with many considering them a treasure.

It saddened me that our reindeer were being exterminated as part of the National Park Service's non-native animals policy. This might be the last time we would see our reindeer here. For certain, my daughters would never share this moment with their children.

We watched the deer, and my heart warmed with the memory of how Mom and I had discovered this hidden natural paradise fifteen years earlier. I felt her standing with Angela and me, sharing this moment.

Peaceful as a sweet dream, the mama and baby slipped back into the forest, and the fog began to thin.

"Mom?" Angela said. "Why did Grandma have to die?"

The pain welled up inside my heart, causing my breath to

catch. For all of my training and experience, I had no answer for her—or myself. My mom shouldn't have died. She had been in perfect health and a young fifty-seven. There hadn't been any signs of vascular disease. It was absurd to think that Mom could have had a heart attack. It wasn't fair. She was a good person. God had cheated us.

I gazed, unseeing, down the estuary toward the ocean. The fragrance of salty air drifted past in bland mediocrity. The vibrant blues and greens of water and forest shifted to a colorless blur. The wild blossoms that sprinkled the meadows with scent and color became lost to me. My mind wandered through clichés, platitudes, and religious axioms, aching for the perfect answer or some biblical passage that would make all of Angela's hurt go away, along with the spiteful unfairness of death.

There were no perfect answers, only faith that there was a reason, a plan. To tell my daughter it was God's will would be to invalidate her anguish, trivialize her grandmother's life, and lay blame where none existed.

"I don't know," I whispered.

Angela sank to the sand and began to sob. I knelt in front of her, put my arms around her, my head resting on hers, and we wept.

For two hours, we sat on the damp sand and talked of love and family. Of ancestors long forgotten and descendants we would never know. Of the roles we played in life, the miracle of life, the circle of life, and the sacredness of life.

The sun warmed our rift valley and the sand we shared. In the distance, seagulls called to the ocean, and the far-off surf replied.

A gunshot echoed from the forest—then another. Visions of the mommy and baby fallow deer raced through my mind.

Angela shot to her feet with more anger than I had ever seen in her and screamed at the forest.

"NO! NO MORE DEATH!"

She kicked sand high into the air, turned, and stomped back toward the parking lot. As she approached the car, her shoulders slumped and she began to sob again. I followed, wishing for my mom's wisdom and advice.

Mama. I need you.

Chapter 2
Best Friends
Evelyn

It was Saturday and by now I knew all the normal sounds and scents of my family's comings and goings from the sanctuary of my room.

The excited silence creeping down the hall was definitely *not* normal, with Grace's sainted giggles escaping her precious little lips. I thought maybe the kids were bringing me breakfast. I remained motionless under the comforter, pretending to sleep while barely contained merriment and light footsteps surrounded the bed.

The high-pitched, playful screams of Grace and Angela filled the room. Their ruckus was immediately followed by the Gaelic trill of my best friend, Felicity. Before I could pull my head out from under the quilt, the bed turned into a trampoline, with two young girls and one "adult" bouncing and screaming with glee. With the first bounce, the quilt billowed like a tent above me. The second sent me airborne. Like a wave, their bounces tumbled me to the edge of the bed where I rolled onto the floor with the poise of a walrus and a loud thunk.

Before I could figure out which way was up, Felicity was hugging me.

"I'm sorry, I'm sorry, you okay?" Felicity asked.

After righting myself and pulling one of Sam's old stinky socks out of my hair, I looked past Felicity at the girls standing on the bed, their faces filled with concern. It felt good to hear their laughs and giggles again—really good.

"Last one on the bed is an ugly toad," I yelled.

I pushed Felicity down and made for the bed. Felicity caught my leg and tried to keep me on the floor. The girls caught my arms and tried to pull me onto the bed.

"Come on, Mom!" the girls cried while they pulled. "You can

do it!"

I kicked gently and felt Felicity pretend to lose her grip so the girls could win. With a lunge, I landed on the bed, with Felicity clambering after.

"Felicity's the toad, Felicity's the toad," we chanted, as she exaggerated a pout.

After breakfast, Felicity insisted on taking me to her art studio in Richmond. She said it was "crucial to the survival of the world," which meant she had finished another bronze statue she was especially proud of.

I worried about her living and working alone inside a condemned 1930's era factory, but the building had a two-hundred-ton overhead crane with a bronze casting furnace that she used for her art—not something she was likely to find elsewhere. A huge bonus was that she didn't have to pay rent because the owner was somehow related, and the city let her live there as a "security guard."

She drove into the dim light of a maintenance shed on the side of the warehouse and parked between her rusted forty-year-old flatbed truck and a ten-foot-tall pile of casting mold remnants.

We walked through an inch of plaster dust toward her main work area.

"Cover your eyes," she said, excitement in her voice.

I covered them and let her lead. The sound of our steps was magnified, echoing through the vast emptiness of the four-story-tall warehouse, each step answered by the flutter and soft coo of pigeons nesting high above. The building's unusual fragrance had become familiar to me—a mix of salty ocean mist, damp musty rooms, pungent burnt plaster and bronze, with a hint of sulfur, gear oil, and acetone left over from the war years. We stopped, and she turned me a little to my left.

"Open," she said, her voice bubbling with excitement.

The late morning sunlight streamed downward from high, dirty, and broken windows, casting perfect squares of brilliant light, marking the middle of her warehouse. Glistening in seven of the natural spotlights sat identical five-foot-tall bronze mermaids. They were perched in a classic pose on a wave-worn rock, looking off into the distance. In one hand, they ran a comb through their long, windblown mane. In the other, each held an ornate, round mirror.

I gasped.

"Oh my. They're beautiful," I said, reverently.

We walked closer.

"No!" I said. I looked at Felicity in disbelief.

"Hope you don't mind, because it would be a real pain to put warts on the noses and give them buck teeth."

"It's me!"

She chuckled. "Yes. I couldn't think of a more perfect face for my mermaids than yours."

"I'm honored," I said, and threw my arms around her.

We walked around one of the sentinels of the sea, with its polished bronze glistening like a golden treasure in the beam of sunlight. The details were flawless: every scale perfect, the hands so real they seemed to move, the breasts big and voluptuous, and the face ... I was looking into a mirror.

I frowned. "The breasts are definitely not mine."

"I modeled those after me," Felicity said, pushing out her chest.

"I should have guessed."

"You get one."

"Huh? What?" I knew I couldn't have heard her right.

"You get one ... a statue."

I laughed.

She looked puzzled for about five seconds, before laughing with me.

In jest, she pushed out her chest again.

"You mean you wouldn't want one of these?"

"Thanks, but I'm happy with mine."

I looked back up at the bronze. Her last piece this size, a young Italian woman stomping grapes, had weighed in at around three thousand pounds. I loved her new statues, but adding one to my obsessive collection of mermaid art would be over the top.

"I don't think it will fit through my front door, and I'm not sure Sam would like it on our lawn."

She looked confused for a second and then shook her head.

"No, no. Not those." She took my hand and led me into her "apartment," an office in the derelict building she had converted with a hodgepodge of second-hand furniture, crates, and castaways. On her crate coffee table sat an eighteen-inch exact replica of the bronze statues that glistened in the warehouse.

"This is my concept model. It's yours," she said.

I held the statue in the light and turned it, admiring the detail.

"I love it. Thank you."

"I've already sold three of them, but you need to help me with the base plaque. I know you've told me before, but what's the symbolism of mermaids, mirrors, and combs again?"

"What version of mermaid lore are you looking for?" I asked, still marveling at the intricacy and beauty of her art.

"Something touristy."

"Touristy? As in *Tavern* touristy or *Fisherman's Wharf* touristy?"

"Tavern. Earthy." Her eyes twinkled with mischief.

"Earthy, huh?" I bit my lower lip and thought for a moment. "Mermaids were seen as a symbol of vanity, woman's sexual power, temptation of the flesh, and deadly sin."

Her eyes gleamed. "Yeah. That's it."

"She was a temptress or a rapacious soul-eater who seduced men, leading them down the path of carnal lust, so she could steal their immortal souls."

Felicity snickered and blushed with pride. "I've done that a few times. Not that it's all that hard, especially when you have big boobs and long, sexy legs to wrap around him."

I chuckled and continued. "She was also portrayed as seducing sailors from the safety of their ship. Once in the water, in childlike innocence, she would pull the sailor to her home at the bottom of the sea, where he would drown."

"Like marriage," Felicity added, with a wry smirk.

I laughed. "Something like that. In Christianity, the dual symbolism of the sailor/mermaid is death through lust and rebirth through water baptism. Her abundant hair symbolized fertility and the act of combing it was believed to cast a spell upon the pious man, causing him to lose his virtue.

"In patriarchal myth, the mirror is vanity. In religious symbolism, it reflects the soul, allowing you to see your true self."

Felicity looked at me with concern, the playfulness gone from her voice.

"What do you see when you look in the mirror, Eve?"

I set the heavy bronze down. Felicity was rarely serious about anything except her art.

"Many things," I said. "But mostly, I see a woman living the only life she ever wanted and never expected to have. A woman blessed with a wonderful husband and three miraculous children."

My eyes asked her the same question.

"I don't know. Your mom's death …" She knitted her brows. "I shouldn't be talking about …"

"It's alright," I said.

She studied me for a second before continuing.

"I really liked your mom. When she died …" She sighed. "I'm not married. I don't have kids. I'm running out of time to have one. Except for my stepmom, my family hardly talks to me. I don't have anyone but you. What if something …"

"You have Dwayne," I said.

She looked down. "I guess. But it's not what you and Sam have. The way Sam looks at you, even when he knows he can't get any. Dwayne only looks at me that way when he's horny. Besides, he's seeing other women."

"I thought you wanted an open relationship."

She shrugged. "The boundaries get so damn blurred, and I'm never sure where I stand with him. There is no commitment. It used to be enough, but now …"

Felicity scrunched her face and slumped forward a little.

"I've felt Dwayne drifting for a while. He was even *too busy* to come to your mom's funeral with me. I expect any day he'll tell me he doesn't want to see me anymore."

"I'm sorry," I said. I gave her a hug. "When you're ready, opportunity will present itself."

Felicity picked up the statue and smiled, but her eyes were still troubled. "Let's put this in my car and go get some tea."

Chapter 3
Unwanted Past
Evelyn

By the sixth week after Mom's funeral, life was getting back to normal. Chris was cooperative again, Angela was less moody, and my dad didn't seem as lost. As a clinical psychologist who worked with families and children, I understood the grieving process. Still, concentrating at work could be a problem, and I sometimes found myself sinking into my own grief when a client talked of personal loss.

A patient had canceled her appointment, so I was going to use the hour to pull myself from thoughts of Mom and pray for the strength to guide my next client safely through his troubles.

My office receptionist rang me and said a young lady wanted to talk with me. I went out to meet her. She was a bit skinny for her five-foot height, looked healthy, and didn't have an adult with her. Her trendy, upscale dress and rainbow hair said she was a typical Marin early adolescent—except for one thing.

"Hello. I'm Dr. Irving. I understand you wanted to see me."

I offered her my hand.

"I'm Clarissa. I'm pleased to meet you."

My smile widened. It was refreshing to meet a young lady with refined manners.

"Clarissa," I said, letting the name settle gently around us. "That is a very pretty name." She smiled with shy pride. "Is your mom or dad here?"

"No ma'am," she said, turning her face away. "My mom went shopping but she said I could talk to you."

Without parental consent, I couldn't treat Clarissa. I retrieved a new client information and history form from the receptionist and handed it to her.

"Let's talk while you fill out the form."

She looked at the clipboard like it might bite, then her eyes darted to the door. I hoped she would fill out the form so I could try to find a way to help her, but was concerned she would flee with the troubles that had brought her to me. She took the clipboard and filled in the blanks with a shaky hand.

"Is there some specific reason you wanted to talk with me?" I asked.

Her hand steadied a little and the corner of her mouth rose into a smile.

"My friend, Makila, on Facebook, said I should talk to you. She said you're super smart and nice ... that you could help me."

Makila had been seeing me for three years. When I first met her, she was failing school, in constant trouble, and had been labeled bipolar and ADHD. Now, she earned A's and B's and showed no signs of behavioral or serious psychological disorders.

My impression was that Clarissa had yet to manifest secondary symptoms—and wouldn't if she received the care she needed.

Clarissa's name, address, and phone number were filled in when she stopped and stared at the medical history section. I had all the information I needed at that moment and took the clipboard. She looked hopeful.

"Are you and Makila sisters-in-spirit?"

Her eyes sparkled with innocent hope. She knew what I meant and nodded yes.

Gently, I challenged her. "And your parents don't know about your friend, Makila, and your mom didn't drop you off ... did she?"

She winced and looked down at her purple fingernails, then folded her hands in her lap. She shook her head no.

"Please look at me," I coaxed. She looked up, worry and fear filling her young eyes.

"I would love to help you, Clarissa, but we can't talk without your parents' permission." She trembled and sniffled back tears. For a second, I saw that vacant look in her eyes, the look children get when they feel life has stripped them of all possibilities except one. Her hopelessness touched a long-ago part of me.

"I can call your mother or father and talk to them. Maybe get their permission."

She shook her head no. "They don't care. They hate me. They

would be happy if I had never been born."

I could see the pain and anger in her eyes, but it was typical teen anger, not the deep, soul-killing despair of a child who isn't loved.

"Really?"

She looked down again and shook her head no.

"If it's okay with you, I will talk with your parents," I said. "But I can't promise anything."

In little more than a lost whisper, Clarissa said, "My dad. Mom will never say yes."

"Sorry I'm late," I said, setting my purse on the breakfast bar. I could smell the over-cooked broccoli, and the macaroni with cheese and hotdogs. Sam caught my sleeve and pulled me into his embrace where I melted into his loving arms and warm kiss. Oh, he felt good.

It's been a while. Maybe tonight.

He loosened his hug, and we stood in each other's arms.

"My mermaid have a long day?"

"Yes. A young girl dropped in. She wanted to see me, but I needed parental consent. Her father couldn't come until late, and we ended up talking two hours."

"Two hours? Sounds like a hard sell," he said. "Or crisis."

"A little of both. But he agreed." I grinned. "He was one of those anti-therapy types."

Sam smiled. "But you won him over?"

"More like sold him on it." I puffed out my chest. "I impressed him so much with my close that he offered me a job selling new cars. Said I could double my income."

Sam chuckled. "When do you start?"

"Tomorrow, of course. But it does mean you will need to fix all the dinners, and you won't see me on weekends anymore."

He made a show of thinking about it. "All the dinners?"

"Yes." I said, with a playful smirk.

He sighed loud and heavy, then made a show of looking mournfully at the stove.

"Think the kids will survive my cooking?"

I winced at the macaroni-and-cheese boxes scattered on the counter, the milk still sitting out, and the burnt splatter on top of the stove. I knew *I* wouldn't. I grimaced and thoughtfully shook my head no.

"Probably not, and it would be awfully quiet without them

around. Maybe I should reconsider?"

"Yeah. Probably," he said, feigning disappointment.

Sam turned toward the stove to reheat dinner. "By the way, your dad called. He wants us to drop by Saturday. Said your mom left you some things."

"Like what?" I asked, as fear shot through me. My words dripped with accusation and suspicion.

"Don't shoot me. I'm just the messenger," he said, turning his head and raising his eyebrows. "And it's not a big deal; sounded like your mom's jewelry, her books, and old stuff from your childhood."

I trembled and stared blankly at the milk carton on the counter.

"Childhood?" I whispered.

Sam turned back toward me, looking worried. He placed his gentle hands on my shoulders for support.

"Are you okay?"

I closed my eyes and took a deep breath. "I'm fine," I said, trying to sound calm and convincing.

I opened my eyes and saw "BS" written all over his face.

"I know what 'fine' means. What's going on, Eve?"

"I don't need anything," I said, trying to sound indifferent as tears clouded my vision.

"No. You don't," he said, his voice calm and protective. "But it's not about needing things. It's about memories."

"I'm sorry," I said, stepping back to free myself from his care. "I'm ... just having a hard time. Drop it ... please."

He clenched his jaw and tension filled the space between us. He turned back toward the stove.

"The kids ate. I'll reheat. You change."

I checked on the kids to make sure they were busy. Chris was engrossed in an online video game. Grace was memorizing and practicing the lines to her community play of *Beauty and the Beast*. Angela was on her phone demeaning a boy from school; I sensed a first crush in bloom.

I went to my room, closed the door, and called Dad.

"Hi, Eve. How ya doing?" Dad asked, in his deep, gravelly voice.

"What stuff?" My words were sharp, and stabbed in anger. I immediately regretted my outburst. "I'm sorry, Dad. I didn't mean to snap."

"It's okay, Eve. You're still adjusting to your loss." His tone was firm and reassuring.

"Our loss," I said.

"Yes. Our loss," he said, with a catch in his voice.

Memories of Mom swam through my mind and tears flowed unchecked. Helpless, I sank into the yearning that Mom's death had left inside me. I knew Dad could hear my muffled sobs.

"Let it out, Eve. Let your grief go. It's okay."

In a few minutes, Sam would come to let me know dinner was reheated, so I didn't have time to wallow.

"I'm alright," I said. I took a deep breath to calm myself. "And I don't need or want anything. I have my memories and her love. That's all I want."

"I went through everything, Eve, and your mom left specific instructions with her will." His voice was as thick as cough syrup, with the pain we shared. "There are things she wanted you to have, and I thought you should go through her clothes. I know you don't wear the same size, but you might want some of her wraps or scarves. I boxed up most of her jewelry, but kept a few pieces that have meaning for me. She wanted Sam to have her first editions and rare book collection."

Being a bibliophile, Sam had hit it off with Mom the first time they met. When the two of them got to talking books, Dad and I would wander off to play Trivial Pursuit or talk about the latest research in clinical psychology. I already missed that time with Dad.

The line fell silent for a few seconds before Dad continued. "I packed away the things you're worried about. They're all in a footlocker in my closet, and a key is in your mother's jewelry box. If anything should happen to me, everything is in one place for you."

I had made the decision long ago to forever deny my past. I could accept that my history had been important to Mom, but to me, my early childhood did not exist—could not exist—would not exist.

My past didn't need a caretaker; it needed a funeral pyre. I had told Mom to throw her mementos of my past away so many times that she had threatened to give them to Sam. I knew she never would, but I had gotten her point and hadn't mentioned them again.

It didn't matter what I wanted. Dad had picked up the torch. He was now the unwanted caretaker of my past and would carry it with the same loving and obstinate dedication as Mom had.

The only living blood relative of mine that Sam knew about was my birth father. He also knew I had nothing but contempt for the man and wisely avoided bringing him up. Sometimes I prayed for the tolerance to forgive my mom's first husband, only because I knew that when you hated someone, you gave them power over you. I hated the idea that he had power over me as much as I hated him, so I prayed I could forgive him, but only for me. It hadn't worked yet.

If Sam were to find out about my past, most of me believed he loved me enough that he would stand by me. But part of me feared. He was a man—a good man—but men just don't understand some things.

"Please, Dad. Just burn it all."

"We can't see the future, Eve," he said, his voice gentle, but resolved. "Someday you may want those memories. For now, I will keep them safe. I'd love for you to come over and look through her things. Take what you want."

This weekend was too soon. I needed to figure out how to make sure Sam wouldn't find anything.

"Alright, Dad, but I have a journal article I need to finish writing this weekend, and we're going to Golden Gate Zoo the following week. The weekend after that is free. How would eleven on Saturday in three weeks work?"

"Sounds perfect." The tension in his voice dissolved, replaced by his normally cheerful tone.

"Would you like to come to the zoo with us?" I asked. "The kids would love to have their Grandpa Nick along. We're leaving about nine and making it a full day."

"Love to. A week from Saturday at nine."

"Thanks, Dad. I love you."

"Love you, too, Eve."

The phone went silent, and dread saturated every cell of my body. Despite Dad's assurances that he had gone through everything, I was frightened of what he might have missed. One report card or one photo and my perfect world could be washed away.

I heard Sam coming down the hall and realized how tired I was of the secrecy, the fear, the worry.

An old saying popped into my head.

"We don't have secrets, our secrets have us."

Chapter 4
Abalone Diving
Evelyn

Sam finished his breakfast and leaned back in his chair to watch me fix the kids' lunches. His contemplative frown grew defensive, so I knew he had made plans to go diving with Dad.

"We doing anything special on Saturday?" Sam asked.

"I have a journal article I need to finish. Why?"

"Nick called yesterday, wants to go diving."

I hated their abalone diving. I knew my phobia of the water intensified my concerns, but there were real risks associated with the sport. No matter how he minimized the dangers, I couldn't ignore the fact that every year a good number of divers drowned, fell off the cliffs, got bashed against the rocks by the surf, or were bitten by sharks.

"I thought we might go to the Exploratorium," I said.

He was accustomed to my evasion and held my gaze. He half smiled. "Let's wait on that. You and the kids could come."

I shivered. "And watch a great white eat you? No, thanks."

His look of annoyance was met by my glare.

He repeated his mantra. "In over a hundred years, there has only been one confirmed kill of a diver north of the Golden Gate—"

"Five years ago—when you were out diving."

We had danced this dance too many times, and he wasn't going there. Tight-mouthed, he studied me for a few seconds.

"I will tell Nick it's a go for tomorrow."

I glared and nodded.

Chris stepped into the doorway, bouncing with hope. He glanced back and forth between me and his dad. I knew what he wanted, and he knew my answer was NO! He hung his hope on his dad.

"Can I go?"

I turned back to the lunches and stabbed the peanut butter, trying to pretend it was just between them. Naturally, Chris wanted to dive for abalone with his dad and grandfather. I knew Chris was growing up. I knew that Sam and my dad were the safest of divers. Some days they would come back without even getting wet because the water was too rough, too murky, the seals had all hauled themselves onto the rocks so they wouldn't be shark food, or they just "had a feeling." I was being paranoid and unfair to Chris, but …

In the reflective silence, I could feel both of them watching me. Sam would have let Chris go two years ago, but I had begged him to wait until Chris was older. I was a little surprised Sam hadn't already pulled rank.

"Sorry. Not this time, buddy," Sam said.

I had held Chris back for too long. I forced a smile and turned to face them.

"Why don't you take him? You've taught him everything he needs to know about abalone diving. You can rent a wet suit and I can get him an abalone card and tags after school."

"Thanks, Mom!" Chris said. He bounded over and gave me a bear hug. "I'll bring back a big one for you."

Sam smiled and winked at me. I smiled back, but inside, my heart was pounding like surf in a winter storm.

I checked on the girls to make sure they were ready for school. Angela was ready and working on some calligraphy, which meant she had finished another poem that held special meaning for her.

I loved her penmanship. On Angela's eighth birthday, she had taken notice of the beautiful script her Grandma Louise used when she wrote personal notes in birthday cards. A couple weeks later, we were at my mom and dad's for a barbeque when I noticed she and Mom had disappeared. I found them in the library, Angela with quill in hand imitating an Old English script.

Watching them from the door, I remembered when Mom had tried to teach me. I had no patience or talent, with my letters looking like refugees from a paper shredder. But even from eight feet away, I could see Angela's steady hand already turning simple letters into things of beauty. Before the visit was over, Angela had fallen in love with quills, colored inks, handmade paper, and the magic of turning letters into art that spoke.

"A new poem?" I asked.

"I'm almost done." She nudged the printed version toward me on her desk. I picked it up.

My Mother is a Mermaid
by Angela Irving

My mother is a mermaid, of that we're all agreed,
But mother is a mermaid, of seas and waves aggrieved.
She will not swim in water, nor even get toe wet,
My mother is a mermaid, her fear I just don't get.

My mother is a mermaid, who sits upon the shore,
She looks to seas and oceans, heart longing to explore.
I long to see her swimming, for her I do adore,
A mermaid in the ocean, who swims with great splendor.

Why won't she swim in water, like all her tadpoles do?
My mother is a mermaid, so dry and oh so blue.
I wish that Mom would join us, with the fishies in the sea,
My mother is a mermaid, from surf and sea does flee.

None of my family—not even Sam—knew the origins of my fear of the water. All they knew was that not even Poseidon himself could drag me in.

I thought my kids had given up trying to get me into the water, but Angela's poem showed that my belief was more hope than reality. I, too, wished I could swim with them, but I just couldn't. Twice I had almost drowned. Twice the waters had spit me out. I knew beyond knowing that the "third time would be the charm."

"I do so get my toe wet, every time I take a shower," I said, with playful indignity.

She finished the last word in her beautiful script and began cleaning the ink from the pen's nib. By her tense body, I knew she had taken me too seriously.

"That's not what I meant, Mom. I know you get your toes wet. It's poetic license."

"I know, sweetheart," I said. "I was just teasing." I bent down and kissed the top of her head. "It's a beautiful poem. I love it."

She held her finished work up, and we admired it. I kissed her cheek and wondered if I really wanted to check on Grace. It seemed as if everyone had swimming on their minds and I didn't want to hear it.

Grace was dressed and stuffing her backpack.

"Hi, Grace, sweetie."

Her face lit with expectation. "Marla's having a swim party in two weeks. Can I go?"

I looked up at heaven and said, "Very funny, Mom."

Chapter 5
Beauty and the Beast
Sam

Eve had taken Grace to the children's community theater to get ready for the opening night of *Beauty and the Beast*. I was home editing a client's business proposal for yet another drive-thru coffee stand and waiting for the time to leave.

I went to check on the kids. Angela was reading an English assignment in the living room. She was also wearing a black T-shirt with blood red vampires and skulls which Eve hated and forbade her to wear outside of her bedroom. Once a week, Angela put it on, hoping to whittle us down.

"No. You're not wearing *that* to the play," I said firmly.

Angela snapped her book shut. "What's wrong with it? All the other girls wear it, and it's not like I'm going to go around biting boys."

I gave her my "Don't-argue-with-dad" look. She huffed and stomped off to her bedroom.

I looked in on Chris. He was hiding in his room.

"Hey, buddy. You need to get ready."

Chris turned from a history paper on his computer.

"Please, Dad. I don't wanna go. It's just a dumb kid's show, and I didn't even like the movie."

I agreed with him about it being a dumb kid's show, but Grace was in the play and it was important that we all be there.

"It's just a couple hours, and we're going for pizza after."

Chris frowned.

He frowned at pizza?

"But, Dad. I need to get this paper done."

"When's it due?"

He scrunched up his face. "Next Thursday."

"You're going."

"But it's such a boring and lame story, Dad. He's a jerk, so some witch turns him into a beast, but he's still a lame jerk. He would have let Belle rot in the tower if he hadn't thought she could break the spell."

I leaned against the door jam, pleased with his insight.

"You might like the older version by Marie Le Prince de Beaumont."

He nodded with questionable interest.

I continued. "You're right about the movie being shallow. Marie's story is about honor, kindness, and virtue. In it, Beast values Beauty's happiness above his wish to be free of the curse. Because of that, she saw his heart and fell in love with him."

Chris slumped. "Do I still have to go?"

I was about to say, "Yes," when Angela stopped next to me at the door wearing her "Girls Rock" T-shirt.

"Katelyn just called my cell," Angela said to Chris, while giving me her best cold shoulder. "Said yours was off. Wanted me to tell you she's going to the play."

Angela headed off to finish dressing, while I watched a sappy teenager smile congeal on Chris's face, and the hormone level rise in his glazed eyes. While he shut down his computer, I closed his bedroom door so we could talk about desire, respect, being responsible, and always acting with honor.

My parents, Rich and Rose, drove us to the play. Grandma Rose sat in back with the kids.

"What are you reading? Homework?" Grandma asked.

I looked back at them.

"No, Grandma," Chris said. "It's *Beauty and the Beast* by de Beaumont. Dad had it in his library. The wording is a little weird, but Dad's right; it's a lot better than the movie."

"I read it in high school … I think," Grandma said. "Too long ago to remember for sure."

Angela looked over and started reading. She scowled.

"Her sisters are losers."

Chris held up his hand and they high-fived.

After we found seats, I decided to slip backstage to see how Grace was doing and wish her well.

Trouble.

Eve was on the other side of the stage talking with Barbara. Even from fifty feet away, I could see the protectiveness boiling up inside Eve. I didn't know what it was with those two, but every time they met, they ended up trying to scratch each other's eyes out. It was so unlike Eve. Normally she would let insults from stupid people go, but not with Barbara.

I saw Barbara turn white and knew Eve had just won another victory. I also knew Eve would feel guilty and ashamed of it later. I decided to let her save some face and waited another five minutes in the shadows before wishing Grace good luck.

Chapter 6
Backstage
Evelyn

In the well-ordered chaos backstage, I helped Grace adjust her arm in the costume's spout so she could articulate it for emphasis. Ms. Simms, the children's theater director, shouted last-minute instructions, the adult volunteers attended to last-minute stage and prop adjustments, and the parents helped their kids dress and rehearse their lines one last time.

"I wish I could have been Belle," Grace said, pouting slightly.

I smoothed her hair and said, "But I'm really excited about seeing you play Mrs. Potts. You make such a wonderful teapot, and your British accent is perfect."

She hugged me. "I love my costume, and I'm going to be the best teapot ever." Grace wiggled with delight. "In rehearsals, Ms. Simms said I was perfect."

"And it was wonderful of Angela to help you memorize and practice your part."

"Yeah. She's the best big sister in the whooooole world." Grace's smile glowed.

The closeness of my girls brought me immense joy. Even though three years separated them, they were always there for each other.

Like usual, all us moms exchanged compliments on the costumes we had made, purchased, or just thrown together.

"Oh, what a darling teapot costume," Barbara Stark cooed in her usual condescending tone. I felt my blood pressure rise.

"Thank you. I'm happy with how it came out." *Now please go away.*

I knew Barbara from the PTA. We had a history of running debates concerning age-appropriate educational material for our children. Since I had a Ph.D. in child psychology, and she spelled cat with a K, our debates were always a bit one-sided.

The name on Barbara's driver's license was Barbie-Sue, but she rarely admitted to it. On top of being a petty sleaze, she was too skinny—probably anorexic. She tried to look twenty years younger than she was by nursing a copper-pot tan and painting her face with too much blush, caked-on eye shadow, and enough eyeliner to reprint *War and Peace*. The only things that seemed to matter to her were status and money. And everyone but her husband seemed to know she was doing her handyman, Stanley. People like her annoyed the heck out of me.

Rumor was that she had been a porn star before she married her first husband, Barry, and moved to Marin. Barry was a nice, hard-working man. Once settled here, he worked while she shopped for someone better—*better* being defined as *richer*. Three husbands later, she married a CEO, the current and apparent last stop in her career. Her only child was eleven-year-old Madonna, a quiet and respectful girl who needed therapy nearly as badly as her mom did.

Madonna came up to Barbara wearing her Belle costume. Her dress was mesmerizing. Even in the poor back-stage lighting, the sequins, Swarovski crystals, beads, and gems sparkled like stars in the night sky. The body material looked like fine silk and was embellished with what appeared to be custom Point de France needle lace. The gown had that perfect, professionally tailored look, but like everything Barbara did, it was excessive to the point of absurdity.

"Excuse me, Barbara," Madonna said, in her flat, monotone voice. "I need some help with my zipper."

"Crap, Madonna," Barbara said. "Can't you even do a zipper?"

"Your costume is exquisite, Madonna," I said. "You look like a beautiful princess."

"Thank you, Ms. Irving. It is kind of you to say." Most girls her age would beam or blush, but she acted indifferent.

"Her costume is silk taffeta," Barbara said, raising her head in smug satisfaction. "I bought it from a luxury importer my husband knows. The silk is a custom weave and dye. Only fifty dollars a yard."

Fifty dollars a yard? I tried not to gag.

"And my seamstress did a wonderful job. She's such a perfectionist, but she's not cheap." Looking disdainfully at Grace's costume, and taking on a haughty tone, she continued. "And as I'm sure you know, silk taffeta is hard to work with. Much harder than cotton." She grinned to herself. "And the decorations are, of course, top quality, so she had to charge me four thousand to make it. But even at that, it's a bargain."

I saw a couple other moms roll their eyes or drop their jaws in disbelief. I stood there steaming.

Barbara blabbered on. "Of course, this is the peasant dress she wears at the beginning of the show."

Peasant, my eye.

The director called all the children to the center of the stage for one last round of encouragement. With the kids occupied, I turned back toward Barbara and sharpened my claws.

She continued her inane chatter. "Her ball gown is simply exquisite." She raised her eyebrows with amused contempt, cracking the foundation of her makeup, and added, "And your child's costume? Did you make it yourself? It looks homemade."

I knew my smile was acidic but I didn't care.

"Her name is Grace, and yes, it is. Cotton. Jo-Ann's bargain rack for three dollars a yard. As much as I might like to spend extravagant sums on children's costumes to impress other people with my wastefulness, I never got into the habit of trading up husbands, so I can't afford it."

She glared at me.

The little voice inside told me to act like an adult and bite my tongue, but the words just tumbled out.

"And by the way, *Barbie*, if you want to borrow it sometime, I recently came across an old VCR copy of *Barbie-Sue and the Banging Big Boys* at a garage sale. Has your husband—I mean the current one—ever seen it?"

Her sun-wrinkled, dull bronze tan turned whiter than her new Rolls. Her eyes fluttered, and I thought she might faint for a second, but then a pink blush began to appear. Within a few seconds, she reached a flattering shade of crimson. The red of her blush and the metallic green of her eye shadow gave a nice Christmas lights effect to her face. She tried to look angry, even defiant. But I could see the fear behind the mask.

My stomach knotted at my cruelty. I wanted to pull the words back, but it was too late.

Barbara pushed past me toward the children.

Sam showed up a few minutes later to wish Grace good luck.

I worked my way through the ocean of kids and adults to find my family. I settled in between Sam and Sam's mom. To my right, Angela was basking in the warmth and attention of

Aunt Margarita and Grandma Rose while she shared some of her poetry. Grandpa Rich sat on the other side of Sam, and my dad beyond him. They were talking about tide tables and diving. I cringed.

"Where's Chris?" I asked Sam.

"Top," he said, pointing over his shoulder without looking.

I craned my neck. Katelyn and Chris were near the top of the auditorium with her parents. I stood for a better look. They were holding hands and staring with adolescent longing into each other's eyes—one hundred percent infatuated. Katelyn's mom waved and I waved back. She nodded her head toward them and shrugged. I chuckled and nodded back.

Barbara and her husband, Frank, stopped at the seats in front of us. She and I exchanged viperous smiles, then she gave Sam a come-hither look and batted her fake mascara-encrusted eyelashes before settling into her seat.

Sam chuckled, leaned close, and whispered, "You been picking on her again?"

"Me?" I whispered back. "She started it."

The lights dimmed and the orchestra began playing.

Grace's performance was flawless, every line perfect and every move on cue. Madonna had done an excellent job as well, delivering her lines with impeccable dramatic flair and voice inflections. It puzzled me that in real life she spoke in flat monotone.

In the backstage disorder after the show, we found Grace and Madonna with a large group of girls who were chattering in nonstop excitement. Barbara and Frank were standing with a dozen other parents, encircling the pool of adolescent estrogen, congratulating each other and complimenting the children.

"Barbara, what is chl ... amy ... dia?" Madonna said, her flat monotone cutting through the delirious squeals and chatter.

The parents were instantly silent, with all eyes on Madonna, Barbara, and Frank. The squeals and nimble chattering from the bevy of girls slowed, as the awareness that something was amiss coursed rapidly through the group.

Barbara scowled and said, "What?"

"Stanley picked up his tools at the house today," Madonna said. "I heard him on his phone. He said he needed to get out of town because he probably gave me chl ... whatever it is."

Barbara stared at Madonna—frozen in disbelief, while Frank

glared at Madonna as if she were the perpetrator.

Frank turned toward Barbara and raised his hand like he was going to hit her. Barbara reflectively cringed and braced herself. Sam bristled and began moving toward them. Seeing Sam, Frank stopped and lowered his arm as he stole glances at his audience.

Glaring at Barbara with his nostrils flared, Frank said, "You stupid bitch. You would pick a pedophile to screw. You have any idea how this is going to make me look?" He turned and stormed off.

Madonna watched her stepfather for a moment, then turned her attention back to Barbara. Uncertainty, confusion, and fear slowly painted a frown on Madonna's face as she watched her mother staring blankly at her.

In the backwash of Frank's departure, parents quickly pulled their daughters from the group and hurried away. Sam took Grace out while I remained.

Knowing that I was probably the last person on the planet Barbara would want support from, I stood to the side, hoping that someone would step forward to help her. It didn't happen. All the parents and children had left—a few even grinning with perverted satisfaction at Barbara's situation. I wasn't too surprised. I had seen Barb antagonize nearly every parent with her childish arrogance and conceit.

I waited another minute, praying Barbara would be able to pull herself together.

Ms. Simms came over and said to me, "Shelly said there was a problem."

I nodded and softly said, "Yes. Could you have Madonna help with something while I talk with Barbara?"

"Sure." Walking over to Madonna, Ms. Simms studied Barbara's blank stare. She turned her full attention to Madonna and smiled. "Could you help me put away some of the props?"

Madonna looked back and forth between her mom and Ms. Simms.

Ms. Simms said, "Your mom needs a few minutes alone. Ms. Irving will take care of her."

Madonna looked at me and nodded yes, before following Ms. Simms to prop storage.

I crossed over to where Barbara stood and gently asked, "Are you okay?"

She slowly raised her head toward me. Her eyes remained

glazed and unfocused.

"Barbara, I will need to report this. Do you understand?"

She flinched and then slowly nodded yes. Her eyes focused on me as tears drew long, black lines of mascara down her cheeks.

"He hurt my baby," she said, in a soul-anguished whisper.

I took her hand. "I'm sorry. Is there anything I can do?" Her eyes began to glaze over again.

My mother-in-law, Rose, came up to us. "Sam wanted me to tell you that Frank took off, so Barbara and Madonna are stranded."

"Thanks, Mom."

In Barbara's eyes, I saw a lost and bewildered soul.

"Would you like me to take you and Madonna home?" I asked.

Barbara partially focused on me as a deep questioning frown formed. She seemed as surprised at my offer as I was. She nodded yes, then her eyes rolled back into her head and a violent shudder thrashed through her body. I broke her fall.

Chapter 7
Chris's First Dive
Evelyn

The early-morning sky glowed in hues of violet, and the high horsetail clouds shone with a vibrant white. Like the inspired colors that painted the heavens, Van Damme State Park was gorgeous as always.

Its beauty had infused life into some of Angela's finest poetry. It was here she had found the words to evoke the aroma of the rich, damp, and fertile forest soil. Where her prose echoed with the chaotic beat of water dismantling itself against barbarous rock outcroppings. And where seagulls were transformed from noisy poop machines into a symbol of life and dignity, their cackles and sharp pulsating calls a heavenly choir.

My fleece jacket killed off the bite of the cool, damp morning air. Sam still hadn't put on the top half of his wet suit. I smiled and shook my head, envious of his ability to withstand the cold. No matter how chilly it was, I could always cuddle in his arms and feel his soul-soothing warmth restore me. He would joke that his body thermostat was set ten degrees warmer than normal, and that mine was set fifty degrees too low.

Chris applied liberal amounts of talcum powder to his body and his wet suit, mimicking his dad and Grandpa Nick. The powder was to make the suit easier to put on. Chris had managed the pants, but despite the groans escaping his gritted teeth as he shoved with all his strength, his arm was stuck halfway down the sleeve. Chris had borrowed the suit from his friend, Bobby, and it looked way too small. Frustration was stealing his excitement.

"Mom. I can't get my arm in."

His voice carried echoes of the little boy who used to come to me and say, "Fix it, Mommy," with absolute confidence that I could and would.

"Maybe it's too small," I said, trying to hide the hope in my voice.

"Bobby is a little bigger than me. It has to fit," Chris said, shaking his head no.

"It's the right size," Sam said, stepping over. "Has to be tighter than skin tight to keep the water from circulating inside it too much so that he can stay warm." Sam took the end of the sleeve. "I'll blow. You push. Just try not to punch me."

Sam put the sleeve to his mouth and blew, like he was the big bad wolf trying to blow over the brick house. I could see the sleeve slightly expand like a balloon, allowing Chris's arm to slip through.

Fudge.

"What do you do if you get into trouble?" Sam asked Chris.

"I'll be fine."

Sam raised his eyebrows.

Chris looked away and mumbled, "Drop my weights."

Sam studied him for a second.

"What's the problem, buddy?"

"They're expensive," Chris said, concern clouding his face.

"Not as expensive as a funeral," Sam said, his voice unyielding. "When things go bad down there, you literally have only seconds before bad becomes very, very, very bad. I've dropped my weights twice in my life and I don't regret it. You got it?"

Chris relaxed and nodded.

"Yeah. I've got it."

Sam glanced over to see my wide eyes and got an oh-fudge expression.

He looked back to Chris. "Got your ab-iron and caliper?"

"Yeah. They're on my kayak with my other gear."

"Good. Go help Grandpa Nick get his things to the water."

Chris hurried off, and Sam turned to face me. I trembled.

"Is that how you *lost* your weight belt last year?" I asked.

He tensed, took a deep breath, and slowly let it out.

"Yes. I didn't pay attention and ended up in some thick kelp. My fin strap got tangled."

It was rare that a tangled fin strap was more than a minor nuisance, so it obviously wasn't the whole story, but I didn't really want the whole story. I nodded and glared at him.

"I'm not a child, Sam. You don't need to protect me. The

next time you drop your weights, don't lie about it. How can I trust that you're being safe if you don't tell me the truth?"

We scowled at each other for a few more seconds. He wasn't going to volunteer any more information, and I didn't want to think about his "very, very, very bad" comment.

"Dive safe," I said.

I turned and headed to where the girls were looking for pebbles and driftwood. After a few steps, I spun around and trotted to catch up with him. He heard me coming and turned toward me. I stood on my toes and gave him my traditional "good luck" kiss to keep him safe. His eyes sparkled with love and appreciation. I let my hand rest on his chest for a moment. Our hearts touched.

"Dive safe," I said.

"Always."

With Sam leading on his orange diving kayak, I watched the guys disappear around the treacherous rocky point to the north.

The girls and I wandered south on the gravel beach, watching the seagulls and sand pipers.

"Hi, girls," Felicity yelled from behind us. She jogged over, hugged me, and then gave Grace and Angela big hugs.

Felicity quickly scanned the ocean. "I saw Sam's parents headed into the forest. Where are your intrepid abalone … or should I say, snail hunters?"

"North. Around the point."

"Good," Felicity said, her playful gaze holding Angela's eager smile. "We can have fun without condescending looks from the grouch squad."

Angela laughed and distorted her face; Felicity did the same. They tried to out goofy-face each other. Grace and I joined in.

"Mom wins," Angela announced.

I tried to unlock my jaw.

"Relax," Felicity said, reaching into my mouth.

"Mom's jaw is locked open again," Grace announced to the whole world.

"You know better than to open your mouth so wide," Felicity said. Her huge grin and the sparkle in her eyes told me I wasn't going to like her next statement. "When was the last time? Oh, yeah. When you and Sam were—"

I punched her arm. She feigned hurt, but was beside herself

with delight.

My jaw had been locked open from the TMJ long enough for the muscles to begin to spasm. I closed my watery eyes and tried to relax, while she worked the joint into alignment. With a parting stab of pain, the jaw slipped back into place.

Felicity and Grace headed south to the tide pools while Angela and I picked through the green serpentine, white quartz, and polished agate pebbles on the beach.

"Mom," she said, her tone extra grown up. "Am I old enough to date?"

Her first crush had blossomed into a delicate orchid. The correct answer was, "Absolutely not!" but when you're thirteen going on eighteen, such dictates are often taken as a challenge or dare. We stood, woman to woman for the first time.

"What do you think?"

"Oh, yes. Definitely," she said, standing proud.

"And where would you go on this date?"

She frowned, then shrugged in contemplative slow motion.

"The mall?" Another idea flashed in her eyes and she glowed with excitement. "Six Flags."

He was probably thirteen, too. At least he'd better be.

"Has he asked you out?"

"No. But I know he wants to," She said, blushing a little. "He's really cool and gets good grades."

"And who is this wonderful young man?"

"Daniel Wilson. He's really smart and he's in my history and math classes."

I remembered him from last year. *She could do better.* I closed my eyes and flogged myself. I didn't want to be one of those "no one is good enough for my little girl" mothers. He was a good and responsible boy. Besides, he hadn't asked—maybe he wouldn't. I opened my eyes.

Angela was staring at me, her eyes moist and fearful.

"You don't like him?" she sputtered.

"Of course I like him, sweetheart," I said, taking her in a hug. "He's a wonderful young ... man."

She pulled away and excited hope filled her voice.

"Then I can date?"

"If he asks you, you can go to the mall and a movie with him. If he wants to take you to Six Flags this summer, I will talk with his mom about him joining us when we go."

"Oh, thank you, thank you, thank you," she said, jumping up

and down.

There was nothing to thank me for. A first crush is nature's coming of age ritual—as unstoppable as the tide. It rises on the tip of hormonal flames and gloriously outshines the sun, while we euphorically drown in an ocean of self-doubt, bewilderment, and fear.

With the rush of hormones comes our introduction to the confusing, thrilling, painful, and disappointing realities of intimate relationships and adulthood. Too soon, the flames die away, being replaced by a sea of tears, confusion, and feelings of betrayal.

My job would be to guide her and be her safe harbor when the uncertainty and swirling storm of emotions crashed down on her. I knew the storm clouds were looming just beyond the horizon of her perfect sunny day. Before Monday, I would talk with her again about boys, becoming a woman, wants, desires, peer pressure, and responsibility.

We found several pieces of smooth white quartz and pink agate, perfect for Angela to make into jewelry. With treasures in hand, we joined Felicity and Grace and explored the shallow tide pools, watching the starfish, sea anemones, and urchins.

I looked up and stiffened.

"What's wrong?" Felicity asked.

"They're coming back," I said, pointing north. "Less than an hour. They did really well—or something is wrong."

Felicity bumped shoulders with me. "You're all just Little Miss Sunshine today, aren't you?"

"Sorry," I said.

"It's okay. I'm sure they're fine," she said, putting her arm around my shoulders.

Chris picked up an abalone from his kayak and held it high for me to see.

"Looks like it's about eight ... maybe nine inches," I said. "What do you think?"

Felicity held her hand up with her index finger and thumb about four inches apart.

"Men keep telling me this is six inches, so it's hard for me to say."

I snickered and glanced around to make sure the girls weren't within earshot. In a tone that demanded strict confidence, I said, "I know what eight inches is. Sam says he won't take an abalone under eight. Says it isn't manly."

Felicity swatted me. "Bad girl. Bad, bad, girl,"

We jogged back up the beach to meet the men. In Chris's excitement to get off his kayak to show me his catch, he stumbled, fell into the surf, and flailed as he struggled to hold onto his prized abalone. We tried not to laugh. Unfazed, he regained his footing, scrambled up the beach, and held out his abalone for us to admire.

"Eight and a quarter inches, Mom. I got the biggest." He bubbled with excitement.

"The biggest?" I said. "Wow. That's wonderful."

It was heavy and slimy. I turned it over and admired the rough shell so I wouldn't have to look at the poor thing struggling to breathe.

"Very nice, honey," I said. "And it looks like the shell is going to be a gorgeous souvenir. You going to eat the whole thing yourself?"

He blushed. "No. I want everyone to have some."

I hugged him, getting my jacket wet.

"Thank you, honey. I'm looking forward to it."

"How'd your dad and grandpa do?" I asked.

"Dad got two and Grandpa got three."

Sam came over and held up his catch—just a little over the legal size. I grinned. He shrugged and grinned back. Felicity turned away from the guys and snickered.

"Chris got the biggest his first time out," Sam bragged.

"Isn't that great, Mom?" Chris said, pushing out his chest.

I kissed his salty cheek. "Congratulations. It's absolutely wonderful."

After a fried abalone lunch, we heard stories about the fish, crabs, and plants the men had seen on their dive. Angela listened with rapt attention, and I could see dreams of joining them next year swimming through her thoughts.

Later, Sam and I went for a stroll in the redwood forest. I stopped and turned toward Sam. "In weather like today, you stay out until you get your limit. Why'd you come back so soon?"

"Didn't want Chris to get too tired."

Something in the way he said it made me question his reason.

"Why did you really come in?"

Sam grimaced. "I saw a dolphin."

"Dolphin?"

"Yeah. I know they come this far north, but I've never seen one close to shore." He paused in thought. "It was alone and came right up to my kayak, bobbed its head out of the water and looked at me for the longest time. It was like it knew me or something. Made me uneasy."

"Dolphins are good luck."

"And they keep away sharks," Sam added.

He knew it wasn't true, and he was only saying it to appease my fears.

"Nice try, dear. Urban legend. Sharks eat dolphins. The only way a dolphin will take on a shark is if it doesn't have a choice, or if its baby is threatened. You know that."

Sam shrugged. "I guess that explains the crescent-shaped bite out of the front of its dorsal fin."

Crescent? It couldn't be the same one after more than twenty years. Could it? I shivered.

"You okay?" he asked.

I nodded. "Yeah. You know how easily I chill."

Chapter 8
The Inheritance
Evelyn

I woke to the silent scent of doom invading the sanctity of our bedroom. The sound of Sam's soft breathing stood like a slumbering sentinel, forcing the invader to remain hidden in the shadows.

It was *the* Saturday. We were supposed to go to Dad's to pick up the things Mom had left to me.

I strained to hear any noises from the kids' rooms. Nothing. They were still asleep.

I knew Sam had assumed we would all go together, but I wanted to go through everything first and make sure nothing had been missed. I was afraid Sam would object and say it was silly if I suggested that I go by myself. I needed him in a really good mood, and besides, it had been awhile.

My fingers trembled on the bedroom door lock as I watched Sam's chest slowly rise and fall. My nightie surrendered itself to the floor and the cool air awakened my senses. I slipped between the silky sheets, where his warmth filled our bed with happiness and his intoxicating scent pulled me into a Cinderella dream.

My hand flowed, like unending love, through his forest of curly, dark chest hair. I delighted in the soft, childlike sighing sounds he made in his simmering sleep. With his eyes still closed, still halfway between his dream world and me, he caressed my face and smiled. Our lips met like clandestine lovers and we shared the breath of life. Basking in our shared pleasure, he slowly opened his eyes to reveal a river of love that only we shared.

"We need to be quiet, so we don't wake the kids," I whispered.

The desire in his eyes and the smile on his lips said, "That won't be a problem."

We kissed and he pulled me into his strong embrace.

The smell of bacon and hash browns filled our home. I tended breakfast while Sam cut up the ham, spinach, and bell pepper for the scramble. I was ready to pour the eggs into the sizzling skillet, when Chris shuffled into the kitchen.

"Smells like blueberry muffins," Chris said through a yawn.

Chris and his dad were blueberry muffin vacuums. Two dozen were in the oven, and every last one that the girls and I didn't lay a claim to would be gone before we left the table.

"Yes," I said. "They'll be out in five and breakfast will be ready in ten. Could you go wake Grace for me?"

I glanced up from the bacon and didn't like his mischievous grin. Grace had been teasing him about Katelyn for the last two weeks, and I knew he wouldn't mind a little payback. Sam must have seen it too.

"I'll get her up," Sam said to Chris. "You set the table."

"It's not my turn." Chris whined.

I knew to stay out of it. This was another alpha male skirmish. They had become more frequent as Chris tested his boundaries.

"If you want muffins, you'll set the table."

Chris opened the cupboard for the dishes and mumbled, "Mother Hubbard," which meant the cupboard was bare. He tried the dishwasher.

"Mom. Grace didn't run the dishwasher last night."

"I know. I thought it was a short load, so I told her not to. Use the dolphin dishes."

He took the dishes out of another cupboard and looked at them for a moment.

"Where did you get these?"

"Cinnamon, a friend of mine, made them for me. She wanted to be a commercial artist."

"She's good. Is she?"

"No," I said.

Cinnamon had made the dinner plates in her tenth grade ceramics class and given them to me for Christmas. I had always adored the design of two dolphins swimming in an undersea grotto, filled with coral reefs and bright, colorful little fishies. She had said one of the dolphins was her and the other was me.

"Cinnamon's kind of a funny name," Chris said.

I smiled at distant memories. "It was perfect for her."

Cinnamon and I had met in seventh grade and instantly knew we were sisters-in-spirit. We had planned to share our lives, careers, and families—always being there for each other.

I closed my eyes and sighed.

"She's up," Sam said, coming back into the kitchen. "And what was that big sigh for?"

I had been thinking about how Cinnamon and I were going to live to be one-hundred-and-two years old. How we had planned to live in the same retirement home and glue silk daisies, pansies, and roses to our bedpans and use them for hats.

My smile was impish.

"Bedpan hats and silk flowers."

Sam and Chris both looked at me like I was a few seahorses short of a rodeo.

"Sorry I asked," Sam said.

I wasn't. Except for the rare nightmare, my memories of Cinnamon were mainly happy ones now. The deep pain and longing I had never expected to survive when she died had diminished with the years. Now only a mild wish that she could have shared my life remained. I prayed the pain of my mom's death would age to the same mild longing.

I had never seen any point in telling Sam about Cinnamon or her murder, so I changed the subject.

An hour to fix and twenty minutes to inhale—breakfast was over. All the muffins had been devoured and the only food left was two shriveled slices of seven-grain toast. The kids cleared their dishes and headed off.

Sam was sitting at the head of the table, with me at his left. We sipped our coffee and smiled like conspirators who had dug up a pirate's chest but were keeping it a secret.

"That was a fantastic breakfast, Eve. Thank you."

"Thank you for your help. I enjoy it when we cook together."

"Me, too," he said. His smile now held a hint of questioning. "So. Why the special morning?"

"Special?" I said, feigning coy innocence. I could feel the heat on my cheeks. He knew me better than I wanted him to. "I just felt like making love to my husband and fixing a nice breakfast. Would you rather I didn't?"

He continued smiling with a way too smug "Well?" expression on his face. I was a little put off. He was old enough to know a man shouldn't question a woman's motives.

Doing my best Mae West imitation, I leaned close and whispered, "I'm having an affair and I didn't want you to get suspicious."

He wasn't smiling anymore. "Don't tell me you dented the van."

"Did what?" I pulled my hands away and sat bolt upright. "If that's not a nice how-do-you-do. *No, dear.* I didn't dent my car. If I had wrecked it, I'd tell you. I don't play those games."

He looked annoyed and only a little guilty. "Anyone I know?" he asked, stone-faced, but with a twinkle in his eye.

"What?"

His mouth was straight, but his eyes were laughing. "The affair. Anyone I know?"

I rolled my eyes.

"I just wanted to go see my dad this morning without family around."

He looked puzzled. "Is that all?"

I sighed and slumped. "Yes."

"Why would I mind?" he said, leaning over the corner of the table to kiss my cheek. "It's been two months. You two probably need to talk. We can do the barbeque another time."

"Thanks, honey," I said. The tension fell from me. "We'll still barbeque. I'll call when we're ready."

Chapter 9
Vanishing Memories
Evelyn

The boxes Mom had left for me didn't have anything that would make Sam question my past. As I closed the last box, Dad came in with two cups of coffee and his "we need to talk" look. I took the cup, sat in the warm sunshine streaming through the living room window, and waited for him to start.

"Your phone call three weeks ago concerned me. I'm worried about how hiding your past is affecting you."

My eyes narrowed, my body tensed, and my heart raced. "I'm not hiding anything. Sam knows everything that he needs to know. My childhood is irrelevant."

Dad held my glare. "Do you think Sam would agree?"

I knew Sam wouldn't agree, but it wasn't his choice to make.

"Don't play therapist with me, Dad."

He grimaced. "I'm not. I'm just concerned."

Anger shot from my eyes. "It's none of your business, Dad."

He took a slow deep breath while he studied me.

"You're a psychologist, Eve. You know how blinding denial can be. I heard desperation and fear in your voice—"

"No! When we talked, I was upset about Mom. It has nothing to do with Sam."

Dad sighed. "Then why are you so afraid?"

"Because you and Mom won't let it go. I know you agree with Mom. I understand why you think I should tell Sam. But you're wrong, and it's my life. I need to live it the way I see fit. And I don't need a bomb sitting in your closet waiting to destroy my life."

His patient gaze held my glare. "Yes. It is your life, but—"

"No, Dad! It's not open for discussion," I said, shaking my head. "From the day I was old enough to think about marriage until the day I met Sam, I struggled with whether or not to tell.

Most people don't have a realistic frame of reference. They would view me through myths and lies. Condemn me because they believe I'm something that I am not."

I leaned forward, my anger driving me on. "I *won't* be a victim. I *won't* live that way. I *won't* spend the rest of my life apologizing for who I am. It's *my* choice. It's *my* life. It's *my* family. I made the right decision for *me*. End of discussion."

Dad nodded his understanding. I thought he was going to drop it.

"But Sam knows you better than anyone. He wouldn't judge you based on myths and lies."

I scowled. "You're right. He wouldn't judge me, so there isn't any point in telling him, is there?"

He gently repeated his earlier question.

"Then why are you so afraid?"

I was going to say, "I'm not afraid," but froze, mouth half-open. A vision of my birth father—more real than the air that I breathed—appeared before me. He was drunk, roaring profanities, and beating Mom because she had tried to stop him from beating me.

For the first time I understood why my past had to remain a secret. In the false logic of a child's world, I had come to believe that since my birth father hadn't wanted me for his daughter, then no man who knew my past would want me for his wife.

Before the logical understanding of my past could find root, my fear vaporized it like a drop of water on a hot skillet. Both the memory and rational thought were gone. The only thing that remained was a misty recollection that *something* important had just slipped from my mind.

The room staggered as if I had been spinning wildly and suddenly stopped. I clutched the couch to keep from falling. The room calmed and I stared at Dad through blurry eyes. I knew we had been talking about my childhood and that I had been angry, but I couldn't remember what we had said.

"I'm sorry, Dad. What were you saying?"

"Nothing." The word was filled with deep concern.

A pile of books by Dad's chair coalesced some of the fuzzy fragments of thought that were floating through my mind.

"I still have the library to go through."

Dad seemed puzzled by my statement.

"There are over two thousand books in her library," he said absentmindedly. "It would take weeks to go through them."

I looked toward the library. The haze and discomfort in my mind cleared. Going through the library was a huge chore; I was wishing Mom hadn't given her books to Sam.

"Yeah." I said, half-heartedly. Even a quick flip through the pages would take weeks, and to check every page for misplaced photos or notes would take months, if not years. I felt a headache coming on.

Dad came over to the couch, sat next to me, and took me in a bear hug.

"Love you, Eve."

Despite my anger at his meddling, his hug soothed my worries.

"Love you too, Dad."

He sat back and stared out the window.

"Sam told me he needed to build new bookcases," Dad said, seeming to be distracted by some thought, "so he would have room for your mom's collection."

His eyes cleared and his smile held the promise of a conspiracy.

"Since you don't want to risk damaging them, you could leave the bulk of the collection here for now. Give you time to come over and see your old man while we go through them.

"There are about three dozen extremely rare and valuable volumes which make up the centerpiece of her collection." Dad's eyes filled with joyful sadness, and his thoughts seemed to visit a cherished memory. "When Louise bought a new book, she'd make me wash my hands and put on white cotton gloves before she would share it with me." His smile tightened. "I know she would never have put anything in one of them. Take those for now, and we'll go through the others later."

I took a deep breath and hugged him. My secret was safe.

"Thank you," I said. "Why don't you start the barbeque, and I'll call Sam and tell him to bring the kids over."

Chapter 10
Annual Family Reunion
Evelyn

The grayed and worn redwood deck was solid and reassuring under my bare feet. For eighty years, its ancient wood had been imprinted with the memory of Irving family footsteps, crawling babies, and sun-worshiping bodies.

Sam's great-great-grandfather had built the beach house back in 1932, using hand tools and a Ford Model-A pickup. His wish was for the Salmon Creek house to become the summer gathering place of the Irving clan and relations. Over the decades, his dream bore fruit, becoming an annual pilgrimage for many. As was the custom, the clan wives and daughters came two days early to prepare the house for the annual gathering.

I was taking a short break when Sam's cousin, Annie, came out and leaned on the deck railing beside me. She was in her mid-forties and was responsible for coordinating the gathering. She always did a brilliant job.

"Taking a break?" Annie asked.

"A short one."

Concern settled onto her face as she studied the ever-restless ocean.

"I wonder what's going on with Georgette," Annie said.

I looked behind us through the huge front picture windows at Georgette's son, Patrick, sweeping the great room. There had been an unsaid rule that the base camp prep crew could only be the women and daughters, but because Patrick was suffering from kidney failure, we had readily made an exception this year.

I looked back out to sea. "I'm sure she is just having a hard time with Patrick's illness. I would get a little testy, too, if one of my kids had renal failure."

Annie shrugged. Georgette had been far beyond testy, to the point where we were all getting close to taking her up to Bodega Head and pushing her off the cliff. Annie knew I was making excuses for her, but she dropped it.

"Do you think Patrick will make it?" Annie asked softly.

Georgette had been secretive about the details concerning the search for a donor or the severity of Patrick's kidney failure. We all wanted to be there for her and support them both, but she was holding back and making it hard for us. Her reticence mystified us.

"Yes. He's young and looks healthy. He can do dialysis for a long time, and they will eventually find a match."

She nodded in concerned thought.

"Why do the women have to do all the cleaning?" Annie's seventeen-year-old daughter, Hannah, whined behind us.

We turned. Hannah was standing in the doorway with a rag and cleaning bottle in her hands.

"Because if the men did it, the house would be filthy," Grandma Rose called from the kitchen.

"And all we would have to eat and drink are steaks, chips, and beer," Georgette added.

By this time, my girls had gathered with everyone else in the great room or on the deck.

"Besides," Annie said. "This way we get to have our cleaning day splurge of ice cream and chocolate, and then our one day girl's—" she glanced at Patrick then back at Hannah. "A one day party with just us down on Doran Beach, getting our feet wet and hunting for sand dollars before everyone else gets here."

With the chores done, we luxuriated in our annual ritual of shared decadence. The kids ate their ice cream and chocolate in the house. All of us "old ladies" lay out on the deck chairs with our favorite beach sunglasses sitting lazy over our eyes. A rainbow of flip-flops hung from our toes. The shadows grew long while we nursed our personal pints of Ben & Jerry's ice cream, sipped on expensive chardonnay, and took furtive bites from a large selection of chocolate bonbons.

"What are the girls doing?" Annie asked.

"And Patrick?" Georgette added.

"In the back bedroom," I said, motioning toward the back of the house.

"Doing what?" Annie asked, with disinterest.

"If it were me, I'd be sharing a pilfered bottle of wine." Margarita said.

"Not if Hannah wants to see her eighteenth birthday," Annie said, with serious jest in her voice and a little more interest.

Grandma Rose started to get up, but I heard the kids coming.

"They're coming, Rose," I said.

She settled back down and picked up her wine.

Georgette craned her neck to see the kids. "WHAT THE HELL?"

Except for Georgette, who was on her feet and charging for the door, we all simultaneously sat up like a drill team, swung our legs off the right side of our lounge chairs and turned to see what was going on.

Aunt Margarita let out a hearty laugh, Rose snickered, and I repressed a chuckle. The girls had dressed Patrick in one of Hannah's dresses, done full makeup, and "styled" his hair. He was even wobbling on a borrowed pair of two-inch stiletto sandals. They looked like mine.

It was harmless fun, and Patrick's grin showed he was clearly a willing volunteer.

Georgette stopped inches from Hannah. "What in the hell do you think you're doing?" she screamed.

I was shocked. Georgette could be pretty strict but this was over the top. Annie and I scrambled inside.

"It's supposed to be a girl's party," Hannah said, her voice trembling. "We were just having fun."

"You don't yell at my daughter," Annie said, inserting herself between Hannah and Georgette.

Visibly shaking, Georgette turned away from Annie and the kids. Tears poured down her face. I cautiously stepped over, put my arms around her, and pulled her to me. Annie glared at Georgette with the proverbial look of death as she herded the kids into the bedroom.

After a few seconds, Georgette pulled away. By this time, Margarita was pretending to pick lint off the couch, and Aunt Jewel and Rose were pretending to clean the spotless kitchen as they stole glances.

"I'm sorry," Georgette said.

Her voice contained what I call "the sadness." It is a tone and resonance that rises like unblemished innocence from the well of the soul, carrying with it the pain our minds cannot hold. I hear it in those who have suffered the death of a dearly loved one, the infidelity of a spouse, the unfairness of terminal illness, and the betrayal of unwanted divorce.

"Would you like to talk?" I asked.

She wiped her eyes and looked to see if the bedroom door was closed. It was. She glanced at Margarita, Rose, and Jewel.

"Henry's leaving me. He found someone else."

Everyone gathered around, offering sympathy and commiserating about how much of a fool Henry was to give her up, and how she would find someone better. I felt for her, but knew it was a cover story. She had confided in me last year that she expected to be a single mom by this vacation. "The sadness" had come from somewhere else. I wondered if Patrick's illness was worse than we were being told. Perhaps the renal failure was being caused by cancer.

Annie checked to make sure it was safe and then let the kids out. Patrick was back in his own clothes, his face red from scrubbing off the makeup, and his hair plastered down from washing out the hair gel. Georgette apologized to the kids and Annie.

"Anyone want s'mores?" Rose asked, holding graham crackers, marshmallows, and chocolate bars high in the air.

Aunt Margarita followed her with a bottle of Pinot Noir and a box of instant hot chocolate. Dinner was served.

The surf crashed onto the soft sand only feet from where we stood.

"Mommy is a scaredy cat. Mommy is a scaredy cat," Angela and Grace chanted.

"That's right, and if you girls want to get all cold and wet, there's the whole ocean," I said, motioning to the protected stretch of Doran Beach.

"Come on, Mom. You never go in," Angela said, bouncing with the limitless energy of youth. "We want to swim with you. Besides, you're a mermaid and mermaids like the ocean."

"Not this one. You two go have fun."

Knowing it was a lost cause, the girls ran out and splashed into the chilly waves. Georgette stepped next to me, with her eyes fixed on the kids.

"Most of the time, I think I've got you figured out," she said. "But other times ..."

I looked over at her, unsure what she was talking about.

"Oh?"

"Yeah. You're perfect," she continued, her eyes still fixed on the kids. "The perfect husband. The perfect kids. The perfect job. The perfect body. The perfect life. And the perfect answers when someone has a problem."

Her voice held the scent of old bitterness and a shade of jealousy. I couldn't tell if it was aimed at me or at life in general.

I said, "I'm not—"

"Perfect," she finished for me. "No. None of us is, but you always have the perfect answers. I need one."

I didn't say anything. I looked back out to sea and thought about Ted, a sixteen-year-old client who committed suicide three years ago. I hadn't had the answer he needed—much less the perfect one.

I waited for her.

"You afraid of the water?" she asked.

I knew that wasn't her real question. "Yes. I had a bad experience."

Grace was knocked down by a wave. We watched in silence for her to stand back up. She emerged from the water smiling and then threw herself into the next wave with Angela.

"So why do you wear a bathing suit?" Georgette asked.

I blushed and knew that wasn't her real question either.

"Partly so I can tan. But it's mainly because I like the way Sam looks at me when I'm wearing it."

She nodded, as a bittersweet smile shadowed her face. We continued looking out at the kids. I sensed her guilt and grief slowly boiling to the surface.

"The Bible says God will punish our children for our sins. Why is God so hateful? Why does he hurt my son for what I did?"

She needed to talk, and here wasn't the right place. "Annie and Jewel can watch the kids," I said. "Let's go back to the beach house. It'll be empty for a few hours."

I pulled two mugs from the cupboard and reached for the pot of well-aged coffee. Georgette snatched up a bottle of wine.

"That won't help," I said.

She sneered at me. "Like hell it won't."

Her grief was turning vengeful. I had seen clients going down hard and fast before. Georgette's guilt was trying to push her in that direction. I wasn't her therapist, and there wasn't a quick fix.

"You need to see someone," I said. "Talk about the stresses in your life."

She huffed and took a long swig off the bottle. "I'm that fucked, huh?"

"No," I said, unsure I wanted to continue. "Your son needs a kidney transplant and your husband is divorcing you. They are both extremely stressful. Having to deal with both at once is brutal. An objective person who understands life's problems can help you navigate the pain and confusion so you don't end up on the rocks."

She turned away and took another long gulp. I was ready to tell her to find me after she sobered up.

She spun around and glared at me.

"Patrick isn't Henry's," she blurted. "Henry wanted to donate his kidney, but the tissue match wasn't even close. He did a DNA test."

I had heard several such revelations over the years.

"Is that why he's divorcing you?" I asked.

She shivered. "Things have been bad for a long time. It's his excuse to stop trying."

"Does Patrick know?"

"No. None of the kids know." Her eyes brimmed with tears of guilt and shame. "They can't know it's my fault."

She slowly closed her eyes and lowered her arm in defeat. The wine dangled at her side for a moment, then the smooth glass bottle slipped from her fingertips and thudded heavily on the floor. A spray of fruity alcohol erupted, dotting our legs with purple and filling the room with its earthy scent.

Only the sound of the surf outside intruded on the silence in the room.

I handed her a cup of coffee and we sat on the couch. For the next two hours, she cried, cursed, justified, blamed, rationalized, and despaired as she purged herself of her affair, told me about her fears for Patrick, and condemned herself with a litany of could-haves, should-haves, and would-haves.

She closed her eyes and leaned her head back as if in surrender. "I used to pray that God would make Patrick well, but then I realized how ludicrous it was to pray to the God who made him sick and might even kill him just to spite me. What kind of God is that?"

"It's not God," I said. "Experts believe that four to seven

percent of children are attributed to the wrong father. Statistically, the incidence of birth defects, illness, injury, and death is the same as for any other child. The facts don't support the idea that God hurts our children to get back at us."

Her frown deepened. "But ..."

"The myth that God hurts our children comes from men who claim God is vengeful and cruel so they can manipulate us through fear," I said. "Some promote the myth believing that fear makes people do what is right. But mostly, the belief comes from our need to feel that we have control so that we can feel safe.

"Our emotional logic says, 'If I had been good, this wouldn't have happened. So if I am good from now on, nothing else bad will happen.' It's not God punishing you. It's just life."

Georgette opened her eyes and nodded. Sadness hung heavy in her voice, "I used to believe in the American dream: get married, have kids, the white picket fence, growing old together. Then he cheated, I cheated back, and now my life is crap.

"I don't know what to believe. There is no happily-ever-after. If he hadn't ... If I hadn't ..."

"If you hadn't had an affair, you never would have had Patrick," I said. "If you had a choice, would you choose Patrick and the problems of divorce and dialysis, or would you choose for him to never have been born?"

She stared blankly at the far side of the room for several minutes. Without a word, she went to the picture window, leaned against the warm glass with both hands, and looked out at the calm seas. I moved near. Her eyes were filled with sadness, but a slight curl graced the corner of her mouth.

"Perfect," she whispered. Tears slipped down her cheek. "I need to be alone for a while."

The traditional last night bonfire cast long, wavering shadows along the beach and filled the night air with the smell of campfire, wet bathing suits, and potato chips. With Sam's strong arms wrapped around me, I was at peace. I snuggled against him and we watched the last hokeypokey dance around the bonfire.

When it ended, the kids swarmed the s'mores table, snapping up the skewers and marshmallows before charging back to the bonfire to roast their treats and make s'mores.

Half of the marshmallows were turned into torches as the kids watched them burn in giddy fascination. Grace carefully checked her marshmallow every few seconds until it was a uniform golden brown. She came running over to me, just like she had the last two years, with a perfect epicurean delight on her stick.

"Here, Mom. I cooked this one for you." I jerked my head back to avoid being impaled.

The caramelized sugar coating called to me, and after my thoughtful daughter had gone to such trouble, I couldn't refuse.

"Thank you, sweetie. It looks perfect."

I gently pulled it from the stick, feeling the delicate caramel shell wanting to collapse into the molten core. I took a careful bite, letting the warmth and sugary sweetness fill my senses. I closed my eyes and smiled in ecstasy.

"Mmmmm. That is so delicious." I opened my eyes to see her bouncing with delight.

"Want another one, Mom?"

"Thank you, but no, sweetie. I bet your daddy would like one—nice and black."

Grace spun and charged back to the fire. I flinched under a playful pinch.

"Black," Sam said. "You know I don't like them burnt,"

I craned my neck to look up, and smiled.

"But you're such a good daddy; you will eat it to make her happy."

He shook his head, then gave me a quick peck on the lips.

I settled back into his arms and watched Grace trying to blow out the burning marshmallow, before shaking it in a frenzied effort to extinguish it. Helplessly, we watched the flaming ball of sugar rise in the night sky and then plummet harmlessly back into the fire. Before I had a chance to move, Grandma Rose was beside her, giving instructions on the safe way to burn her daddy's treat.

"Rumor has it you cured Georgette of being a bitch," Sam said.

The tone in his voice told me I was being baited.

"And you believe rumors?" I cautiously said.

He snickered. "I was just thinking, if you had some of that magic left over, I've got this wife—"

I elbowed him hard enough to hurt but not hurt too much, then jumped up.

"You bugger. I'm going to tell your mommy on you."

His smile was smug—too smug. I kicked sand at him and then took off running down the beach. Within seconds, he caught up, grabbed me, and with little effort lifted me over his shoulder. He headed for the ocean, his tone playful.

"Bad girl. I'll teach you to kick sand."

It wasn't a game anymore. My voice was trembling and my scream drowned out the roar of the surf.

"No, Sam. Don't you dare!"

I could hear his feet tromping through the shallow water towards the breakers. The cold wet spray assaulted me. In the dark, I saw the reflections of light off the menacing black water that surrounded us.

"God—don't, Sam!" I screamed.

A truck was moving slowly beside me as I walked along a dark road. Someone was calling my name. I looked over and saw Sam. I stared at him, trying to understand why he was holding a beach towel to a bloody nose and why his left ear looked swollen.

He's hurt.

Staring at him, the long-ago nightmare receded. I looked around and realized I was walking along Salmon Creek instead of the flood control channel—unsure why I was here.

The fragmented memories returned. I remembered Sam carrying me to the ocean. I remembered the panic rising up in primordial desperation. I remembered flailing with all my strength. I remembered the burning water stealing the air from my lungs. I remembered fleeing over the dunes, and the gravel cutting my feet.

I remembered Cinnamon.

Aware of the pain, I looked down. In the reflection from the truck's headlights, I saw the crimson blood and stinging salt water pooling around my chipped pedicure.

"I'm sorry, Eve. I didn't mean ..." Sam said, his voice filled with worry and regret.

I looked up at him, and for a millisecond saw Cinnamon's lifeless eyes.

"Take me home, Sam. I need to go home."

Chapter 11
A New Friend
Evelyn

I loved San Francisco's Fisherman's Wharf. The salt smell of the ocean. The tourists speaking dozens of different languages. The excited children pulling their exhausted parents in every direction. Fresh seafood. And the Ghirardelli chocolate factory. A city paradise.

Barbara had arrived early to hold a table. We hugged.

"How are you doing, Barbara?"

"Pretty good. I've ordered for us. Shrimp for you, right?"

"Yes. Thank you."

After Barbara had collapsed backstage, I accompanied her to the hospital. In the hours we spent together waiting for tests and filling out police reports on her handyman, I had seen someone hiding behind a lifetime of hurt that I thought I might like to know.

Barbara launched into her pet peeve.

"Even with the best lawyers, the state won't let me drive for a year. Damned seizure. The only one I've ever had. And like, who wouldn't have one if that happened to them? Now I have to take a cab, bum a ride, or find a chauffeur if I want to go anywhere."

She wasn't tanning anymore and her skin was approaching a natural warm flesh color; it looked good on her. Barbara had also cut back on the heavy makeup she had used to hide the bruises. She was beginning to look like an average, middle-aged mom.

"Frank reconsider?"

"Nah," she sneered. "Said I caused 'irreparable damage to his public image.' Even if he had, it's like you said—I'm probably better off without him."

I didn't bite my tongue fast enough. "So, who's your next

victim?"

She scowled at me.

I blushed. "Sorry, old habits die hard."

She waved her hand to say no-big-deal and took a sip of her chardonnay. Her grin was impish and I knew it was payback time.

"And how's that hunky husband of yours?"

I returned her scowl.

"Just kidding. He's so stuck on you, I wouldn't stand a chance. Besides, I'm not his type. He likes nice, intellectual girls."

I feigned insult. "'Nice, intellectual girls?' You make me sound like a nerd."

"Nah. Nerds aren't as pretty and don't dress as nice as you.

"Anyway, I've been seeing that shrink you told me about—Dr. Sharma. She said I should be a human being before I look for another sugar daddy."

I was incredulous. "She said that?"

"She put it real nice, but that's what she meant."

She paused. Her eyes narrowed with concern as she studied me and searched for words. She untied and retied her scarf in silence. Putting her elbows on the table, she leaned toward me. Her eyes softened and her chin quivered.

"Thank you for being my friend, Eve. You're the only one I have."

She jerked back into her chair, looking like she had bit into a lemon.

"All those other bitches I thought were friends were nothing but a bunch of backstabbing social climbers."

"I'm sorry."

Her anger evaporated, and she sank down into the chair.

"I woulda done the same to them."

I had grown to like Barbara. She could make you laugh so hard it hurt, was more unpredictable than the weather, and was remarkably easy to talk with when she wasn't trying to impress or belittle you. And sometimes her simple childlike view of life made me rethink what I thought I knew.

But because she had no moral boundaries around men, and was only beginning to learn what it was to be a mother or real friend, I was taking our friendship slow.

She sat up straight with a huge smile, her eyes wide with excitement.

"The cops think they caught him."

"Who? Stanley, your handyman?"

"Yeah. San Diego. Some guy caught him poking his wife and beat the living crap out of him. The wife thought her husband was going to kill the bastard and called the cops. Shame he didn't kill him. Stoned on pain killers, the prick gave his real name and told the police he had lived in Marin. After lunch, I'm going to see a dick and do a positive ID."

I frowned, not sure I should ask.

"See a dick?"

"Yeah. A dick. Like Dick Tracy. Detective. My dad had all the old Dick Tracy comics and read them to me when I was little." She glared at the table. "Dick's girlfriend, Tess Trueheart, was just as screwed up as me. They had an eighteen-year courtship, during which she married a baseball jock who offed himself." She sneered and shook her head. "Some courtship, huh?

"After forty five years, Tess threatened to divorce Dick's self-absorbed ass, but chickened out." She looked at me with pain and frustration on her face. "Why do we do it, Eve? Why do we put up with assholes and jerks?" She slumped into her chair again.

"They're not all jerks," I said.

She sighed. "Yeah. Just the ones who want me."

I wasn't going to tell her she had thrown away a good one when she divorced Barry. I was going to tell her that if she were patient, she would find a nice guy when she was ready. But she shot up out of her seat, causing our drinks to shimmy on the table.

"I want some chocolate. Ya wanna go to Ghirardelli's?"

I chuckled. "They haven't brought our lunch yet."

"Oh, yeah." She looked disdainfully at the waiter coming with our food and sat down.

She grimaced and shook her head. "Ya know. It's hard being a mom."

I nodded in agreement.

"I thought my nannies and governesses were doing a great job with Madonna, but she's as fucked up as me."

She leaned over her lobster toward me, her scarf slipping into the butter.

"You have three. They're great kids. How do you do it?"

"Lots of love. Lots of attention. A firm, but not crushing hand. And a lot of luck. Even with luck, it's hard work, and you never, ever get it perfectly right."

She leaned back, pulled off her scarf, and dropped it on the table.

"Yeah. Tell me about it."

"How is Madonna doing?"

Her lips quivered, her eyes reddened, and a worried smile graced her lips.

"Last night at bedtime, she told me she liked calling me Mom. It's so weird to be called that. I feel like a fake. I don't know how to be a mother, but her shrink says I need to try. I'm just going to fuck her up more than she is."

I understood her fears. "The natural mother is a myth, Barbara. We need to learn how to be good parents. Most people spend more time learning to use their cell phone than they spend learning how to raise their child. There are a lot of classes and good books out there—"

Barbara sat up, her face aglow.

"Yeah. My shrink gave me a book. I'm halfway through it. I never would have guessed half that crap, and it really does work better when you don't scream at your kid." She grinned. "It confuses her."

I couldn't help chuckling.

"Keep reading, Barbara, and Madonna will have the best mother she could ever want."

Barbara frowned again and looked down.

"I guess," she said. She looked over the top of her sunglasses. "Do you believe in God?"

"Yes."

She raised her head so she could look directly at me. "Which one?"

"Most people agree that the Jews, Christians, and Muslims worship the same God," I said. "I take it further. I believe that as long as it is a compassionate and loving deity, it is the same one."

She slowly nodded, and said, "I believed in God when I was little. I went to church, prayed, and tried to be a good girl. My Sunday School teacher said that if I prayed and believed, God would answer my prayers.

"Well, I prayed He'd make my parents not drink and fight anymore, and He didn't do crap. My dad would still get drunk and hit Mom, and she'd still get drunk and hit me."

Barbara glared at some absent person.

"My shrink said it would help to find," her voice filled with bitter mocking, "a spiritual connection." She looked at the sky as if to say, up-yours. "If God doesn't answer prayers, what the fucking difference does it make?"

I said, "You don't have to do it just because Dr. Sharma said it was a good idea."

She scrunched up her face and looked down. "But I ... I feel so alone, even when I was married. Something is missing and the booze doesn't keep the loneliness and pain away anymore."

She sat back, scowled, and looked me up and down for a moment. "You're a lot smarter than me. Why do you believe in Him?"

"Lots of reasons."

Barbara's eye twitched, and her brow furrows deepened.

"But He fucking lied about answering prayers. He didn't do shit."

I was ready for that chocolate.

"I'm not a Bible scholar or theologian," I said. "Do you know someone who is?"

She shook her head and sneered. "I went to church with Frank because he wanted me to and I figured it was probably good for Madonna. But I know when I'm being conned. Hell, churches can't agree if baptism is drown you, dunk your head in a bucket, throw some water in your face, or spit on you. So how can you trust them when it comes to the important crap? Most preachers can out snake-oil a lawyer." Her anger softened to concern. "I trust you, and you aren't trying to sell me anything. I want to know what Eve thinks."

"Most people would say I'm wrong."

Barbara chuckled. "So, I'll join 'em."

I looked down and sighed as a tide of old memories pulled on my heart. "Just before I turned seventeen, two very close friends of mine were killed. I tried to save one and prayed for God's help. He didn't help."

Barbara cringed and said, "Sorry."

"On the other hand, I should have died twice, and I believe my mom's prayers saved me."

She frowned and nodded.

"We could speculate until the end of time as to why God does or doesn't answer prayers, but it would be pointless," I said. "The workings of the world are too complex for us to understand what would happen if God gave us what we wanted.

"So when God doesn't answer my prayers, I take it on faith that there is a good and loving reason, even if I never know what that reason is."

Barbara nodded and then said, "I'm sorry about your friends, but why pray if He is going to do whatever He wants anyway?"

"Because sometimes prayers are answered," I said.

She scowled and poked at her lobster. "It sounds like snake oil bullshit to me."

"I can understand that," I said. "Since it appears random, it is easy to say that prayers don't work. But there are other reasons to pray."

She huffed. "Like what?"

"People who believe in a loving God and pray are happier. I pray to remind myself that I'm not alone. That there is someone out there, bigger than me, who does care. That there is a reason for everything.

"It gives me hope. It comforts me when I feel the pain of loss. It helps me to become the person I want to be."

Barbara slumped in her chair and studied me. "All I ever wanted was to be rich and famous."

I snickered. "You *are* rich Barbara."

She grinned. "Yeah. I guess one out of two ain't bad." She sighed. "But I don't want to be famous anymore. I don't know what I want."

"To be a good mom?"

"Ain't that the fuckin' truth!"

"Prayer helps give me patience and insight so I can be a better mom," I said.

She chewed on her lower lip for a moment as she thought.

"So what does one of these prayers sound like?" she asked.

"Like most. Please keep my family safe and feed the hungry. Give me the strength and wisdom to forgive those who've hurt me. Guide me as I go through my day. And I always end by asking that all things be for the greatest good.

Barbara scowled. "The what?"

"What is best for everyone, not just me. God's will be done. Not mine."

She frowned. "So you pray for nothing, and that way you're not disappointed."

I chuckled. "I guess from a certain viewpoint, maybe. What do you want, Barbara?"

Her voice shaking, she said, "For Madonna to be okay."

"And what would that take?"

She thought for a minute and then smiled softly. "Dr. Sharma said that me being alright would help Madonna. Maybe the bitch is right."

She nodded to herself, and whispered, "For the greatest good."

After a few seconds, she pulled herself from her thoughts, winked at me, and said, "You ready for that chocolate now?"

"Oh, yeah."

Chapter 12
Louise's Journals
Sam

"Her grave is to the left, Eve," I said.

"I know, Sam," she snapped.

An annoyed frown flooded her face as she turned left on the winding and poorly marked cemetery road. She seemed to hold onto the irritation. I assumed it was so she didn't have to feel her grief. Today was the one-year anniversary of her mother's passing. She was hurting, but trying to hide it from the kids. Or maybe from herself.

Despite her annoyance with me, I smiled. I loved having her in my life. Our first meeting had been the classical fairytale love-at-first-sight. We had barely known each other when I asked her to be my wife, but I had known in my heart that it was right. Our life together had been good—better than good. Nearly perfect.

The only gray cloud had been her secretiveness about her past. I knew Nick was her stepdad, and that both she and her mom hated her birth father, but that was all. The silence about her past had bothered me because my first wife, Clora, had started lying and hiding things before she made my life hell.

I had asked Eve something about her birth father one day. Instead of evading like usual, she had turned to me with her eyes narrow and mouth so tight that her lips had turned white.

"I'll make you a deal, Sam," she had said. "You tell me everything about your first wife, and I will tell you about the bastard who fucked my mom."

I stared at her, unable to respond. I had never heard her use the f-word before, and hadn't since. After a few seconds, Eve had turned and stomped off.

Clora and the hell she had put me through—and my part in it—was in the past. Eve's knowing the details could only hurt our relationship. I had learned, grown, and moved beyond those days. I had my secrets. It was only fair to let her have hers.

As the years passed and our family grew, I buried my uneasiness with the knowledge that I knew Eve's heart and that we were perfect together.

Eve parked the van. The low overcast was thinning and the sun was trying hard to break through. A heavy dew blanketed the lawn and soaked our shoes. As we approached Grandma Louise's grave, a ray of sun graced it, causing the dewdrops to sparkle like a million rainbow diamonds. We all stared in amazement.

"Grandma's saying, 'I love you,'" Angela said, in a soft reverent voice.

Eve trembled and struggled to hold back her tears. After a minute, the glow faded. Eve and the girls placed a spring bouquet just below the marker, then sat on blankets, while Chris and I stood watchfully over them.

"The girls and I want to go to Muir Beach," Eve said as I pulled out of the cemetery. "It was one of Mom's favorite places to meditate by the ocean. If you and Chris want to come along, we would be happy to have you."

I checked the rearview mirror and saw Chris roll his eyes and slump down into his seat.

"I wanted to get the garage straightened up a little," I said. "It's getting hard to get in and out of the van."

"We'll get dinner out. Will you two be alright?"

I winked at her. "Oh, yeah. I'm sure we can find a bag of chips and a six-pack."

She gave me a playful "yeah-right" look. "Maybe you can find a pizza and soda instead."

I made a show of my smug smile. "Great idea, honey. Wish I'd thought of it."

After the girls left for the beach, Chris went to Katelyn's house to do homework, and I started on the garage. I had cleaned the garage three years ago, with the vow that I would keep it neat and organized. I hadn't succeeded.

The best place to start was my workbench so I could get to my tools and work on Evelyn's honey-do list, not to mention some maintenance on the kayaks.

An hour later, the bench was clear, a large trash bag was threatening to explode, and two boxes of charity donations sat in the middle of Eve's parking space. It was time to tackle the mystery boxes stacked against the north wall.

I always labeled storage boxes, something I had never been able to get Eve to do. Granted, she could look at ten identical boxes five years after packing them and list just about every single item in them, but that didn't help me when she wasn't around.

With felt-tip marker in hand, I attacked the stack at the garage door, intending to work my way to the back wall. The fourth cardboard box was small, ragged, water-stained, and had a big black X on the side. It was definitely not Evelyn's and not mine. I popped the folded flaps open and saw old fiction books: *Tom Sawyer, The Grapes of Wrath,* and *Treasure Island.* These particular copies didn't look familiar and were reprints in fair condition, not worth more than a dollar or two apiece.

I remembered the box from Louise's library. It had been under a small lamp table, hidden by a tablecloth. When I showed the box to Nick, he checked the top layer and said he thought it was unwanted volumes Louise would donate to charity. He wanted to look through the box before I took them, so I had set it aside. Somehow it got mixed in with the other cartons and I hadn't noticed until I got home. I had stacked it in the garage intending to check it for Nick, but had forgotten.

Checking for first editions or any book that caught my interest, I picked through the box. Only the first two layers were fiction; the rest was a collection of diaries and journals.

I laid them out on my workbench and pulled up a stool. The oldest was an inexpensive child's diary, with faded orange and yellow stripes across the water-damaged cardboard cover. The bookplate said, "This Diary Belongs To: Louise Elizabeth Santoro, 1964."

Santoro? Must be Louise's maiden name. Seems strange I never knew.

It was easy to recognize Louise's penmanship, although it was a little rough compared to her refined and fluid adult handwriting. I loved her elegant script and appreciated that she had taught it to Angela.

Louise's letters and words were graceful, flowing, artistic, and legible. I had never met anyone who took more pride in her writing.

Let's see. 1964. That would have made Louise about 13.

I knew it was wrong to go through other people's diaries, and if she had been alive I wouldn't have dreamed of it. But she wasn't alive, and Evelyn had so many secrets. I was curious, so I thumbed through the oldest one and saw references to Elvis and the Beatles, schoolwork, her parents, a brother, and a sister.

Hmm. Evelyn said she didn't have any aunts or uncles. I guess they could have all died in a car crash or house fire. It happens. Still, she never mentioned them.

The journals ranged from the 1964 child's diary to a 1994 leather-bound hardcover with a gold leaf imprint that said, "Louise E. Strand" on the face. Evelyn would have turned seventeen that year. The '65 through '68 and '81 through '85 journals were missing, which made it a set of nineteen. I thumbed through a couple and discovered Louise hadn't been consistent in keeping them. She rarely had entries running for more than a full week, with days, weeks, or months between them.

I had at least three hours until Evelyn got home, so I decided to take a break, grab a coffee, and browse the journals to find out what had happened to her relatives.

Dead? Disowned each other? Witness protection? Abducted by aliens?

In the '65 diary, Louise wrote at length about a Thanksgiving at her grandparents. She mentioned all four of her grandparents, three uncles and five aunts, her brother, her sister, and close to a dozen cousins.

That's a lot of family.

The phone rang. Katelyn's mom asked if Chris could stay for dinner. Pizza was out. I'd find some leftovers in the fridge later and nuke them.

The rest of the '65 diary was adolescent girl talk, so I moved on to the '69 journal. Louise talked about high school senior year events, her boyfriend, her senior prom and what they did after ... A little too personal. I flipped to the next page.

Maybe I had better read less and skim more. I'm looking for family history, not intimacies. Although, it is those intimacies that get a lot of families started.

The rest of 1969 held predictable life events. She broke up with her boyfriend over the summer and started college in the fall. She made occasional mention of her immediate and extended family, but nothing out of the ordinary.

The 1970 journal had very few entries. Most indicated she was occupied with schoolwork and having fun with her friends. Just before Christmas 1971, she had an entry that was barely legible and tear-stained.

> *December 21, 1971 Tuesday*
> *"Grandpa Adam died yesterday from a stroke. It still doesn't seem real. I know we grow old and die, but he was always bigger than life. He seemed immortal. He can't be dead. It has to be a mistake."*

I kept flipping pages, but the rest of the diary was blank. The next journal was dated 1973.

> *June 19, 1973, Monday*
> *"I started my new job in the auditing department. I'm their first woman accountant at this level. Some of the men resent me, but they need to learn it's a new world and women can ..."*

> *July 9, 1973 Monday*
> *"There was the cutest electrician in my department today, rewiring the offices for some new type of phone system. He reminded me of David Cassidy, but all cute guys remind me of David. He kept checking me out, and I was having a hard time just adding two and two. I'm still a little distracted. Before he left, he introduced himself as Duke Grant and asked me if I would go out with him. He seemed a little rough around the edges, and I said no of course. I know he will be here all week, so if he keeps asking nicely, I might go to lunch with him Friday."*

Duke? I had a vague memory of someone saying that Louise's ex was Duke.

> *July 13, 1973, Friday*
> *"Duke took me to lunch. I couldn't eat. All I could think about was being a bad girl with him. He's so perfect. I'm in love. We are going to the zoo tomorrow and then dinner and dancing. I bought new lacy panties and a skimpy bra on the way home."*

I never would have guessed that Louise was that, um, passionate. I decided to skim again.

May 12, 1974, Sunday
"At lunch after church, I told Duke I was pregnant and he yelled at me in front of everyone in the restaurant. I guess I was pretty stupid to let it happen. I asked him what he wanted to do. He told me to get rid of 'it.' He wants me to get rid of our baby."

I began to understand why Evelyn hated him.

May 18, 1974, Saturday
"I haven't heard from Duke since last Sunday and he doesn't return my calls. I don't know which is worse, being an unwed mother or having an abortion. I don't want an abortion, but if I keep my baby, my company will fire me. How will I support us?"

May 19, 1974, Sunday
"Duke came by this afternoon and proposed. I was so happy and wanted him to take me to tell my parents, maybe go to dinner to celebrate. But he said he had a rush job and needed to get back to work. I should be happy. Why am I crying?"

May 30, 1974, Thursday
"I had my last wedding dress fitting today and Mom asked me how far along I was. She tried to be happy for me, but I know she was disappointed. I felt dirty. How can Mom shame me with just a look?"

June 9, 1974, Saturday
"In a week I will be Mrs. Louise Grant. It is killing Mom that I won't be married by a priest, but Duke refused to join the church. I love him dearly but I know he would never have proposed if I wasn't pregnant. He's a good man and did the right thing. I'll be a good wife and make him happy. Mom will see I'm not a slut."

Eve and I had been married by a minister. I'm not sure Eve or Louise would have had it any other way. I personally didn't care. Touchy feely bothered me, and religion was all about touchy feely. I liked hard provable facts. No one had yet proven that God existed, much less that He belonged to their church.

I checked the time; it was late. I assumed Eve and the girls were having dinner somewhere, and Chris was displaying his best table manners for Katelyn and her parents. I wasn't hungry, so I went and grabbed another cup of coffee.

Until now, I hadn't realized that Louise was nearly as secretive as Eve. I had known Louise for eleven years and yet I didn't know her at all. She was Eve's mom, Nick's wife, and a nice person. We shared a love of old books. She worked as a CPA and had great penmanship. She loved her grandchildren and was overly protective of Eve. Other than that, I knew nothing about her, even though she had been an important part of our lives and our family. I knew so little of Eve's past.

I guessed Eve would be home in about an hour, and I had too much junk strewn across the garage for her to park the van.

If Eve found the journals, I suspected they would disappear. It seemed like a good idea to "forget" about them until I had a chance to finish reading.

What would the harm be?

Chapter 13
Love Eternal
Evelyn

I took Angela's clean laundry into her room and set it on her bed. She was so engrossed in her calligraphy that I wasn't sure she even noticed me.

Perhaps I was just a proud mommy, but I admired Angela's poetry and how she blended it perfectly with her art. Numerous examples of her work were scattered throughout the house, like kisses of happiness. I decided to risk the wrath of her moodiness of late and took a peek over her shoulder.

She had selected handmade paper in mottled shades of light pink with watermark hearts. I read the title: *"Grandma Louise."* Our visit to the cemetery last weekend had left me raw. I forced back the tears.

With great care, Angela wrote "consoles" in perfect script.

"This is for Grandma," she said, with sad, comforting love floating on her words.

"That's very sweet of you."

I stood behind Angela, wiping a few stray tears from my cheek as I read her poem.

Grandma Louise
by Angela Irving

My Grandma's gone to heaven, far above the clouds she flew,
But in my room, beneath the stars, I feel her love anew.
In my dreams she speaks to me, and holds me in her love,
We laugh, we play, we talk and sing, and share the stars above.

I tell her of the many things, my secrets no one knows,

What's in my heart and on my mind, and in my silly prose.
She laughs, we hug, and then she says, "with you I'll always be,"
"I'll watch you grow from high above, and always be with thee."

She kisses me, we hug again, and dreams they fade away,
And to the stars, she goes again, while here below I stay.
I rise disheveled, my mind a jumble, love and grief combined,
Grandma's gone, but she's still here, how strange our love's entwined.

But in my dreams, in her love, my heart and soul consoles,
Then warmth and peace, they come to me, her love within me grows.
Forever she will be with me, of this I surely know,
For in my heart and in my soul, her love will always glow.

After she finished writing the last word and set her pen down, I hugged her.

"It's beautiful. Thank you, sweetheart. I'm sure Grandma loves it as much as I do."

I turned to leave.

"Mom? Could you close the door?"

It wasn't a "close it on the way out," it was an "I need to talk in private."

I closed it and sat on the edge of her bed. "Yes?"

She turned toward me and struggled to find words, then stared at her hands and fidgeted. I waited. She looked up, her eyes moist with fearful yearning.

"I really, really, really like Daniel." Her fear faded quickly, replaced by anger. "Brad, an older boy at school, said it was puppy love. That by next year, we would hate each other. I hate Brad. He's a doofus."

The anger faded, and she looked imploringly into my eyes.

"I looked up puppy love," she said. "They said it wasn't real, that it was childish foolishness. That it goes away." Concern filled her eyes. "I don't want to not love Daniel."

I held out my arms. "Come here, sweetheart."

She came over and I held her.

"You love him?"

She nodded. "Yes."

"Does he feel the same way about you?"

She smiled warmly and nodded again.

"Then it doesn't matter what Brad or anyone else thinks ... except me and your father, of course."

She chuckled.

"You're growing up and becoming a woman. It's not always easy and it's never simple. You love me. You get angry with me sometimes. And sometimes I disappoint you. It's part of life and living with other people. You won't always be enamored with Daniel. At some point, you will see him as an individual—"

"Oh, but I do. He's so smart and athletic and hot. He's perfect."

The rest of my sentence was going to be, "—and that he isn't perfect." I didn't finish it.

"That's wonderful, sweetheart."

Worry caressed her brow. "The web says that if you marry your puppy love, you'll end up leading a dog's life."

I frowned. "You're right. Brad is a doofus. Ditto for the dog's life thing." I shifted, so we could easily look at each other. "A lucky few fall in love when they are young—like you and Daniel. They grow up together, marry, and live long and happy lives. No one can know if you and Daniel will be one of those rare couples, but I know one thing for sure."

She looked eagerly into my eyes.

"If you try to be what you think he wants," I said, "the love will die. You need to be yourself."

She nodded in foggy understanding, her face aglow with misty-eyed hopes and dreams.

Angela hugged me. "Thanks, Mom."

She went back to her art, and I started to leave.

"Angela Wilson. Mr. and Ms. Daniel Wilson," she said to herself.

"Mr. Daniel and Dr. Angela Wilson," I corrected.

She looked at me and frowned. After a moment, a smile lit her face.

"Dr. Daniel and Dr. Angela Wilson," she proudly announced.

I smiled. "I like your thinking."

Chapter 14
Easter Service
Evelyn

Felicity considered herself a "non-practicing Buddhist," but always joined us for Easter and Christmas services to make her stepmom happy. As Sam pulled into the church parking lot, I noticed her rusted hulk of a truck; her car must have died again.

Despite her claims of being a starving artist, she was a savvy businesswoman and the most frugal person I had ever known. She could easily pay cash for a top-end luxury car and a modest house on Nob Hill with plenty left over, but that lifestyle wasn't her.

Felicity's eyes sparkled with infatuation as she walked toward us on the arm of someone whom I assumed to be a new boyfriend.

I frowned. *What happened to Dwayne?*

Two weeks ago, she had found the receipt for an engagement ring when she was doing Dwayne's laundry. When we talked on Thursday, she was giddy with expectation because he had planned a special date with her for yesterday. I had expected to see her, Dwayne, and the engagement ring at Easter Service this morning.

She glowed as she snuggled up to her new beau. "This is Mark Antony, no relation to Cleopatra's flame. Mark, this is my best friend, Eve, her husband Sam, and their absolutely incredible kids, Grace, Chris, and Angela."

With one-inch heels, Felicity stood even with Mark. His suit was good quality with no wear, his oxfords weren't broken in, his shirt looked like it was ironed straight out of the package, and his tie looked brand new. He was tanned, like a man who worked outdoors all year, and his calloused hands said he didn't spend much time behind a desk.

After basic introductions, Sam asked him what he did.

"I'm an outdoors sports and recreation instructor mainly," Mark said. "Fishing, rafting, backpacking, cross-country skiing, surfing, diving, kayaking. Whatever is in season that I can make a buck doing while getting people out-of-doors and active."

I caught Sam's smile. Most people would have thought he was pleased to hear how talented and versatile Mark was. But I knew he was thinking something like, "Perfect. He's just as irresponsible as Felicity. Do what they want when they want."

Sometimes I envied free spirits like them, but I wouldn't trade the stability of a family and home.

After introductions, Chris went to find Katelyn, and the girls hurried off to find their friends and show off their Easter dresses. As we walked to the sanctuary, Sam and Mark talked about the best abalone diving spots, while Felicity and I talked about how pretty and grown-up the girls looked.

Before the service started, I took a quick trip to the ladies' room. Felicity accompanied me.

"So what happened with Dwayne and the ring?" I asked. "And what's with Mark?"

She glared at far-off thoughts. "Dwayne suggested we take a kayak class. I already knew how to kayak but figured he was setting up a grand proposal and went along with it. The class was a half-day paddle in Tomales Bay.

"I was thinking that after kayaking in the ocean, he'd take me to our favorite seafood restaurant and ask me to marry him. But nooooooo. We're out there paddling around, and he casually says, 'Oh. By the way. Gloria and I got engaged.'"

She glared at the sink, her whole body quivering with anger. The words rumbled out from between her teeth like an 8.0 magnitude earthquake. "Before he knew what happened, I rolled our tandem kayak, dumping him in the water. While he was still kissing the fish, I Eskimo-rolled it upright again and took off for shore, leaving his worthless ass to swim back." She stopped shaking as smug satisfaction overwhelmed her tight smile.

"Oh, my. I'm so sorry," I said.

She nodded back over her shoulder. "That's where Mark comes in. He was our instructor. He cut off my escape and said I couldn't leave Dwayne out there. I told him there was no way in hell—" She looked up sheepishly and mumbled "Sorry, God," then went back to her story. "No way in *heck* I would let him back in the kayak with me." She smiled. "I expected Mark to argue with me, but he smiled so sweet and said, 'It's illegal to dump your trash in the ocean. The fine will bankrupt you. So I'll tell you what …'" Her smile quivered and tears came to her eyes. "He's just so sweet. He gave me his beautiful wood strip single and took the screaming-yellow plastic double back to pick up the garbage."

I laughed.

She grinned and continued. "On shore, Mark and I got to talking while Dwayne took off, leaving me stranded." She blushed. "Mark asked me to dinner, and I spent the night. He's just so, so … perfect."

"You met him yesterday, and he came to church with you today?"

Her face softened as a peaceful bliss enfolded her. "Yes. Last night, when we were lying in bed, it was like I had known him my whole life, and I think he feels the same. It's scary. I haven't felt this way about anyone since junior high."

She pursed her lips. "Do you think he felt it?"

The chances were good that Mark was feeling a lot of things, but I doubted love was one of them—but then, you never know. I hoped it was something more than another rebound relationship for her and a conquest for him.

I shrugged. "Don't know, but I do know that for him to be here says he's very interested."

"Is that my friend Eve, or Dr. Irving talking?"

I smiled. "Both."

Chapter 15
The Journals Continued
Sam

I stayed home while Eve and Felicity took the kids, Katelyn, and Daniel to the Exploratorium in San Francisco. I loved the gadgets and science magic as much as the kids, but with Felicity going, it was a good excuse to get back to the journals without the risk of being discovered. It had been over a month since I had found them, and my curiosity was killing me.

I fixed myself a full pot of coffee and settled into my chair in front of the fireplace.

November 11, 1974, Monday

"We brought our son, Peter Samuel Grant, home today. He was six pounds, three ounces, born on November 7, 1974 at 6:32 a.m., and was sixteen inches long. Duke thought it was funny how they measure babies like fish, with bragging rights going to the mom with the biggest one.

"A busybody nurse asked me about my bruises. When I told her I was clumsy and fell down a lot, she said clumsy and babies don't mix. Told me I need to get some help for it, so my baby doesn't get hurt. The bitch needs to mind her own business."

Peter was Eve's brother. I hadn't known him long, but he and his wife Gwynn were a great couple. One day they were leisurely exploring the back roads of the North Bay when an old eucalyptus tree fell on their car. They called it a "freak accident." I shivered at the thought.

I looked at a picture of Grace on the wall. Such a beautiful little person. She was only two and a half at the time and riding in the back seat. She said she didn't remember the accident, and it had been eight years, but she still screamed, turned white, and started shaking if someone set a plate of spaghetti with tomato sauce in front of her.

She had Eve and me now, and I couldn't imagine our lives without her.

February 14, 1975, Friday

"Mom offered to babysit Peter so Duke and I could go out for Valentine's Day. I told her we were going to have a romantic evening at home. I hate lying to Mom, but there's no point in telling her.

"Duke says if I wasn't so lousy in bed, he wouldn't need that bitch. The idea of what he wants me to do feels so degrading, but I'll do what he wants. That way he won't need her and come back to me and Peter."

September 11, 1976, Saturday

"Duke said he had to "work" today. Yeah. Sure. I didn't tell him I'm pregnant. I can't believe I was stupid enough to let it happen again. Duke's right, I'm nothing but a dumb bitch. I hope it's his and not Randy's.

"I might rot in hell for it. I deserve to. But when it's born, I'm going to have my tubes tied."

March 14, 1977, Monday

"I brought my second son home today. Adam Randolph Grant. He was five pounds, six ounces, born on March 10, 1977 at 1:09 p.m. and was fourteen inches long. Everyone was surprised that being full term, he was so much smaller than Peter, but he is perfect the way he is, so small and delicate. Everyone says he looks a lot like me."

Son? But Eve was born on March 10. She had a twin brother?

I flipped to the next page. No mention of Evelyn. I scanned the rest of the journal and found no mention of Eve.

I flipped back to the first page. "This journal belongs to Louise Elizabeth Grant." It didn't make any sense. *That's Eve's birthday.* I thumbed through the journal again to make sure I hadn't missed something—that two pages hadn't stuck together or pages hadn't been torn out.

Not one mention of Eve. *Weird. Why would Louise leave her out, and why didn't Eve tell me she had a twin brother?*

And with that "Randy" thing, maybe I should rethink Eve seeing these journals at all.

Eve's tone rang on my cell phone.

"Hi, good-lookin'. What's up?" I asked.

"Felicity ran into Mark in the biology section—"

I finished the sentence for Eve. "And she decided to run off with him to work on the practical application."

She paused. "Um. Yeah. Something like that."

I always enjoyed those rare times when I was one step ahead of Eve. "And you were thinking?"

"My dad called. Said that since it was such a nice day, he was wondering if we would like to come over for a barbeque. He'll have it ready by the time we get there."

"Sounds good."

I stashed the journals, stopped at the store to pick up some potato salad, soda, chips and dip, and beat Eve to her dad's by about ten minutes.

Chapter 16
The Scent of Doom
Sam

The barbeque lasted until three-thirty, when Eve had to take Chris to baseball practice. The girls liked to go so they could cheer for Chris's team, hang with the other sisters who got stuck at practice, and tease the boys. The practice would run until about six, which would give me time to get back to the journals. But first I wanted to talk to Nick. I made excuses to hang around when Eve and the kids left.

"What's bothering you?" Nick asked, after we finished cleaning.

"Nothing."

He grinned. "I've been a psychiatrist for thirty-five years. I've known you for eleven. Something's eating at you, Sam. If you don't want to talk, I'm fine with that, but I doubt you stayed to wash the dishes just for the practice."

"Got a beer?"

Nick frowned. "That serious?"

I pursed my lips and shook my head. "Don't know."

Nick got both of us a beer, and we parked at his dining room table, grazing on the leftover chip rubble and warm crusty dip.

"When I picked up Louise's books last summer, there was a box you thought was library donations that ended up with my boxes."

Nick's neck muscles tightened, and his breathing stopped for a moment.

I continued. "It wasn't donations."

"Oh?"

"I found journals."

His voice broke slightly and I saw a flash of fear in his eyes. "And?"

In horror and thrillers, there comes a point in the movie

where the dark lighting, muted colors, ominous music, and halting images palpably portend doom. I was sitting in a well-lit room, drinking rich German beer, while grazing on cardiac-terminating potato chips and onion dip.

Drifting in from a neighbor's home was Louis Armstrong, singing *What a Wonderful World*. Yet I had the inescapable feeling that the hollow, decaying scent of doom had just wrapped its tentacles around me and that I was sinking into a hole from which I might never return.

I sat up straighter and shuddered to displace the feeling.

I said, "I haven't read them—"

"I didn't realize they were in there. I'd like them back. Mind if we go over to your house and get them?"

I stared at him. I had expected … I don't know what I had expected. Certainly not fear.

I watched him for a moment, trying to decide if I wanted to continue.

"I read the seventy-seven journal," I said. "Louise said she had a son, Adam Randolph Grant. There was no mention of Eve."

He took a long, slow breath and let it out. "Sam. Do yourself and your family a huge favor. Give me back the journals and forget you ever saw them."

I respected Nick's opinion, but I couldn't let it go.

"Why didn't she mention Eve?"

"Some questions are best never answered," he said. "If you love Eve and your children, let it go and give me the books."

Nick was almost as protective of Eve as Louise had been. If I refused to give him the journals, I gave myself a fifty-fifty chance that he would call Eve while I was heading home and tell her about them.

"I need to think about it. I'll let you know tomorrow."

He spent another twenty minutes trying to persuade me to give him the books. He almost succeeded, but I needed to know. I headed home to finish the journals before Eve got back from baseball practice. If Nick called Eve, I wouldn't have much time.

Chapter 17
A Secret Revealed
Sam

After returning from the barbeque, I settled into my chair in the family room. The 1978 and 1979 journals were pretty sparse. Louise made constant references to being exhausted from working, taking care of the house by herself, and chasing after Peter and Adam.

April 23, 1980, Wednesday
"Yesterday Duke caught Adam with one of my barrettes in his hair. He said that if I didn't give Adam a haircut, he would. I tried to cut Adam's hair, but he wouldn't let me. I even tried to bribe him with the promise of another fish toy, but he kept fighting me. When Duke got home from the bar, he screamed at me for being more stupid than a three-year-old, then duct-taped Adam to a chair and gave him a buzz cut. Adam cried half the night, and today he just sits curled up in a ball sobbing, with one of my scarves and his tiny hands covering his head. He won't eat and I don't know what to do. I don't understand why a toddler would care so much if he has short hair."

November 8, 1980, Saturday
"My neighbor, Kate, babysat Pete and Adam for me today so I could grocery shop. When I went to pick the boys up, Adam was wearing Kate's daughter's dress and a tiara. When I asked him why, he said it was because he was a girl. Kate thought it was cute. I didn't."

December 6, 1980, Saturday
"Mom asked Adam what he wanted for Christmas. He said, "To be a girl." My heart stopped but it didn't faze Mom a bit. I asked Mom about it

later, and she said my brother did the same thing when he was five and now he's a macho fireman with a wife, four kids, and a fifth in the oven. Unlike me, he's a good Catholic. She said it was only a phase."

December 29, 1980, Monday
"My insurance covers shrinks so I snuck the ten-dollar co-pay out of the grocery money and went to see a child psychologist my Mom knows from her church.

"He told me that toddlers relate strongly to their mother because she is the one that feeds, protects, and cares for them. He said that because my husband and I fight all the time, Adam is mimicking me and saying he is a girl so that I won't abandon him. I would never abandon Adam or Peter. He said that if I am a good wife, Adam won't be afraid, and he will stop wanting to be a girl. I am so happy my son isn't gay."

I stared at the wall as a mild queasiness pulled me down. There still wasn't any mention of Evelyn and I didn't like where this was going. I couldn't accept where this was going. It *had* to be something else.

I took a break to get some antacid.

The 1981 through 1985 journals were missing. I started the next one.

January 1, 1986 Wednesday
"I've tried so hard to be a good wife for Peter and Adam's sakes, but I'm too much of a stupid bitch to do things right. Last night when Duke stopped and picked up his new girlfriend so 'we could start the new year as a threesome,' I lost it. As I tried to storm off, he grabbed my arm, and I turned and slapped him so hard I drew blood. Clumsy me. Of course, he gave me a black eye, but I deserved it for not being a good wife. He left me lying on the sidewalk with four-inch heels, no coat, and no money—not even a quarter for a phone call. A woman who saw it gave me a dollar in change so I could call Mom.

"It's almost lunch and he's still not home. Maybe I'll get lucky and that bitch he's been screwing will keep him."

January 6, 1986 Monday

"The bullies beat Adam up at school again. I liked it when Peter was at the same school and could protect him. His father says it's no big deal and that it'll make a man out of Adam. If being a man means being like Duke, I don't want my boys to be men."

March 10, 1986 Monday
"Adam turned nine today. We had a birthday party yesterday with his school friends. When Duke saw Adam had only invited girls, he turned red and stomped out of the house. I didn't expect him back until the bars closed, but being the stupid bitch I am, I was wrong, like always. After the last guest left, Duke showed up with two shopping bags filled with toys we can't afford—guns, swords, bulldozers, robots, and a G.I. Joe. As I watched, he dumped the toys in front of Adam and said 'These are boys' toys and you will not play with girls unless you're playing Fuck the Bitch.'

"Duke got a trash bag and started throwing most of Adam's new toys into it. Then he went to Adam's room and started throwing all of Adam's stuffed toys and mermaid things ..."

Mermaid? Oh, God! No. It has to be something else.
I got myself a shot of whisky to steady my nerves. She couldn't be. It wasn't possible. Eve couldn't have been ...

June 11, 1986 Wednesday
"It was a stressful, but good day. I filed for divorce, got a restraining order against Duke, and talked Grandma Grant into leaving the stinking bastard in jail. I hope he rots in hell."

Her June Fourteenth entry ran for several pages. I was cold, so I wrapped the quilted comforter Evelyn had made around me and continued reading. Heartburn gnawed at my chest.

June 14, 1986 Saturday
"We went to the beach six weeks ago, May 3rd. It was supposed to be a fun day. Every night, I pray that I will never again feel the terror I felt on that day. Only now is my hand steady enough for me to write about it.

"It started when Adam refused to take off his T-shirt. Duke, who had already downed a six-pack, tore it off, leaving bloody scratches on Adam's arms and back. I started pounding on Duke as hard as I could. As we fought and screamed at each other, Adam ran off.

"Our fighting was interrupted by people yelling, 'Call the Coast Guard.' A man asked if we knew how far out our son was; he pointed far past the breakers. I couldn't breathe. Adam was further out than I had ever seen anyone. A man was trying to swim to him, but Adam loves the water and is a strong swimmer. The man was so far behind that I knew he wouldn't catch Adam.

"In a terror only a mother can know, I knew what Adam was doing. He was going to go live with his beloved mermaids and dolphins.

"With the man over a hundred yards behind Adam, I watched, knowing that God was punishing me. As Adam slowed, floundered, and vanished, I stared at the ocean and prayed to God to save my son. I promised I would go back to church. I promised I would never again do the things my ex had made me do in bed. I begged for a second chance that I didn't deserve.

"Time stood still as an icy numbness possessed my body. I was oddly aware of a high-pitched humming in my ears. The sounds of people shouting and the waves crashing became a confused, meaningless whine. Then as clearly as the cloudless sky above, Duke said, 'I guess that takes care of our little queer problem.' I looked at him, stunned. I couldn't believe he was that heartless. That he was incapable of loving his own son.

"Someone yelled, 'What's that?' I looked back to the ocean and saw a large group of dorsal fins moving toward where Adam had been. 'Sharks,' someone screamed, but I knew it was a pod, and sharks don't travel in pods. They were dolphins. I felt a sudden peace as the breath of God caressed my face, and the warmth of his sun began to chase away the cold. I knew Adam was with his dolphins and in God's hands.

"The dolphins disappeared below the water. Seconds later, one reappeared with something lying on its back. It turned toward shore like a motorboat at full throttle, and I knew.

"I splashed into the surf as I watched Adam clinging to the damaged dorsal fin. God's angel was bringing my baby back to me. I was in waist-high surf when the dolphin turned and brushed against me. I caught Adam and pulled him to my bosom as he coughed up seawater.

"I hurried up the beach with my baby, where Duke grabbed Adam from me. He said, 'They're not throwing the little queer back that easy.' He headed back into the water, with Adam screaming for me. It wasn't a driftwood beach, but there in the sand was a piece of battered and splintered wood about the size of a baseball bat. Without thinking, I swept it up and charged into the water after them. The thud of the stick hitting the side of Duke's head was sickening and liberating. They fell into the water. I grabbed Adam and ran for our lives.

"Unfortunately, someone dragged Duke's unconscious body out of the surf. He had a concussion, but was drunk enough, angry enough, and stupid enough to admit in front of the paramedics and police that he was trying to throw Adam back into the ocean to drown.

"A long time ago, when I was saying bedtime prayers with Adam, he told me God had made a mistake when he made him a boy. He told me his real name was Eve. When I corrected him, he said, 'No, Mommy. I'm Eve. God made Eve out of Adam, so if I'm Eve, he can make me right.'

"I understand—a little. Adam has always been a girl inside. Everything about him has always been soft and feminine. On that day, Adam became Evelyn, my daughter. I love Evelyn and am happy for her, but I grieve for my son who is no more."

"Shit!"

Chapter 18
Beer, Prostitutes, and Parents
Sam

I sat staring at the words "Adam became Evelyn" as a putrid tremor rose from my stomach and lodged itself in my head. My disbelief withered as the tremor exploded with the force of a hurricane inside my skull, obliterating my thoughts.

Even in the brutal numbness that now possessed me, it didn't make sense. Everything about Evelyn was so ... soft and feminine. I couldn't believe it. I wouldn't believe it.

"It can't be true," I said, as if debating it with the devil. "No! Evelyn wasn't a boy. She couldn't have been. She's the most honest person I know ... she would have told me. No! This is a lie. Fantasy. Fiction."

I hurled the book at the confusion and pain that was battering me. The journal slammed into one of Evelyn's ceramic mermaids and some picture frames on the fireplace mantel. Splintered porcelain and shattered family pictures lay scattered on the hearth and rug. I stared at the fractured mermaid. A myth. A lie.

I didn't want to believe the journals, but I knew. Little things over the years. Little inconsequential misfit pieces slammed together like a head-on collision. Random fragments of her past that were said and unsaid. A story that didn't ring true about a scar from a playground accident. Her passion for the transgendered, as if she had a private stake in it. A well-masked, deep-seated *personal* anger that was reserved for parents who rejected their child's gender choice.

I couldn't deny it any longer. I wished I were still blind. I wished I had listened to Nick.

My body was locked with tension. I struggled to contain the boiling anger and believing disbelief. I wanted to hit something and scream. I wanted to pretend it wasn't true. I wanted to somehow make it all go away. I wanted it to be a lie.

With agonizing effort, I pushed my rage down. I needed to beat back the anger that caged me. I needed to run; get away. I hurled my oxfords at the wall and grabbed my running shoes. At my usual two-mile turn, I kept blindly winding down the street. Thoughts of "us" rose and fell.

My phone rang with Evelyn's ring tone. I started to answer it out of habit, but why? The idea of talking to her threatened to rip my guts out. I stumbled, turned off the phone, and kept running.

My mind spun with thoughts that would begin to make sense and then shatter under the brutal lie that crashed blindly through my head. Our life had been a lie. Our love. Our relationship. All of it. But it had all been so undeniably real ... but a lie.

The sun was getting low in the sky when a truck pulled out in front of me and I came to a startled, winded halt. I looked around as my emotions receded into the shadows that surrounded me. Exhaustion stripped me of hope. I wiped away the sweat that was stinging my eyes and checked the street sign. I had run over ten miles. Flashing beer advertisements in the window of a bar across the street caught my attention. I went in.

After two beers, the swirling thoughts of "us" had exhausted and numbed me.

"Divorce." I mumbled to myself. But what about Angela, Chris, and Grace? They loved Evelyn ... or should I say, Adam.

"She cheating on you?" I heard a woman ask in the beguiling way that turned men's heads and drew the scorn of women.

I looked to my left. Standing one barstool over was an attractive woman my age, dressed to get a man's attention and looking for business.

"Huh?" I grunted.

"You said divorce. She cheat and you find out?"

I started chuckling. If only it was that easy—that normal—I could handle it. I wanted to blurt, "I just found out my wife used to be a man," but she would think I was crazy or queer. I turned back to my beer. She sat on the stool next to me.

"I'm not interested," I said, as my anger at Evelyn rose in livid indignation. I continued trying to curdle my beer with my glare.

"If you were, you would have offered me a drink. You're a

nice guy. Not the cheating kind. You always have been a prince."

I looked over at her, wondering what her game was—other than the obvious.

She smiled in amusement. "Don't remember me, do you, Sam?"

"Should I?"

She shook her head no. "Hannah Smith. We went to the same junior high and high schools. I had a thing for you. Tried to get your attention a couple times, but you never noticed me. You only had eyes for Clora. Sorry things turned out so bad for you."

"What do you care?" I snapped.

She winced and leaned back a little. "Okay, okay. You don't need to bite my head off. Things are slow at the moment and you look like you could use a friend. Heard you remarried. Bet your wife is pretty and nice. Bet she makes everyone eat at the dining room table, and makes the kids eat their vegetables and do their homework."

I looked at her like she had sent her brain out to be dry cleaned and forgot to pick it up, and then went back to staring at the cigarette burns on the bar.

She snuggled up against me. I pulled away.

"I see all kinds, Sam," she said, practically purring. "Guys like you have morals, ethics. Even when you're pissed, you think with your head instead of your dick, until you get drunk. A couple more, *stud*, and you'll be glad I'm here for you. We can relive our high school days the way I always imagined them."

I looked her up and down. I remembered her. She'd gotten prettier with age, or maybe it was the beer.

"You applying for Mrs. Irving number three?"

Her smile widened. "Sure. Where do I sign up?" she said. She ran her long fingernails up my thigh in a playful tease.

"Get lost."

Unhurried, she looked me over with pretend hungry eyes and turned the simple act of standing into a beguiling seduction. Nearly all the men in the bar watched her sashay to the ladies' room. Several minutes later she returned, sat down next to me again, ordered a diet soda, and started rambling about her mother, high school, and the cost of lingerie, while I ignored her.

Twenty minutes later, my dad walked into the bar. I stayed

seated because I wasn't sure it was safe for me to stand.

"What are you doing here?" I asked, as Dad sat next to me, craning his neck to get a good look at Hannah.

"I called him," Hannah said, handing me my cell phone. "It's getting late. You're too drunk to drive, and if you try to walk home in your condition, you'll get run over. I didn't figure your wife would appreciate me giving her a call, so I went with 'Mom and Dad' in the contacts." She leaned over and kissed me on the cheek. "If things don't work out, I sure wouldn't mind a shot at being number three. For real."

Dad and I watched her slip off her bar stool and mince out the door in five-inch stilettos, with a swivel that would put Mae West to shame. My dad looked back at me and said, "How do they walk in those things?"

I frowned. "Damn, Dad. You *are* getting old."

Chapter 19
Mom Knows Best
Sam

I didn't want the kids to see me drunk and I couldn't face Evelyn. My parents' house was the only other place I could think of to go.

"Can you take me to your place?"

Dad nodded. "Ya wanna talk?"

I shook my head no and tried to get comfortable against the door. I had never been much of a drinker, and Eve hated alcohol, so I rarely had more than two beers or a sip of hard liquor. Between going without dinner, the whiskey, and four beers in less than two hours, I fell asleep on the short drive. Dad helped me into his living room and dropped me onto the couch, where Mom took my shoes and cell phone.

"A hooker called me to pick him up," Dad said. "I was in the middle of staining the hutch I just finished and I need to get back to it or the stain won't be even."

Mom stared at me with her mouth half open. Dad headed to the garage.

I didn't want to think about how she took Dad's hooker comment, and the last time she saw me even close to drunk was when I divorced Clora.

"Sorry, Mom."

"You should be sorry, Samuel. I didn't raise you to be a drunk."

I loved my mom, but she wasn't the most understanding or nurturing woman to grace the planet. When I was seventeen and Clora broke up with me, I went to a friend's house and got falling down drunk for the first time in my life. Someone called Mom to come get me, and she gave me her "getting drunk doesn't solve anything, only makes it worse" speech. When I needed my butt kicked, Dad always left it to Mom—said she did it better.

"So why'd you go and get hammered, Samuel?"

Through the blur of the alcohol, I was a little confused and looked around to see if someone else was drunk in the room. Outside of formal introductions, Mom hadn't called me Samuel since I was sixteen and got caught half-naked necking with Clora in the bushes at school. Oh, and when I was twenty-four and denied my ex was a druggy.

"Don't know," I said, annoyed with her meddling. The sole reason I was here was that I didn't want the kids to see me toasted.

Mom looked more annoyed than I felt.

"Don't know, my eye. The truth, Samuel."

She loomed over me, dripping with irritable impatience. Time stripped away my will. If I had been sober, she never would have pried it out of me. But drunk, I shrank and became eight again. I was a child tortured, because I didn't want to tell but knew I had no choice. If I lied, she always knew.

"Evelyn was a boy," I slurred.

She looked as stunned as I had felt.

"You didn't know?"

My brain screeched to a mangled halt in the slush and muck that filled it as the room became eerily silent. I halfway expected to see the Cheshire cat pulling on a bong.

I stared at her. "You knew?"

She shrugged. "Yeah." Her "yeah" sounded like one huge sarcastic duh. "I figured it out eight years ago, and I don't sleep with her. I always assumed you knew, and like a priest in a whorehouse, knew it was a dumb idea to advertise."

I blinked and wondered if I was dreaming.

"Does Dad know?"

Her normally absent mother-instincts kicked in. She sat down and took my hand with uncharacteristic sympathy.

"I don't think so; he's denser than you. The only things he ever notices are big boobs and nice round asses. I never discussed it with him."

"Who else knows?"

"Don't know. Half your relatives range from closet to outright homophobes. You know the ones. They are barely civil to Eve because she works with transpeople. If they knew she was a transsexual, there would have been a family uprising long ago."

"She's a man," I said, trying to understand what that meant. The whine in my voice shuddered through me.

Mom dropped my hand and looked pissed enough to hold the tide at bay.

"That's an oxymoron, moron, and she's not a man." Her eyes flickered with electrified vexation. "You know me. I'd rather go camping with your dad than shop for clothes. I prefer my motorcycle to the car. I rarely wear dresses or makeup. The tallest heels I have are three inches, and those are on my motorcycle boots, so I can reach the ground. I keep an untidy house. I don't sew, knit, needlepoint, scrapbook, or any of that other girl crap.

"I'm your mother and I could take lessons on being a woman from your wife." She stood, pursed her lips, and stared down at me. Her face softened and her body relaxed. "They say a man marries his mom, but both Clora and Evelyn are so girly it makes me nauseous sometimes. Maybe Eve can't have children. Maybe she was born a boy. But she's more of a woman than I am, and you and the kids are damned lucky to have her."

A putrid tremor awakened again, deep in my guts. It must have shown.

"If you throw up on my carpet, Samuel, you're cleaning it," she said, the annoyance back in her voice.

I collapsed into the cushions, exhaustion numbing my mind.

"Come on, Sam," Mom said. "This is 2010. You live across the street from San Francisco. There have been all kinds of documentaries on it. There is even a good-looking transsexual woman … um, Candis Cayne, I think. Not as pretty as Eve. She played in a bunch of movies and on soaps. And Oprah has had a couple shows on it. You watch Oprah? Dumb question; of course not, it's a chick show. I'm surprised I watch it."

Mom was sounding further and further away, and I wondered if Evelyn had found the damn journals.

Chapter 20
Shattered Secrets
Evelyn

The kids and I came in the house through the mudroom, where Angela tripped over Sam's oxfords lying in the middle of the floor. I was puzzled, since he insisted we keep the shoes neatly lined up and out of the way. Sam's truck was out front and his jogging shoes were missing, so I assumed he had gone for a run. The kids streamed off into their parts of the house, and I called for Sam in case he was home and just hadn't changed shoes.

"Hey, Mom," Chris called, from the family room. "Someone broke your blue mermaid, and it wasn't me." By the tone of his voice, I knew it wasn't.

The porcelain mermaid and two photo frames which had been on the fireplace mantel lay shattered on the hearth and rug. The girls joined me and we surveyed the damage. I assumed it was Angela's cat, Kitty, who had knocked everything to the floor.

A book which looked unfamiliar lay open and face down by the wall. Stepping over pieces of debris, I picked it up and instantly felt the blood drain from my face. A chill colder than death rolled down my spine. I knew the handwriting. The year at the top of each page was 1986.

"Oh, Gawd!" I gasped.

"What's wrong, Mom?" Chris asked, his voice tense and high.

"Sam!" I shouted.

The only replies were from the crunch of broken glass under my feet, and the ice coursing through my veins. The kids had heard the fear in my voice and were looking wide-eyed at me. I noticed a large stack of journals on the end table next to Sam's recliner. I trembled, trying to hold back a wave of nausea.

Grace snuggled up against me and wrapped her arms around

my waist. Glass snapped under her feet.

Her voice was tense. "What's wrong, Mom?"

My body stiffened as I beat down the growing panic. I tried to sound calm and reassuring. My heart raced. "Nothing, sweetie."

I kissed her forehead and gently freed myself from her hold. More crunches and pops escaped from the shattered glass under our feet.

The journals tottered in my arms. The faint smell of Mom's jasmine perfume escaped their pages.

"Everything is fine," I said, trying to sound reassuring. "Mom needs some alone time. Please don't disturb me for a while." I started for the office.

"Where's Dad?" Chris asked. His voice reflected the concern I saw in the girls.

"He went for a run. He'll be back in a little while."

I hurried into the office and closed the door before the tears could come.

How could you, Mom? He wasn't supposed to know. Damn you! You should have burned everything, like I told you.

I sat at the desk, took the top journal, and opened it to May 3, 1986. A blank page stared at me. *But ... that was the day.*

I turned the page. No entry. I kept turning pages until I got to June 14. My fear was real. Sam knew.

I needed to hear his voice, have him say "I've always known, and it's fine, Eve. I love you," but Kitty hadn't thrown the book. It wasn't "fine."

But he loves me. He's tolerant and open-minded. It might upset him at first, but once I explain, he'll understand.

I called his cell phone.

"Please, God. Please let it be alright."

It rang five times and then went to voicemail. I tried again. It went straight to voicemail that time. He had turned his phone off.

My mind spun in a panic. I couldn't think. I didn't know what to do.

I heard the kids' feet shuffling outside my office door, followed by a light knock. Trying to sound calm, but failing miserably, I said, "Yes?"

"What's for dinner?" Grace asked, her voice weak and pleading.

I shivered to release some of the fear so that I wouldn't

sound as upset as I was.

"Order a pizza and have it delivered. The money is in my purse and the coupons are on the refrigerator. I need to be alone for a while."

I could hear the three of them whispering outside the door and knew they were trying to figure out what to do. After a minute, their footsteps headed for the kitchen. Mom and their worries would wait until after pizza.

There was only one way Sam could have gotten the journals. My dad picked up on the third ring.

"What in the hell have you done," I screamed. "He knows. You said he wouldn't. You said you had it all locked up. Damn you, Dad. Damn you!"

After my initial outburst, I realized the kids could probably hear me. I lowered my voice and turned the radio on loud enough that my words would get lost in the noise. Dad let me batter him like a rowboat in a typhoon for almost half an hour. As despair settled in, I began to listen to him, between outbursts of hurt and accusation.

I heard the doorbell ring, followed shortly by the smell of pizza, heavy with garlic, the way Grace liked it.

Dad gave some lame excuse about a mix-up with boxes of books. He and I had spent weeks going through the library. I never saw any journals. And once Dad knew Sam had them, he should have called me immediately.

The smell of pizza had grown cold. I could hear whispers and shuffling slipping in from the hall, as the kids tried to be quiet outside the office door.

I looked at the clock. I had been talking to Dad for over an hour.

Dad's apologies and assurances that it would all work out for the best left me seething, almost as much as his giving Sam the journals had.

"I've got to go," I said, and hung up.

I used the tissue on my desk to clean myself up as best I could. I needed to burn the journals, but I didn't want the kids to see me do it; it would raise too many questions that I didn't want to answer. I needed an excuse to confine them to their rooms.

I snuck to the door and pulled it open. Grace and Angela fell onto the floor. Chris caught himself on the door jam. They all looked guilty.

Busted.

Once they were tucked safely in their rooms, I grabbed the journals and hauled them back to the family room, where I threw them with savage abandon into the fireplace and doused them with lighter fluid.

The house phone rang. I hoped it was Sam, and ran to answer it. Dad was on the caller ID. For a second, I thought about letting it go to voicemail, but dousing the journals had put me in the mood to rake him over the coals again.

"Yes?" I said, my words pure acid.

"How are you doing?"

I wanted to bite the phone. "Just peachy keen, thanks to you. Doing what you and Mom should have done years ago."

"Oh?" His voice was urgent and filled with misgiving.

"Yeah. Burning the friggin' journals."

"You burned them?"

I had never heard near panic in Dad's voice before, and it shocked me out of my self-pity for a moment.

"I was just lighting the match."

"Don't, Eve. If you want Sam back, don't do it."

I stood there in silence while my logic and emotions warred. I knew what he was saying. Sam needed to know the truth. The journals were his only impartial witness of my life. But they had betrayed me already. *They hurt my Sam.*

"No, Dad. Not this time." I was seething. "We tried it your way, and it didn't work. Now we will do it *my* way."

After five minutes of arguing, I knew in my heart he was right, but it still took him almost half an hour to talk me out of my anger and fear so that I didn't light the match. I heard the kids coming and checked the clock. It was their bedtime.

I soothed their fears as best I could and said goodnight to them. Once they had settled down, I put the journals in a garbage bag, tied it shut, and hid them in my closet.

I tried Sam's cell phone again and flinched when Sam's mom answered.

"Rose?"

"Hi, Eve. Sam's as drunk as a frat boy at a keg party and sleeping it off on my couch. I think we need to talk."

I was silent. I didn't know what to say. I loved Rose. She was a great mother-in-law, and the kids depended on the security of her no-nonsense approach to everything, but she wasn't known for her tact or for her tolerance of opposing views on life's matters. She could make things a lot harder than I was afraid they already were.

"I've known for eight years, Eve, and I don't give a rat's ass," Rose said, breaking the silence. "Sam, on the other hand, is pretty messed up over it. I suspect he will want to move out when he sobers up, and that would be a worse idea than a poodle at a pit bull convention. The kids need their mom and dad. He needs to grow up and get over his childish male pride."

She knew? I shuddered, and my mind blanked for a second under the stress. How could she know? Only Mom, Dad, Felicity, and my doctor were supposed to know.

Who else knows?

Outside of my very small circle, I thought my secret was safe. A long-ago deathly fear rose up as the illusion of secrecy which had given me comfort was stripped away, baring my soul and leaving me feeling naked and feeble.

"What do you suggest?" I asked, not sure I wanted her help, but not sure I had a choice.

The kids had been asleep for several hours, and I was trying to sleep, but my mind wouldn't stop thinking about all the possible things that could happen. What I would say. What Sam would say. What I would say back. What we would do. What we would tell the kids.

I tried to clear my mind with prayers, meditation, and gratitude lists so I could sleep. I needed a clear head tomorrow when I saw him and explained.

I beat my pillow and pounded my head into it, trying to get comfortable, and thought about Sam, Mom, Dad, and Rose.

Rose had suggested we meet at my dad's tomorrow morning and work out a plan. I didn't want to. I wanted to keep it between Sam and me. I wanted to run over and talk sense into him. But I had never known Sam to throw things or get drunk. He had taken it far harder than I ever would have imagined, as hard as if I had had an affair—maybe harder. I hated to admit it, but I needed to give him space, and give myself time to soothe my fears—if not for me, for the kids.

I gave up trying to sleep, got up, and dragged the garbage bag out of my closet and into the family room. I opened the sliding glass door to let the stink from the lighter fluid out into the fresh night air, sat in Sam's chair, and started reading. I had finished with the ones that would matter by the time I heard

Chris get up.

I re-bagged the journals, hid them back in my closet, and got dressed.

The kids wanted to know where their dad was. I told them he had spent the night at Grandma Rose's but didn't elaborate. They knew I was withholding and became grumpy as they played off my fear and anger. When it was time for me to leave, I told them to fix themselves whatever they wanted for breakfast. Chris grabbed a chocolate bar and a soda just to tweak me. I ignored him, left him in charge, and headed over to Dad's.

When I saw Dad's house, I felt my blood pressure rise. How could he have been so careless? He said … He promised … and then he just handed Sam the journals like they were dinner rolls. I parked next to Rose's motorcycle and went in.

I could see the guilt and concern in Dad's eyes. He tried to hug me, but civility left me.

"How could you, Dad." My vision blurred and lips quivered. "I told you and Mom, but you wouldn't listen. Noooo. You had to do it your way. Now? … Oh, God. Why? Why didn't you—"

"I didn't take you for a quitter, Eve," Rose said, with as much sympathy as a hangman.

I spun and glared at her. I wanted to call her something really, really nasty, but she was right. With effort, I slowed and deepened my breathing. Rose took me in a hug and held me.

"I'm so sorry, Eve," Rose said. "He's being an ass, and if you take him head-on, that stupid male pride of his will just dig in and he'll fight you harder."

"Go to him," my heart was screaming. "Tell him you love him. Tell him you're sorry. Explain everything. He'll understand. We'll kiss and make up." But the part of my head which was still functioning with something that vaguely resembled rational thought knew Rose was right. Her being here was proof of that.

I glared at Dad. "What do I do?"

Chapter 21
Jumping Ship
Sam

I awoke from a nightmare of drowning, screaming "*Eve.*" My head was throbbing, and the vertigo was trying to rip it off and send it rolling across the floor. Several seconds passed before I realized where I was. The sun's glare through Mom's front window drove spikes of pain through my head. By the angle of the light, I knew I had slept all night and then some.

"Bad dream?" Mom asked with detachment from the overstuffed chair across the room.

My breath was rapid and deep as I tried to scour my lungs of the burn left from the nightmare of me drowning. The dream and pain receded, and reality took hold of my mind. I wanted to say yes to Mom's question and pretend everything was alright, but my body folded in on itself, with the brutal pain I hadn't felt since Clora. I struggled to hold back the tears which could not be held. Mom knelt next to me and stroked my hair.

After several minutes, the tears vanished like a switch had been flipped. I sat up, numb and displaced from my body, with an ocean of pain crushing my chest. Yesterday I had a perfect life. Now?

Nothing made sense anymore. The one person in my life I could always count on was gone; or maybe she never existed. I had been living with a stranger—a lie.

"Do you want to talk?" Mom asked.

"About what?" My intention was to somehow bluff my way out.

Mom sneered. I hated it when she did that. It meant her guns were loaded and I was a sitting duck.

"Oh, I don't know. How about the fact you're acting like a hypocrite—"

"She lied."

"*Omitted.* How much of your life with Clora have you omitted? The drugs? The police? The time she was high and slugged Chris so hard he lost a tooth, and you had the gall to defend her?"

I folded as if I had been stomach-punched by a prizefighter. Clora hitting Chris had been the low point of my life. Somewhere inside, I had known his injuries weren't an accident, but I hadn't wanted to believe Clora could do something like that. The guilt of standing up for her stuck to my conscience like barnacles to a shipwreck. I'd carry that guilt into eternity.

But my omissions didn't matter. They were normal mistakes. Mistakes made out of love, trust, ignorance, and inexperience. Lessons learned the hard way. Evelyn had deliberately betrayed and used me. She'd played me for a fool.

"It's not the same," I mumbled.

Her eyes flashed with anger. "What are your intentions, Mr. High and Mighty?"

Divorce was the obvious. The kids would be a problem. They loved their ...

I needed to clear my head and think.

"I don't know," I said.

"You going back home? Going to talk it out?"

"No! There's nothing to talk about."

"What about the children?"

"They'll ..." *Shit.*

My history with Evelyn flashed through my mind in seconds. Evelyn had adopted Chris and Angela. She was legally their mom. With what Clora had done and my reluctance to face it, I'd be an easy target for her lawyers. With Evelyn's squeaky-clean professional standing as a renowned child psychologist and her familiarity with child custody law, it would be a cakewalk for her to take my kids.

But she had lied to hide a secret. With something like that in her past, there had to be other secrets, other lies. I needed to find them. I needed to find out who I had been married to.

"I don't know." Slowly I looked up. "This sucks, Mom."

She nodded in agreement. "When you have children, you make a pact with God to place them first. Before your spouse. Before you. No matter what, you need to do right by them."

Mom had never been religious, so her statement seemed nearly as unreal as the idea that Evelyn had been born a boy. I had definitely fallen down a rabbit hole.

"God?"

She scowled. "It has nothing to do with religion, Sam." She leaned closer making me feel small on the couch. I could see fear in her eyes. "Don't finish what Clora started, Sam. Don't hurt my grandchildren."

She stood. "You have some soul-searching to do, mister. I'll go fix you some breakfast."

"I need to go ..." *Go where?* I didn't want to go home to Evelyn. I didn't want to face her. I was too angry, and she would just say, "We need to talk about it." I didn't want to talk. I didn't want to hear her excuses. And I especially didn't want to say something mean or stupid in front of the kids. I needed time to unscramble my brain.

Mom stepped toe-to-toe with me and bumped my knees with hers. I looked up.

"While you were sleeping it off, I got with Eve and Nick—"

"What? It's none of your business."

She leaned close enough that I could smell the coffee mocha she had been drinking.

"My family *is* my business, mister. Eve is the best thing that ever happened to you, and I will kick your butt to the moon and back if that's what it takes to keep you from screwing it up."

I leaned back on the couch and glared at her. More calmly, I repeated, "It's none of your—"

"Bullshit, Samuel. You, Eve, Chris, Angela, and Grace are my business, and I won't—" She stopped and stared at me for a few seconds while she chewed her lip. In a tight, authoritative monotone, she said, "It was a dark, sad day when Clora went to jail leaving you, Chris, and Angela alone. I couldn't fill the void she left in my grandchildren's lives. Eve did. Do you really want to do that to them again?"

"No," I whispered. I looked down at the floor. This was another no-win just like when Clora left.

"This afternoon," Mom said, her voice calm. "Eve is taking the children to Bodega Bay for the week. She is leaving the journals at the house so you can finish reading."

I scowled at Mom. Evelyn would never let me read the rest.

Mom sat back down and took my hand again.

"She had thrown them in the fireplace, intending to burn them. Nick talked her into giving them to you. It took a lot of courage and trust for her to do that. She loves you—"

I pulled my hand away. "If she trusts me, why didn't she—"

"Would you have married her?" Accusation dripped from her question.

I wouldn't have. I knew that. Back then, I thought transsexuals were freaks, mentally unstable, or dickless gay men. I would have assumed she was too.

"Is the week so I can move out?"

"If you want to be a moron, you could do that. Or you can read the journals and find out why she kept it a secret. Think about my grandchildren, Sam, and think hard. Decide what you want, without the pressure of a blurry-eyed wife and scared children clinging to you. Get your head and heart in a place to talk to her, without letting your bruised ego make you do something we will all regret.

"You're an adult, Sam. The future of four people I love as much as I love you is waiting on your decision."

"It's not fair," I said.

Mom stood and walked toward the kitchen as if she wasn't listening. She stopped, turned, and leaned against the door jam.

"She loves you with all her heart. She'd walk into hell for you and the children. You know that, don't you?"

I nodded yes. But that didn't change what she was or the fact she had lied to me.

Chapter 22
Future Uncertain
Evelyn

"Mom. I can't go," Chris said from his room. "We have a big game Wednesday and I'm pitching."

"Take your equipment. We'll come back down for the game."

"But I'll miss practice."

"We can practice on the beach. I'll pitch and catch."

I could hear the frustration rising in his voice. "You pitch like a girl, and you can't catch. Can I stay at Katelyn's instead?"

I stuck my head into his bedroom. "Absolutely not."

"How about Bobby's?"

"You're coming and that's final."

Angela called, "Mom, I can't find my bathing suit."

"It's in the bottom drawer on the left," *where it has been for the past five years.*

"Thanks."

I was pulling some extra towels from the hallway linen closet when Grace snuck up behind me, wrapped her arms around my waist, and hugged me.

"Why didn't Dad come home?" she asked.

Chris and Angela stopped packing as silence echoed through the house. I turned and looked into her big brown eyes, which were pleading with me to bring her dad home and make everything better. I settled onto the floor and took Grace in my lap, even though she was too big. Chris and Angela were standing just out of sight behind their doors, listening. I tossed two of the folded towels out in the hallway like they were throw pillows.

"Have a seat, kids."

They peeked out at me, with uncertainty filling their eyes, before slipping into the hall and settling onto the towels.

"Your father and I are going through a difficult time right

now. He needs a little space to think about things. We still love each other and, no matter what happens, we both love all of you."

Grace curled closer against me, while Chris and Angela battled with their desire to be close and the need to run away and hide from the world that was inexplicably crashing down around them. I held out my arms, inviting them to join me and Grace in a group hug. Angela scooted over. Chris shifted backwards. Tears filled his eyes.

"Are you divorcing?" Chris asked.

I didn't expect him to jump to that conclusion so quickly or be that direct. I stretched out my hand and caught his shirt, then pulled him to me.

"No, honey. No. We can't. We love each other too much."

"That's what my real mother said before she went away," he said, pulling away. Hurt and anger flashed in his eyes.

I was shocked. He was two when Clora left. He couldn't have any conscious memories of her.

He did a backwards crab-walk to distance himself from me, until he ran into the wall.

"I love you, Chris. I won't leave you. I won't leave any of you."

He stood and glared for a second before slipping into his room and slamming the door.

Angela and Grace were crying. I held them as we rocked and I told them over and over that everything would be alright. I prayed it would be.

With the kids in the car, I took the journals out of the trash bag and stacked them on the hearth. The sharp smell of lighter fluid called for me to strike a match. In my mind, I could see the match sizzle to life. I could see flames leaping from the books' pages. I wanted them to turn to ash, so I could pretend they never existed. But my dad and Rose were right. If I burned them, I would be burning my hopes for us. Sam needed to know everything. He needed to understand. And he wouldn't trust me to tell him the truth. Mom would have to do that and I would need to trust Sam to her.

I looked to heaven. "Why, Mama? Why?"

I set the letter it had taken me all night to compose on top of the journals.

"Please, God. I know I don't have a right to ask, but please, just one more miracle. For the greatest good."

Chapter 23
The Tip of the Flame
Sam

Evelyn's text message said the house was mine. When I opened the front door, I was mugged by the smell of barbeque fluid.

Doesn't she know she can blow up the house with a stunt like this? Maybe that's what she wants.

Leaving the door open, I stepped back outside. I knew a static spark or light switch could easily ignite the fumes, leveling the house, so I considered doing the smart thing, which was to call the fire department; they would safely air the house out. But I wasn't in the mood to deal with their questions. I took a deep breath of good air and charged through the house to the family room, where I opened the sliding door to get a cross breeze that would clear the fumes.

The smell rolled out of the open doors while I stared at the stack of journals on the hearth. They were covered with fluid stains. The bindings were ripped free. Mutilated pages hung loose.

They looked as beaten as I felt.

A plain business envelope was perched on top with "Sam" scribbled across its face in Eve's messy script. I expected it to contain a lengthy, tear-stained essay of regret, pleading, excuses, and proclamations of her undying love. Maybe even a "for the children."

I noticed the bronze mermaid Felicity had made, sitting on an end table with Evelyn's face looking at me.

The real Evelyn. A myth. Make-believe.

After the stink dissipated a little, I carried the stack outside, plopped down in a patio chair, and opened the letter.

My Darling Sam,

I'm sorry. I was wrong. No more secrets. Call me when you want to talk. If you need to leave, I will try to understand.
I will love you always,
Eve.

I read it three times, trying to figure out if it was some manipulative therapy technique, then crumpled it and threw it into her flowerbed with her pansies.

With the journals laid out on the patio table to dry in the sun like beach towels and bathing suits, I sat down with a notepad and began where I had left off. I started taking notes—dates, names, places, so that I could put the puzzle together and see the whole picture instead of the disjointed fragments Evelyn had given me. I needed to know all her secrets.

The 1986 journal said that Evelyn had been diagnosed with gender dysphoria by Dr. Nicholas Strand. His workload was too great, so he referred Evelyn to a psychologist and an endocrinologist and stepped out of the picture.

As the year progressed, Louise wrote about her adjustment to having a daughter, the predictable family dramas, challenges with school administrators, Duke's trial, and legal entanglements with child protective services over what was best for Evelyn.

The 1987 journal had references to Duke getting a year in county for "aggravated assault" on Adam, and a passing reference that indicated Louise had been granted full custody of Evelyn and Peter.

February 9, 1988, Tuesday

"Nick happened to come by the therapists today while I was waiting for Eve to finish. We got to talking and he said he wanted to take me to dinner and a movie on Friday, if I was interested. Interested? I was interested the first time I saw him, but I had rushed into my relationship with Duke. I wouldn't make that mistake again. I couldn't for my kids.

"It's been a year and a half since I last saw Nick, and to be honest, five since my love for Duke died. I think I'm ready, and despite how much I'm attracted to Nick, this time I'll do it with my eyes wide open."

March 21, 1988, Monday

"Evelyn started hormone therapy today. She's happier than I have ever seen

her, dancing and singing all afternoon and talking about how she is going to be a movie star or supermodel or princess when she grows up.

"I'm terrified that I'm making a horrible mistake. I've read all the articles and research papers Nick and Eve's doctor gave me. In my head I know Eve is transgendered, born in the wrong body. In my heart, I know she is a girl, but, as Duke would always remind me, I'm just a dumb bitch and I'm always wrong.

"The doctors say they are delaying puberty to make sure she is trans. Their hesitancy only feeds my fears and doubts. They said that the hormone blockers are a pause button that only delays puberty, but what if they aren't? What if they're wrong? What if next week, Eve comes to me and says, "Mom, I want to be Adam now," but it's too late?

"Even though I know in the depths of my soul she's a girl, I can't shake the idea that I'm wrong. We're wrong. That we've made a mistake. I don't know if I could survive that.

"But Nick says it's the right thing. He has no doubt she's a girl. Said we need to start the hormone therapy once the doctors are sure so she'll be better accepted by her peers. So she can have normal girl experiences and look like a real woman when she's grown up.

"I'm scared."

March 26, 1988, Saturday

"I had to laugh when I overheard Nick's great aunts saying how disgraceful it was that Nick was seeing a "divorcee with children." I remember those days when I was growing up in the fifties. Divorcees were poison, soiled. Little more than a legitimized mistress if they remarried. Now no one cares much except for old biddies. Live and let live. I wonder if some day people will accept children like Eve the way they accept divorcees now."

October 10, 1988, Monday

"Eve has a new friend, Cinnamon. She's like Eve, except she's not on hormones or seeing a doctor and her parents won't let her wear girl's clothes. I know they're sharing outfits, because Cinnamon's clothes are always in Eve's laundry and I've seen Cinnamon's wig in Eve's backpack.

"The school hasn't said anything about it, probably afraid to after what I *put them through last year. Cinnamon comes over almost every day after school. When I get home, I make sure they've finished their homework before they can go to Eve's room to play. They dress up and experiment with makeup and hair, just like I did at their age.*

"Sometimes I hear them talking about cute boys at school. It makes me sad, because they can't ever have children, and I wonder if they will ever have a normal life.

"Normal. Such an odd word. Was my marriage to Duke normal? With all the books on how to survive an abusive relationship, and all the women's shelters, it sure seems like it.

"Maybe I should hope they don't have a normal life. Maybe I should wish for them to have a Hallmark or a Norman Rockwell life. Or a life with something new and different that is even better.

"Maybe for Eve to find a man like Nick, who will understand and stand by her, no matter what."

Other than the growing romance between Nick and Louise, and a couple of steamy passages that I skimmed, there wasn't anything else of interest. I realized I was getting sunburned and moved to the shade.

Her engagement to Nick occupied most of the 1989 journal. Nick wanted to get married on the beach in Hawaii, but Louise said it would be in a church or not at all. Evelyn was a bridesmaid and Peter was a groomsman. Evelyn would have been twelve, and Peter fifteen.

I remembered the wedding photos hanging in Louise's home. I guessed that the homely-looking girl with reddish brown hair and freckles was Cinnamon. When I had asked particulars about her, Evelyn had evaded my questions. At the time, I had assumed it was one of those ugly girlfriend breakups that guys are well-advised to stay out of. Now that I knew she was trans, I wasn't so sure.

The 1989 through 1993 journals were sparse, except for frequent references about Louise trying to overcome her negative attitude and how hard it was for her. At least every other day she would write a gratitude list. At first, the lists included things like, "I'm grateful I wasn't a stupid bitch today." In the later journals, she wrote, "I'm grateful to have a husband who is kind to me." "I'm grateful for my beautiful son and daughter." "I'm grateful for all the challenges I had today. They are teaching me patience, acceptance, and courage."

I had only seen Louise be negative a couple of times. Despite the way she put herself down in the early journals, I had a hard time picturing her as ever having been a negative and bitter woman.

At thirteen, Evelyn's hormone regimen was changed and the effects became irreversible. Louise talked about Cinnamon having to use black market hormones and how concerned she was. At one point, Nick tried to intervene, but Cinnamon's parents threatened to sue him, and ordered Cinnamon not to see Evelyn, which was impossible, since they had classes together at school.

In 1993, Peter left for college, and Eve had her first serious boyfriend. That same year, Cinnamon's parents accepted that their son was "gay" after she nearly died from contaminated blackmarket progesterone.

The last journal was from 1994, when Evelyn was a high school junior. It was an expensive, black leather bound, gilt-edged work of art, a gift from Nick. In January, Louise had written a gratitude list every day, with occasional references to normal life events.

January 31, 1994, Monday

"Nick called this afternoon to say everything is set for July eleventh. They make most girls like Eve wait until they're eighteen for the surgery, but since Nick's a doctor with friends in the field, they will do the surgery after Eve turns seventeen.

"Sometimes I wonder if we're wrong, then I look at Eve and there isn't any doubt. I'm happy for her, because she will be able to finish her senior year as a real girl.

"There's a part of me, though, that feels like I'm losing Adam again. This time forever."

The February first page was blank. I thought nothing of it and started thumbing. The last entry in the journal was on February 7, 1994, a Monday.

"Cinnamon's funeral was yesterday and Evelyn is devastated. The paper this

morning said the police have released the men who killed her and Zack. The newspapers are suggesting that there was a love triangle and that Eve did it. The truth is that no one cares because Cinnamon was trans and Zack was Eve's boyfriend. We need to leave here before they kill Evelyn, too."

The last sentence seemed like hysterics, but it would explain why Evelyn had refused speaking engagements in Southern California, and sometimes acted like she was in some sort of witness protection program.

I almost missed the yellowed newspaper clipping pressed between the back pages. It was dated February second.

"Brandon Jones, Jr., son of prominent Los Angeles Pastor Brandon Jones, Sr., is being held in connection with a double homicide, along with a second suspect, Billy Jackson. The two men, both eighteen, are charged with the slaying of preoperative transsexual, Kelly "Cinnamon" Bandeau, and his boyfriend, Zachary Taylor. The two men are also being held for the attempted murder of a third person, whose name is being withheld because she is a minor. Lawyers for the suspects claim the two men were at a private religious retreat with Pastor Jones at the time of the murders."

I wondered if that was the reason for Evelyn's nightmares. It would make sense. She saw her friends murdered, and had someone try to kill her. It also made sense that she wouldn't tell me, because a simple newspaper archive search would have revealed her secret.

The news article was on the second of February, and the journal entry was on the seventh. That meant the men were innocent or the police had lacked the evidence to charge them.

Love triangle? Evelyn had always been very traditional regarding relationships and I couldn't see her going so far off the deep end that she'd kill someone. But I never would have thought Clora was capable of doing what she did either.

My stomach rumbled into my throat and then settled as the throbbing in my head increased. I didn't want to bother with the journals and notes; I just wanted out. But custody would be a problem and I didn't know what to tell the kids. The truth? "Your mom used to be a guy and then cut it off." *Yeah. Right.*

I needed to follow it through to the ugly end, and Evelyn had given me a week to find the truth, hoping we would kiss and make up. I figured I had a week to find a way to get full custody of my kids.

At this point, there was a pretty good list of names from her past. I could look up Cinnamon and Zack's families. Evelyn's doctor, therapist, and endocrinologist. Louise's sister and brother. Evelyn's grandparents. A few uncles, aunts, and cousins.

Another possible source of information was Nick. We had a good relationship, and it was obvious he knew things, but I was hesitant to start there. I wasn't sure how honest he'd be, and anything I said could get back to Evelyn. But then, he hadn't called Evelyn and told her I had the journals after our little talk.

The phone rang; caller ID said it was Evelyn.

"Have you finished the journals?" she asked, her voice soft and scared.

"Yes."

"Do you want to talk?"

"No. Not to you, and I thought I had a week."

Her fear saturated the phone. "You deserve some answers."

"No shit, Sherlock."

She was silent, except for muffled crying. "I need to see you."

"It's late. I don't have time to drive up to Bodega."

"I'm at my dad's. Felicity took the kids up. I'll meet them later."

I liked Felicity. She was hard not to like. But I wasn't sure she was mature enough to look after the kids. But then, Chris was old enough and responsible enough to look after his sisters and Felicity.

"I don't know."

"What about the kids?"

I squeezed the phone so hard that my wedding band cut into my finger.

"Shit. You bellyache for years about parents using kids as pawns, and now? ... Fucking bitch."

The words "f-ing bitch" seared through my heart. I had never once called her anything even close to that, and it seemed so incredibly wrong, even if technically ... almost correct.

"I'm sorry. You're right. I wasn't thinking," she said, with pain in her voice.

But I was hurting too, and it was all her fault. I sneered at the phone. "Damn right, I'm right."

"Please," she pleaded.

I wanted to hate her. I could never make love to her again. *The kids*. I needed info. She was being emotional. Maybe she'd let something slip.

"Okay."

I grabbed a slice of cold pizza out of the refrigerator, brushed the excessive garlic into the sink, and headed over.

I glared at Mom's motorcycle in Nick's driveway. She was still meddling. Evelyn had lied to me about something this important and everyone was acting like the whole thing was my fault.

"Go in, or drive off?" I asked myself.

Lies. Our life had been lies. Ten damn years of lies. It hurt. Gut-wrenching, soul-stomping hurt. Hell, my mom knew! Why hadn't I figured it out? Was I that stupid?

"God, this sucks," I yelled, slamming my fist on the dash.

What did I do to deserve this? I had never been this angry with Evelyn, and I hated it.

I looked at the house and could see her watching me from the front window. It was time to get it over with.

Chapter 24
Choose?
Evelyn

Through the window, I watched Sam hit the dash of his truck. I had known that if he ever found out I was born in the wrong body, there would be some adjustment, but the depth of his anger surprised me.

I had expected him to be more understanding. Tolerant. Even accepting. He was close to coming unhinged, and I wondered how well I really knew him. Had I just seen what I wanted to see? Had I been lying to myself about us? Was he afraid of transsexuals—transphobic, deep down? Was there no hope?

I checked myself in the entry hall mirror. Bloodshot eyes. Exhaustion hanging from me like a rag dress. Hair frizzing. Dark circles under my eyes. I had looked better.

I met Sam at the door. He looked worse, was horribly sunburned, and smelled of barbeque fluid. The anger, hurt, confusion, and fear in his eyes scared me.

I started to hug him, but he pulled back with a barely perceptible shiver. My face warmed and my vision blurred. I turned away and led him to the living room.

Rose and Dad excused themselves, leaving us to sort out our *little* problem. Sam took the easy chair so I couldn't sit too close. Avoiding eye contact, he drummed his fingers on the plump brown fabric. I ached to sit close to him, feel his warmth, and let him feel my love. But I knew I was being clingy and he didn't like that. I went to the couch and sat.

His anger boiled to the surface. When he looked at me, an image of my birth father, drunk and ugly, flashed through my mind. I pulled back before I could catch myself.

His eyes narrowed, the unsaid message, "You think I would hurt you?" He turned his head to look out the front window.

No. I knew he never would.

He stared outside, while callous silence stood between us. Slowly, his rigid wall of anger softened, and I could feel the man I loved coming back to me.

"You should have told me you chose to be a girl," he said.

With calm assurance, the therapist Dr. Irving, would have said, "You've heard me speak on the subject. You've read my articles and research papers. You've heard the stories of how difficult it is for trans children. Do you honestly believe it was a choice?"

But I wasn't Dr. Evelyn Irving. I was Eve. A wife terrified that her husband would leave her. An exhausted woman, who had been up all night reading, crying, and praying. An emotionally overwrought bundle of desperation, indignation, and fear.

I clenched my fists and glared at him. "CHOOSE?" His eyes snapped to me, surprised and angry.

I was spitting venom. Not at him, but at my father and all the other sanctimonious and barbarous people who had judged and condemned me for being me.

"No, Sam. It was NOT a choice. I did not *choose* to be a girl at two years of age. I did not *choose* to have my father hate me because I couldn't be the boy he wanted. I did not *choose* to make my mom's life hell by being an effeminate boy. I did not *choose* to be the outcast that everyone in school ridiculed, bullied, and beat up."

I leaned forward and glared. "Being a woman wasn't any more of a choice for me than being a man was for you. I was born a girl. My physical gender was a mistake. I could kill myself, or I could become the woman I was meant to be. There were no other choices. I'm not making excuses for it, and I'm not apologizing for being me."

With my fury drained, I realized I had just blown it. Forcing a much calmer, but still hard and petulant tone, I said, "I didn't tell you about my past because there was nothing to tell. I had a birth defect and I fixed it. That's all. The sex change was no different than amputating a deformed and useless limb that gets in the way."

He cringed and pulled his knees together.

"I'm not a bigoted Neanderthal," he roared. His neck veins bulged and his sunburn turned purple. "You lied to me. I had a right to know."

My vision narrowed and the room became shades of black,

white, and red.

I yelled loud enough for the world to hear. "I didn't lie to you! I have always been a girl!"

His fist slammed into the arm of the chair with a dull, thunderous thud, and he shot to his feet. His towering, virile energy shocked me back into rational apprehension, and caused me to pull back.

"Bullshit, Eve." He stomped around the living room, his arms beating at invisible demons. He stumbled over grunts, incomplete words, and incoherent sentences, stopping with his back to me. He lowered his arms and his body slumped in exhaustion. After a long silence, with his back still to me, he calmed and said, "You were born Adam Randolph Grant. It's not a difference of opinion or point of view. You deliberately deceived me."

He turned to face me, the anger of his glare incinerating my hope for us. "You hid things, and a lie of omission, intended to deceive, is the same as a flat-out lie."

I struggled not to cry.

Sam took a deep breath. He looked like a man who had won a war where there were no winners—or survivors.

"I loved you, but love isn't enough. I need to trust, and I don't trust you anymore."

We both flinched as his words drew blood from both of our hearts. It was impossible to stop my tears. In pain, I curled into the corner of the couch.

"Let's say it wasn't a choice," he continued, his voice filled with agony. "That it was a *birth defect*." The word "birth defect" was drenched in contempt, driving me further back into a little ball.

"It's not that simple, and you know it, Evelyn. You misled me and hid things I should have known. You lied." His body slumped into hopeless despair. "You said you loved me and trusted me, but you didn't tell me. Actions speak louder than words. What else? What other secrets and lies?"

"There isn't anything else," I whispered.

"How can I believe you?" he said, his voice now calm and filled with a sense of loss.

I forced myself to uncurl from my fetal position, sit up, and look him straight in the eyes. I tried to blink back the unrelenting tears.

"You're right, Sam. I lied to you, and I understand why you

don't believe me."

"Don't play mind games with me, Evelyn," he said, his anger flaring. "I'm not one of your clients. I'm your …"

He couldn't say *husband*. I saw the confusion and pain crash through his mind as he struggled with the idea of who I was and what a small and closed mind would make him.

I shook my head no and looked down at my pink tennis shoes so he wouldn't see my tears.

"I'm not playing games, Sam. You are right. I lied to you and I lied to myself. I told myself it wasn't important, that I am who I am and my past was no one's business … not even yours. But my mom was right. Our past is always a part of us. You had a right to know. I was wrong. I'm sorry."

He was silent for a minute. I didn't want to look up. I didn't want to see his eyes and know I had lost him.

"So what do you expect now, *Evelyn*?" His words flooded the room with bitterness and ridicule. "Kiss and make up? I don't think so."

I heard him moving toward the door.

My voice was tight and imploring. "Physical gender and gender identity are two different things. I am and always have been a woman."

Sam dropped into a rocking chair near the door. I looked up. He had put his face into his hands. He did that when he needed to unscramble his emotions, understand facts, and find a compassionate solution.

He hadn't walked out. *Maybe …*

I needed to reign in my emotions—be rational and factual for him. I knew he had heard it all before in my lectures and conversations, but perhaps he'd hear it in his heart this time.

"Most people used to think the earth was flat. The truth is, the earth is round. Most people think that physical gender and gender identity are the same thing. The truth is, they are separate and distinct aspects of who we are.

"I was born knowing—not thinking—*knowing* that my spirit was not the gender of the body God gave me. Current research in human physiology, brain structure, behavior, and genetics is proving more conclusively every day that we no more choose our gender identity than we choose our eye color. It's—"

He looked up, the anger in his eyes burning my hope once more.

"The time for this biology lesson was eleven years ago,

Adam."

His words impaled me, stealing my breath and racking me with pain. My Sam, my soul mate, my husband, hated me for being different. Shaking, I pulled my knees to my chest and curled up again, as the light of my world faded to twilight shadows.

I heard him walk out.

Chapter 25
Why?
Sam

I closed the front door with the knowledge that I was through with Evelyn. It pulled open behind me.

"Hold up for a second, Sam," Nick said.

I guessed he was going to try to talk me into going back inside so he could play marriage counselor and "fix" things. I kept walking. He followed me out to my truck and leaned against the hood on the passenger's side. I continued to the driver's door.

"You probably need a drink," he said. "How 'bout I be your designated driver?"

Behind him, I could see Mom comforting Evelyn through the front window of the house—*the traitor*.

I started to tell Nick to go—but he knew stuff that I needed to know if I was going to keep my kids. There had to be other lies. Maybe he'd let something slip.

"Sure. Your watering hole or mine?"

"Yours. The female clientele are better looking."

I wasn't sure how to take his comment about the women. It had been over a year since Louise had died. If he was looking, he could do a hell-of-a-lot better than a sports bar, and right now seemed to be a lousy time to be looking.

I was on my second beer, which helped my hangover from yesterday. I had half expected Nick to give me a lecture or justify Evelyn's deceit, but all we had done for over an hour was drink, play pool, talk abalone, and rate the women who came in. It was a nice Sunday, so there hadn't been many women. Since they had all been with men, it was harmless fun.

I had heard a lot about transgendered children from listening to Evelyn over the years, but had never paid a lot of attention, nor taken anything but a passing interest in the subject. Now I was interested. Like Evelyn, Nick was an expert on it.

"I saw a television show on kids like Evelyn," I said. "One of them was into mermaids, like she is. What's with that?"

Nick leaned back in his chair and thought for a minute. "Shallow or deep?"

I knew he was asking if I wanted the shallow thirty-second version suitable for short attention spans, morons, and voters, or if I wanted something with a little meat. When he and Eve talked shop, they quickly got into a technical vocabulary that left me feeling like they were speaking alien. But I wanted more than just a "cuz they like 'em."

"Deep. Just not too technical."

He nodded again. "Some male to female transgendered children love mermaids, but the fascination is far from universal. Girls in general are captivated by fairytale figures: unicorns, fairies, princesses. Mermaids are just one of the many archetypes they relate to.

"In *The Little Mermaid,* Ariel is magically transformed from a mermaid into a girl—the perfect fantasy for a gender dysphoric boy.

"On the other side of the gender coin, females who are gender dysphoric tend to be attracted to superheroes like Superman, the Incredible Hulk, and G.I. Joe.

"Their bodies are one gender and their minds another, so they are naturally attracted to things which interest the brain's gender."

Evelyn had fretted over whether a child was truly gender dysphoric or if there were other medical or emotional reasons for wanting to be the opposite sex.

"It's not that easy," I said.

"You're right. It's not easy," he said, his frown filled with reflective concern. "Some children are trying to please a parent who wanted a child of the opposite sex; some hyper-feminine boys and hyper-masculine girls claim to be the opposite gender to escape the disapproval of adults and peers; some children are just uncomfortable with their body and think they would be more comfortable if they changed it; some want to enjoy toys or clothes traditionally reserved for the opposite gender and believe changing sex will allow that; some boys claim to be female so that their parents will be as demonstrative with them as they are with their daughters; some girls claim to be male so that they can enjoy the attention and privileges their brothers receive; and some children want to escape the disapproval of a parent who is a misogynist or misandrist. Then there is—"

"A what?"

He thought for a second. "Oh. A woman hater or man hater."

"Got ya."

"Sometimes other underlying or associated psychopathologies cause the dysphoria. Then there is the possibility of hormonal imbalances, a chromosomal abnormality, or other physical disorders.

"On top of all those factors and possibilities, many of the children who are gender dysphoric cease to be so at puberty. It takes a lot of dedication, experience, and compassion to effectively treat these children."

I remembered Evelyn saying that trans children were more at risk for suicide than any other segment of society. The most common reasons were rejection by family, sexual assault, and the unwanted biological changes of puberty. She had lost a client to suicide a few years ago. His death had hit her hard, and she had considered giving up her work with children.

"In the diaries," I said, "you seemed pretty damn sure Evelyn was a girl. How did you know?"

Nick took a deep breath and let it out slow as he waded through old memories.

"I could rattle off all the classic symptoms and behavior patterns she exhibited. I could list the personality and gender test scores. I could tell you we couldn't find any endocrine, genetic, or physical abnormalities. But when you've been working with the transgendered long enough, you sometimes just know.

"There was something unequivocal and genuine in the way Eve moved through the world. In her eyes and in her words, I could see that she had an absolute knowing and understanding of who she was. Few of us ever attain that depth of understanding.

"Even without all the clinical evaluations, like her, I just knew."

He paused and took in a slow, deep breath and then let it out.

"Regardless of the cause of the dysphoria and the eventual outcome, intervention results in lower suicide rates, less substance abuse, fewer secondary or symptomatic psychiatric symptoms, fewer entanglements with law enforcement, and generally greater academic achievement. A win–win for everyone."

Everyone but me.

Chapter 26
Helping?
Sam

After another game of pool that Nick let me win, we sat at a booth and started talking abalone again. I noticed a woman who was trying to be inconspicuous slip into the bar and head to the back. She was alone and her clothes reminded me of Evelyn's old baggy garden work clothes. Her hair was uncombed and she didn't have any makeup on. Nick motioned to her.

"Three," I said.

"Nah. At least a six," Nick said, grinning.

"Three," I reiterated. "It's a known scientific fact that the more beer you drink, the prettier a woman gets. I should be two points higher than you by now."

"Look at those breasts. Even through the baggy shirt, you can tell they are Cs, leaning to Ds, and have very little sag. The jeans are baggy, but you can still tell she has a very nice derriere. Put her in something tight, and she'd be at least a six … with good makeup, maybe even an eight."

I started undressing her with my eyes to see if Nick was right. "Hmmm. Maybe."

"She's looking for someone to keep her warm for a while," Nick added.

I stared at Nick, wondering where he was getting off with a comment like that.

"How ya know?" I asked, trying to figure out if he was serious.

"I've been working with people for over thirty years. It's written all over her. Look at her ring finger. She has a fresh tan line. Took her wedding ring off less than a week ago. Uncombed or windblown hair is normally compacted on one side and fluffed out on the other. Hers is artistically disarrayed.

She's dressed in baggy work clothes, but they are clean, and given the length of those acrylic nails, she's not planning on doing any tree stump pulling in the near future.

"My guess is that she dressed down and made herself look unattractive so she could check out the bar scene without being hit on. Based on her rapid, shallow respiration and how her eyes are darting around to take everything in, I doubt she has spent much time in a bar.

"She's desperate to feel wanted and loved, but she's in too much pain to figure out a healthy way to get it. She's vulnerable. An easy target for a guy looking for a one-nighter or a short fling. I'd guess she's even about five years younger than Eve."

She sat at the end of the bar away from everyone and ordered a lite beer. Everything Nick said about her seemed accurate. She probably was an easy score.

"What the hell do you think you're doing?" I asked, glaring at Nick.

"Helping." His look was serious and confident.

"Helping? This isn't exactly helping."

He looked back at her and sipped his soda, a contented Cheshire grin on his face.

I tired of waiting for an answer and looked back at her. He was right ... she was an eight. Looked like a nice person. And she did have that hungry look.

"You've been thinking about it, haven't you?" Nick said. "Which justification, Sam? That will teach her for lying to me. It'll prove I'm a real man. It'll prove I'm not gay."

I was so close to hitting him, it surprised me. I slammed my fist down on the table, knocking my beer bottle to the floor. I glared at him. *Yeah. All three, and then some. So friggin' what?*

My capped molar began to ache under the force of my clenched jaw. I stood and marched out of the bar, with all eyes on me. I paced the parking lot and debated whether I should wait for Nick or call a cab and tell him to get lost.

Five minutes passed, then ten. The four beers in two-and-a-half hours had mellowed me. After fifteen minutes, I went back in to see what had happened to Nick. Sitting at the end of the bar with his number six, he was handing her a napkin. She was crying, like Evelyn had earlier. I never would have guessed he was into picking up women younger than his daughter. But then, there seemed to be a lot of things I never would have guessed.

"What is it with women and their crying." I muttered to myself.

I headed down the bar to where Nick was and sat on the stool two up from him. I wanted to find out if I should hang around for a ride, or call a cab and let him rock the cradle.

"Call the divorce support group on the back of the card and ask to talk to Marlene." Nick said. "If you wish to talk with someone privately, Marlene can recommend someone good."

"Thank you, Doctor Strand," the woman said, drying the last of her tears. She stood and hurried past me, avoiding eye contact. Up close, despite the red and swollen eyes, she was at least an eight; and that was after subtracting the two-point intoxication bonus. Nick turned toward me.

"Looks like your day to be doing good deeds," I said.

He smiled and shrugged. "Sorry you missed your opportunity. If you want to hang around, the night is young. We might get lucky and find another easy score."

I shook my head no. "I've had all the help I can use from you today. Why don't you just take me home? I'll drop by tomorrow for my truck."

"What are you going to do with your free week?" Nick asked.

I knew he wasn't stupid enough to put himself in the middle of Evelyn's and my fight—although he was dangerously close to it.

"We … I don't have any plans at the moment," I said, cautiously.

"Do you want to know who the real Evelyn Louise Irving is?"

I scowled at him. "I've already read the journals." I was going to hit the newspaper archives and do web searches on all the people listed in the journals, but he didn't need to know that.

"I haven't," Nick said. "But from what Eve told me, the journals don't tell the whole—"

"She read them?"

He hesitated. "Yes. Last night."

I wondered if I should go back through and look for torn out pages. It wouldn't make any difference.

Nick continued. "There were important things, too painful, too private, for Louise to write down. A journal is *one* person's viewpoint and opinion. Reading the journals and thinking you know everything about Eve is like reading one article on abalone mating and thinking you know everything about oceanography."

I turned toward the bar and flagged the bartender for another beer.

I needed to play dumb. *Play? I am dumb.* "I know too much already." *Damn journals.*

Nick turned toward the bar and ordered another soda, and we both looked straight ahead.

"What was with the 'easy score' shit?" I asked.

"Just seeing if you still loved Eve."

My body tensed, and I had the urge to hit something again.

"How can you be in love with someone who doesn't exist?" I said.

He frowned and gave a solemn nod but didn't say anything.

"Besides, you should know better than anyone that cheating only makes things worse. Until the judge signs the papers, I'm still married, whether I love her or not. But the main reason I'm not interested is that I want my kids to believe in honor and integrity. If I was irresponsible enough to cheat, how can I expect them to be responsible?"

Nick nodded again. "It's unlikely they would find out."

I knew he was playing devil's advocate, and as tempting as it was, I couldn't let it be an option. I looked down the skinny neck of the beer bottle. It reminded me of a sink drain. The realization that I was trying to drown my anger—and maybe my life—in alcohol didn't seem all that appealing. An image of Clora flashed through my mind. I pushed it away, leaned back, and gawked at the ceiling. It needed painting.

"I made a friggin' big mistake once," I said. "And it almost cost me my kids. I swore that I would always—*always*—do the right thing after that. I won't judge others, but for me, adultery is wrong. And telling my kids to be honorable and have integrity when I don't is wrong. Just … plain … wrong."

The second the words were out of my mouth, I regretted saying them. I had come here to get dirt on Evelyn, and I was giving Nick dirt on me. *Stupid, stupid, stupid.*

I caught a glimpse of the jukebox and went over.

"Patty Smyth, Patti Smyth," I mumbled to myself. I flipped through the jukebox menu. "Yes." I plugged in a buck and hit L42. I walked back to the bar, while Patty started whining that *Sometimes Love Just Ain't Enough.*

I sat down and ordered a soda as she whined about the danger of loving someone too much and how we can't trust our hearts.

I could relate. Really relate.

Staring ahead I said, "She was scared and wanted to believe a lot of things that weren't true. She should have told me."

"It's about a lot more than a bruised ego and a lie," Nick said.

I dug in. "She lied. Period. The end."

"Baby, sometimes, love … it just ain't enough." Patty finished.

Nick went over to the jukebox and started flipping the menu. I tried to ignore him. After a couple minutes, he plugged in his dollar and came back with Dolly Parton singing, "You ask me if I love you …"

I crossed my arms on the bar and set my forehead on them as Dolly talked of honest hurt and misleading lies. About judging and how she was just beginning to "see the real you."

See the real you.

I leaned back in my seat and scowled at Nick. "Why didn't I see the real Eve?" I asked. "My mom knew. Why didn't I?"

Nick shrugged. "I could argue that you did see the real Eve, but that isn't what you are really asking.

"Eve's surgeon was one of the best. The reconstruction is so good, a gynecologist might not notice without looking close." Nick blushed and then mumbled. "At least that's what her surgeon told me."

He took a sip of his soda and cleared his throat before continuing. "As for your mom knowing, I don't know. Louise may have let it slip, though I doubt it. She may have figured it out from a pregnant pause during a conversation or little pieces of history picked up here and there.

"What I do know is that women are better than men at putting things like that together. They have around fifteen areas of the brain that read body language and vocal tones. We only have about five. That ability—their *women's intuition*—tells them things that go right over our heads. They naturally pick up on little details, while our male brains are stuck staring at soft curves and pretty faces. You could ask her how she knew."

Yeah. Like that was going to happen.

I pushed the soda away and headed for the door. Nick was close behind me this time.

Nick was signaling for a left out of the parking lot toward my home.

"Right," I said. "Take me to my mom's."

I didn't want to go home. I couldn't face seeing all the pictures on the walls of us as a happy family, knowing that was about to change and how hurt the kids would be. No whispered poetry from Angela. No video game music from Chris's computer. No humming or singing or dramatically read plays from Grace. No Eve. No us. Just an empty house full of loneliness.

"You've got it." Nick said, and turned right.

As he drove, I stared out the window at the now dark San Francisco Bay. The city lights twinkled in San Francisco, Berkeley, and beyond. All the sailboats that wandered aimlessly around the bay during the day had been put away for the night. The lone occupant of the water was a small container ship, making its way through the dark waters to the Golden Gate Bridge and then on to some far-off port.

"Getting back to my earlier question," Nick said, interrupting my thoughts. "Do you want to know who the real Evelyn is?"

I sat silently mulling it over through my slushy brain. Part of me didn't care; I just wanted her out of my life. But I had the kids to think about. Evelyn was the only mother they had ever really known. A divorce would devastate them, and I could lose them. *Dirt*. I didn't have anything to lose.

"Sure."

"By the time you pick up your truck tomorrow morning, I will have airline tickets, maps, news articles, photos, car and hotel reservations, and an itinerary with a list of people who will be expecting you. Your plane will leave before noon."

Nick was manipulating me. I glared at him.

"You've been planning this for a while."

He nodded yes. "For about a year. After Louise died, Eve came over to my house to go through her mother's things. I questioned her about her choice to keep it a secret. She had a severe stress reaction. I expected her to somehow let it slip." He sighed and looked annoyed. "And then I let it slip.

"After you told me about the journals, I started pulling the rest of it together. There will be loose ends, but you'll manage."

"You're butting in where you don't belong. Why?"

He thought for a second. "You deal with facts, Sam. You value honesty and integrity. What would you do if I didn't offer you the chance to find out firsthand why she kept it a secret?

Web and newspaper archive searches? Call a few people listed in the journals? Walk away?"

I didn't like that he knew me that well. I glared and didn't answer.

"I want you and Eve to work this out. To do that, you need answers. Los Angeles is where you will find some of them."

"Does Evelyn know?"

"No."

"Would she approve?"

He winced. "I wouldn't want to be in the same state when she finds out, but once she calms down, she'll understand."

We stopped in front of my parents' house, and Nick turned off the car. We both stared straight ahead.

"There may be some satisfaction in outing Eve to people around here," Nick said, "but what do you think will happen to the kids?"

I nodded. Even slush-brained, I understood. Ignorance and prejudice were still commonplace—even in a community a stone's throw from San Francisco. They'd be treated like lepers. Shunned, ridiculed, and possibly even beat up. Evelyn had me by the balls, and doing anything about it was going to hurt—a lot. I closed my eyes and asked God for deliverance, even knowing it was wasted effort.

Nick continued, "Most everyone in L.A. knows about Eve. My sister, Tanya, was always extremely supportive of Eve and Louise. My brother, Dave, and several other family members came around eventually. But most of my family acted like Eve had the plague."

"Evelyn will need to know where I am, in case of an emergency. What do I tell her?"

Nick shrugged. "It's your call."

"I could tell her we're diving, so she won't call home."

He chuckled. "She knows I'm going out of town for a seminar."

I frowned at him. "What's the chuckle for?"

"Life's little ironies, Sam. I'll see you when you get back. Take care of yourself."

I got out of the car and watched Nick drive off. As I turned toward Mom's house, I understood his "irony" statement and wanted to crawl under a rock. *Lies.* Now I would need to tell Evelyn where I was going.

Chapter 27
Declaring War
Evelyn

I cried and talked with Rose for hours after Sam left. It was late in the day before I was able to pull myself together enough to drive up to Bodega Bay. Exhausted, I parked in front of the beach house and opened the van door. My cell phone rang with Sam's ring tone.

Maybe he wants me to come home.

"Hi, honey." His silence was excruciating. "Are you alright, Sam?"

"Yeah. Um ... I just called to tell you that you won't be able to reach me at home. Text my cell if you need me."

My stomach felt hollow, and I shivered. "Where are you going?"

"Los Angeles. I leave in the morning."

I started trembling. "No, Sam. Please. I'll tell you everything. Please don't go. I beg you." My plea was more an old reflex and the fear of what I had run away from, than any fear of discovery. His going wouldn't make any difference to us. It was more important that we talk. He needed to understand. We needed to rebuild trust.

"Tell me everything?" he said, his voice cold. "Just like you did when we were dating?"

"I'm sorry. So, so sorry. I'll tell you anything you want to know. What do you want from me? I'll do anything you want."

His tone was cavalier. "Go away and don't come back."

I frowned in confusion. "What?"

"Move out. Go. Leave me and the kids. That's what I want. I want you out of our lives."

He wanted me to walk away from *my* kids? As if they meant *nothing* to me? *My* Sam wanted that? NO ONE takes my kids away from me!

The fear vanished, and the fires of rage seared the cell towers from Bodega to Marin.

"Screw you, Sam. I'll see you in hell before I walk away from my kids. You want to be a bastard? Well, I can be a bitch. Whether you believe it or not, I was born to be a bitch, and if you think Clora made your life hell, you don't know what hell is."

His tone was acidic. "You're not taking my kids, Adam. They're mine, and I will do whatever it takes to keep them."

When he called me Adam, I found myself sitting in a dark tunnel that extended out the back of my head. My eyes had become picture windows on the far side of a house, through which I watched the world outside. I was the clumsy operator of some exoskeletal robot, driving a human machine that I called me, only vaguely aware that I had lost the physical sensation of touch.

I didn't feel fear or anger. No emotions except the curious awareness of the absence of emotions, and the discomfort of the odd, sluggish perspective through which I was seeing myself and the world. Sam's voice sounded like a distant radio, set to a hatemonger talk show, spouting ignorant, spiteful tripe. I held the phone away from me as if it were a rabid dog.

Sam had threatened to take our children away from me. He wasn't the gentle, kind, thoughtful, and reasonable man I thought I had married. He didn't love me enough to want to try to understand.

I realized I didn't know him any more than he knew me. Maybe both of us had been a lie in our own personal way. It didn't matter now. Only our children mattered.

I held down the power button. The phone turned off, and like a childhood dream of falling, I was slammed back into my body with a turbulent jolt. Pain, grief, anger, fear, self-pity, and self-righteousness all flooded my consciousness—all focused by my protective mother instincts. Icy chills swirled across my skin as heat surged like a tsunami through my veins.

He didn't want to save our marriage. That donkey's behind was going to that poop-chute of a city to find a way to make me look like an unfit mother. He had declared war.

Chapter 28
Falling Apart, Falling In Love
Evelyn

Felicity had been watching me from the beach house and came out after I hung up. The surge of adrenaline subsided, and I stepped out of the van—hanging onto the door to steady myself.

"I'm so sorry he found out." Felicity comforted me in her arms.

Between the meeting at my dad's house and the phone call with Sam, I was completely drained and physically numb. I didn't have the energy to feel my justified rage and so I sank into a puddle of self-pity and tears.

"He doesn't love me anymore."

Felicity held me as I tried to calm myself. I looked up at the house and said, "The kids can't see me like this."

"Mark took them into Bodega for dinner. We waited until they were starving hoping you would get here," she said.

"You what! You let him take my kids?" I pulled away and looked wide-eyed at her, as renewed energy surged through me, trampling my self-pity.

Her tone was defensive. "He's a great guy. I know practically everything about him. We haven't been apart for more than a couple days since I met him, and he even took me to dinner with his parents Friday night."

Glaring at Felicity, I tried hard to sound cheerful as I called Chris.

"Hi, Chris. Where are you and the girls?"

"Lucas Wharf with Mark." His tone said he was still angry.

"Is everyone alright?"

"Yeah," he said, like it was a dumb question. "We want to go home."

"We'll go home tomorrow morning. Felicity and I will be

down to join you in a few minutes."

"Good. I won't miss practice." His tone was more upbeat.

"See you in a few. Love you. Bye."

Felicity made a sad grin. "Sorry. He's a good guy and very responsible. Really. I wouldn't have let him take the kids if I wasn't absolutely sure."

I was still peeved, but Felicity had meant well. We climbed into my van and headed south to Bodega.

"Since Easter? That was five, six weeks ago." I said.

Her smile was radiant. "Yeah. After church, I took Mark to my place. He loved my art, but I could tell he didn't think it was a good idea for me to be living there."

"Duh," I said. I'd been telling her that for years.

She scowled at me, and continued. "He suggested that we would be more comfortable at his place. I packed an overnight bag, and he thought I should take hiking clothes in case we wanted to go hiking, and swim clothes for diving, and something for a nice dinner out." She chuckled. "By the time I had packed for all the possibilities he was suggesting, half my stuff was in bags and boxes."

Felicity stared wistfully at the winding road, looking content. "I knew it was silly and irresponsible to move in with him, and if I had said no, he wouldn't have pushed it, but it was so much fun. It was like when we were in high school and would just throw together a day bag and run out to the ocean with friends. The only things that mattered were being together and having fun.

"I've never felt this way about anyone," she said. Her sigh was long, soft, and blissful.

My heart ached with memories of Sam and me. "I'm happy for you."

I pulled onto the wharf and noticed the girls were sitting in a new jeep that had two gorgeous wood strip kayaks strapped to the top. Chris and Mark were standing next to it. Mark's uncomfortable suit had been replaced by top-end outdoor clothes, and the kids seemed to be enthralled with Mark's story.

I frowned at Felicity. "Where does a kayak instructor get the money for a brand new Jeep with fancy ornaments on top? Or did he borrow it?"

She nudged me and grinned proudly. "He and his dad started an outdoor recreation store while he was working on his MBA. They have three stores now. His dad works the in-store business end and Mark runs the educational and field operations."

At the church, Mark had been so modest and unassuming that I never would have guessed—especially when he was riding with Felicity in her beater truck. I wanted to be there for her as she explored her new relationship, but she had sure picked one heck-of-a-time to find the perfect guy and fall in love.

I parked next to Mark and the kids. He handed greasy bags to me and Felicity.

"They were closing," Mark said. "So I ordered both of you cod and fries to go. Hope they aren't too cold."

Mark entertained us with stories of how stupid some of the people who took his classes were while we ate our dinner on the hood of his jeep. After Felicity and I finished our fish, she and Mark headed home. The kids and I went back to the beach house.

After the kids were asleep, I went out on the deck to watch the dark surf. I tried to call Sam but he didn't answer either his cell phone or the home phone.

He had sounded like he had been drinking, and once I cooled off, I realized—or hoped—it had been the booze talking. He was hurting and had lashed out without thinking. He couldn't have meant it when he said he wanted me gone; he loved me too much. I decided to pretend I hadn't noticed how late it was and called Rose.

"Your dad got him drunk again and dropped him off a couple hours ago. He's sleeping it off in the guest room."

"How is he?"

"Stupid and stubborn. He's still mad at me for siding with you, as if that's not the best thing for him. Other than that, he'll live. How are you and the kids holding up?"

"I'm alright," I said. There wasn't any point in telling her I was falling apart. "The kids are having a hard time, but that's to be expected."

"If you need anything ..."

"Thanks, Mom."

Chapter 29
Los Angeles
Sam

After seeing my lawyer and starting the divorce paperwork, I caught a plane to L.A. It was just after noon when I landed at Los Angeles International Airport. Nick had thought it would be a good idea if his brother, Dave, showed me around for a day or two while I got my bearings. After that, I could get a rental car and drive myself.

Nick had said not to be surprised if Dave was late; he was right. I stood in the pickup area of the airport, gagging on diesel exhaust for nearly half an hour, waiting for Dave's car—a mint, royal blue, 1969 Dodge Charger RT. It was easy to spot him. I tossed my bag in the back and handed him the short list of contacts that Nick had set up.

"Ashley must be doing good," Dave said, looking at the first name on the list. "Thousand Oaks is a nice area. Expensive."

Within minutes, we were on the congested San Diego Freeway heading north. The smell of diesel exhaust hung with us.

"Hey, Dave. What's that smell?"

He scowled. "What smell?"

"It smells like diesel exhaust and rancid jock strap."

He looked confused for a moment, then he chuckled.

"It's the smog. We have a saying here, 'Don't trust air you can't see.' That way, you know the politicians didn't steal it." After he finished chuckling at his joke, he said, "They say there was smog way back before the Spanish settled here. The mountains and trade winds held the campfire smoke in, just like they hold in the smog.

"It's not normally this bad anymore, but we've had an inversion layer and no wind for a few days. The weatherman said it will last all week." He grinned. "Wouldn't it be nice to have a job where you can be wrong half the time and still get paid good?"

"Yeah. It would."

"Evelyn didn't tell you, huh?" Dave asked, looking pointedly at me.

I flinched and shook my head no.

He grinned one of those what-a-dope grins. "She always was good at pretending. You know."

"Uh. Yeah."

I didn't like Dave's insinuation that I was an idiot, but it seemed based more on immaturity than malice, so I ignored it.

"I was going through the itinerary Nick set up for me," I said. "He has me meeting with Pastor Jones. I understand his son was a suspect in the murders."

Dave grimaced and shook his head no. "Pastor Jones died seven years ago. You're seeing his son, Brandon, Pastor Jones *Jr*. He went to college and took over his dad's business."

"Evelyn said he killed Cinnamon and Zack."

Dave shrugged. "Police said he didn't."

"Did he?"

"Eve never struck me as a liar, and Nick was one hundred percent behind her. People like Eve freak people out, and she's a nobody. Nick isn't rich or connected.

"Brandon's dad was famous and worth millions. A great American success story. Poor preacher becomes televangelist and the Lord showers him with millions and political contacts. You question his word and you're questioning God. He gave them an alibi."

I was beginning to doubt the wisdom of coming here, but Evelyn could take my kids.

I leaned back and watched Los Angeles fly by. San Francisco could get congested and had a lot of high-density neighborhoods, but despite the sprawl, L.A. seemed far more crowded. Maybe it was because the houses, shopping centers, and ten-lane roads seemed to sit on top of each other and went on forever, without large expanses of water and green mountains to break up the congested brown.

"So this is the City of the Angels."

"Yep," Dave said. "Los Angeles. Spanish for *The Angels*. It was originally called something like *The Town of Our Lady the Queen of Angels of the Little Portion*, but people got hand cramps trying to address envelopes, and it didn't fit on government forms, so they shortened it to Los Angeles—the angels."

I was more than skeptical. "And when was this?"

He shrugged. "Not sure. Back when California belonged to Mexico; before Abe Lincoln wrote the constitution."

Uh. Right. This was going to be an interesting trip.

I noticed a freeway sign to the San Fernando Valley. "My son, Chris, made a sugar cube model of the San Fernando mission in the fifth grade. Did a great job."

Dave chuckled. "His school book probably said the monks named it San Fernando after Saint Ferdinand."

"Sounds about right." It had been awhile so I wasn't absolutely sure.

He grinned. "They're wrong. It was actually named after a Spanish prospector."

I was dubious, but rested against the door and listened.

Dave continued, "These two prospectors were on their way back to Mexico after a big gold strike up in the Sierras. When they crested the San Gabriel Mountains, they looked down on the valley. One of the prospectors said, 'What's that, José?' to which José replied, 'It's sand, Fernando.' And from that time forward, it was known as the Sand Fernando Valley—until the monks showed up and messed up the spelling."

I chuckled out of politeness and wondered if he was going to help or send me on snipe hunts.

"Can you tell me anything about Ashley?" I knew Ashley was a cousin, or second cousin, but that was the limit of the information Nick had given me on her.

"Don't know," he said, his brow furrowed deeply. "She was one of those relatives that I just kind of avoided or ignored. She made me nervous."

"Why?"

"Don't know," he said, shaking his head. "She was nice enough. A head-turner and loved to flirt. Harmless stuff, but she still made me nervous."

"Did she and Evelyn get along?"

He thought for a moment. "Never saw them talk beyond polite manners shit."

I pulled some notes out of my pocket and quickly reviewed them.

"Nick couldn't find where Billy Jackson is. Would you know?"

"No. Heard he got knifed in jail, but don't rightly know."

"Know about when or which jail?"

Dave shook his head no. His face brightened. "I do know where his dad lives." He slumped. "Course that was like fifteen years ago."

"Do you know his dad's name?"

He thought for a second and hesitantly said, "Mr. Jackson?"

It was obvious Nick got all the brains.

"Louise had a brother. A firefighter. Know anything about him?"

He thought hard for a few seconds. "Oh, yeah! He lived back east somewhere and came out for the wedding. At the rehearsal dinner, he got real weird when he met Eve. You would have thought he'd been introduced to the devil. He and Louise went outside, and you could hear them screaming at each other. Nick went out, and it got real quiet in the restaurant. Everyone was straining to hear what was being said without looking like they were listening. Her brother came back in, got his wife and eight kids, and left before the food was even served. Can you imagine? Free food and he left. Didn't show for the wedding, either. That's all I know."

The dead ends were stacking up fast.

"How about your sister, Florence? Would she know any of Evelyn's old contacts?"

He shook his head no. "She married a career Army man, early seventies. Lived all over the world. Seen her maybe eight times in forty years. They retired in Italy. Don't think she ever met Louise or the kids."

"Anyone else who knew Evelyn?"

He shrugged helplessly. "Not that I know, except Tanya, and we'll be seeing her later." He glanced over at me. "You look like you've been on a bender. With this traffic, it's over an hour to Thousand Oaks. The seat leans way back. You could catch a few winks."

I was out of questions for the moment and exhausted from the last two days of shit.

"Thanks. I will."

When Dave slowed on the freeway off-ramp, I woke from my nap. Thousand Oaks was obviously a planned community. Architecturally blended and aesthetically harmonized retail businesses and offices flanked the main road, with organized high-density, urban sprawl beyond. Eucalyptus, pine, pepper, and ornamental trees were scattered along the streets and through the parking lots. Dead grass and scrub brush in dull grays to golden browns sprinkled the mostly barren hills beyond the developments. The tan grass, dry air, and open meadows reminded me of the picturesque oak-studded valley around the Sonoma Mission north of San Francisco. It almost felt like home.

"Where are the thousand oaks?"

Dave smiled and pointed. "There's a Scrub Oak. Looks more like a bush than a tree." He pointed beyond some houses. "There's a California Live Oak, probably more what you expected. They're around. Some areas are thick with 'em."

As he drove, I saw oak trees scattered throughout the city, with some small groves and meandering flows of oak bordering the housing developments. After a few wrong turns in the rat maze of streets, Dave found his way to Ashley's house.

We both studied her two-story McMansion, which took up most of the lot. It had massive windows that sparkled like a window cleaner commercial, and a small but professionally landscaped and manicured front yard. The walkway was garnished with trendy solar bug lighting and brightly colored gnomes that looked dangerously proud.

"Dang postage stamp lots," Dave said, studying the house with his face scrunched in disapproval. "If I could afford a house like that, it'd have an acre of land around it. Hell, you could piss from her porch to the street without getting any on the lawn."

I liked having a big yard, too, but sometimes a postage stamp yard that didn't require mowing, raking, weeding, fertilizing, trimming, pruning, mulching, and two days of spring flower planting every year seemed like a pretty good idea.

I didn't like being here or doing this, but I didn't have much choice. I stepped out of the car.

Chapter 30
Cousin Ashley
Sam

Hollywood movies often promote the myth that all Southern California women are beautiful. Standing on Ashley's porch trying not to gawk at her, I could believe that she was the origin of that myth. She looked like a sex symbol straight out of the Golden Age of Hollywood movies, with her perfect hair and makeup, a low cut nothing of a red dress, incredible cleavage outlined by the top of her lace bra, a skirt barely long enough to be functional, and legs that went on forever, finding infinity in a pair of five-inch bedroom stilettos.

It had only been a couple days, but with everyone thinking I was gay or something less than a man, my eyes were possessed by her seductive cleavage and the possibilities it held. I forced my eyes to meet hers.

Her strained smile and questioning, wary eyes told me she wasn't sure she wanted to talk to me. Nick had set up the meeting, so I wondered if he had warned her I was looking to divorce Evelyn and she was being protective. Maybe Dave had been wrong, and they had been close after all.

"So you married *Evelyn*." She made the name "Evelyn" sound dirty. "Don't like a real woman?" Her face curdled with contempt. She didn't let me answer, not that I would have. "No. Gay men don't like the real thing." She turned almost dismissively and said, "Come on in, girlfriend."

I followed. She continued talking, her voice a mocking come-hither. "Are you gay, Sam? Or are you bi, and don't care where you shove it?"

"I'm not gay," I said, as indifferently as possible.

She stopped and spun around. I almost ran over her.

"You're not?" she asked. Her strained wariness was gone, replaced by a hopeful flirt.

She leaned toward me, so her breasts brushed my chest. She looked up with a smile that drained the blood from my head. She gave me a quick kiss on the mouth with her moist, shimmering red lips. The taste of mint on her breath, mixed with her tantalizing, fruity perfume stirred my mind. At the same time, I felt her hand on my crotch. I stepped back.

"Well, well, well. Aren't you the eager one." she said. Her smile widened and her eyes sparked with playful seduction. "So if you're not gay, why did you marry *him*?"

With my brain a quart low on blood, I spoke before I thought.

"I didn't know."

She studied me while swaying seductively. Amusement slowly reshaped her glistening lips. Her eyes slipped to my chest, then south. Her smile blossomed.

Our eyes met again, she winked, and tilted her head.

"How long since you've had the real thing, Sam?"

"I'm sorry. I'm not here to play games."

She frowned for a second, seeming to question my claim of being straight. Then her blue eyes twinkled with the excitement of a child playing a game she loved.

"Surely you can't blame a *real* girl for trying," she said. Her mocking pout was sugarcoated with amusement. She pushed her chest out a little more. "A hot stud like you. I'd think you'd be dying to indulge in the finest there is after being married to a man for ten years."

Her "to a man," jab made me flinch. I frowned and stared at her, unsure if I wanted to continue.

She took a half-step back, and the playfulness receded. She cautiously reappraised me.

"After Nick called, I had some friends check up on you," she said. "They told me the basics. First marriage ended badly—you poor dear—but you came out of it squeaky clean. Evelyn is your second. Married ten now. Three kids. Two by the ex and one through adoption. You are a business consultant that is well thought of, but not very successful because you spend half your time helping non-profits pro bono. The basics."

It was all "public" information, available online for a few dollars, but it still felt like she had invaded my home and snooped through my dresser.

I stared at her for a moment. "I think I need to go."

Her frown bordered on a contempt-filled glare. "You were

lied to, and she's really a man. No sane person would consider your marriage valid. A straight man would be eager to prove he wasn't queer, and you're not interested in messing up the sheets with me. So are you really straight, Sam?"

I started to turn, but she caught my arm. Her contempt folded and she shook her head no.

"You have three kids. If you are straight, I would guess you are looking for a way to lose him and keep the kids."

Something was seriously wrong. She was too eager. As homophobic as she was, she never would have agreed to see me if she didn't want something.

"Why would you want to help me?"

Her smile turned smug. She knew she had guessed right about the kids and that she had me—for the moment. She turned, with a victorious whip of her long, blond hair, and I followed her to the family room. She offered me a drink, and I declined. She fixed herself something that was heavy on the brandy.

"I worked to pass the California Marriage Protection Act, because marriage is the union of a man and a woman. Eve's not a woman. He's a freak."

I clenched my teeth. Normally, I would have told Ashley she didn't know what she was talking about and then walk out, but I needed information so I could keep my kids. She acted like she might have some.

She continued. "Marriage is the union of a man and woman who make a permanent and exclusive commitment to one another for the purposes of having and raising children. Not for perverted sex acts between queers.

"Kansas and Texas courts have both ruled that a marriage to a transsexual is a same-sex marriage and therefore illegal. A Federal Court overturned the California Marriage Protection Act. If the damn liberals kill it, your situation could set a new precedent and achieve at least some of our goal.

"Since *she's* XY chromosome, you should have had to do a civil union, so the marriage is invalid. We would back you if you claim in court that he deceived you and that the marriage was a fraud from the start. If we win, we could invalidate all marriages to transsexuals. Then, if we play it right, we could use the public outrage at Evelyn's deceit to roll your annulment into a ban on civil unions."

Her suggestion would become a major news story. Even if I

succeeded and had my marriage declared invalid, I still faced the problem of the adoptions. The publicity would make the kids' lives hell and they would be forced to choose sides. I couldn't be sure who they would choose. I didn't like her line of thinking, but I needed to consider all possibilities.

"So you agreed to meet me, hoping that I wasn't gay and was looking for a divorce."

She glowed with amusement. "Didn't care if you were queer. Just hoping you wanted a divorce. You being straight is just the cherry on the whipped cream." Her smile widened and I thought she was going to laugh. "And I have the cherry, if you have the cream."

As tempting as it was, I wasn't going there and shook my head no. Only slightly disappointed, she sat down across from me, slipped off her bedroom heels, and draped herself on the sofa, like eye candy in a glossy furniture ad.

"An Oklahoma politician said that embracing homosexuality would be the death knell of this country, that they are a bigger threat to America than terrorism or Islam. Americans agreed with her and reelected her."

She studied me for a moment. "We need more politicians like her. You have the look, the presence, the intelligence, and I have it on good authority that you speak well to groups. You go public with Eve's deceit, and I have friends who are willing to put you in the state legislature.

"With the public knowing that Eve lied to you to gain intimate access to your children, voters would be sympathetic to our call to deny the queers and trannies marriage. When you say they are a threat to our family values and our children, people will listen and believe. The voters will understand how devious and evil they are."

I hated how she wanted to smear Evelyn.

"You make it sound like Evelyn's a pedophile. It's not true."

Her contempt and arrogance disappeared behind a well-practiced look of thoughtful, righteous concern.

"Truth is a point of view, Sam. From Clinton's point of view, a blow job wasn't having sex. From Bush's point of view, Iraq posed an imminent threat. From their viewpoints, they told the truth. From other viewpoints, they were lying.

"So what is true, Sam. Is it true that she is a woman? Or not?" She huffed. "From my viewpoint, for a man to do something like that to himself is proof of a sick and twisted mind. A mind that would prey on our children and betray our country. And I'm not the only person who feels that way. The passage of the Marriage Protection Act proves that.

"Maybe Eve isn't a pedophile, but as a group, they are perverts," she said, her voice somewhere between a plea and desperation. "If we paint her a little worse than she is, it's for the good of the country. In the end, we will all be safer and better off without them.

"Besides, you don't want her, so what difference does it make? Everyone villainizes their ex."

I didn't like her proposal and just stared back.

She sighed, her tone filled with tender reassurance. "You will have your kids, Sam. You can find a real woman to be their mother."

I shook my head no. She hadn't sold me.

She looked down in thought and then smiled pensively.

"Maybe we could even get your ex-wife, Clora, out early if you would like." Her grin widened. "Or make sure she never gets out."

She had that bedroom smile and longing look in her eyes again.

"And there are benefits, Sam. Perks. A good-looking man like you in a position of power never has to worry about being lonely."

There were so many factual errors in her arguments, I couldn't count them. Her proposal went against everything I believed about right and wrong. Most of the people who voted for laws like the Marriage Protection Act were good and decent people. They voted for those injustices because of ignorance, church doctrine, and fear—not vindictive malice or sadistic hate.

But she was right about America being a situational nation—a nation where expediency usurps principles and morals if a situation makes doing the right thing inconvenient. A nation where people cast votes based on fear or blind adherence to some *-ism* instead of votes based on facts, compassion, and what is best for the country.

So why was I hanging onto the idea that truth and justice are the American way? The only thing that mattered was my kids.

My stomach churned. "And how do you know these people?"

"I'm a political strategist."

"How connected?"

She demurely said, "As connected as I would like to be with you, Sam."

"You don't know me," I said, annoyed by her advances. "And you obviously could have any man you want, so why the interest in me?"

She looked down in deep thought for a minute.

"Do you know about Zack?" she asked.

"I understand he was Evelyn's boyfriend in high school and was killed."

Her eyes dulled. An old sadness pushed down her delicate shoulders.

"Yes. Zack was the only man I really loved." She glanced up, regret at her disclosure masking her face. She quickly added, "In high school."

"So you and Zack dated?"

She took a long sip on her drink. "Yeah. We had something extraordinary. He gave me his ring and I gave him my virginity." Her smile was bittersweet. "Not really, but he thought I did."

With prideful embarrassment, she added, "I made him feel real guilty about it after we broke up."

A serious frown settled above her perfectly arched eyebrows. She slumped back into the couch and sighed. Her voice carried tired resignation.

"Political spin and love are alike, Sam. We say trickle down. They believe it. What is real doesn't matter. *Perception* is all that matters.

"Eve said he was a girl. You believed he was a girl. Then one day you find out it was all a lie, but it's too late. He owns you, and the price to get rid of him is astronomical. *Perception*. The people with the smoke and mirrors win. The people who didn't bother to check the facts, pay."

She shrugged. "None of that matters."

"I know revenge is deplorable," she said, her seductive smile alive again. "But politics has taught me how good it can taste. That skank, Eve, took Zack from me. I would love to take you, just to get even."

She saw my ego bruise and shook her head no.

"You're a desirable man, Sam—very desirable. Even if I had never met Eve or Zack, here, today, right now, I would want you. Knowing you were his is just a cherry on the whipped cream.

"You can go places. I can see us in the governor's mansion, maybe even Congress. I could make you very happy, very powerful, and very rich."

"Not the White House?" I smirked.

She scowled, more at my flippant tone than the question.

"You're too honest, Sam." She studied me for a moment, her bedroom eyes now cautious with what seemed to be a genuine want. "If you're divorcing Eve, why not have a little fun with me? I'm clean. I'm more than willing. And my last three husbands will attest to the fact that I'm a real live wet dream."

The caveman inside my head wanted her. "I'm still married."

She shrugged. "It's not a real marriage. So why not, Sam?"

I was getting tired of her game and shook my head no, making my annoyance clear.

She sneered. "You must have someone on the side. Who is it? Coworker? Wife's best friend? Best friend's wife?" She shook her head. "Doesn't matter. My husband has done all three."

"You're married?"

She shrugged. "Yeah. He's traveling."

I grinned. "Permanent and exclusive commitment?"

She glared at me. "It's an ideal, Sam. Half the country has been married at least twice, and we both know that most men and half the women cheat at some point. It doesn't change anything. Marriage is still between real men and real women."

My smile was too smug and her glare turned to contempt.

"I gave up believing in monogamy and love after I caught my second husband screwing the neighbor. Benny and I married for convenience, public appearance, tax advantages, and to leverage our assets. If we keep it discrete, nothing is said about what we do when the other isn't around. When we find something better, we dissolve the partnership with no hard feelings."

Her contempt melted and her thoughts seemed to be elsewhere. A sadness crept onto her face and I thought she was going to cry. I was ready to leave.

Without looking up, she said, "My first husband left me for my best friend." Her voice was choked with old pain. "I caught the second one screwing the neighbor in our bed." She looked at me with curious confusion. "I didn't think there were any men like you. I thought the whole idea of *monogamy* and 'till death do us part' was a childish fantasy, an ideological rallying cry. But you're real. If Eve weren't a boy, you would have stood by her until the sun stopped shining." Her eyes brimmed with tears. "What I wouldn't give for a man like you."

A sad emptiness permeated the air around her, and she looked away. After a few moments, she went to fix herself another drink.

"What do you know about the murders?" I asked.

Lost to her thoughts, Ashley stared at her half-prepared drink and shrugged without saying anything. After a minute, she stood taller, shook the old emotions off herself, and turned back to me with an inviting smile and clear eyes. But the playful eagerness was gone, replaced by well-practiced sociable pretense. She sat with coy flair and empty solicitation.

"She wasted them. Everyone knows it."

Before the journals, I would have said Evelyn was incapable of killing someone out of jealousy, but I had seriously misjudged my first wife and I had no reason to believe my judgment of Evelyn was any better.

If Evelyn had killed them, I could get the kids without having to play Ashley's game.

"Oh?"

"Zack got what he deserved for dumping me for that freak," she said with indifference. "And there is one less queer in the world. He should get a medal for killing them, but you don't give medals to rabid dogs for killing their own."

She stared blankly at the rug.

"Why do you believe she did it?"

She shrugged. "Eve's a tranny, so of course he did it. What other proof do you need?"

Seeming weary of the discussion, she sighed and shook her head. Her luxurious curls floated back and forth, calling me. There was futility in her voice.

"Come on, Sam. Let's get to know each other better. I promise you won't be sorry. I know I won't be."

My patience was running thin. "So you don't know anything else about the murders?"

She half sneered at me. "God, you're no fun."

"Do you know if Evelyn did drugs or anything illegal?"

She chuckled. "Boy, have you got a hard-on for him. What'd he do to piss you off so bad? Other than marry you."

In a hard monotone, I repeated, "Do you?"

She shot me an annoyed glare and shook her head no.

"Everybody smoked weed and drank their parents' booze.

Beyond that, I didn't hang with the queers, so I wouldn't know. As far as illegal, if he did, he didn't get caught."

She leaned forward, making sure her cleavage was clearly visible and lively.

"I can probably get the murder investigation reopened, but why? It's history. It could take decades before there's an indictment. Getting your marriage declared invalid would do the same thing and further your career *now*."

She leaned back, with a deep, concerned frown.

"Or do you have a fetish for seeing all your ex's behind bars?" She looked away in thought for a moment. "You make it to the legislature, and your backers could probably arrange it."

It felt like I was negotiating with the Godfather—or Godmother, but she was low-level bait. She was probably intimate enough with the system to know what was possible. And she knew if I was elected to the state legislature and wanted Evelyn in jail, someone would try to make it happen so they could own me.

I was way past my comfort zone, but if her contacts were real and did have the power she inferred, they might be able to make Evelyn go away and get me sole custody. Being a politician, I wouldn't have to worry about how I was going to support the kids without Evelyn's income.

Ashley smiled expectantly.

I'd married a man and everyone thought I was gay or clueless. Clueless? Yeah. Lied to? Yeah. Played for a fool? Yeah. Still playing the fool? The jury was out.

I stared at her powdery breasts with my heart pounding. I shifted so my pants weren't so tight. She saw, and undulated her chest like bait, with renewed interest.

I wanted to walk over to her, pull her to me, and feel those full glossy lips on mine. I wanted her to melt into me. I wanted to unzip that patch of a dress and watch it drop to the floor.

I wanted desperately to prove to everyone that I wasn't gay. That I was a real man, a virile man who loved women and loved taking them to a place most only went in their fantasies.

But I knew that if I bedded her, it would only prove I wasn't a man of my word or a man of moral conviction. But so what? My wedding vow was based on a lie, and we are a situational nation. Expediency and winning are the only things that matter.

I realized my hurt and testosterone were talking. I knew it

would be wrong and that fools rationalize and justify wrong. I had already played the fool long enough.

I stood. "I need to think about your offer … offers. Thank you for your time."

My feet wanted to walk over to her. I walked out the door.

"You were a while. How'd it go?" Dave asked.

"Don't know. Kind of weird," I said, buckling in.

"She a friend of Eve's?"

I shook my head no. "If I were the police, I would have her name at the top of the suspect list for Zack and Cinnamon."

He fired up the Charger and snickered like a ten-year-old kid. "You have lipstick on your face."

Chapter 31
Moral Support
Evelyn

Sam had texted me, so I knew that the house would be mine after eight on Monday. I stood on the deck with a cup of coffee, watching the early sunlight paint the sky a rainbow of blues and violets. But even in the brightness of the morning light and freshness of the crisp air, a desolate darkness clung to me. I wanted to stay in Bodega and pretend we were a happy family, but Sam wasn't here to find sand dollars with me, and the kids wanted to go home.

Even though I had already canceled my Monday appointments, the kids needed to be in school and I needed to tend to other business. Sam had said he wanted me gone. I wanted to blame the alcohol, but he had made it clear he was going to L.A.—and he hadn't called to apologize.

When we got home, the journals were scattered across the patio table where the kids could have easily found them. They didn't stink as much as when I had pulled them out of the fireplace, but enough that I double-bagged them in trash bags before hiding them in my closet again.

After dropping the kids at school late, I went to see a lawyer that Barbara had recommended. I really, really, really didn't want to. My better judgment screamed NO, but Sam seemed hell-bent on a divorce and I couldn't take any chances that he would take my children. Felicity met me so I would have some moral support and an objective opinion.

Doris Aureus was smart, personable, and experienced. She had that belligerent, alpha-female edge to her personality that I had seen pay dividends in child custody cases where I had been a professional witness.

"Money is always a big issue in divorces," Doris said. "Who controls the assets?"

"We both do."

She nodded approvingly. "What kind?"

"Some savings and bonds. IRAs. The house."

"Move whatever you can into accounts you control."

"What?" I asked.

"You said he's serious about divorcing you. A lot of men bleed the joint assets dry, mortgage the house to the limit, and then hide the money in a girlfriend's or close relative's account before they say the word divorce. In a situation like yours, the property settlement gives the wife half the debt and he gets all the assets that aren't supposed to exist. A year later, she's struggling to feed the kids, while he's buying new trucks and taking long vacations with his new girlfriend. It happens all the time."

"Why doesn't she sue him?"

"It takes money to hire a lawyer and detectives to prove he hid assets. She's broke."

"So she and the kids just lose."

"Yep. The beauty of no-fault divorce. A system built by men for men. It's no wonder that a year after the divorce the man's standard of living has risen and the woman and children's has plummeted.

"If you think Sam is trying to make you look like an unfit mother," Doris continued, "you need to document any incriminating history he has that would make *him* look unfit.

"Has he ever hit you or the kids?"

I hated the question, but understood it.

"No."

"Drugs or gambling?"

"No. He's a good man."

"It doesn't matter. Given the circumstances, and the possible gray legal area you are in, if he tries for full custody, it could go his way with Angela and Christian. We will need all the skeletons you can find. I have a private investigator who could find dirt on God. Shall I turn her loose?"

I knew he had skeletons. Clora was in jail and child protective services had been involved when they were together. I suspected Sam's past held enough "evidence" to make him look like the most unfit father who ever walked the face of the planet, even though it would be a lie.

I admired Sam's parenting skills. He had a rare mix of protectiveness, patient understanding, intuition, wisdom, and attentiveness that made for a perfect father.

Digging into his past was the same as digging a grave for our marriage. He was doing it, but I couldn't. I was praying he would come to his senses and be the compassionate and understanding man I had married—that we could still work it out.

The legal system moved only slightly faster than the San Andreas Fault, and if things went bad, there would be time later.

"No investigator. Not yet."

Felicity didn't know Barbara, but knew I needed support and that Barbara and I were becoming friends. She had told her that Sam and I were having some marital problems and had arranged for the three of us to meet at a restaurant in Sausalito. When we arrived, Barbara was sitting at a table by the window looking across the bay to San Francisco's financial district. She was sipping on a Sea Breeze.

Barbara and I hugged, then we sat down and ordered.

"The kids know something is seriously wrong," I said. "I don't know what to tell them. Chris even asked about divorce. He's slamming everything, Angela is ignoring me, and Grace does everything she can think of to stay with me. Even begged me to let her sleep with me."

Felicity smiled. "You let her?"

"Of course. Then I lay awake watching her sleep."

"Divorce? He get a girlfriend?" Barbara asked, emerging from her uncharacteristic silence.

I shook my head no, but wasn't sure what to tell her. "Sam thinks Eve is someone she isn't," Felicity said.

"What kinda double-talk crap is that?" Barbara said, glaring at Felicity. "It doesn't make any sense."

"Sam wants me to be someone different than I am," I said.

Barbara chuckled. "Yeah. My second husband was into role-playing, too. Some really weird stuff." She shrugged. "But if it keeps him happy and the money keeps coming in, what the fuck." Her smile turned wicked. "Besides, the movies of him tied to the bed begging me to—."

Felicity held her hand out for Barbara to stop.

"Too much information."

Barbara shrugged and took a quick sip of her drink. "I was just going to say it really helped get me a sweet divorce settlement. Maybe you could video Sam, too."

"That's not what we were talking about," Felicity said, tension filling the space between them.

Barbara looked confused, then her eyes slowly got huge.

"He knows?" she gasped.

Felicity and I both stared at her. I couldn't breathe. Surely Barbara didn't know, too.

"Knows about what?" Felicity asked, with the charm of an inquisitor.

Barbara looked back and forth between me and Felicity, seemingly unsure if she should say what she was thinking.

"You know," she said, wincing.

Except for the protective anger, Felicity was stone-faced.

"Know what?" Felicity's voice was demanding.

Barbara shook her head and looked down. "Nothing. Just silly stupid thoughts. I'm good at those."

Barbara knew. I didn't know how or when she found out, but she knew. I shivered. Felicity's eyes met mine, both of us asking how.

Barbara looked up, and took a long swig on her drink. We all pretended the conversation hadn't happened, as a jittery silence filled the space around us.

The waiter brought us our drinks. Felicity squeezed the lemon slice into her chamomile tea and watched me like a mother watches a sick child. Barbara was trying to nurse her Sea Breeze and failing. I added cream and sugar to my coffee. I needed the caffeine and sugar to keep me awake and going.

"I can't imagine a life without Sam. I know he loves me. There has to be a way for us."

"How much was in your mom's journals?" Felicity asked, without thinking.

Our eyes snapped to Barbara. She was looking down at the table but we could see a knowing look. She nodded ever so slightly to herself.

No point in pretending. I sighed. "I thought I knew my mom, but she had secrets, too."

"Oh? What?" Barbara asked, rising from her melancholy stupor.

"My mom was having an affair when she got pregnant with me."

Barbara leaned back and sneered. "So what? If he thought it was his kid and paid child support, who gives a—"

Felicity elbowed Barbara. Barbara stuck her tongue out, and then went back to sipping on her Sea Breeze.

"I'm sorry," Felicity said. "It's not like you don't have enough going on right now."

I let my gaze come back to Felicity. "She should have destroyed them."

"She didn't." Felicity leaned forward—care in her eyes. "You need to face it and move on. How many times have you told me, 'What is meant to be, will be?' If it's meant to be, you two will work things out. If not, you need to think about you and the children."

"He's so angry," I said.

"He's a man." Felicity said. "Men do that. They get mad, get drunk, hit something, feel better, and come back. They're simple creatures with three loves in life: food, sex, and themselves."

"You can say that again," Barbara said. "You'll get over the shithead, Eve. Find something better."

Felicity elbowed Barbara's arm.

"Ow! What was that for?" Barbara asked, scowling.

"For being stupid."

"I'm good at stupid," Barbara said. "Only thing I ever got right." Barbara scooted her chair several feet from Felicity and turned to me. "Sorry, Eve. I forget not all men are shitheads." She looked at Felicity with narrow eyes and added, "And some women are."

I had hoped they would be friends, but that wasn't looking likely.

"We're here to help Eve," Felicity said. She glared at Barbara.

"I said I was sorry. I haven't been laid in three weeks. It's hard for me to concentrate on anything." Barbara pouted like a scolded child.

"You want to get laid?" Felicity asked.

Barbara leaned back a little in her chair, frowned, and looked Felicity up and down.

"You offering?"

Felicity clenched her jaw and rolled her eyes. After a good huff, she pursed her lips and pointed to the bar. "I'm talking about *him*."

We looked over. A lone man sat at the bar, watching golf on the television. He looked like he spent some time at the gym, and by his black Armani suit, perfect hair, and well-polished shoes, it was obvious he wasn't doing bad financially.

Barbara turned back to Felicity. "What makes you think he's interested?"

"I used to date him." Felicity said. "He's interested."

Felicity marched over to the bar, sat next to the man, and put her arm over his shoulder. She pressed her shining monuments to womanhood into his arm and whispered in his ear. He looked over his shoulder at Barbara and me a couple times, making sure to catch the view of Felicity's cleavage that was straddling his biceps. When Felicity came back to the table, he strutted after her like a barnyard rooster.

He stopped next to Barbara. "Hi, Barbara. How 'bout I buy you a drink?"

Barbara looked at Felicity, then me, then back to him.

"Yeah. Probably a good idea," Barbara said. She looked at me. "Sorry, Eve. I just wanted to help, but I don't ... I'm sorry about Sam. Really I am." She gave me a quick hug. "You two were perfect together."

She took the guy's arm and led him to the exit.

After the door closed behind them, Felicity turned back to me.

"Damn. Now I feel guilty," she said.

"What'd you say to him?"

She held back a snicker. "That Barbara makes Dallas Debbie look like an amateur, and that she needed to get laid worse than he did."

"Are you sure he's safe?"

"I dated him a few years ago." She grinned. "He's as loyal as the only bastard in a breeding kennel, but he's safe, and when he's through with her, she'll be sated for a month. Gawd, he was good."

"Oh," I said, with distracted disinterest.

"But we're here to talk about you," Felicity said, tapping her short, ragged fingernails on the table. "I'm sorry I invited her. I thought she would be supportive. And how in the hell does she know?"

"I don't have a clue. And Rose knew, too. I thought it was a secret. Is it that obvious?"

Felicity shook her head. "No. It's not obvious. Sam didn't know and he sleeps with you. There's nothing masculine about you. I don't know how anyone could have figured it out."

I shivered. "But they did. How?"

"I don't know."

The concerned mom look returned to Felicity's face. "I'm praying that Sam wises up and you two work it out. But if he doesn't, you have ten years of wonderful memories and three great kids. That's special. A lot of people never have that much."

"Yeah." It was true enough, but I thought we would always be together, and right now, knowing how good I once had it didn't help.

Felicity leaned closer. "Before you met Sam, you told me you doubted you'd ever marry and that your one dream was to adopt a child. You did marry. You have three children, all legally yours. No one—not even Sam—can take that away."

If I had been born right, she would be right. But I lived in a legal gray area, where small-minded people worked viciously to deprive people like me of life, liberty, and happiness. I couldn't assume anything.

"But the kids will hate me when he tells them."

"Will they?"

My chin quivered. "Chris might."

Chapter 32
Family History
Sam

Dave was hungry, so our first stop after Ashley was a restaurant he knew in the San Fernando Valley. He sucked in his gut and slid into the booth, his ample portions spilling onto the table.

Being Nick's brother, I figured he might know some history. "How well did you know Evelyn?"

Dave held up his hand for me to wait a minute and took a puff from an asthma inhaler.

"Dang smog. Screws with my asthma."

"I thought you liked air you could see."

"Just making the best," he said. His face twisted into a sour grimace and then settled into annoyed resignation. "It was a lot worse when I was a kid. Back then, there were weeks when every breath burned your lungs like you were sucking on a bottle of chlorine, and your eyes watered like you rubbed onion in them."

After a couple wheezy breaths, he continued. "I didn't run in Nick's circles, and I worked seven days a week, so I don't know a lot. Heard rumors. Most said she was gay and they didn't want anything to do with her or her mom.

"Back then I didn't know shit about queers and trannies. Thought they were all perverts, freaks, and whores." His frown deepened, and he stared at the table. "I said something like that to Nick once. He rode me up one side and down the other. Only time he's ever chewed me out."

Dave looked out the window. "Nick is six years older than me. I had always looked up to him and wanted to be just like him ... until that day." He stared blankly at the street and shook his head. "After he dressed me down, I wouldn't talk to him. About a year later, he showed up at my place and said he was going to marry Louise and adopt Eve and Peter. Said he wanted me for his best man."

His wince was infused with regret. "I said no. That it was a bad idea to get mixed up with people like them." Dave's face brightened and his eyes lit with amusement. "Nick asked me what I was afraid of. I was ticked. I ain't afraid of nothing ... except my ex. Then Nick flashed that big brother grin of his and said, 'It's not contagious, Dave.'" Dave laughed. "I remember I was freaked out by his statement. He was right. I was scared shitless I'd catch it. Don't know why. Just was.

"I offered Nick a beer. We talked 'til supper. He's always been a good talker. I said yes. Glad I did."

Dave looked down, began fidgeting with his napkin, and slouched. "I still don't understand it, and it gives me the creeps if I think about it too much."

I could see the deep furrows on his forehead.

"I just can't imagine a man wanting to ..." He shivered and then looked up with a forced grin. "Nick said that's what proves Eve's a girl, but I just don't get it. Do you?"

A week ago I would have said "Yes," but I wasn't sure anymore. I had picked up a lot of the biology and psychology over the years. When it had been an intellectual exercise, I thought I had understood and accepted. But now?

"I don't know."

He started in on his triple bacon cheeseburger.

"After Nick and Louise married, did you have much contact with Evelyn?"

He shook his head no and wiped the grease and barbeque sauce from his face with his hand. Despite a vague family resemblance, I wondered how Nick and Dave could have come from the same gene pool.

"I was working seventy-hour weeks back then. Eat, sleep, and work was all I did. I'd see them at family things sometimes. Eve would disappear with some of the other girls, and Louise hung in a corner with a few women who would talk to her."

"Did you know her birth father?"

"No. From what little I heard, he was a first-class scum bag, but it was just gossip." He grinned. "And to hear my ex talk, you'd think I was a useless slob. Said I never spent enough time with her, but she sure didn't complain about the overtime money."

"What do you know about her friends, Cinnamon and Zach?"

He shrugged and the front of his shirt dipped into his french-fry ketchup.

"Didn't know they existed until after the murders. All I know is newspapers and gossip, and there isn't a whole lot of difference between the two, if you ask me."

I glanced back at the notes Nick had written.

"Nick said both Louise and Evelyn were close to Tanya."

"Yeah," Dave said, smiling through a mouthful of burger. "Nick told me to make sure you saw sis today."

"Nick said she's seventy two. That's quite a bit older than either of you."

Dave shrugged. "Tanya's the oldest. A year later, Mom had Florence; almost killed Mom. The doctor said she couldn't have any more kids. Ten years later, surprise! The doctor said Nick was a miracle child and not to expect a repeat performance. Six years later, she had me."

"After that Mom found a new doctor."

Tanya's ranch style tract house was similar to the tens of thousands of such homes that dotted the brown valleys and crumbling foothills. It was tucked away in a little canyon in the Verdugo Mountains, east of the Los Angeles basin.

Dave dropped me at the curb and said he would be back at seven. I didn't think my visit with Tanya would take three hours, but I didn't have much choice.

Tanya was maybe five feet tall, her smile a thousand hugs, and her hazel eyes majestic lights that shone with unconditional love. In her presence, there was a serenity I could only remember from my childhood, when I lay in my mother's arms. I was at peace for a moment, and then it was gone.

She moved with the fluid grace of a woman decades younger and carried herself with such poise and dignity that for a second, I was watching Grace Kelly in all her 1950s wise and compassionate elegance on the silver screen.

She reached up to take my face between her hands and, with a gentle lead, pulled me down to her height without a word. She looked deep into my eyes as if looking for something, nodded to herself with a contented smile, and released me.

"Welcome at last to the family, Sam," Tanya said, taking me in a hug.

"Thank you," I said, uneasy at being called family when I was going to divorce Evelyn.

"I'm sorry it's sadness that brings you." She took my hands into hers. "Nick said you are a seeker of answers and truth. I will do what I can, but you know Eve far better than I do."

In the living room, I noticed a small table under the front window covered with a lace tablecloth on which stood last year's Christmas photo of Evelyn, Chris, Angela, Grace, and me. Just in front of it, a white candle glimmered inside a cut crystal holder. Tiny shimmering rainbows sparkled on the table.

She motioned me to an overstuffed chair while she took the couch.

"Do you believe in God, Sam?"

"Yes." The truth was, I didn't have strong convictions and only went to church because of Evelyn, but I wasn't here to discuss religion.

She smiled and nodded with contented pleasure.

"Good. What would you like to know?"

"Nick said you were close to Evelyn and Louise. What can you tell me about them back then?"

"Eve was a typical teenager. Her mom was understandably over-protective, but well-intentioned. I think she indulged Eve too much, but considering what they went through with Duke, it was probably what Eve needed."

"Did you know Duke?"

"Saw him once. I was over at Louise's. He had just gotten out of jail, ignored the restraining order, showed up at Louise's apartment, and demanded that Louise give him Peter.

"We went out a back window, while he kicked in the front door. When the police got there, he was stuffing her jewelry in his pockets. Claimed it was his.

"For the breaking and entering, burglary, parole, and restraining order violations, they gave him six months in county."

That incident confirmed Duke's violent temper and gave credence to what the journals had said about him.

"Nick went to see him there." She smiled impishly. "He wouldn't tell me why, or what they talked about, but Duke never tried to contact Louise again."

"Do you think he threatened him?"

"With child support maybe." She grinned. "But that's not his way. He helps people find their heart and see what the smart thing to do is. Then they just do it.

"Nick probably helped Duke see he was better off leaving

Louise and the kids alone."

"What about the shooting?"

She frowned and studied me. "Why are you here, Sam?"

"Nick didn't say?"

"He said you recently found out Eve wasn't born a girl and that you were troubled by it. But that isn't reason enough to fly down here and ask such questions."

It wasn't any of her business, but I was the one rattling the skeletons in the family closet. I leaned back in the chair and studied her. She held my gaze.

"I just need to know."

Her eyebrows rose. "Really?"

"Yes," I said, sharply.

She nodded. "Have you filed?"

I flinched. "I spoke to my lawyer."

"Does Eve know?"

I shrugged. "She's not stupid."

Her face was infused with concern. "No, she's certainly not." She stood, and I thought she was going to ask me to leave.

"I could use some tea," she said. "Would you like some? I have just about every kind made."

"Sure. Whatever you're having would be fine."

The tinkling of fine china and spoons bounced in from the kitchen. My palms were damp. *I shouldn't be here. I shouldn't need to be here. Evelyn's lie shouldn't be this big a deal.*

I stood and looked at the photos on the wall. A few were old tintypes of men in bowler or top hats and women in bustles and bonnets. Other photos were of flappers, doughboys, servicemen from various eras, bellbottoms and tie-dye, beehives and mullets, and the infamous powder blue polyester suits.

In a corner were several photos of Evelyn, Peter, and Louise. In one, Louise was standing next to a beat-up 1967 Shelby Mustang holding a toddler, with Peter standing next to her.

"That's Evelyn she's holding," Tanya said, behind me.

She set the tea tray down to a melody of china and silverware chimes. The earthy scent of mint filled the room.

"You ever see a picture of her that young?"

"No," I said. "In the earliest I've seen, she's a teenager."

Her eyes sparkled and she went over to a bookcase filled with photo albums. She peered at them through thick reading glasses.

While reading the labels, she said, "When I retired, I set up a family webpage. Relatives I never heard of started calling me and sending me genealogy information, old photos, and family records. Without meaning to, I became the unofficial family genealogist and photo archivist. Every picture and document in this house has been scanned, with copies given to at least six relatives. You probably want to see one of my newer acquisitions."

Holding an album with the pride of a new mother, she sat on the couch and patted the seat next to her. I sat down and she opened the album on my lap.

"Guess who."

I didn't need to guess. The first photo was a black and white hospital snapshot of Evelyn. Under the photo, written in Louise's fine script, was, "Evelyn Louise Grant" with all the statistics listed below—*girl* replacing the technically correct *boy*.

"She was a cute baby, wasn't she?" Tanya sounded like a proud aunt.

"How'd you get this?"

"Nick sent it to me after Louise died. Said he didn't care what the purists wanted, Eve and Peter were his children, and Grace, Angela, and Christian were his grandchildren. He wanted them listed as *his* in the family history."

"But aren't family trees supposed to be about bloodline?"

She smirked. "*Supposed* is the operative word.

"We all know that not all children are the biological offspring of the father of record, but they still go into the hereditary family tree."

"Someone born a hundred years ago could have easily spawned a whole branch of two hundred and fifty descendants—maybe four times that.

"If that *someone* was the child of a president or royalty, do you think the current heirs would care, or want to know, that they were not direct blood heirs? Would it make a difference?"

I shook my head no.

"The real question is: are we chromosomes to be catalogued like purebred dogs, or are we people with love and a common history that join us?"

"What about hereditary disease?"

Her look was disapproving. "What about Grace?"

"Point taken." Grace was my daughter, bloodlines be damned.

She nudged me. "What are you smiling for?"

"Just wondering how many people want to see Nick's branch sawn off the family tree."

She grimaced. "Quite a few, I'm afraid. I know for a fact that some of them have children they parented, but won't admit to. They don't want them in the family tree, either."

"Are they?"

Her smile held mischief. "If it won't bring harm to the child or others in some way, they are family and belong."

I frowned. "Aren't there potential legal implications?"

She chuckled. "Wouldn't it be horrible if they were held responsible for their actions?"

"You make it sound simple."

"It is, Sam."

She took the photo album and closed it. "In my great-grandmother's time, Western Europeans married Western Europeans, Catholics married Catholics, Republicans married Republicans, rich married rich. It was all very simple, and all children were deemed the husband's, regardless of actual parentage.

"Then Catholics started marrying Protestants. Northern Europeans married Mediterraneans. Such scandal.

"Then it was white males marrying Asians and Hispanics. Of course, many states had laws against such "perversions" of the race, but time moved on and prejudice and racist laws were pushed aside.

"Now, instead of debating whether interracial and interdenominational marriage is moral or legal, we debate gay marriage."

I nodded. "In your genealogy, is Evelyn a girl or boy?"

"Girl of course."

I pointed at the photo album. "Can I see the rest?"

Chapter 33
Banana Splits and Mermaids
Evelyn

Grace had been underfoot since she got home from school. After setting the table, she sat and said, "I heard a joke today, Mom."

"Oh? Do tell," I said, mimicking her impish smile.

Her eyes sparkled with delight.

"A mermaid was sitting on a rock, eating, when a prince on a magnificent steed came by." She frowned. "Hannah didn't say what the mermaid was eating."

I suspected this was going to be a very long story and sat down with her.

"What do you think she was eating?"

As if pondering the woes of the world, she said, "Hmm. I don't know. Some of my friends say mermaids eat fish, but she's half fish so that would be gross. Probably seaweed." She beamed. "She's probably a vegetarian and eats things like sea cucumbers and seaweed. Isn't that right?"

I pretended to think hard. "Hmmm. Cucumbers and seaweed. I bet you're right. And maybe watercress and algae."

She smiled. "I like cucumbers, but I like ice cream better. Do mermaids eat ice cream?"

"I don't know why not."

Grace glowed. "I bet she was eating ice cream." She looked expectantly at me. "Can we have ice cream for dessert tonight?"

I had eaten the last quart of chocolate fudge after I got home from the lawyer.

"Sorry, sweetie. We're out. I'll pick some up tomorrow."

She nodded. "Well, she was eating—. Can we have it with nuts and marshmallow goo? I like them. They're good."

"Nuts and marshmallow goo it is."

"Well, she was eating the ice cream with nuts and marsh—I

want vanilla. You always get chocolate fudge. I want vanilla. French vanilla.

"French vanilla it is. Anything else?"

She thought hard for a second. "A banana split with three flavors of ice cream and sprinkles. And strawberries and blueberries and pecans."

The aroma of a rich vanilla ice cream buried in sugar-drenched fruit, with butter pecans, danced in my mind. Sam liked his swaddled in whipped cream with maraschino cherries on top. I looked at the clock. Not enough time to run up to the store.

"Alright. I'll get everything for banana splits tomorrow."

Grace went back to her story.

"The mermaid was eating a banana split and tanning herself on a rock when a prince on a magnificent steed came by. The mermaid thought he was very handsome and would make a fine husband.

"The prince said, 'Tell me, mermaid. Are you magical?'

"She knew he wasn't real smart because *everyone* knows mermaids are magical. But he was still handsome and she thought he might make a good husband anyway. She said, 'Yes I am, kind sir.'

"He said in a very gruff voice, 'Then you will grant my wishes.'

"The mermaid thought he was very rude for bossing her around, and that maybe he wouldn't make such a good husband after all. She thought about turning him into a toad, but that would have been even worse manners."

I laughed.

Grace pouted. "That's not the end of my story."

"I hope not. I'm really enjoying it. That sounds like a very smart mermaid."

She sat up straighter and smiled. "The prince said, 'I want to be the wealthiest man in the world.'

"The mermaid shrugged and said, 'You already are.'

"He thought about it for a moment, and then said, 'I want to be the most handsome man in the world.'

"The mermaid frowned at his foolishness and said, 'I find you quite handsome, but handsome is a matter of opinion. Old women like old men. Shall I make you old and bald?'

"The prince shivered. 'No, no. Of course not. Make me young forever.'

"Sorry. Immortality is not mine to give.'

"The prince thought and thought and thought, while the mermaid finished her banana split and waited patiently. When the sun touched the water, the mermaid said, 'It is late. I must go home or my mom will ground me.'

"The prince sat up tall upon his steed and proclaimed, 'Make me ten times wiser than the wisest man in my kingdom.'

"The mermaid scowled. 'That is not a wise wish.'

"The prince drew his sword. 'Don't trifle with me, magical creature, or I shall have your tail for my dinner. I command you to make me ten times wiser than the wisest man in all the world.'

"The mermaid had been trying to be helpful and didn't like the way he was acting. She had also decided he would make a *lousy* husband. She said, 'Very well. You are now ten times wiser than any man in the world,' and she turned him into a woman."

I laughed with her. My heart cringed.

"That was a very good story and an interesting paradox. Thank you for sharing it with me. I need to finish fixing dinner."

Grace looked quizzical. "Paradox?"

"A paradox is a statement that contradicts itself. If someone said 'I always lie,' it would be a paradox, because if he did always lie, he would be telling the truth, which would mean he had told a truth and therefore didn't *always* lie.

"The idea that a man can be ten times smarter than the smartest man is a contradiction, because no matter how smart he was, if he is a man, he could never be ten times smarter than himself.

"The mermaid cleverly fulfilled his wish by making him a smart woman. Though I guess she could have turned him into a wise frog or owl that was ten times smarter than the smartest man."

Grace grinned and nodded. Her grin faded to a frown, and dark clouds of concern skirted her brow.

"Someday I will get married and go away. Will you be sad?"

"Yes. But I will also be happy that you are happy."

Her question seemed to come from a sad place, deep in her heart, but I didn't know where.

"But you won't go away for a very long time, and only when you want to," I said.

"Dad went away."

"It's just a little trip. He'll be back by next Monday."

Her frown deepened. "Yeah."

Her "yeah" sounded lost and battered. The oven timer started beeping.

Chapter 34
Photo Albums and Dolphins
Sam

I continued thumbing the dog-eared pages of Louise's photo album. Most of the early shots were Polaroids, the red hues faded to watermark or brown, leaving a depressed, muddied image.

In the photos where Duke was absent, I could see a spark of life in Evelyn's eyes. In the photos with Duke, she looked lost, or had a pasted-on smile, her eyes always dull and desolate as they stared through the camera.

Holding Evelyn's hand through her mom's, brother's, and sister-in-law's funerals had acquainted me with that desolate place inside her. I couldn't imagine a child having to live there. The closer I got to when Evelyn would have been nine, the more lost her eyes became. I shivered.

I flipped a couple more pages. There was a picture of the ocean surf. No people or boats or birds or anything. "What's this?" I asked, pointing at it.

She glanced over. "If you look close, you can see a dolphin. Someone at the beach took a picture of it, just after it brought Eve back to shore."

I squinted at the photo. The coloring of the dolphin blended with the water, and you could only see its back and dorsal fin. I mumbled, "Can't be."

Tanya peered intently at the picture. "What can't be?"

Goose bumps hatched along my arms, and I tried to tell myself it was a splash of water in front of the fin. That I was imagining things. "Nothing."

"The dorsal fin? It's a shark bite."

This was too weird. If I didn't know it was impossible, I would say her dolphin and the one I saw during Chris's first dive were the same one.

"How'd she get this photo?"

Tanya smiled. "Happenstance. A woman at the beach was taking pictures of her family when she saw the dolphin bring Eve back to shore. She took a bunch of pictures, but this was the only one that came out. Two weeks after the beach incident, Louise started going to a new church. The woman who took the picture went to that church, recognized her, and gave her the picture."

She smiled like she had just scored a touchdown.

"Three-and-a-half million people in Los Angeles and Louise just happens to join the church where someone has a photo of Eve's dolphin."

By her smug smile, I knew she believed the coincidence was a minor miracle or some sort of a sign. I took a deep breath to settle my nerves and turned the page.

The faded Polaroids were gone, replaced by brilliant color snapshots. The dates jumped from the dolphin to a year later, with the first photo showing Louise standing with Evelyn and Peter in front of a church. Evelyn wore a pink eyelet dress, Peter a dark blue suit and tie, and Louise a plain white summer dress. A joy that had been absent in all the previous photos shone brightly in Evelyn's, Peter's, and Louise's eyes.

Evelyn's hair had bangs and butterfly hair combs. The combs were still in her jewelry box, though their luster was gone; I had never seen her wear them. Her hair had been one of the things that attracted me to her—long, shiny, and elegant. She'd complain about all the work of taking care of it sometimes, but when I suggested she cut it, she glared at me like I had forgotten our anniversary before storming off into the bathroom to finish fixing it.

I touched her hair in the photo. It looked like Eve, but the short hairdo gave her a different look. Long was more flattering on her, and I was a sucker for long hair.

"She never missed church," Tanya said.

"Huh? Sorry?"

"After Louise divorced Duke, she never missed church."

When Evelyn and I had first met, the kids and I didn't go to church. Even with Mom's help, my weekends were consumed with cleaning, shopping, and doing laundry. If I had time left over, it was special time with the kids—not church time. But church was important to Evelyn, so when we became serious, the kids and I joined her for Sunday services.

The kids made friends at the church, and I found a supportive and caring community I could trust and lean on. After we married, we went about seventy-five percent of the time. Her mom, though, was always there, even when she should have been at home in bed.

I mumbled, "Hm. Right. I guess she kept her promise."

"What promise?"

I looked at Tanya, unsure again of why I was here.

"In her journals. Louise promised God she would go back to church if he saved E ... Adam."

Her question was warmly leading. "Was that when the dolphin saved Eve?"

I nodded.

Tanya studied me with concern.

"Quite a miracle, wouldn't you say?"

I knew she was really saying something like "God saved her for you," or "Aren't you lucky to have her?" She was looking for a half-full glass. I knew it was empty and broken.

I shrugged. "Dolphins have been known to save drowning people." I turned the page.

There was critical skepticism in her voice.

"Is it just this miracle you doubt, or do you not believe in miracles?"

I looked at her with more annoyance than I should have.

"There might be real miracles, but I've never seen one. Most of the things we call miraculous are natural phenomenon, psychosis, selective memory, wishful thinking, random chance, or a scam.

"Dolphins save people. It was dumb luck. Goody for her. God didn't save her for some great humanitarian cause ... or for me."

I wanted to believe in a god that cared for and helped people, but there wasn't one. When Clora got hooked on drugs, I prayed like I had never prayed in my life for a miracle. I didn't get it.

Evelyn said that everything happened for the highest good. I agreed that we could learn from our personal and collective tragedies, but I didn't believe there was a divine plan. Clora's drug use wasn't some great cosmic conspiracy or a devil whispering in her ear. She went to jail because she screwed up. I wasn't going to make excuses for a god that didn't give a shit, or give him credit for random chance.

She frowned and nodded. I went back to the album, beginning to wonder what I was really looking for. I didn't know what other information she had. Other journals. Legal documents. Photos.

Yeah, photos. Teenagers are real stupid about photos. That could give me some leverage.

Tanya stood. "It's getting warm and stuffy. It's a beautiful evening, and it will be a little nicer out back."

On the way out, she picked up a fat manila envelope that lay on the dining room table and handed it to me without a word.

The mixed scents of honeysuckle, jasmine, and roses sat heavy in the air. A prayer labyrinth in red brick and grass adorned the center of the yard. In the shade of Japanese maples and gingko trees, stone paths led through the flowerbeds. Near the labyrinth stood a birdbath made to look like an old tree trunk. Tucked in with some camellias, Mother Mary stood erect and serene, holding her baby with angelic love. Under a small ginkgo tree, Buddha sat laughing with heavenly joy. On a white sandstone shelf behind a small reflecting pond stood some sort of Hindu statue. I remembered seeing one like it in Evelyn's office but had never asked about it.

She set her tea down.

"You're not allergic to flowers are you?"

"No." I motioned toward the yard. "An interesting collection of statues."

She smiled with modest pride, then said, "I've always been open-minded. I was one of those crazy California New Agers fifty years ago, when New Age was new. I believe that all the major religions have something to offer if you look past the politics, greed, and egos. Usually it boils down to respect; treat others the way you want to be treated."

"They say you should keep an open mind, but not so open your brain falls out," I said. "Where do you draw the line?"

Her smile bordered on a smirk. "That is the question, isn't it?" She motioned me to a lounge chair. "Have a seat, Sam."

I sat and pointed toward the Hindu statue.

"What's that one?"

She seemed amused by my question.

"I'm surprised you aren't familiar with Ardhanari. It is a Hindu god, composed of the gods Shiva and Shakti. Half male and half female. The 'lord who is half woman.' It illustrates how the male and female principles of God are inseparable."

I was annoyed with her subtle meddling and shifted my attention to the envelope. It contained copies of various legal documents, including Evelyn's original birth certificate, the transcript from Duke's first trial, a psych evaluation of Evelyn when she was fourteen, newspaper clippings about the dolphin rescue, and articles about the murders.

I looked over at Tanya. "The journals said Evelyn was a strong swimmer, but she's terrified of the water."

With numbed emotion, Tanya said, "When she was little, she loved the water and was always the first in and the last out."

I looked back down at the article.

"What happened?"

She didn't answer, and when I looked up, she seemed to be off in her own world, her eyes unfocused.

"It's in there."

I thumbed through the documents while Tanya sat quietly watching the sparrows feeding on seed and bathing themselves in the reflecting pond. Three hours wasn't enough time. I concentrated on the police reports about the murders.

"That would be Dave," Tanya said.

I looked up and became aware of the low rumble of a sixties V-8 muscle car in the background. It was seven-thirty and I hadn't finished going through the envelope or the photo album.

Tanya stood. "You can take them with you, if you promise to return them."

"Yes, yes. Of course. Thanks."

"And if you get tired of fast food or want to talk, give me a call. I'd love to cook you a meal or two and chat some more, hear about your children. You're even welcome to stay in my guest room, if you want. My address and phone number are on the envelope."

Chapter 35
Old Dreams - Old Terrors
Evelyn

I had hardly slept for almost two days, and it was catching up to me, so I laid down to rest before getting the kids to bed.

I've been here before. I'm dreaming. I need to wake up. I don't want ...

The thought that I was in a dream drifted away, and I sank deeper into the archetypical symbols of my long-ago, familiar nightmare.

In the radiant glow of a hot pink Jacuzzi, Cinnamon and I squealed, soaking each other in a furious water fight. While we jousted, the bitter chlorine in the water did battle with the smells of burnt sugar, greasy fries, and teriyaki noodles from the megamall food court that surrounded us.

We were oblivious to the presence of mall shoppers, who sat around us eating, with complete disinterest in our antics.

My boyfriend, Zack, jumped into the pool, deliberately splashing us. Cinnamon and I joined forces and enthusiastically attacked him with a chaotic volley of water. After a minute of mock battle, our warm pink Jacuzzi morphed into the neglected, slimy duck pond at the park near our high school. The warm and bright mall dissolved into cold winter gloom. I shivered.

Clouds sulked like bad-tempered children at treetop, spitting chilly gray mist down on us. Goosebumps arose on my arms as the putrid water dripped from my hair onto my breasts. People were standing around us, staring—morose aberrations with faces as gray as death. The demonic rage in their festering red eyes threatened to dissect us.

The apparitions were as close as thirty feet and as far away as the dark shadows that possessed the distance. I choked on the smell of the fetid, brackish water and the baleful scent of death that filled the air.

Out of the corner of my eye, past Cinnamon, I saw two malevolent shadows, moving toward us like sharks closing for the kill. They lacked physical shape or features but they carried an energy, an odorless stench that I knew. Zack charged toward them, my knight on a magnificent stallion, protecting his princesses.

I saw the flash, like the flames of a dragon's breath, and heard the explosion of thunder. At the place where the thunder struck Zack, a radiant angel now tenderly cradled him.

The dragons turned to face us; Cinnamon stepped between me and them. The flames hurtled toward us, and the thunder struck Cinnamon, driving her backward. I tried to catch her, but she slammed into me with the force of a fifty-foot wave and we were thrown from a cliff. We tumbled in weightlessness to the turbulent dark river below. I clung to her.

The savage river instantly swallowed us and tried to rip Cinnamon from my embrace but I wouldn't let her go. We surfaced momentarily. Flames and thunder rained around us once again, but the brutal current sucked us back into its murky depths. My spirit weakened and my heart accepted that Cinnamon and Zack were no longer with me.

The spirits of the water called my name, as they had when I was a child.

"Evelyn. There is nothing to fear. You are a creature of the sea, a mermaid. Join us. No one will ever hurt you again in the safety of your grotto. At the bottom of the sea, you can be who you were meant to be."

I held Cinnamon, like the angel had held Zack. I wouldn't let her go, even as her body drew us deeper into the frigid cold, and the taste of her blood tortured my soul. I looked into my sister's lifeless eyes—eyes that once shared so much joy with those she trusted enough to let past her guarded glare. My grasp weakened, and I knew we would find peace—Sister Mermaids, free from the hate at last.

I shot up in bed, my pillow crushed to my chest in a death grip. I tried to pull air into my body. I could still feel Cinnamon against me, taste her blood, and smell the stagnant stench of Brandon and Billy. The air drew hard and stung my lungs. My sob seemed to shake the universe.

I was cold and alone. Sam's arms were no longer here to encircle me and pull me to his warmth. He wasn't here to say,

"It's okay, Eve. You're safe. It was just a bad dream," like he had so many times before.

It had been sixteen years, but it felt as if Cinnamon and Zack had just died. I sank listlessly back into Mom's quilt, sobbing.

"Do you want to talk about it?" Sam would always ask, and I always said, "No." I never told him about Cinnamon and Zack. They were another "something" about my past he didn't need to know. Another secret.

Mama, I need you. Why did you have to leave me, like everyone else?

Chapter 36
Murders, Strangers, and Offers
Sam

I was up late at the hotel, going through the photo album and documents that Tanya had loaned me. The police reports on the murders were limited. The partial autopsy was merciless in its details and so drenched in technical terms and legal mumbo jumbo, that it left me both queasy and wondering what I had just read.

The report held few conclusions beyond the cause of death and what a chunk of lead traveling at over 1000 feet per second does to your body. I understood Evelyn's nightmares now.

The document package included censored reports from neighbors who heard the shooting but saw nothing, and useless reports stating that there were no footprints or other physical evidence. The only conclusion the report made was that Cinnamon and Zack died from physical trauma inflicted by a Smith & Wesson .38 caliber revolver and a Colt .357 revolver. I was surprised the bullets could tell them that much.

More questions were unanswered than answered. Objective evidence that would incriminate Evelyn didn't exist. There was no "dirt" that would portray Evelyn as an unfit mother, but the documents contained new names I could check.

After another three hours on the phone and the web, my original long list of names was down to six, with the others dead, moved away, giving short useless phone interviews, or falling into a hole I couldn't follow them down.

Cinnamon's father, Kelly, had agreed to meet with me at a cemetery. Zack's mom, Sarah Strother, had tried to say no politely, until I told her I was a friend of Evelyn's. I was still waiting for Zack's father to call me back.

The names of Billy's parents were given in one of the newspaper reports, but I was unable to locate him or his parents.

It looked like my week could end up pretty short.

The people in the room next to mine partied until three, so I hadn't slept well. At the hotel's breakfast buffet, I chugalugged my first cup of coffee trying to kick-start myself, and then sat down to eat the bizarre square of "scrambled" eggs and a do-it-yourself waffle. A man walked up to my table.

"Sam Irving?"

"Yes," I cautiously answered.

"I'm a friend of Ashley. May I sit?"

I nodded as I took in his expensive wool suit, silk shirt, manicured nails, and perfectly cut hair. He wasn't smooth enough to be a politician or slimy enough to be a lawyer. He did have that "I'm God" aura that I saw in a lot of CEOs, but he somehow just didn't fit that label.

"What can I do for you?"

His projection of being relaxed, friendly, and concerned with my well-being was well practiced. "Ashley is a wonderful person, isn't she?"

He was trying to build rapport and gain my trust before going for what he wanted. I decided to have fun and maybe even pump my bruised image.

"Yeah," I said. "Quite the passionate woman."

His smile widened. "Yes, she is. Many admirable qualities."

I chuckled at his game. "Yes. Fine indeed." I'm sure he thought I was chuckling at fond memories with Ashley.

His smile slipped to an excellent facsimile of the real thing.

"She thought that we could be of benefit to each other."

I had expected him to spend more time trying to become my "friend."

"I'm sorry," I said. "I didn't catch your name."

"Jim Regan." He had paused just long enough for me to question whether he was telling the truth.

My guess that Ashley was a low-level player in their little political espionage game appeared to be accurate. "Jim's" interest meant someone further up the power and money ladder thought I might be of use. I assumed he was my second interview, with a dozen more to come while they played me.

Despite his slick dog and pony show, I knew he wasn't the power broker with the final say. I didn't have the time or patience for their ego games.

"Well, *Jim*," I said, leaning long and heavy on the name, "you're not the one with the final say, so make your offer. I'll think about it, while you do your background checks."

I had expected signs of insult, but his mouth curled up in pleased delight.

"Smart. Direct. Cool. Perceptive. Ashley may be right about you." He smiled and his eyes narrowed. He was getting serious. "Real name is Bernard Dillinger. Most people call me Benny."

He acted like I should recognize his name. "Yeah?"

He chuckled. "Ashley's husband."

Oh, shit!

He chuckled again. "It's cool. She said you didn't do her, not that it would matter one way or the other.

"She said that you have a problem and we might be able to help. If..."

If I played along and did their hatemongering.

"I didn't catch what you do," I said.

"Activist. Organizer. Lobbyist."

I watched him carefully. "Who with?"

"Various pro-family groups and corporate interests."

I knew that was all he was going to give me, so I nodded.

He continued. "I did the first round of background on you last night. It would appear you have the history and situation we need. You have the presence and intelligence. The question is, are you willing to come over to our side?"

That would depend on what happened with Evelyn, but he didn't need to know that.

"You're a lobbyist. You buy politicians all the time. What do you think?"

He scowled. "I think you're being evasive."

I held his gaze. "I don't agree to something when I don't know the details. What exactly are you offering?"

He smiled again. "Good. A realist and a pragmatist.

"We will give you the best lawyers and push to get you a sympathetic judge. Whether or not a new precedent is set, if you do well in the public eye, we will run you for political office. Which office will depend on the political landscape at the time. Our intent would be to get you into the state legislature where you will support bills like the Marriage Protection Act and oppose domestic partner laws."

I leaned back and studied him. It was possible they could help me. If I rolled over too easily, they would use me, and then dump me. If I played too hard to get, they might walk. I didn't like the game so I decided to play hard—real hard.

"You don't have the authority to make that offer and I'm not interested in sitting through ten interviews on the way to seeing whoever can. Doing it your way is harder and more expensive than a simple divorce. I want the kids for myself, but Evelyn will be reasonable if the worst happens.

"You seem to need me more than I need you. Do your background on me, while I wait for a real offer … or not. If you decide you are interested, I will need something more substantial than a 'we will try' and 'if.'"

I could tell I had hurt his ego. He was supposed to be the demigod, and I was supposed to be the lowly mortal, eager to kiss his ass. Wasn't going to happen.

He collected himself. "Understood. I will see what I can do."

Yeah. You do that.

Even though they might be able to get me my kids, I didn't like the direction they were taking this. I watched Benny drive off, not expecting to see him or his owners again. I was okay with that. They were looking for a fool. I had been a fool for Evelyn but I'd never be a fool for them.

Chapter 37
A Family Falling Apart
Evelyn

Through a storm of teenage hormones and domestic uncertainty, Chris and Angela had been going out of their way to teach me patience and understanding, while Grace had been underfoot all morning and unusually quiet.

Eager to get away from me, Chris and Angela were ready for school early, but Grace bore the wrath of her siblings, dawdling and finding excuse after excuse to delay our departure for school.

I had barely stopped in front of the school when Chris and Angela jumped out of the van without our customary "Bye, Mom. Love you," to which I always replied, "Love you, too. Have a great day." The slam of the van door rattled me out of my swirling emotions. The way Chris had been banging everything around all morning, I should have expected it.

"Can I get a T-shirt like Angela's?" Grace asked.

I looked at Angela and Chris double-timing it away from me. My heart stopped. She was wearing that tasteless vampire and skull vulgarity. While a popular and harmless fad in isolation, it cracked open the door to a subculture where children were encouraged to become irresponsibly rebellious and self-destructive. People had accused me of being puritanical because of that view. Me? Puritanical?

I started to step out of the van to yell, "Angela! Get back here now!" but felt the van begin to roll forward. White knuckling the steering wheel, I pulled myself back into the car and slammed on the brakes. If the car in front of me hadn't been pulling away, I would have hit it.

With my heart pounding, I shifted to park, set my head on the steering wheel, and tried to slow my racing heart.

"Are you okay, Eve?"

I looked up and saw Angela's history teacher, Sheila, standing in the open door.

"Yeah. Angela ..." It was pointless to go into details.

She smiled. "Yeah. I noticed the T-shirt. I was a little surprised."

"How could I not notice?"

She frowned in concern. "Are you sure you're okay?"

"Yeah. Just a little distracted. I'll be fine." I took a deep breath and sat up straight.

I headed for Grace's school. Grace said, "Mom, I have a stomachache. Can I stay home?"

Normally, my Tuesdays started at ten and went until eight, but today my appointments didn't start until two.

"Sure. What do you want to do?" I watched her in the rearview mirror. She scrunched up her face, trying to figure out why I had folded so easy, or if it was a trick question.

At ten, she felt like my baby sometimes, but in her child's body, I saw the promise of a young woman. Soon she would be more than a girl and struggle to find her independence as she grew to adulthood. I would no longer be her sun, but her safe harbor, while she explored her ever-expanding world.

At that moment, I wanted to stop time, even turn it back. Have my babies with me for eternity. But I knew Henry David Thoreau was right: "You must live in the present, launch yourself on every wave, find your eternity in each moment."

The past is gone. The future is unknown. All we really have is now and the people we love.

"Ice cream sometimes helps a stomachache," I said.

Her eyes lit up. "Yeah. Ice cream."

I took Grace to a restaurant that was always open and served ice cream desserts twenty-four-seven. Grace ordered a banana split with extra sprinkles and nuts. I ordered a single scoop of chocolate in a bowl; it was one of my favorite stress foods. Actually, for stress food, just about anything sweet, chocolate, calorie-laden, and consumed in excess, was my favorite.

Halfway through her treat, Grace seemed to lose interest in the ice cream. With slow deliberation, she opened and closed her sticky fingers, watching the sugar pull the skin. A look of sad worry knitted her brow.

"Mom. Is Dad coming back?"

"Of course. Why wouldn't he?"

She seemed lost in deep thought, so we sat in silence. She stared intently at her dessert, and played with the oozing marshmallow fluff that was sliding off the untouched chocolate ice cream.

"I could go away, if it made you and Dad happy again." Each word was filled with deep sadness.

Even though it was Psychology 101 that children blame themselves when parents are having difficulties, I was surprised at the depth of her self-blame. I scooted my chair over, hugged her, and kissed her. She dissolved into my embrace.

"No, sweetie. Your going away would make us very, very sad. We love you. Your dad and I are just having a little disagreement. It's stuff between him and me. We'll work it out. It has nothing to do with you."

"My ice cream is melting," she said, pulling away.

She finished the extra-berry strawberry and scooped up a spoonful of flabby whipped cream and soggy sprinkles.

"Can I get a cell phone, like Chris and Angela?"

"No, sweetie. You know the rule. Not until you're in junior high."

She pouted before taking another bite of her strawberry ice cream.

"Did he go away because I tease Chris? I don't mean to."

I took her free sticky hand into mine. The innocence in her eyes begged for me to bring her dad back and make everything alright.

"No, sweetie. He just had to go on a trip. It wasn't because of you. He'll be back soon."

Grace pulled her hand back and scraped some nuts from the sugary goop at the bottom of the dish.

"Chris said you are going away like his—" Her brow furrows deepened and she looked like she had said something she shouldn't have.

My breath caught. "It's alright, sweetie. You can tell me."

With the slow reluctance of a child squeezed by peer pressure, she said, "That you were going away, like his other mom. That you were going to take me with you. He said his other mom is in jail and he'll never get to see her. He said that when we go away, he'll never see us again, either."

Chris was two when his mother went to jail. He had claimed he remembered her when he asked if Sam and I were divorcing. Now Grace was telling me he knew his mom was in prison, though he was wrong about her never getting out. Someone had been talking to him. Sam was the only person I could think of—or maybe Clora's mom, Grandma Suzy.

I leaned close and made every word clear and confident. "We're not going anywhere. Nothing could take me away from my babies."

Grace scowled at the "babies" choice of words.

"His mother made some bad choices and she is in prison because of them. She will get out some day, and he will get to see her. Alright?"

Grace nodded and stuck her finger in her mouth to suck off the strawberry sticky.

"Please use a napkin."

She pouted, then started wiping her hands.

"When does she get out?"

"Not for a very long time."

"Why doesn't Chris go see her?"

Sam had been adamant about cutting Clora out of the kids' lives. I was divided, concerned about them being exposed to the brutality of the prison environment, possibly seeing their mother as a role model, and the belief that, when possible, children should have contact with their biological parents. Between my uncertainty around what to do, and my respect for Sam's position as their father and my husband, I had taken the easy road and defaulted to his wishes. Now I questioned if it had been the right thing.

"There are a lot of grown-up reasons, but maybe it's time your dad and I talk about it again."

She looked sad. "I wish I could see my mom."

"I do too, sweetie. She was very special, just like you. She loved you so, so much. If she could be here, she would."

Grace stared intently at the napkin in her hands.

"Why did Grandma Louise go away, like my mom and dad?"

Grace, Chris, and Angela were asking the hardest questions about life. These were the same questions I saw all the time in my practice, when the storms of a death, a divorce, or some other major disruption in the status quo pulled the whole family into an inescapable rip current.

The strong emotional surge would pull all the hidden hurts, insecurities, and secrets from the muck at the bottom of their private oceans and send them crashing onto the beach. Some were quickly sucked back into the depths by the next wave.

Others became stuck in the sand—immovable and impossible to ignore.

I didn't need this right now. I should have expected it.

"You miss Grandma?"

"Yeah."

"What do you miss the most?"

She scrunched up her face, unhurried and thoughtful.

"I miss her cookies. I miss telling her my stories. She liked my stories and listened to me when all the other grownups were too busy. And she had good hugs." A melancholy smile settled onto her lips. "Mostly I just miss her. It makes me sad."

"It's alright to be sad sometimes," I said, stroking Grace's hair. "We all miss her. But we also need to remember the good times. Like the red and green velvet Christmas dress she bought you. How much fun we girls had shopping for it."

Grace smiled and her eyes sparkled. She said, "And the time Chris hit a home run, and she jumped up and spilled her drink on Dad."

We laughed.

She bounced with excitement, and said, "And the time she put the wrong tags on the Christmas presents, and gave Chris the Barbie doll and me the baseball glove." She melted into a ball of giggles.

I leaned close, my heart filled with her innocent love.

"Good memories, huh?"

Some sadness returned to her eyes. She nodded yes.

I took her hands gently in mine. "I don't know why God takes people when he does. But I do know that I was blessed to have known and loved Grandma, your mom, and your dad. That my life was happier and better because I was able to share their lives for a while.

"I also know that death is not the end of life here on earth. We live on through our children and grandchildren. You have Grandma's blood in you, alive, moving with every beat of your heart. As long as you are here and remember her with love, she is alive, just as her mother, and her mother's mother, and all your other ancestors are alive in you, all the way back to the Garden of Eden."

I touched Grace's heart. "Her love and her memory are still alive in here … and always will be."

She reached over and set her small hand on my heart. "And here."

Chapter 38
Zack's Mom
Sam

Being forced to discuss my pending divorce and child custody with Benny, I realized that Evelyn would never try to take my kids. She understood better than most how much kids need both parents.

I didn't know if it was the coffee or Benny, but my guts were as inhospitable as my mood when I walked out of the hotel. The smoky-brown sky and orangish-yellow sun didn't do anything to improve my mood. Dave was waiting in the parking lot listening to Pink Floyd.

I handed him Sarah's address. "She's expecting me at ten."

I had checked the distance on the web, and we had time to spare.

The Charger's massive 440 cubic inch, cast-iron V-8 caught on the first turn and rumbled to life.

"Better call and let her know you'll be late," Dave said.

"Google maps said it's only fifty minutes."

He laughed. "And you believe in Santa Claus, too?" He launched the Charger out of its parking space, the g-forces pushing me back into the seat.

"Could have done it in thirty-five minutes thirty years ago. Today? Ain't gonna happen."

Zack's mother, Sarah, had remarried since the murders. Her house was a nice, two-story Spanish Mission style home, with a small fountain by the front door leisurely trickling water. The lawn had enough yellow dandelions smiling at the sun to make me feel at home.

We settled in the living room.

"How is Evie?"

"She's doing well. She's a psychologist in Marin."

Her smile was tranquil and she seemed lost in old memories.

"She always was smart and so pretty. It was easy to see why Zack loved her." Concern shadowed her eyes and the tranquility passed. "You weren't very clear about why you wanted to meet. You said you're a *friend*?" The word friend was sharp enough to prick.

"Yes. A close family friend." I paused for a second. "I wanted to say how sorry I am for your loss. If Evelyn cared for him, he must have been a special person."

Sarah's eyes reddened and I stiffened in preparation for the tears. She looked down but the tears didn't come.

"Thank you. He was. But that was a long time ago. What about Evie?"

"When her mother passed, about—"

She stiffened and leaned forward, her eyes huge with disbelief and pain.

"Louise? Gone?"

"Yes. A year ago. I'm sorry. I assumed … Were you close?"

Her voice was so soft, it was almost lost in the silence of the room.

"In some ways." She looked at me, a wall of resolve holding back her emotions. She forced a smile. "I didn't mean to interrupt you, Sam. Please continue."

"After her mother passed, questions came up about the … um—"

She frowned. "Murders?"

"Yes. Evelyn left because she didn't feel safe here."

"She wasn't."

I hadn't expected that answer. "So, Brandon and Billy would have been stupid enough to try again?"

She glared at invisible demons and her voice carried absolute certainty on every word.

"Brandon, no. Billy, yes."

"Do you know where Billy is?"

She nodded yes, anger burning in her eyes. I waited for her to say. The words were hard and bitter.

"His remains are at Forest Lawn. I pray his soul is burning in hell."

My expression asked how and why he ended up there.

"He went gay hunting in East L.A. with some friends. April 1st of '97, I believe. They were beating a man they thought was gay because he was wearing a scarf, but he wasn't gay. The scarf was his gang color, and the hunters became the hunted. The rest of the gang was in a house nearby. Their lookout tipped them off, and the gang jumped Billy and company. Billy got his head beat in. He was a vegetable for three years before a stroke killed him."

The anger slipped from her eyes, leaving a sad emptiness.

"God's justice, I suppose. If it is Billy and Brandon you are worried about, they aren't a threat anymore."

"Could you tell me about your son?"

She went over to the fireplace mantle and picked up a photo. She handed it to me.

"Good looking young man," I said. "Looks athletic and strong."

"Yes, he was." She smiled and sat back down. "Took after his father. He was a typical boy. Loved soccer and track. Girls, cars, and astronomy. He wanted to be an astronomer with NASA or JPL. His dad wanted him to be a doctor, but if you don't have a 4.0 GPA in high school, both of those aspirations are a long shot. He only had a 3.6. I was hoping he would end up with a high-tech company, inventing things. He had a great imagination, was a natural with techie stuff, and would have been happy."

Her smile faded. "His father wouldn't believe he loved Evie. Said Zack was just studying her in preparation for being a doctor. At first, it was a little hard for me to understand how Zack could be attracted to her, too, but after I got to know her, I knew what Zack knew. His father never got it."

She looked at me. Her eyes narrowed.

"Last night after you called, I googled you and found out you are a business consultant with three kids and a wife named Eve. I googled Evelyn Strand and didn't find anything. Then I googled Evelyn Irving. Do you know what I found?"

Shit. Busted.

I nodded yes. The web had multiple links to her papers and video taped presentations on the transgendered. There were even some photos of me and the kids that other people had put up without our permission. To protect the kids from someone who might act on their homophobic paranoia, fanatical religious beliefs, or political partisanship, we had tried to get the photos taken off without success.

She studied me for a moment, her smoldering contempt heating the room.

With barely contained hostility, she said, "Perhaps you know the term—I forget. It's when a transsexual leaves their past behind and doesn't tell anyone they were once the opposite sex."

"Deep stealth."

She nodded, and slowly said, "Yes. Deep stealth." Her voice and her eyes held accusation, condemnation, and righteous anger. "You didn't know, did you?"

I shook my head no.

"You don't get it, do you?"

I wasn't sure how to answer, but she didn't wait for me to.

"So why ..." her voice trailed off, and she seemed lost in thought. She nodded to herself.

Sarah took a deep breath and looked at me with an odd mix of disgust and pity.

"My son was not gay, Mr. Irving. My son saw the real Evelyn and loved her with all his heart. When I asked about children, he said they would adopt. If my son had lived, Evie would be my daughter and I would be proud to call her family.

"If you want someone to berate your wife and accuse her of killing Zack and Cinnamon, like Brandon said, go see my ex. The great Master Sergeant Richard Taylor would be happy to oblige."

I wanted to crawl under the chair cushion.

The front door opened and a man walked in, carrying one of those man-bags. I stood to greet him. He was only about five-foot-four, which made him several inches shorter than Sarah. He wore a turtleneck sweater under a plaid sports coat, with chino slacks, and looked the part of a stereotypical, intellectual nerd, with thick glasses, pale waxy skin, and a bad haircut.

He offered his hand. In a soft voice, he said, "Hi. I'm Jimmy Strother, Sarah's husband." His handshake was clammy, soft, and limp.

"I'm Sam Irving. A fr ... Um. Eve Strand's husband. She is a girl your wife knew a long time ago."

His eyes brightened and he clasped my hand between his and held it.

"Oh, yes. Sarah told me all about Evelyn. Sounds like such a wonderful girl. You must feel very lucky." He looked over at his wife. "Isn't that right, sweetums?"

He let go of my hand and she dryly said, "I would have thought so." She stood. "I think Mr. Irving was just leaving.

Weren't you, Mr. Irving?"

"Yes. Of course. Thank you for your time."

I offered my hand, but she remained motionless, so I dropped it. Jimmy looked back and forth between us, somewhat confused.

"Glad to help, Mr. Irving. Do give the Sergeant a call. I suspect you'll love what he has to say."

Chapter 39
Email from the Past
Evelyn

After her ice cream, I took Grace to school and then stopped by the store to pick up banana split makings for the kids.

When I got home, I checked my email and tried to call Felicity but couldn't get ahold of her. I was about to call Rose to see if she had heard anything from Sam when Barbara's Rolls pulled into my driveway. She had a new chauffer—again.

I was already overstressed from the email I'd received and wasn't up to seeing her if she was in a needy mood.

Fudge. I don't need this. Maybe ...

Barbara waved at me from the driveway. It was too late to hide. I grabbed my purse and headed for the door, where we met.

"Hi, Barbara. Good to see you, but I was just on my way out."

She smiled and shrugged. "I'm not doing anything. How 'bout I go with you. Keep ya company. Where ya going?"

"I'm going to work to catch up on some stuff."

She looked dejected. "I was hoping you were going shopping. That's what I always did when my husband was being a scumbag."

I raised my eyebrows. "Excuse me?"

She waved her hand in the air like she was chasing away flies.

"Not your husband, of course. I was talking about the scumbags I married. That cute hunk of yours wouldn't even know how to be one."

I wasn't sure how to take her comment and I wasn't going to spend time trying to figure it out.

"Didn't you take the week off?" Barbara asked.

"I was going to, but when Sam went to L.A., I decided it would be good to stay with my routine. If you will excuse me, I need to get some work done."

"Hold on, Eve." She felt my forehead and feigned concern. "No fever. Now why would someone as sophisticated and professional as you go to work in fuzzy bunny slippers?"

I closed my eyes in defeat and slumped.

"Where do you want to go?"

Barbara's amused grin faded and a lonely sadness bore down on her.

"I like you, Eve. You were my only friend when I needed someone bad." She looked down, and a tired sigh drained her. Talking to my slippers, she said, "I'm not smart like you, and I know I say stupid things all the time."

She looked up, her eyes red and sad. "And I know when people don't want me around. Call me sometime if you feel like it."

She turned to go. I reached out and hooked her arm.

"I'm sorry. It's not you. It's just been hard with Sam gone and the kids being difficult. You want some tea?"

She looked over her shoulder and grinned. The light was back in her eyes.

"Bermuda Triangle?"

"What?"

"Rum, cranberry juice, and orange juice. I like mine half rum."

Sometimes being around her felt like the Bermuda Triangle.

I frowned. "It's ten-thirty in the morning."

"Margarita?" she asked, giving me a sad, puppy-dog look.

"Tea."

"Okay," she pouted.

I filled the teapot and got out cups, while Barbara sat in the dining room and talked about Madonna. She expressed her frustration at Madonna giving her a hard time with homework. I couldn't help chuckling.

"The little brat asked me if I knew if A equals B if B equals ..." She was quiet for a moment.

I looked over and my stomach dropped.

I had left the email from my high school sweetheart's mom on the table. Barbara was reading it.

I turned toward the cupboard. "Why don't you read it out loud?"

I sensed her eyes silent on me for a minute as I breathed the scent of chamomile tea that was escaping from the box in my hands. She rustled the paper with dramatic flair and began.

> Dear Evie,
> I hope this letter finds you and your family well.
> There is so much I want to say that I don't know where to start.
> I guess I should start by telling you I'm Sarah Taylor, Zachary's mother. (The email header name is Sarah Strother because I remarried.)
> I'm very sorry to hear about Louise. She was such a wonderful mother and friend. I wanted to stay in touch with her but she said it was best if she broke all ties with L.A.
> I guess I should get to the point of why I'm writing. I know you left to be safe and start a new life, so I honored your mother's wishes, but your husband dropped by to see me this morning. Perhaps he's told you that Billy is dead and Brandon is satisfied with fomenting others to carry on his work.
> I don't know about the history questions. Sam said he didn't know until recently, so I am assuming your children don't know.
> I'm rambling. Sorry.
> I saw the photos of your family on the web. Your children are beautiful and I'm so happy for you. I would love to hear all about your family and all the wonderful things you're doing with your life.
> I don't want to intrude or complicate things and will understand if you don't write back.
> You are frequently on my mind and always in my prayers. Every time I think of Zachary, I think of you, and miss you both. I just wanted to offer my hand in friendship. My phone number is below. I'd love to hear from you.
> Love and Prayers,
> Sarah

I could feel the hairs on Zack's arms and smell the scent of his skin, as if he had been with me only moments before. The warmth of his lips—my first French kiss—lingered in my mouth. In that moment, he was as real and present as the teapot in my hand.

"Who's Sarah?"

His image faded from my mind, but the scent of his skin lingered. I started pouring the tea.

"Zack's mom."

"No shit. And who's Zack?"

I looked over at her, somehow expecting to see Mom.

"An old boyfriend."

"Why'd you have me read it if you don't want to talk about it?"

I handed Barbara her cup. "Should I call her?"

"Hell. I don't know. Ya got some vodka or whiskey to warm this up?"

I scowled at her.

"And what's with the dead guy and the troublemaker?" she asked.

I looked at Barbara, and a question that had haunted me since the restaurant spoke out.

"How did you know, and why didn't you out me?"

Her look was blank. "Huh?"

"Back before we were friends—"

She reached over and touched my hand, her eyes aglow.

"So we *are* friends?"

I smiled. "Yes. I guess we are."

Barbara leaned back, looking like a contented cat stretched out on a sunny windowsill.

I said, "Back when we were … uh—"

She winked. "Dissing each other?"

"Yeah. You knew but you never outed me."

She looked down in deep thought and mumbled, "A little brandy in the tea would help."

"I have some leftover chardonnay in the fridge."

She looked up, her face aglow like a child offered candy.

"Perfect. I'll get it."

Most of her tea swirled down the sink drain before she filled the cup to the brim with wine.

"You have a problem, Barbara."

She huffed. "Yeah. Not enough sex. With a population of about eight million people around here, you'd think I could find a good-looking single man."

"What about Mr. Sausalito?"

"Told me he was single. I was half-naked in his bedroom when his wife walked in. She got back early from wherever."

"Ouch."

Barbara sneered. "Tell me. When I got home, I locked myself in the bedroom with my vibrator. Burned the damn thing out."

I decided to tease. "Only one?"

"Nah. I've got six. The batteries went dead on four of them, and then Madonna got home."

"And needed help with her math?" I added.

"Yeah. The little brat. And when did they start using letters for numbers? What's with that crap?"

"A long time ago, Barbara. You just got lucky and missed it."

With serious contemplation, Barbara refilled her teacup with chardonnay and impassively said, "Back to me and why I didn't out you.

"About the time I got interested in boys, I found I could tell if someone was gay, lesbian, tranny, or bi just by looking at them. All the girls were after a really hot football player. I knew he was gay and blackmailed him into being my boyfriend. In high school, he fell for some egghead. I got pissed and outed him. His jock buddies beat him up so bad, they crippled him."

She cringed and shivered. "I had thought it was a cool superpower, but it was a super curse. I never outed anyone after that."

"I'm sorry. That had to be horrible."

She shrugged. "Despite all that, I was real tempted to out you a couple times, but I was scared of you."

"Of me?"

She huffed. "Yeah. No matter how hard I tried or how much I planned, you'd come off the cuff with some smart-ass remark that put me in my place and showed I was nothing but a low-life skank."

I winced at the memories of our cat fights. "That was mean of me. I'm sorry."

She waved her hand dismissively.

"History. Besides, I deserved it. Lousy wife. Lousy mother. Fucked my way to the top. A nobody, trying to be important."

"You're not a nobody. You have a good heart. If you didn't, you wouldn't be my friend."

She covered her face, and her eyes filled with tears. "Oh, gawd. I'm going to cry."

I handed her a napkin.

She sniffled and looked thoughtfully at me.

"I knew that your Stud Muffin was more homophobic than he thought and that if he found out ... Well, let's just say I wouldn't have been doing the handyman."

She realized what she had said and turned beet red. I gave

her a stern, don't-go-there look.

After another gulp of her *tea*, she said, "I have secrets, and not just the movie." She became lost in thought for a second, and then shivered. She looked at me with concerned fear, and then looked away. "I was afraid that if I outed you, you would find them and hurt me back ... because that's what I would do."

I reached over and touched her hand. "I don't believe in 'an eye for an eye,' because it's like they say, the whole world would be blind and toothless."

She nodded in agreement and took another sip but I could tell she didn't really agree.

"So what happened to Zack?" Barbara asked, holding up the email.

"He was murdered."

She winced and nodded. "Mr. Dead and Mr. Trouble?"

"Yes."

"And they wanted to smoke you, too?"

"Smoke?"

She rolled her eyes. "Dick Tracy. Back in the old days, when you shot someone, you smoked them. Like the smoking gun thing."

"Yes. They wanted to *smoke* me."

"Crap. I would have disappeared, too."

"I still should have told Sam."

"So this Sarah would have been your mother-in-law?"

I nodded yes.

"How long ago?"

"Sixteen years."

"And she's writing to say, 'Hey. Let's chat?' That's creepy."

"I thought it was sweet."

"Then why don't you call her?"

A shudder ran through me and the thought of holding Cinnamon's dead body threatened to smother me.

"I left L.A. behind. I don't even take speaking engagements or go to seminars there. It's as if I have anything to do with that place, it will swallow me up."

Barbara nodded thoughtfully. "Yeah. When I was a kid, my dog, Cat, got hit by a car when he was crossing the street by the park. After that, I just couldn't go to that park anymore."

It took me a moment to make the connection between her story and mine. I leaned over, hugged her, and started chuckling.

"What's funny?"

"How you put things in perspective in the most unexpected ways."

She frowned in puzzlement. "Oh. So you going to call Sarah?"

"Yes. I think I will."

"So what ya doing with the rest of your day?"

I smiled. "I have to be at work before two, but I think my friend, Barbara, mentioned it would be a great day to do some shopping. We have a couple hours."

"Short day?"

"No. Don't get off until eight."

She looked disappointed. "Damn. I was hoping you, me, and our kids could go get pizza tonight."

"Some other time."

Chapter 40
More Leads
Sam

Dave was waiting when I left Zack's mom's with my tail between my legs. When I opened the door to the car, I was assaulted by the smell of sour cream and onion potato chips. Dave leaned the mega bag toward me.

"Like some?"

Two broken chips and a pile of crumbs sat in the bottom.

"No, thanks."

He upended the bag into his mouth and finished it off.

"Where to next?" Dave asked.

Zack's dad still hadn't called me back, and I was having second thoughts about continuing my search for Billy's parents. If I did find them and they were radically homophobic like Billy, they could put two and two together the way Sarah had, and things could get real ugly.

"Do you know any of Louise's family?"

"Yeah. Ruby and her kids."

"Ruby?"

"Yeah. Um. Louise's sister. Ruby's her middle name. Her first name is Ursula, but she never used it." He snickered like a twelve-year-old and sarcastically added, "I wonder why?"

"She's had a half-dozen last names. One of them was almost Strand."

"You dated her?"

He nodded. "Yeah. I would have been number four. She's eight years older than me. When we started dating, it pissed a bunch of people off." His smile carried wistful lust. "It's true what they say about older women making beautiful lovers."

His tone was inviting me to pry.

"What happened?"

"I dropped by one day for some afternoon delight and caught

someone else poking her. That woman had balls. When she saw me standing in the bedroom door with my chin on the ground, she told me that they were almost done and she would be out in a few minutes."

"Ouch. Sorry."

Dave shrugged. "Probably for the best."

"You know where she is?"

"Yeah, but it's a waste of time. Imagine. Sixty-two and so senile you can't remember your own kids. I'd rather be dead."

"What about her kids?"

"Her son was killed in the Gulf War—Senior Bush's, not Junior's. Her daughter, Martha, lived in Orange, last I heard. Saw her and Eve play sometimes. That's all."

Sisters usually have children about the same age, so Martha would have probably known Evelyn when she was Adam. "Got a phone number?"

"Nah. Haven't seen her in years. Tanya will know."

I called Tanya. She had the phone number and said the genealogy showed Martha was married with two daughters. She hadn't seen Martha in over ten years and had never been close to her. She also noted that Martha had worked as an extra in movies and commercials.

With hope in his voice, Dave said, "It's almost lunch."

"Your pick."

He grinned from ear to ear. "I know a great burger place in Eagle Rock."

After Dave ordered the one-pound bacon cheeseburger with chili cheese fries, and I ordered the comparatively miniscule standard cheeseburger, I excused myself from the table.

I called Zack's dad, Richard, and got the answering machine again.

"Hi. This is Sam Irving again. I just talked with Sarah and she said you could tell me who really committed the murders. If you could give me a call back—"

The line picked up. His voice was drill sergeant assertive. "Hello, Mr. Irving. This is Master Sergeant Richard Taylor, retired. You want to know the truth?"

"Yes."

"My house, tomorrow, at 1900 sharp."

He gave me the address and directions.

After watching Dave eviscerate his burger like a wolf

devouring a deer, we went back to Tanya's.

Dave headed for the kitchen while Tanya led me out to the patio.

"I called Eve. She's worried about you."

It wasn't any of her business.

"I'll call her tonight." *Not going to happen.*

I knew she was looking right through me, like my mom used to.

"I wanted to ask you about some photos," I said.

"Ask away."

"These four girls show up in a bunch of the later photos. Do you know who they are?"

"They were high school friends." She stared at the photos, thinking hard. "That one was Rosalie Garcia, that one was Cinnamon Bandeau, and I think this one was ..." she closed her eyes and scrunched up her face. She mumbled, "Started with an f. Flirt, Flirtatious." She relaxed her face, "Felicity. Sorry, but I don't remember the other one or the other last names."

I stared at the picture. She had looked familiar, but in the photo, she had short permed hair and extra weight, so I hadn't made the connection.

"Felicity Summers?"

Tanya frowned. "Yes. I think so. Do you know her?"

I nodded yes. "Do you know where I could get a high school yearbook?"

She shrugged. "The high school?"

My plan had been to talk with her friends, but what would I say? What pretense would I use to pry information out of them? I could hear the phone conversation in my head. *"Hi. I'm Sam Irving. I married your high school friend, Evelyn Strand ... Yeah, the transsexual ... She's doing well ... Yes, we have three children ... Why I called is, I wanted to meet with you and discuss what you and she did in high school. You know. The boys you partied with. The drugs. The orgies. The criminal activities."*

I knew Evelyn had always been squeaky clean. With a high school 4.0 grade point average and advanced placement classes, she wouldn't have had time to get high and party all night. The best I could hope for would be a minor instance of poor judgment or some spiteful gossip.

My only real hope was the murders, and I knew that was pretty much a dead end. If I used Ashley's version, I'd be playing off lies, speculation, and homophobia, without any facts to back it up. I wanted her out of my life, but it wasn't looking like that would happen.

I flipped to the next marked page in the photo album. It showed Evelyn and another girl dancing. The date placed Evelyn at fifteen, and the title read, "Evelyn Strand and Suzanne Grouse at Grandma Clarisse Grouse's birthday party."

I pointed at it. Tanya nodded.

"Suzanne is a cousin once removed on Eve's paternal side. She moved to Texas after finishing college. Oil company lawyer. Married and two kids, if I remember right."

"Were they close?"

She thought for a second. It looked like one of those, do-I-tell-or-not thoughts.

"Don't know. You could ask Eve when you call tonight."

"I'll do that." *Not.*

I was curious if Tanya knew anything about Evelyn's paternity, since the journals had cast some doubt. As a society, we had moved past the traditional values where we punished children for their parent's indiscretions, so it wouldn't matter who her biological father was. I suppressed my idle curiosity and moved on.

With the album finished, all that was left was the envelope of information she had given me. I glanced at the documents again. My hope to gain full custody was evaporating like morning fog in bright sunshine. I stared blankly at the Buddha in the garden, knowing I had nothing on Evelyn. I could dredge up the accusations that she had killed Cinnamon and Zack, but her lawyer would shred my story faster than a congressman shreds the evidence of a kickback. Unless Ashley and gang came up with a plan that I could live with, I was stuck with Evelyn in my life.

"Do you still love her?" Tanya gently asked.

I wanted to hit something again.

"She lied."

"Yes. She did. Do you love her?"

I frowned. Everyone else had made excuses for Evelyn, and I knew Tanya was on her side.

"What difference does it make?"

"It makes a difference, Sam. You know that." She leaned back in her chair and closed her eyes.

I had worshipped Evelyn, but it had all been an elaborate illusion.

The smell of potato chips preceded Dave. The patio deck shifted under his weight and one of the boards let out a painful creak.

"How's it going?"

"Fine," Tanya said. "Sam and I were just discussing what a wonderful family he has. Have you ever seen pictures of his kids?"

"Not recent. What you got?"

She stepped past Dave.

"I'll get the ones I have. I'm sure Sam has a few in his wallet."

I was tempted to say no.

"That's my son, Christian."

"Nice. Looks like you."

"And my daughters, Angela and Grace."

"Pretty. And that Eve?"

"Yeah."

"She's gotten prettier than when I last saw her. Grace sure takes after her mom, don't she?"

"Yes."

He scowled, and I knew what he was wondering.

"Peter's daughter."

He nodded. "Heard. That sucked, but she looks happy. I guess it was lucky she had you two."

Other people had said she was lucky to have us, but the reality was, if she had been "lucky," her parents would still be alive. Maybe it was the word *luck* that bothered me.

Yeah, that's it. Luck was for fools, not orphaned children.

She was fortunate to have family who could and would take her in. We were blessed by her presence in our lives, but it was never luck. Eve was her godmother. The thought that Grace could or would have gone to live with someone else had never entered our minds.

"Yeah," I said.

Given Grace's age and how Evelyn was the center of her world, Evelyn would need to have primary custody of her. The thought of not having Grace in my daily life opened up a raw, hollow ache inside my chest.

When she kept teasing Chris, I sometimes wanted to lock her in a closet and throw away the key, but sometimes I wanted to lock up Chris and Angela, too. Most of the time, Grace was a precocious little daisy and, except for the teasing, more cooperative and helpful than Angela or Chris.

I pushed back the tears and tried to blank out my mind.

Tanya returned and handed Dave a few photos. He thumbed through them. Our family Christmas photo from last year. A few pictures of our Hawaii vacation two years ago. Camping at Mt. Lassen. A couple diving trips.

"Where'd you get these?" I asked.

"Nick comes down on business a couple times a year," Tanya said. "A few of the family meet him for dinner or an afternoon somewhere. He keeps us up-to-date on what's happening with everyone."

"Did Louise know?"

"Yes."

Given everything, I was surprised Louise would have approved. Or maybe she didn't and he did it anyway. It would make sense. As fiercely loyal as he was to Louise and us, he couldn't have walked away from his family in L.A.

The week wasn't half over and I was already close to done. All that was left was Zack's bitter father, a graveyard meeting with Cinnamon's dad, an appointment with the man who had tried to kill Eve, and a cousin whom I doubted could give me any dirt. I had screwed up bad when I was with Clora. If Eve decided to get even for my Adam comments, I could lose my kids.

Chapter 41
Alexis / Alexander
Evelyn

Alex smiled as he swaggered into my office. "Hey, Dr. Irving. How you doing?"

"Good. And how are you, Alex?"

"Couldn't be better. The hormones are trippy. No more periods or mood swings." He flexed his arm muscles. "And look at these. I'm working out three hours a day."

Alex had been on hormone therapy for four months. It was a little early to judge the mood swings, but it was promising that he wasn't experiencing adverse side effects. I could see his soft skin becoming course, and his muscles starting to grow.

"You're bulking up nicely."

He grinned. "Yeah. It won't be long 'til I look like Arnold Schwarzenegger."

"I see some facial hair."

He blushed, but stuck his chin out and rubbed it.

"Yeah. It's not much yet but it's coming. I was thinking a Fu Manchu would look cool … or a goatee."

Testosterone did an amazing job of masculinizing the female body. Facial hair and body hair sprouted like weeds in a flower garden. The "female form" disappeared as body fat faded and muscles developed. Within a short time, no one could tell that the person had ever been female, and most blended into society with little or no trouble.

The options for coitus were more limited than for a male to female transsexual because the surgical techniques for creating a penis were far less successful than for creating a vagina. Because of the high rate of complications and failures, many transmen only had a mastectomy and hysterectomy. Others accepted the formidable risk and did vaginal closure with urethral lengthening, so they could stand to pee. Some opted to have phalloplasty—male genital organ construction—complete with an inflatable penile implant, which enabled the man to have an erection and penetrate his partner.

Alex scowled in deep thought. "Why do people get so bent when they find out I'm trans?"

"Do we have ten hours?"

He chuckled.

I considered the most pertinent and appropriate answer.

"The bottom line is fear of the unknown."

"Oh?"

I continued. "Our physical gender defines who we are, the roles we play, and the ways we interact with each other. 'I am a girl. I will be a wife and mother.' 'I am a boy. I will be a husband and father.'

"When someone says 'I was born in the wrong body,' many people find the idea confusing and unbelievable. They don't understand, and what we don't understand, we fear."

Alex winced and shifted like he was on the proverbial hot seat.

"But I *am* a guy. Can't they just look at the facts? Understand?"

"It's not that easy. Seeing someone who is transitioning stirs questions and fear in people's minds. They ask themselves, 'Is he/she really a he/she?' 'Are they sane?' 'How do I act around them?' 'What do I say to them?' 'What pronoun do I use?'"

I paused for a moment to let him ponder what I had said before continuing. "People unfamiliar with the transgendered don't know what to say, how to act, or how to relate to you. They fear the unknown."

He frowned. "But I'm just like all the other guys. I like girls, cars, sports, and hunting. And I'd never hurt anyone."

"I know. You have a good heart. You will be a wonderful and responsible man someday."

He seemed to understand, so we moved on to his transition.

"The last time we met, you had an appointment with your doctor."

Alex smiled. "The doctor said I'm in great shape and good to go for my hysterectomy and breast reduction when I turn eighteen. Only 628 more days to go."

"How are you doing at school?"

He looked down and I saw a huge blush. "I've been hanging with Sylvia. I really like her."

"Does she like you?"

He puffed himself up. "Yeah. We date and neck and everything."

"Everything?"

He cringed and pursed his lips. "No. Not everything, but she wants to."

"And you don't?"

He looked down and blushed so crimson that he could have been used for a stoplight.

"Yeah. I do. All the other kids have, but I ..." he trailed off in unwarranted and disappointed shame.

I leaned forward. "Look at me please, Alex." He looked up. "I can tell you for a fact that not all the other kids have, even if they say they have. You're sixteen. You're in transition. It's going to take you longer. It's going to be harder. But you will get there. You will find someone who will love and accept you the way you are."

He nodded. "I know. I just wish I was born right."

"Me too."

He sighed. "Can I be honest with you?"

"I would hope you are always honest with me."

He shrugged. "I really like Sylvia, but I don't love her, love her. The truth is, I date her so I can have a girl."

He was thinking hard, so I let him.

He sighed and continued. "I don't actually love her at all. I date her because she's the only girl who will have me. Kind of pathetic, isn't it."

Many people in the trans community have a weak or nonexistent circle of intimate support. Alex was one of those. His parents had fought him every step of the way—even after he started harming himself. It wasn't until his older brother sued for legal custody of "Alexis" that his parents accepted that he was trans.

"No. It's not pathetic. It's part of dating. We try new people on and if they don't fit, we move on. It can get complicated and messy sometimes, but we all need someone. She's your someone right now and you are hers. If the relationship is respectful, there isn't anything wrong with spending time together, going out, and having some fun."

Alex said, "But it's so hard. I'll never find someone who will love me."

"You've been on the web and seen the stories of transmen

who are happily married. I know it's hard but the reality is that most people don't find their true love until they are in their twenties or thirties. Maybe what you're feeling for Sylvia will grow, and things will work out for the two of you."

He grinned and shook his head. "Nah. The way she tries to get into my pants sometimes, I don't think she even knows I'm trans." He chuckled and then looked me hard in the eyes. "She makes french fries look intelligent. When I marry, I want a smart woman."

His smile faded. "It's scary, but I'm going all the way with surgery."

I was concerned he wasn't being realistic.

"Most transmen never do bottom surgery because of the expense and risk."

"I know," he said. "I have a part-time job, and I'm saving every penny I can."

He was evading the issue of risk. I said, "It's risky and the failure rate is high. What if it doesn't work?"

Worry and sadness filled his eyes. "It'd be awesome if it worked, and a huge bummer if it didn't. I'm not doing it for the sex. I'm doing it so no one can question whether I'm a man. So I can stand to pee."

"I want it bad, but if the surgery fails, I will still be a man. You know that."

"Yes I do," I said. "And I'm thankful you know it too."

"When I'm done and really a man, will I have to tell whoever I end up with?"

Lost to the world, I stared at the wall as my thoughts overwhelmed me. His words, "will I have to tell," mocked me. I had been so, so wrong to keep it from Sam.

His voice sounded a little shaky. "Dr. Irving? Are you okay?"

I pulled myself back. "I'm sorry. Yes. Um. I'm fine." I looked at him for a moment, thinking about secrets and lies.

"In answer to your question, it's your choice whether you tell. But secrets like this never stay secret forever. What happens when a year or two or ten or twenty down the road, she finds out?"

He sighed and nodded.

"And if you were her, would you want to know?"

His frown deepened and he nodded again. "Yeah. I guess it does make a difference."

"To some people. But it won't to the right person."

Chapter 42
9-1-1
Evelyn

On Tuesdays and Thursdays, I worked until eight. On those days, cooking dinner fell to Sam. When he had to work late too, the kids took turns fixing dinner. I had left an oven-ready meatloaf in the refrigerator, with sticky note instructions, and pointed out the microwaveable vegetables in the freezer.

When I arrived home, the kids' coats were lying on the floor; I hung them and went into the kitchen. By the lack of mess and smells, it was obvious they hadn't fixed dinner. I wasn't too surprised. This morning, they had ignored me, been rude, left a mess everywhere they went, and had just generally been encouraging me to give them back to Clora.

I started the oven preheating and went to see what opportunities for growth they had planned for me. Grace was lying on her bed, staring at the ceiling and absentmindedly twirling a princess wand with glitter streamers.

"What are you doing, sweetie?"

She looked at me for a moment as if she were trying to memorize my every feature.

"Nothing."

She went back to staring at the glow-in-the-dark stars she had glued to the ceiling above her and twirling her wand.

Chris and Angela weren't in their rooms. I was about to call out for them when the smell of lighter fluid coming from my closet caused me to wince. I had double-bagged the journals, but must not have tied them tight enough. I opened the closet door and gagged on the fumes. Chris and Angela looked up from the journals, glassy-eyed, their movements slow and uncoordinated. The cool fresh air hit them, causing Angela to throw-up. Chris wobbled as he stood.

"Grace. Call 9-1-1," I yelled.

Angela continued to retch as I helped her out of the closet. Chris stumbled out and collapsed on the rug. He was still breathing, so I opened the window. Grace stood in the doorway with the cordless phone to her ear. Her eyes were wide and her voice was trembling.

"They want to know what's wrong."

I took the phone. "My son and daughter were in a confined space with solvent fumes. My daughter is throwing up and my son's unconscious."

I tossed the phone onto the bed and dragged Chris into the family room, where the air was fresh. His face was pasty white instead of its normal, healthy tan. He was struggling to breathe so I laid him on his side. Grace had followed me and was watching—terror screaming in her eyes.

"They'll be fine, sweetie. I need you to go out front and wait for the firemen. Alright?"

She nodded yes and hesitantly edged toward the door while I went back for Angela.

After the paramedics arrived and gave them oxygen, their pale white complexions turned a little green, but they were alert and responsive enough to be embarrassed. The paramedics took them to the hospital over their plaintive and futile objections.

Grandma Rose and Grandpa Rich met us and sat with Grace in the waiting room while I sat with Chris and Angela and talked with the doctor. After the initial exam, the doctor said the kids would have headaches and feel weak and nauseous for a day or two, but there didn't appear to be any permanent harm. Still, she wanted to keep them on oxygen therapy and monitor them for a couple more hours.

My stomach gurgled. Barbara and I had been so caught up in our shopping that I hadn't eaten lunch, and it was now ten.

Oh, fudge. The oven is still on.

It would be midnight before the doctor released them and one a.m. at the earliest by the time I got them in bed.

Grace was asleep in Grandpa Rich's arms, and Rose hugged me.

"They'll be fine," I said. "The doctors want to monitor them for a couple more hours. Let's go to the cafeteria."

Rose looked concerned. "Have you called Sam?"

I had thought about it a dozen times but I hadn't had—or hadn't taken—the opportunity.

"Not yet." I slumped. "I'll meet you in the cafeteria."

I headed for the exit and dug through my purse for some chocolate. He'd be angry at me and blame me, but I *was* to blame. What was I thinking, storing a bag full of flammables in my closet? The fire chief had graphically pointed out, with a half-dozen different scenarios, how I could have killed all of us.

I didn't expect Sam to answer his phone—he hadn't since Saturday. After the fourth ring, I heard, "Yeah. What do *you* want?" His voice was filled with disdain.

My mind was still on the kids and his pettiness caught me off guard. I was speechless for a second as his contempt swept me into a confusing whirlpool of thoughts and emotions.

Part of me had forgotten he was being a mule's behind, or maybe it was an old reflex that said "He's my safe harbor. He will comfort and protect me in my time of need," and God, did I need him right now.

"Excuse me?" I said indignantly.

"It's late. I have a long day tomorrow," he said, his tone impatient.

I was numb and cold. I trembled. The thought "You should be angry at him" spun through my mind, but I wasn't. His little temper tantrum wasn't important. His rudeness wasn't important. His being a pain wasn't important. Even his going to L.A. wasn't important.

My stupidity and blind desire to keep my secret had nearly killed two of my children. *That* was important.

My spirit calmed, as Mom's words came to me. "I love you, and I am proud of you. Be proud of your past, Eve. Embrace it. Sam loves you. He will stand by you."

The solid ground of my mom's love calmed my mind. Maybe Sam would stand by me and maybe he wouldn't. That was his choice and I couldn't make it for him. I could only be me, in all my human imperfections.

Sam's voice crackled in the phone. "I don't have all night."

I smiled, unsure why. "I called to let you know ..." He'd cancel his trip and come back. The kids were fine, so it would be pointless. He needed to make peace with the demon he was locked in mortal combat with. "... we love you."

I hung up and stared at an old man hobbling through the parking lot, alone, with no one to help him or give him company and comfort.

I whispered, "Sam. You're better than this. Why?"

Chapter 43
What Do They Know?
Evelyn

Sleep evaded me as the memory of finding Angela and Chris in my closet replayed in my head. Meditation didn't help.

The Wednesday newspaper banged into the screen door, pulling me from my attempts to rest. I hadn't let the firemen take the journals so they had put them in the barbeque on the patio, since it was the closest thing to a fire-can we had. I needed to re-bag them and lock them in the garden shed before anyone else got up.

The kids would stay home for a day or two, and I wasn't in any condition to carry a full client load. I cleared my calendar through Friday except for four clients.

Grace was the first one up, but unlike Monday, when she had been clingy, she was now distant, watching her videos and all but ignoring me while I caught up on cleaning.

When her video ended, I sat with her and put my arm around her.

"How are you doing, sweetie?"

Her look was a jumble of troubled, sad annoyance. "Okay."

"Last night was pretty scary."

She shrugged and I felt a wall building between us.

"Do you want to talk?"

She shook her head no.

"Thank you for calling 9-1-1 and waiting for the fire truck. You were a big help."

Worry filled her eyes. "The fireman said they almost died."

I kissed her forehead. "I'm sorry. He shouldn't have said that. There isn't any way for him to really know."

She looked up at me. Her eyes asked if I was telling the truth.

"It wasn't good for them to be in the closet with the fumes," I said, "but God was watching out for them. He made sure I got home."

"Was Grandma Louise watching out for them, too?"

I smiled. "Yes. I'm sure she was."

She frowned. "And my mommy and daddy?"

"They are part of our family, too. I believe so. Just like they watch over you."

She sank into a sadness far too deep and dark.

"I wish they were still here."

I kissed her hair. "Me too, sweetie. Me too."

About eleven, I stuck my head into Angela's room. She quickly closed her eyes and pretended to be asleep, then faked a very bad snore when I sat next to her.

Gently, I pushed some hair from her face.

"I know you're awake. How are you feeling?"

She peeked up at me. "I have a headache, but I'm alright. I'm sorry."

"Me too. But I'm mainly glad that you and Chris are okay."

She shifted and then stuffed her pillow under her head so she could easily see me.

"Are we grounded?"

I had felt so guilty and had been so relieved they were alright that I hadn't even thought about punishing them.

I frowned. "I don't know. I guess it would depend."

Her eyes narrowed, and she studied me.

"Depends on what?"

"On how honest you are with me."

I saw the flash of anger that screamed, "Double standard. Unfair." They knew I hadn't been honest with them about why their dad left, and now I was asking her to be honest with me.

"You're right. It isn't fair." I leaned down and kissed her forehead. "I'll start. Your dad found out something about my childhood that upset him a great deal."

"The diaries?"

I nodded yes. "He needs some time to think about it, what it means to him, and how he feels about me now."

"What?"

If she had read the part in the journal that said I used to be a boy, she would have known "what."

"I wish I could tell you right now, but I can't. I don't know when I can. And that's the truth."

Her lips tightened into perturbed anger, but in her eyes I could see she understood.

"Is Dad coming back?"

"Yes. He will come back, but I don't know if he will be able to stay with me. In my heart, I believe he will, but I don't know. I'm praying."

She nodded, her eyes sad and heavy. "Me, too."

"Your turn. What did you read in the journals?"

She scrunched up her face and huffed. "Your father was mean to Grandma."

"Yes, he was. Very mean."

"Is he still alive?"

"I don't know."

"I hope not. I hope he got cancer and rotted to death."

My heart trembled. That was one of the kinder wishes I had made for him over the years. Vindictiveness had seemed so right and justified at the time. But coming out of my daughter's virtuous heart, it cut me to the core.

Hate was such an insidious virus. I knew that my looks, hesitations, and silence when he was mentioned had conditioned her to hate him. The journals had given her permission. He might deserve it, but it was wrong to teach my daughter blind hate. It was no longer about me and my birth father. I needed to make peace with him for my daughter—for my children.

I shook my head no. "No, sweetheart. It's as wrong to wish harm on him as it was for him to hurt Grandma. He shouldn't have done those things, but wouldn't it be better if he became a good person and spent the rest of his life helping others instead of rotting?"

She scowled. "I guess. But it doesn't seem fair."

I softly smiled. "An eye for an eye?"

She tried not to grin and repeated the line from *The Fiddler on the Roof*, poorly faking Tevya's deep base voice. "Very good. That way, the whole world will be blind and toothless."

And then she said something that surprised me. "Justice without compassion is vengeance."

I smiled. "Very true. Where did you hear that?"

"My history teacher."

"Smart teacher."

Chris was still asleep, for real. It was almost noon so I woke him. He glared and rolled over.

"How are you feeling, honey?"

"Fine. Leave me alone."

"We need to talk."

He buried his face under his pillow.

"We raised you to be responsible and honest, Chris. You can't run from what you did."

He flung his pillow hard against the wall and sat up, anger burning his eyes.

"Dad ran."

I trembled slightly, and then braced myself, trying to appear calm and assured.

"No. He did not run. He needs answers. I hope he will find them in Los Angeles. He'll be back by Monday."

His anger collapsed into resentment and confusion. I could see the emotional black-and-white world of the child within him wrestling with the rational gray world of the emerging young man. His warm hazel eyes glistened with pain as he stared blankly through me.

"A penny for your thoughts."

His eyes went cold and his jaw tightened. My heart flinched. He had a wall I had never seen before. For the first time, I couldn't read my son.

"I have a headache and I'm starving."

"Um. Yeah. Would you like me to fix you something?"

He climbed past me. "No, thanks. I'll get it."

He stomped down the hall. I sat there knowing something significant had just happened, and had no idea what. He was enough like his dad that if he knew about me, he was going to bury it inside and try to find peace with it on his own terms.

His father!

Sam hadn't seen or talked to them since Saturday. He was so caught up in his own garbage that he hadn't even called the kids to tell them he loved them. Or maybe he had called them on their cell phones and they didn't ... Grace would have said something.

Fudge, Sam. Grow up.

Chapter 44
Higher Up
Sam

I woke early thinking about Evelyn and couldn't get back to sleep. There had been something in her voice that wasn't right. Worry? Fear? Probably just upset about me finding out. But I had heard that ... whatever it was ... in her voice before. It nagged at me.

I did a few futile web searches before getting dressed and going down to the lobby for the hotel's free breakfast. It wasn't bad considering the price. I had finished and was grabbing a newspaper when I noticed Benny in the parking lot. He was heading for the main lobby so I waited.

He was sunshine and bright smiles as he shook my hand like we were old friends.

"Great news, Sam. We talked. They loved your background and situation. Our lawyers said that with the right spin, we can parlay your annulment into a Constitutional Amendment which will stand up in court and roll back California's domestic partnership laws."

I thought constitutions were supposed to protect rights, not strip them. The more I thought about their plan, the more I hated it, but I was tired of being a fool. I had been a fool for Clora and then Evelyn. I had been a fool for believing that honor, truth, and justice were worth something. I needed to take care of myself and my kids. They were offering me a deal. I doubted that I would take it, but it wouldn't hurt to hear the details.

"Who do I see and when?"

His smile twinkled like a teeth-whitening commercial.

"You already have it. BJ."

I stared blankly at him.

He frowned. "Brandon Jones. Pastor Jones."

"Oh."

Maybe I shouldn't have been surprised that Brandon would be a major player in the anti-gay political arena, but what were the odds he would be the one offering me a deal? Or maybe they found the connection between Evelyn and him and chose him to make sure I was willing to sell out Evelyn.

I studied him for any signs of deceit.

"So he has the details and the authority?"

"If he likes you, and you agree on the details—yes."

I had intended to tell Brandon that Evelyn was a friend. I could only imagine how much he would pay to make her life hell now that he knew the truth.

I forced a smile. "Okay. I'll see what he has to offer."

My phone beeped. It was a text message from Evelyn's cousin, Martha. I had emailed or texted a dozen of Evelyn's relatives, not expecting any response.

"From Martha Churchill
"In Hawaii wont be back for week. Meet for coffee when back? Love to Eve"

The "love to Eve" told me she was another dead end, so I texted back.

"From Sam Irving
"Sorry. I'll be back in Marin before you get here. Another time. Enjoy Hawaii."

A couple minutes later, my phone beeped with another text message.

"From Martha Churchill
"Sorry can't meet How bout Eve number so I call and catch up? Love to chat."

Seconds later, Evelyn's phone number was bouncing off a satellite or two on its way to Hawaii. I shook my head and mumbled, "Why is Eve so damn likable?"

Chapter 45
Zack's Father
Sam

I took Dave up on his offer to continue being my taxi. Between his gas and food, he was more expensive than a rental car, but he could sometimes answer a question and he definitely knew the best meat and potatoes places to eat.

The main L.A. library was a waste of my morning, with not one bit of useful information about the murders. After lunch, Dave showed me around Evelyn's old neighborhood. The photo albums told me which schools she had attended, and knowing Evelyn, I had a pretty good idea where her favorite places to hang out with friends would have been.

After dinner, Dave took me to see Zack's father. He lived in a three-story apartment building in Chatsworth, at the north end of the San Fernando Valley. It was an older complex but well-maintained, with trimmed lawns and palm trees in front. Between the units, a clean, well-lit swimming pool and a modern glass-front exercise room flaunted the Southern California lifestyle.

I waited outside his apartment until seven p.m. sharp and then knocked.

Richard Taylor looked like he sounded—all military. Five foot nine, stocky, crew cut, military desert boots, and fatigue pants with a camouflage T-shirt that read "An Army of One."

His eyes were more direct than his voice.

"Mr. Irving."

"Yes."

"Were you ever in the military, sir?"

"No."

His look was disapproving, but fleeting.

"Unfortunate. But you are punctual, Mr. Irving. I like that."

He stepped back to let me in. "I'm Master Sergeant Richard Taylor, retired. You can call me Sergeant. Come in, sir."

The contrast between Sarah's testosterone-pumped drill sergeant ex and her current, timid husband was mystifying. I doubted I would ever understand women.

A girl in her late twenties, wearing little more than heavy makeup and cleavage, was standing in the kitchen watching us with mousey eyes.

Without even looking at her, he said, "That's my girlfriend, Sylvia." He called to her, "Get us a couple beers, baby."

"Make mine water."

He looked me up and down with a sneer and said, "Make the civvy's water." He turned. "This way, sir."

He led me to the living room and plopped down in the easy chair. I sat on the couch opposite and we played a game of stare-down to see who would be top dog. Since he appeared to be all ego and I wanted info, I looked away when I sensed he had reached his limit. I knew it was best to let him lead the conversation, so I waited. Sylvia shyly brought our drinks and then disappeared back into the kitchen.

"What's your interest in Zackary's murder, sir?"

"Justice."

He studied me with a poker face for a moment.

"What'd my ex say?"

"Not much. She misses Zackary. Didn't know anything other than what the papers said, what Evelyn alleged, and what little the police told her."

"Evelyn is a liar. What's your interest?" he asked, still hiding behind a blank expression.

I'd hit gold. If he had done a web search and knew I was married to her, he never would have let me through the door.

The story was thin, and if he thought about it for half-a-second he'd know it was bull, but I didn't have much to lose.

"I know Evelyn. She's a lying bitch and I want to take her kids away from her. If she's implicated in a murder, she's an unfit mother."

He smiled. "She deserves it." He stood. "This way to my operations room, sir."

The bedroom had been converted into a television-style, police detective's operations room, with charts, maps, graphs, photos, and documents completely covering the walls, with a few tacked to the ceiling. A large desk and folding table were covered with computers and boxes of documents, the area under the table crammed so tight it lifted the table legs an inch off the floor.

An eleven-by-fourteen, full color, glossy photo of the crime scene hung prominently on one wall. It graphically showed Zack's lifeless body at a park—complete with brain splatter. Tacked up around the photo were a dozen five-by-seven close-ups of the bullet wounds and injuries.

I needed an antacid.

"Welcome to my operations room," he said, with perverted pride.

I looked at the lifeless photos of Zack and realized I hadn't seen any photos of him in the living area. If something happened to one of my kids, this isn't the way I would want to remember them.

He pointed to a map of the park and surrounding area.

"This is the park where my boy was killed. Ballistics confirmed that Ms. Strand was here when she shot Zack," he said, pointing at a clump of bushes and trees. The place he was pointing to had a big dot with two straight lines drawn out from it, which I assumed were the paths of the bullets. From the police reports I had read, I recognized the X where the lines ended as the place where Zack had died.

He pointed to a spot about ten feet in front of the trees.

"And here's where she stood when she shot her friend, Kelly Bandeau. The one they called Cinnamon." Again a dot, with four straight lines which ended at an X near the edge of a flood control channel.

He then pointed to a street downstream, over ten blocks from the park, which had another X.

"This is where they found Ms. Strand wandering. According to the police report, she was drenching wet and in shock."

"What makes you think Evelyn was the gunman?"

"I've seen soldiers go into shock after their first kill. It was Ms. Strand's first kill."

I nodded, unsure of the connection. The police reports had said there weren't any footprints, so I wasn't sure how he could identify Eve as the shooter.

"Did the police find her footprints in the trees?"

"No. It was raining and the soil was sandy. They were washed away before the police got there."

I looked at the map. Another X was drawn next to the flood

control channel, several miles from the park.

I pointed. "What's this X?"

"That's where they found the deceased Mr. Bandeau."

I thought about my drives around Los Angeles. The "L.A. River" had little more than a trickle of water flowing through it, and most of the flood control channels that fed it were bone dry.

"The channels are dry. How'd she get so far down?"

He seemed to sense my doubt about his story and glared at me.

"Let me make something perfectly clear, Mr. Irving. My son was not gay. Contrary to news reports and rumors, neither Mr. Bandeau nor Ms. Strand was dating him. He wanted to be a doctor. Abnormal psychology interested him. His only interest in them was clinical."

He looked back at the map. "As for the flood control channels, most of the time they are dry, as you undoubtedly observed. But L.A. is a rock and sand desert, paved over with concrete and asphalt. There's nowhere for the water to go but the L.A. river and flood control channels. A quarter-inch of rain can generate several feet of water in minutes; a half-inch and they are raging rivers. It was raining that day. He fell into the channel after being shot and was carried downstream by the rain."

His logic still evaded me.

"But how did Ev—Um, Ms. Strand end up in the water?"

"It was a crime of passion, Mr. Irving. She wanted my son. Thought he was gay and that he preferred Mr. Bandeau. In her blind rage, she jumped into the channel to make sure Mr. Bandeau was dead. She even admitted to holding him under the water until she was sure."

I frowned and cautiously said, "And what about Ms. Strand's claim that Mr. Jackson and Mr. Jones were the shooters?"

He studied me, distrust filling his eyes.

"You ever watch the senior Pastor Jones on television?"

I shook my head no.

"Good man," he continued. "The junior Pastor Jones doesn't quite live up to his father's greatness yet, but in another ten years, he just might. Men like them don't kill boys like mine and they don't lie. Both Mr. Jackson and Mr. Jones had solid alibis. Ms. Strand was just looking for someone to blame."

"Have you told your theory to the police?"

"Of course, but that pantywaist D.A. won't do a fucking thing. Says there isn't enough evidence for an indictment." He swept his arm in a broad arch to dramatize the volumes of documentation he had.

"Look at all this. I have all the evidence he needs. It's a cakewalk for them, and the mother-fuckers won't touch it."

"Did he tell you specifically why they won't prosecute?"

"He said they couldn't tie the murder weapon to Ms. Strand."

The newspaper reports had said that no weapons were found at the scene.

"They have the weapons?" I asked.

"One of them. It turned up when a liquor store owner killed some punk trying to rob him three years ago. The gun originally belonged to an old lady that had reported it stolen six months before the murders. The woman lived less than a mile from Ms. Strand. Ballistics tied it to several robberies, two homicides, and a dozen gang shootings."

"Didn't Mr. Jackson and Mr. Jones also live in that area?"

"That's what the D.A. said, but they had alibis, so that leaves Ms. Strand."

With all the documents on his walls, I had hoped for more, but he was just a bereaved father running from the truth. With the loss of hope, my righteous indignation and anger receded. I saw myself reflected in the Sergeant.

Images of Clora's arrest flashed through my mind. The trial. The anguish of holding Angela and Chris as they cried for their mother, knowing they would never see her again. The fear and feeling of helplessness as child protective services tried to link me to Clora's crimes and take my kids. The brutal and painful unfairness of what Clora had put us though.

I stumbled and caught myself on the edge of the table, not wanting to believe myself capable of doing what I was trying to do to Eve and my kids—doing what Clora had done to me.

NO! This is wrong. Even if it was possible to tie Evelyn to the murders and railroad her, I couldn't do this to her or my kids.

"You okay? You're looking a little peaked, Mr. Irving. That water wasn't too strong for you, was it?" the Sergeant asked.

"I'm fine." I stood tall and looked down on him. "What was the time period between the murders and the first ballistics tie to the gun?"

He went over to a filing cabinet and fingered through a folder. He pulled out a few sheets of legal-size paper that were stapled together.

"The first ballistics tie was April 7, 1997. Why, sir?"

"Where, Sergeant?"

"Um. Non-lethal gang shooting in East L.A. Why?"

I huffed. "For reference, Ms. Strand was living in the San Francisco Bay area at the time of that shooting."

He shrugged. "So?"

"You ever hear what happened to the good Mr. Billy Jackson?"

"No, sir. I have not. He's innocent and of no interest to me."

I scowled and shook my head. "On April 1st 1997, he went to East L.A. with the intent to beat or kill gay men. He assaulted a gang member instead, and got his head caved in. He spent the next three years in a vegetative state.

"According to your records, the first time the gun surfaced after the murders was in a gang fight in East L.A. That would have been a week after Mr. Jackson *lost* a gang fight in East L.A. Wouldn't you say that is an interesting coincidence, Sergeant?"

He stared at me for a minute, then at the map on the wall, with one of those fixed, confused stares people get when they find that the beliefs they built their world around are false.

I had seen enough of the pictures. Zack deserved a better memorial.

"Thank you for your time, Sergeant. You have been very helpful. I'll show myself out."

I paused outside the apartment door. "NOOOOO," came screaming from inside, followed by the crash of electronics and the dull thud of heavy boxes.

My anger had burned out. I had failed to find anything on Evelyn. It was time to go home and end the marriage as amicably as possible.

Chapter 46
A Missed Appointment
Evelyn

When possible, I meet with a child's parents before I begin therapy to understand what the parents' expectations are. Clarissa's mom, Helen, had made it clear she did not support Charley's desire to be Clarissa, and had agreed only because her husband "forced" her.

When the family is divided over what is best for a child, it is common for the child to miss appointments, or to face so much animosity concerning the therapy that they stop coming. Clarissa was usually early for our time together, but today she was late. Everyone runs late sometimes or gets caught up in life and forgets, but I was concerned. At fifteen minutes after the hour, I called her home and got the answering machine, so I tried her dad's cell phone.

His tone was angry and upset. "Yes."

I hesitated. "This is Dr. Irving. Clarissa had an appointment. She's late. Is everything alright?"

He paused, while a raspy speaker in the background announced a flight was boarding.

"No. I'm in Detroit. I got a call an hour ago that some kids at her school beat her up pretty bad. They have her at the hospital—she's stable. That's all I know."

My heart sank. I had prayed Clarissa would be spared the senseless brutality I had suffered at the hands of other children.

"I'm so sorry. Do you know which hospital she's in?" I asked.

"No. Helen only said I don't need to bother coming home or trying to see Clarissa."

"I'm really sorry. Is there anything I can do?"

He was silent for several seconds. When he spoke, his anger had been replaced by tired bewilderment.

"I don't know why Helen can't see how much happier

Clarissa is, and her grades were coming up. We could get past this." There was a lost sadness in his voice. "Helen just can't accept that Clarissa isn't a boy. It's like she would rather see our son in a mental institution or dead than happy being a girl."

Barely above a whisper he said, "I always thought mothers loved their children no matter what. But …"

"I'm sure she does love Clarissa. Some parents just take longer to accept that their child is different."

A bitter, absolute knowing filled his every word. "No. She will never accept it. I sell cars and I'm damn good at it. I know when a person will or won't negotiate on some part of the deal. Clarissa's being a girl has never been negotiable to her. After this, you'd have more luck wearing down Mount Everest with a child's watercolor paint brush than getting my wife to accept Clarissa."

That had been my impression when I met her, but people would sometimes surprise me. Some whom I wrote off as unyielding then yielded to incredible compassion and personal growth. Others whom I thought were enlightened and sympathetic were mired in egotism hidden behind a false mask of altruism.

His voice was tight and starting to break. "My plane is boarding. Got to go." He hung up.

I prayed for the highest good to come out of this tragedy.

Admissions directed me to Clarissa's room. I knew Clarissa would have been talking to the hospital psychiatrist, so my concern was for her mom. I stood in the hall where I could see Helen, but was out of sight of Clarissa, so that if she told me to get lost—which she had the legal and moral right to do—it wouldn't upset Clarissa.

Helen looked up from a magazine and glared at me. After a quick glance at her daughter, she came out to the hall.

Her sneer was filled with blame and anger. "You will not see my son. Now or ever. This is your fault, filling his head with the crazy idea of being a woman. It's absurd and wrong. The only future for a tranny is prostitution or being a freak on TV. I want more for my son than that, and I won't let you or my husband do that to him."

That bleak future was Hollywood and urban legend speaking. The reality was quite different, with most transsexuals, like Clarissa, blending with varying degrees of success into society. There were transsexual doctors, lawyers, dentists, politicians, business people, teachers, secretaries, store clerks, waitresses, and managers. The only professions genetic women occupied that weren't shared with transwomen were those where homophobia parading as public or national security prohibited them.

But it didn't matter. Debate and facts were useless at the moment. She was scared and angry. I was an easy and safe target for her rage.

"I'm sorry. Charley is a lovely and intelligent child. I wish you and your family the best."

I turned and walked away, feeling her eyes cursing me and her hate burning the hall. I wanted desperately to go back and comfort Clarissa but my hands were tied. Any attempt by me to talk to her at this point was illegal and considered unprofessional. I could be sued and lose my license to practice. She was in God's hands.

Chapter 47
A Call Home
Sam

What I had seen and learned in the Sergeant's operations room had left me edgy and troubled. As I prepared for bed, the images of Zack occupied my mind. The idea of remembering my kids that way made me shudder.

"My kids!" *Shit.*

In trying to find a way to keep them, I had forgotten about them. I had been so caught up in trying to find people and going through the documents that I hadn't talked to them since Saturday. I called home and got Chris.

"Hi, buddy. How are you doing?"

"Fine. When are you coming home?" He sounded angry and scared.

I tried to sound upbeat. "Probably be a few more days. How'd the game go?"

Definite anger. "Didn't go."

"Why? Are you okay?"

"Yeah," he mumbled. "Just a headache and not feeling good. Mom made me stay home."

"Sorry you missed your game, but there will be others." When I asked about Katelyn, he clammed up, said he had to go, and handed the phone to Angela.

"How's my angel?"

Her "Alright" was filled with annoyance and anger. She was getting that princess thing down pretty good.

"How's school?"

"Alright."

"You write any new poetry?"

"No." I could hear sadness in her voice.

"Why not?"

"It won't come." Her sadness was deepening.

"How do you like your new poetry book?"

"It's okay. Why did you go away?"

We had raised the kids to think things through and speak their minds with respect. At the moment, I was regretting it a little.

"I just needed to take a little trip. I'll be back in a few days."

"Really?" She sounded skeptical.

"I promise."

A chill frosted my phone.

"Grace wants to talk."

Before I could say anything, Grace said, "Hi, Dad," her voice high and filled with tension.

"Hi, Grace, honey. I miss you."

"Miss you too, Dad. When you coming home?"

"A few days."

"Do you still love Mom?"

Her question threw me, and I hesitated while I tried to figure out how to answer. I could hear the receiver clunk onto a table. "Grace? You there, baby?"

The phone rustled. I could hear the protective anger in Evelyn's voice. "What did you say to her?"

"Nothing. What happened?"

"After she asked you if you still love me, she started crying and ran off to her room."

"I didn't say anything. I was thinking." *Shit. Stupid, stupid, stupid.* "I didn't—"

"You're already in over your head, Sam," Evelyn said, her anger boiling just below the surface. "Do us both a favor and don't dig the hole any deeper."

She tried to sound upbeat. "Thank you for calling. The kids have been missing you. How are you doing?"

"Fine."

The upbeat was fading as an angry neediness replaced it. "We miss you. When will you be back?"

"Soon."

"How do you like Aunt Tanya?" Her voice trembled a little. "She's wonderful, isn't she?"

"Yeah. She is."

"How do you like it in L.A.?"

"It's been a long day. I need to get to bed."

Her voice wavered, "Um. We had a little problem last night—"

"You solve it. I need to get some sleep."
I could hear the tears approaching, like a far-off storm.
"Alright. Love you. Good night, Sam."
"Yeah."
I hung up, feeling like a complete ass.

Chapter 48
Cousin Martha
Evelyn

Chris and Angela had moped around all day Wednesday while recovering from having been fumigated in my closet. This morning, they had most of their energy and appetites back, but I decided to keep them home another day.

My hope had been that their closet experience would have left them more cooperative, but Sam's call last night had sent them into a storm of fear, self-pity, and anger that they were venting at me.

By the end of yesterday, I had coaxed Grace a little out of her shell, but Sam's call had hit her hard. She was now completely withdrawn.

My nerves were so shredded that I spilled my coffee when the phone rang. I didn't recognize the number.

"Hi, Eve. It's Martha, your cousin."

"Martha? It's been forever. How'd you find me?"

"Your husband gave me your number. Said he wanted to talk about family history, but I'm in Hawaii shooting a commercial and couldn't meet with him. He texted me your number, so I thought it was probably alright to call."

My cousin Martha and I had been close growing up; she was like a sister when we were little. From the time we were six, she had called me Eve when the grownups weren't around. We had played together almost every week until junior high, when she had moved to Orange County. Except for rare family get-togethers, our relationship had become long telephone chats, as our separate worlds slowly made the distance between us seem real.

After the murders, I had been so sure that Brandon and Billy were going to hunt me down and kill me as well, that I had cut ties with her and nearly everyone else I knew when I fled Los

Angeles. Looking back through the eyes of experience and age, I realized my dad would have protected me. But after so many years of being terrorized by my birth father and then seeing my two friends killed, Mom and I were panic-stricken and desperate to get away. Dad had no choice but to give up his practice and move—or lose us.

Martha's call warmed me like a Hallmark homecoming.

We caught up on husbands, kids, my mom's death, her mom's senility, and our careers.

Martha seemed hesitant. "So Brandon and Billy aren't a problem?"

"Billy is dead and Brandon is too high-profile to risk doing anything."

"Yeah. I catch him on TV when my husband is channel surfing. He has quite the following. Seems like a lot of people are in a mighty big hurry to hate."

"They don't really want to hate," I said. "They're scared and confused. The constant message from government and the press is *be afraid*. When people are scared, they are easily manipulated. So the money and power people keep the *home of the brave* scared to death so that they can steal us blind and have their cowardly wars." I frowned. I didn't like getting on that soap box. "Sorry. How'd we get on politics?"

"I called because I've missed my sister." Her voice smiled. "I'm shooting a commercial next month in San Francisco and would love to get together with you for a day. Maybe go see the vineyards."

I ached to hug her. "I would love to."

Martha seemed distracted. "The director's calling. Gotta go. Love you. Bye."

I had Martha back. I no longer feared Brandon and Billy. I felt more free and alive than I had in years.

Then it struck me. For sixteen years, I had lived in fear. I had allowed that fear to steal my life.

If God is Love, then the Devil is Fear. From now on, I would choose love.

Chapter 49
I Need to Know
Sam

It was Thursday morning and I was almost done. Today, my schedule included lunch with Tanya so I could return the documents, thank her, and say good-bye. Late this afternoon, I would meet with Brandon at his church. Then at sunrise tomorrow, I would see Cinnamon's dad at a graveyard before heading home.

At this point, my interest in Brandon was strictly idle curiosity. I was also having second thoughts about meeting with Cinnamon's dad since he was just another hate-mongering homophobe, but I had committed.

After we ordered lunch, I decided to ask Tanya something I had been wondering since I read the journals. "Do you know the details of the murders?"

"Have you asked Eve?"

Oh, shit. She's back to that. My face warmed with embarrassment.

"No."

Her eyes were filled with a reluctant sadness I didn't understand. It was obvious she could read me the way I could read my kids. I knew she wouldn't judge me, hadn't judged me, so I confessed.

"I'm pretty sure I know what happened; the evidence is all there. But I want to know what Evelyn's version is and I'm not comfortable asking her."

She nodded yes. "Alright, Sam." The sadness was still with her. She looked down in deep thought—maybe even said a quick prayer.

After a minute, she sighed and looked up.

"Brandon and Billy had been harassing Eve and Cinnamon

for years. In January of '94, L.A. was hit by the Northridge earthquake. Six point seven magnitude, seventy some people killed, thousands injured, billions in damage. Most churches immediately reached out to the community to help, but some used it to preach God's wrath and fill their treasuries." She paused for a second. "It's funny how the two seem to go together."

I nodded.

She continued. "Pick your hate. Drugs, sex, gays, non-Christians, communists, Palestinians, Arabs, immigrants—legal and illegal. Regardless of the group they chose to hate, the message was the same. 'God is punishing us for tolerating these people and doing these things.'

"In the weeks leading up to the killings, Brandon and Billy had escalated their verbal harassments to physical assault—first shoving, then a bloody nose, a bruise, or a few scrapes. Because of the quake, L.A.'s infrastructure and law enforcement had been stretched past the breaking point. They didn't have the resources to deal with school fights that didn't involve guns, knives, or hospitalization, so nothing was done. The schools were so traumatized by the quake and preoccupied with trying to glue things back together that they weren't any help either.

"On the day of the murders, Evelyn, Cinnamon, and Zack had stayed after school to help Zack's teacher write a grant to replace computers which were destroyed in the quake.

"It was late and raining, but they stopped to kick around a soccer ball at the park. Their game took them out of the park and into the weeds next to the flood control channel. Eve kicked it wrong and it went high and far back into the park. Zack went after it."

Tanya stared blankly at the table for a second before going on.

"Eve and Cinnamon were watching Zack when she heard the gunshots and saw the flashes. She watched Zack fall and saw Brandon and Billy come running out of the bushes."

Her eyes were unfocused. Her face was tight with pain. Her voice had become tense and carried a barely perceptible tremor. She closed her eyes and took in a slow, deep breath. As she exhaled, I saw peace once again flow through her.

When she opened her eyes, they sparkled with pensive mystery. Her soft words were a reverent prayer rather than the simple transfer of knowledge.

"Eve told me she saw Zack being held by an angel. I feel my angels and they whisper thoughts to me, but I have never seen them. She is surely blessed to have seen his."

She paused. Pain filled the creases in her face.

"This is hard for you," I said. "Maybe we should drop it."

She chased away her pain, smiled with an open heart, and looked into my soul with angelic compassion. The peaceful strength was back in her voice. "No. It's alright, Sam. My angels told me I would need to tell you. I had just hoped they were wrong ... but they never are."

She took a sip of water and continued.

"Eve remembered what she called the crash of thunder and flash of lightning as they shot at her and Cinnamon. Cinnamon stepped in front of Eve, using her body for a shield. The bullets threw Cinnamon backward against Eve and both of them were knocked into the flood control channel. If the channel hadn't been half-full of water from the rain, the twenty-foot fall onto concrete probably would have killed her.

"She was a strong swimmer and certified in water rescue. She knew Cinnamon was dead, but tried to pull her to the surface, hoping to resuscitate her. Cinnamon was too heavy and the current too strong. Eve lost consciousness and awoke a short time later on the bank, coughing up water."

Her eyes filled with sorrow. "That's what Eve told me, and that is what I believe happened. The police didn't find the weapons and Brandon's father gave them an alibi."

"After that, you couldn't drag her into the water."

We sat in silence for a minute.

"Thank you."

Tanya took my hand. "I'm praying for you and Eve, Sam. God bless you both."

Chapter 50
What If?
Evelyn

By three o'clock, I was tired of the moping and cold shoulders from the kids. Considering the grief Angela and Chris were trying to give me, they obviously weren't too worse for wear, so when Felicity dropped by to see how we were doing, I loaded the kids into the van and we all headed to Golden Gate Park's Academy of Science.

I didn't tell them where we were going until we were on the freeway. The wailing and gnashing of teeth was memorable. Once they settled down, Chris went back to ignoring me, Angela seemed lost in worries about a telephone spat with Daniel, and Grace curled up to block out the world.

In the lobby of the museum, Chris said, "I want to see the fish tank."

"Me too," Angela and Grace echoed simultaneously.

"Alright. Stay together. Felicity and I will catch up," I said.

The three of them charged downstairs to the two-hundred-thousand-gallon Philippines salt-water coral reef. It was my favorite exhibit.

Felicity and I dawdled in the main lobby.

"Chris and Angela are certainly in a mood, aren't they," Felicity said. "And Grace didn't say two words all the way here. Is she okay?"

"They're just reacting to me. I'm trying to stay calm and upbeat, but they know me."

Felicity raised her eyebrows. "No. They're throwing tantrums, like their father."

I half glared at her, because she was right—at least about Chris—and I didn't want to hear it. I turned to look at an exhibit on fossils.

Felicity pretended to be interested in the fossils too.

"Sam talking to you yet?"

I shook my head no. "He picked up Tuesday night when I called from the hospital. I talked to him briefly when he called the kids last night, but other than that, he doesn't answer when I call. Rose talks with him every day and says he sounds alright, but I know him. He's good at pretending everything's fine."

"Did you tell him about the kids?"

"I tried but he didn't want to hear it. Told me to solve it." My heart hardened a little. "Our kids could have died, and he didn't want to hear it." *The jerk.*

"I almost killed them."

Felicity put her arm around my shoulder. "They're fine, and it wasn't your fault. You wouldn't deliberately stick them in a closet full of lighter fluid and close the door. It was an unfortunate accident, but it doesn't matter because they are fine."

"What next? What stupid thing will I do next that they won't survive?"

I sensed Felicity's compassionate impatience.

"Life is life," Felicity said. "There are no guarantees. It's a miracle anyone survives childhood. You should have died twice, and god knows I've done a lot of stupid things that should have killed me.

"The kids are alive. They are healthy. If Sam weren't acting like a child, they would be happy. If you need someone to blame, blame Sam. If he had been understanding and supportive, it never would have happened."

She was right about Sam, but it really wasn't his fault either.

I sighed. "But I still feel guilty."

She smirked and took her arm back. "Maybe you should see a shrink."

I couldn't help smiling and swatted her arm.

"I am."

Felicity's smile faded. "What if he decides not to come back?"

I stared at a happy couple about my age, and leaned against a pillar; its coolness felt good on my back. The idea he wouldn't come back threatened to suffocate me.

"He has to come back. He loves us."

She gently repeated her question. "What if he decides not to come back?"

"We'll divorce," I said, looking up with a quick silent prayer for guidance. "Fight over who gets the kids, visitation, the house, money. The usual."

"Did you take the lawyer's advice?"

"A little. I hated doing it, but I opened new accounts for me and put half our assets into them."

Felicity winced. "But if he hides his half before he files, the judge will make you give him half of your half."

I pouted. "You're my best friend. You're supposed to help."

She hugged me. "Sorry. I thought I was."

I fought back the tears that were trying to slip from my heart.

"This sucks. Everyone is saying I shouldn't trust him. I should look out for myself and the kids. But what hope do we have if we start loading our guns and building walls? What is love, if not trust?"

"You're right. It does suck."

"I should have told him."

"I don't know." Felicity slowly shook her head. "You had good reasons, but it doesn't matter. It's the past. It's not as big a deal as he's making it. He needs to buck up and deal with it."

I knitted my brow and sarcastically said, "Yeah. Just a little deformity. No big thing."

Her frown deepened. "Whose side you on, girl?"

I noticed a group of five high-school-aged boys swaggering by. I tried to picture myself being one of them—strutting like a rooster and looking for chicks to prove my virility. My stomach curdled.

"You okay? You don't look so good," Felicity said.

I closed my eyes and nodded yes. "I'm fine."

The naysayers had said that when I was older, I would regret my decision and realize that I was a man. They had said it was "a stage I was going through," "mental illness," and "devil possession."

That was twenty-two years ago. I was now in my mid-thirties. Like most women, I had experienced subtle discrimination in the workplace and blatant sexual harassment. I had been the victim of an attempted rape in college. I was now looking at the very real and very daunting possibility of becoming a single mom.

Nothing. Not one atom of my being said "It was a mistake." At the core of my heart, I could not find even an infinitesimal scrap of regret. Maybe I should have told Sam, but I didn't regret who I was.

Chapter 51
Pastor BJ
Sam

Dave met me after I said good-bye to Tanya and just happened to mention he was hungry. Since we had a few hours to kill before I met with Pastor Jones, I bought him lunch.

I sipped on coffee and asked him about his family history, Nick, and anything else he happened to remember about Evelyn. He told me about the time his mom caught Nick doing the horizontal mamba with his girlfriend when he was seventeen. He also related a story about Nick's college fraternity days. Part of the initiation was to dress like a woman and sell squares of toilet paper in front of a woman's clothing store.

That was back in '69, when it was still a crime to be gay or to cross-dress in many cities. The memory of the '65 Watts Riots was still fresh in people's minds, and the previous summer had seen the Stonewall Riots in Greenwich Village, where the police raided a gay bar and the drag queens, lesbians, and gays fought back. The police didn't have a sense of humor about Nick's initiation and almost arrested him for public indecency. I figured the story was good for a few good jabs at Nick.

About the time Dave ran out of stories, it was late enough to go see what kind of deal Brandon had to offer.

The church was a modern steel and concrete structure, massive and heavy, with few external architectural embellishments. The grounds were professionally landscaped, the lawn an emerald-green—as opposed to most yards in L.A., where the grass was stressed or browned by the intense sun.

"I hate McChurches," Dave grumbled.

"Mc-what?"

"Places like that," he said, motioning toward the church. "You know. Circus sideshows pretending to be a church, turning God into a fast buck." He blushed a little. "I don't go to church much, but my preacher actually knows me and talks to me. I know he cares about me more than my money."

"Unless you need someone to sit on him while you punch out his lights, I'll wait here."

I declined his help. My research on Brandon revealed that he had a hair-trigger temper, and I didn't want a physical altercation. Two of those incidents had nearly cost him his church. The first occurred during a rally when BJ started cursing a woman who supported her lesbian daughter and then shoved her down the State Capital steps. The second was when he slugged a gay man at a Defense of Marriage march. There were many other unsubstantiated stories, three of them with "no admission of wrong" and "undisclosed settlements" having been offered by Brandon or his church.

I just wanted to get in, find out if he had any real information, and get out.

Brandon stood to greet me, with a Cheshire cat grin. The first thing I noticed was his suit. I'd seen suits like it on the CEOs and big-bucks people at various events in the Bay Area. Dave was right. Doing God's work did pay well … at least for some people. We shook hands. It was a confident, firm shake.

"You must be Pastor Jones."

His smile was warmly insincere. "My father was Pastor Jones. Call me BJ."

The words flowed easy, with an offer of friendship, but showed the affected strain of constant use.

He sneered slightly. "And you are Mr. Irving. The … *partner* … shall we say, of a mutual acquaintance." He motioned toward a chair. "Have a seat, Mr. Irving, and tell me about yourself."

"I'm sure you've been briefed. You probably know more about me than I do."

His gloating smile said he did. "Files never tell the whole story. They only tell a little about what kind of person you are. You go to church regularly, which is good. You do charity work. That says you are a religious person and have compassion. But non-Christians have religious services and do good works for their kind. Are you a true Christian, Mr. Irving? Will you stand up against the gay abomination that eats at our country like a cancer?"

This was so wrong, but I was curious to know what he was willing to pay to make Evelyn's life hell. I held his stare.

"What's the deal?" I asked.

"A Judas," he said, leaning back in his chair. His eyes narrowed. "Thirty pieces of silver."

I had done some research on him, too. He was personally worth an estimated hundred million, so who was he to talk about blood money? I didn't blink.

"And what is that with inflation?"

He cautiously eyed me. "A hundred-thousand consulting fee after you file with our lawyers. Win or lose, when it's over, there will be another hundred-thousand and a well-paid appointee position with some visibility at the state level, where you can become known. In three years, we run you for House or Senate. It's as much up to you as us whether you are elected."

I shook my head no. He was playing games, and I wanted to see where his game would go.

"Even with you covering legal fees, my kids won't be safe in public school. We will need a secure home, maybe security. Most of my business contacts are liberal-leaning, so my business would take a huge hit. If I just divorce her, I don't have those problems."

He seemed mildly pleased. "You understand things, and you're not afraid to go after what you want. You're not indispensable, and I would prefer someone who was doing the Lord's work for the Lord and not the money."

My eyes narrowed. "And you are?"

He was silent for a couple seconds. "I was saying, but you can be of value to us. What would it take, Mr. Irving?"

I hadn't expected that much interest. I didn't have any idea what I was worth to them. I wasn't sure what to ask for.

Since we were playing fantasy games ...

"A ten-year consulting contract at one million a year. If we can work that into a political position or the governorship, we will call it a bonus."

I saw him flinch at my bid.

"Half-a-million and five years," he counteroffered.

I liked making him flinch. I shook my head.

"Doesn't work for me."

He thought for a moment and stood.

"Let's take a walk, Mr. Irving. I don't think you understand all that I'm offering. I would like to show you some things."

We walked toward the main sanctuary.

"Benny called you a realist and a pragmatist," BJ said. "He also said you have moral boundaries—weren't willing to do another man's wife."

His well-practiced manipulation was annoying me.

"Maybe I'm gay."

He stopped and looked at me in a way I didn't understand. It wasn't disgust or revulsion or hate. Just ... odd. He forced a smile and tried to chuckle. "Good one, Mr. Irving."

He quickly resumed walking as if to distance us from some felt, but unseen, specter.

I got some small satisfaction out of tweaking him and couldn't help doing it some more.

"Some churches like mine are open to homosexuality and transsexuals. I assume your church is not."

I didn't know if his frown was one of anger, concern, or an ulcer. His reply was guarded.

"It's a sin. The Bible is quite clear that homosexuals and transsexuals are instruments of Satan and enemies of God. Churches that allow such perversion of our faith are instruments of Satan as well."

"What about people who are intersexed—hermaphrodites?"

He seemed annoyed with the question. "I'm familiar with the lies you have been told—the *science*. The Bible is perfectly clear that when we go against God's laws, He will, in His infinite wisdom, sometimes choose to punish us through our children.

"If you accept our offer, we will brief you on all the facts so you can support your assertion that people like your partner are perverts and pedophiles."

My body tensed and my hands balled up so tight they turned white.

He opened the door to the main sanctuary and motioned me in. I walked down the center aisle and surveyed the massive arena. Except for the camera platforms, stage lighting, and media production room hanging over the sanctuary like a sterile incubator, it seemed like a nice, if somewhat ostentatious, church.

Somber stained glass disciples flanked the sides of the room like massive luminous sentinels, sitting high and out of reach. At the rear was a panoramic scene of Mary holding her son's crucified body. The largest and most impressive window stood above the main altar—Golgotha, with a bloody, tortured crucifixion of Christ, and the two robbers flanking him.

I was studying the crucifixion scene, wondering if I could stand to look at it every Sunday.

"He died for us, Mr. Irving," BJ said. "Truly give your heart to Jesus. He will save you. He will open your eyes to the danger they pose to us."

Open my heart and my eyes to hate? I just stared at the bloody thorns.

"Follow me, Mr. Irving," he said, with eager anticipation.

We strode up to the pulpit, where we turned and faced the auditorium. His eyes glistened and he puffed up his chest with the pride of a new father.

"Three thousand, six hundred seats, Mr. Irving. Every Sunday they are full to overflowing. Here to see me. To hear me. With hundreds of thousands more watching on their televisions or online. Every single one hanging on my every word."

He looked at me with giddy joy. "Imagine them sitting there for you, Mr. Irving. From infant to ancient. Janitors to CEOs. Beautiful women. Handsome men. Young minds needing to be molded into the love of Christ.

"Hundreds of thousands—maybe millions—out there hanging on your every word, Mr. Irving. Every last soul saying, 'We love you, Sam. We believe in you, Sam. We will follow you, Sam.'" He was fidgeting like a kid wanting to open his Christmas presents, but waiting for the okay from his mom. "As a politician, you could have millions of people worshiping you. Wanting you to tell them what they need to do to make our country a better place. Depending on you to lead them in the war against gays."

His nervous excitement began to subside.

"You have the presence, Sam. Charisma. You're believable. People will sympathize with you. They will love you. They will do what you say ... what we say. You can make a difference, and everywhere you go, you will be worshipped."

I looked out at the auditorium. I could see their faces. Caring people, concerned with the myriad of things that concern all of us. Devout people, wanting to understand God and what God expects of us. Loving people who want the best for their families but aren't always sure what "best" is. People looking for understanding, and being told by those in authority—by those they trusted—that God is repression and hate.

In the front row, I imagined Chris in his blue suit and tie, smiling proudly at me. Angela in her burgundy and white Christmas dress, scribbling poems in the margin of the church bulletin. And Grace in her pink chiffon Easter dress, looking around to see what everyone but the minister was doing.

I imagined myself standing here, proclaiming that the transgendered were disciples of the Devil. My stomach tied itself into a knot. I had always thought hate was the disciple of the Devil. I shook my head and started for the door. BJ followed.

"What do you think?" he asked, an almost desperate confusion filling his voice.

"I think half-a-million is too little."

"Okay, Mr. Irving. One million for ten years. You do what we want, and it's yours."

I stopped. I couldn't believe he would agree to that. It was absurd. I was a nobody, with no track record in politics or religion.

I looked at him, bewildered by his offer.

Why?

"You went to high school with Evelyn," I said. "Do you remember her?"

The flash of mortal fear, pursued by hatred, passed through his eyes so quickly that I almost missed them.

I understood.

He was as paranoid of what Eve knew as he was of the transgendered. He feared that someday, somehow, her knowledge of what he had done would cost him dearly. If he used me to smear her, she would lose all credibility, no matter how damning the physical evidence. He would be free.

He was buying security and maybe going to make a buck on the bargain. And he wanted me to be the fool who danced for him.

The auditorium chilled.

He cautiously said, "Yes. I remember *him*. Possessed of the Devil. I prayed for *him*, but he chose to lust after the flesh.

"My understanding is that he seduced you and lied to you by claiming to be a woman. You found out and now you want a divorce, because you aren't gay. Is that correct? Or was your little joke earlier the truth?"

I was getting used to people thinking I was gay, but I would never get used to playing the fool, doing other people's dirty work, or listening to people slander Eve.

"It's *her*, Brandon. Feminine pronoun. And yes, I married *her*."

His face contorted and he stepped back. I wasn't sure if it was disgust, fear, or paranoia, but it pissed me off. I had been looking for something to hit ever since I read the journals. My vision narrowed and it took every ounce of my will to hold back.

He quickly straightened his coat and composed himself.

"Give your heart to Jesus, Mr. Irving. He will cure you of your homosexuality."

Primal instincts trampled my civility and my body shifted in feral anger, preparing to slaughter him. I wasn't gay. I didn't need to be cured of anything. And he had NO right to put Eve down or try to destroy her life. I wrestled with my Neolithic desire to club him. My logic and reason rose through the fog of testosterone and forced the caveman back into the dark side of my brain.

Everything about our meeting had been feverishly absurd. I could never do what he wanted me to do to Eve, my kids … or innocent people. BJ's willingness to throw ten million at me to make Eve's life hell was mind-boggling. But then, his personal insecurity aside, he was a businessman. Like me, he understood his market and the potential return on his investment. With me as his disciple, he would be untouchable and would probably recoup his costs and make an obscene profit off Eve's misery.

I opened my mouth to tell the homophobic ass what I thought of him, when a piece of trivia clicked in the back of my mind and I experienced an epiphany.

I knew. Everything suddenly made sense. The proverbial light came on.

Peace settled over me, and my body uncoiled. I smiled—more of a snicker.

"Tell me, BJ. Have you ever heard about the Adams, Wright, and Lohr study?"

He sneered. "Gay propaganda?"

I shook my head no. "An objective, controlled experiment. They had a group of straight men and a group of self-proclaimed homophobes, like you, watch regular porn, lesbian porn, and gay porn, while they measured the men's sexual response. While watching the regular and lesbian porn, the sexual response of both groups was about equal. But when they watched gay porn, the homophobes were about twice as likely to get turned on."

My smile widened. "With that hard-on you have for homosexuals, I wonder if you aren't another anti-gay preacher with a boyfriend in the wings."

Despite his history of violence, I expected his carefully crafted public image, responsibilities, and the wisdom of age to keep him civil. I was wrong. I deflected his blow and gave a hard jab to his soft belly. He folded. I was elated. I was going to leave it at that—then I saw the gun.

He swung it toward my chest, but I stepped toward him and sideways, so his arm was across my body and the gun beyond me. I grabbed his wrist and twisted his arm down, and then up behind his back. My ears rang from the blast of the gun, and the burn of gunpowder flashed across my arm.

With both of my hands holding his arm, I laid my elbow over his shoulder blades and pushed hard across his back. The pop of his shoulder dislocating, and his scream, echoed through the sanctuary. He dropped the gun and started to collapse but I wasn't done with the ass. With all my strength, I slammed my elbow into the back of his head. His face hit the carpet with a dull thud, and he curled up. I kicked the gun into the pews.

After BJ was taken to the hospital, the police watched the church's security video, while Dave and I sat in handcuffs. I was impressed with the quality of the image. The video was in full color and high definition with sound. They were able to hear every word we had said and zoom in. They knew exactly what had happened.

The lead officer turned to me, chewing the inside of his mouth. He had been professional when he arrived but had eyed me like I was the bad guy. It wasn't surprising given BJ's standing in the community.

"Un-cuff them and then leave us for a few minutes," he said to the other three officers. He pointed to Dave. "Take him with you and turn him loose."

After they left, he said, "I have a problem, Mr. Irving. A practical problem that concerns collateral damage." He paused. He seemed unsure of something. Picking his words carefully he continued. "If someone wanted to make an issue of this little misunderstanding, I would need to recommend certain things to the D.A. that many people would find unacceptable."

I knew what he was saying. If I pushed it, he'd have to charge the good pastor with assault, or even attempted murder, and BJ's congregation, business associates, and political contacts would be pissed.

"But there are other things to consider, Mr. Irving. The newspapers would have a field day with you and your wife. You and she would be very unpopular in certain circles. And there are a lot of crazies out there."

His words were either a well-masked threat, or experience giving a warning to the wise. I wasn't sure which. I nodded.

"The taxpayers will spend tens of thousands to try Mr. Jones. Mr. Jones will spend a million in lawyer fees and a public relations campaign. In the end, he will walk and you will be the bad guy."

I nodded again. "Yes."

"So, Mr. Irving. What did you say happened?"

I looked at him for a minute, thinking of my options. I wanted to see his ass burn for what he had done to Eve, Cinnamon, and Zack. But the rich and the powerful were, all too often, above the law. And if I made an issue about our "little misunderstanding," the press would out Eve and make life hell for my kids. BJ held most of the cards, and if I stood up to him, I would be hurting my family for nothing.

"I didn't actually see it, but I think he tripped coming down the aisle, and that when he fell, his gun accidently went off."

The officer grinned and nodded. "That would be consistent with the physical evidence. If Mr. Jones confirms your version of the incident, I think we can put this behind us."

He squinted and added, "Off the record and just out of curiosity, what did he offer you ten million to do?"

"Be like him."

He nodded.

I said, "Off the record and just out of curiosity, where'd the bullet go?"

He smirked. "Through the back wall and into the foyer. Lodged in a portrait of the pastor." He tapped right between his eyes.

Dave had been shaking and sweating the whole time we were inside watching the surveillance video. I had expected him to take off and leave me to my own resources, but he was still there, licking out the potato chip bag from the other day.

Dave's voice was a little shaky. "No bloody nose or black eye?

What happened?"

"We talked about what the smart thing to do was."

"Oh?"

"Pretend it never happened."

Dave scowled. "But he tried to kill you."

I smiled to myself. "I have a sore elbow. He has a dislocated shoulder, a concussion, and a broken nose. All things considered, that will have to do."

"That really stressed me. I get hungry when I'm stressed. How 'bout we go eat?"

"Sure. The hotel? Their free breakfast isn't too bad, and they're supposed to have a nice restaurant."

He grimaced. "Wrong. They give you fancy linen napkins, crystal glasses, and snooty waiters with stupid looking aprons to make it look fancy, but the food sucks and they don't give you enough to feed a baby bird. There's a great ribs place a mile away. Lots of food, real ambulance, and reasonable."

Ambulance? "Do you mean ambiance?" I asked.

He frowned. "That's what I said."

Chapter 52
Mack's BBQ
Sam

Dave drove us to an industrial area that reminded me of Felicity's art studio in Richmond, with its rusty tin buildings covered in ancient grime and decorated with chain link and barbed wire. The air was sullen with the smells of heavy industry: diesel exhaust, oils, solvents, hot rubber, and overworked electric motors.

Dave pulled into a crowded parking lot on the largely deserted street.

"I used to work down the street at a machine shop," he said. "Don't get here very often anymore."

Most of the businesses on the street looked closed, so I was surprised at the number of cars.

"Looks popular."

"Yeah," Dave said. "They have a line out the door for lunch pickup every day."

The sun-bleached sign above the front window read, *Mack's BBQ*. When Dave opened the door, an old bell-on-a-spring chimed our arrival, and the heavy smell of barbequed ribs almost pushed us back out the door. I noticed the concrete showing through the black and white linoleum floor tile just inside the door. With the grimy neighborhood and worn-out floor, I looked around expecting to see fifty years of cooking grease and dust hanging on everything. I was pleasantly surprised that the place was clean, even if well-worn.

Every fixture, stick of furniture, glass, plate, and decoration looked like a well-used refugee from the fifties. Even worn, the furnishings and decorations had to be worth a fair chunk of change to collectors.

Dave nudged me and motioned to a jukebox at the end of the lunch counter. "It's a real, honest-to-god, 1940 Wurlitzer.

Plays vinyl. Mack's pride and joy."

"David," a woman said, the melodious joy in her voice saying, "I'm glad to see you. Welcome back."

"Maureen. How you doing?" Dave asked.

They hugged. She looked to be in her mid-forties, was close to six feet tall, and slender. With her fine features, rich blond hair, and perfect proportions, she had one of those bodies that could light the fire of just about any man.

They exchanged small talk for a minute, while I plugged my quarter into the Wurlitzer and picked *The Tennessee Waltz* by Patti Page from the limited selection of forties and fifties music.

The red-and-white-checked laminate tables were worn through the pattern where people sat, but the table and the silverware were spotless.

"What can I get for you two?" Maureen asked, leaning on the table and smiling warmly.

"The dinner rib special for both of us," Dave said.

"It's really nice to see you," she said, patting Dave's hand. "You need to drop in more often. Let me catch up on what's happening with you."

Dave blushed a little and nodded yes. She scurried off to fill drinks and clear tables.

"Mack and Maureen have been running this place for forty-five years," Dave said. "Quite a couple. He's a short, ugly Pollock and she's a tall, beautiful Swede. They're going to retire soon, close the place down." He looked like he was going to cry. "No more great ribs."

I looked at Maureen pouring coffee. "How old is she?"

He scrunched up his face and mumbled, "forty-six is four less than … plus ten," then opened his eyes.

"About sixty four." He grinned. "Bet you hope Eve looks half as good at that age."

I ignored his comment.

"No kids to take over the business?"

"Nope. Never had children. Doctor said she couldn't when she was a kid, but she didn't really know why until a couple years ago. Had some kind of cancer. The doctor said she had some symptom. Android sensitivity, I think."

"Androgen insensitivity syndrome?"

"Yeah. That's it. Android-gin." He frowned. "What is it?"

It was a genetic disorder where the cells of the developing male fetus were unable to respond properly to the hormones which control male characteristics. In the most extreme cases, the "boy" had the physical appearance of a girl. She might be able to function sexually as a woman, but because she had XY chromosomes, she was infertile.

"A genetic abnormality." I looked over at her. What were the odds? Only something like ten thousand women in America had the disorder.

Dave nodded, not seeming to have any real comprehension. A smile blossomed, and he looked like a child on Christmas morning.

"I talked Maureen into giving me the barbeque sauce recipe. It came out good, but not like Mack's. She laughed when I told her theirs was a lot better. She said it's not just the recipe. It's the whole process and the six hours of slow cooking.

"Ain't no way a piece of meat would last six hours in front of me." He looked over at her. "I wish they'd franchise. People keep telling them they should. The guy who owns the metal supply a couple doors over even offered to help them. Mack says they don't want the hassle, but Mack never got past sixth grade and Maureen never went to college. I think all the legal stuff scares them."

I winced. "I can understand that. I went to college, and legal stuff scares me."

The restaurant was beginning to thin out by the time our ribs arrived. The plates were piled high with enough meat to feed a small country. Dave's eyes glistened and drool formed in the corner of his mouth.

Maureen smiled with the joy of a mom giving her five-year-old a birthday cake.

"You two lucked out. It was slow tonight, so we have a lot left over. Normally we'd use it for tomorrow's barbeque burgers but there's way too much. Enjoy."

I couldn't eat more than a fourth. "You want some of mine? It won't keep at the hotel."

Dave's little boy smile glowed. I shoveled most of the ribs onto his plate, and watched him stuff himself like he hadn't eaten in weeks.

"I'm sure gonna miss you, Sam. Haven't eaten this good in years," he said through a mishmash of sauce and meat.

I had decided to drive home instead of fly, so after dinner, Dave dropped me at the rental car company. One last stop at a graveyard in the morning and then I'd be on the road.

Chapter 53
Cinnamon's Dad
Sam

The morning paper had a small article about BJ falling off a ladder while trying to hang a banner for their latest fundraiser to defend family values. He had apparently taken the deal.

I had thought about canceling the meeting with Kelly Bandeau, Sr., Cinnamon's father, since there wasn't any point in our meeting. Evelyn was a good person, and the secrets she kept and lies she told were out of fear. I could readily understand and sympathize with her secrecy. Still, she should have told me.

I had accepted that my desire to cut Evelyn out of my children's lives was selfish and wrong. My only interest in Cinnamon was to understand a little more about the Evelyn she was before the murders, nightmares, fear, and lies. I wasn't sure Cinnamon's dad could enlighten me much, because he had objected to his son's transgenderism, but I had committed to the meeting. My only hesitation was his insistence that we meet at sunrise at his son's grave. It seemed odd—if not downright freaky.

Sunrise was at 6:23. I decided to get there early.

I parked behind a late-model Toyota, the only other car in the cemetery. About fifty yards away, a man with his side to me stood staring down at a marker, about where Kelly had told me Cinnamon was buried. The sun was close to rising, and I was looking straight into it. I stepped out of my car. Without looking in my direction, he held his arm straight out toward me with his hand up. I leaned against the car, squinting into the light, and waited. The smell of moldy, mowed grass and dying bouquets drifted heavy on the still air. The sun crept over a mountain to the east, the beams of brilliant white dropping down with silent warmth and all but blinding me. He stood there, seeming to pray for about five minutes, before turning and walking to me.

His thinning hair was the same cinnamon color as his son's, and his medium height and stocky build carried an aura of tenacious power a smart man would be well advised to avoid tangling with. He walked like a man with authority and purpose.

"Samuel Edward Irving," he said, in a monotone.

I frowned. "Uh, yes."

He stood so he blocked the sun shining in my face and held my stare with fixed intensity. Like an old, bad detective movie, he said, "Married Evelyn Strand in 2000. You have three children, Christian, Angela, and Grace. Your wife was a friend of my son." He frowned slightly. "You're looking into your wife's past, and she's not here. You've been married ten years, so I assume you want a divorce. California is a no-fault state. What do you want with me, Mr. Irving?"

It was obvious he had spent some time digging into my past. That, on top of his wanting to meet me at the cemetery, made me very uncomfortable. He must have sensed my uneasiness.

"I'm a detective with the L.A.P.D." He showed me his badge. "When someone I don't know calls me and wants to meet, I find out who they are and we meet on my turf."

I looked around puzzled. "Your turf?"

Kelly said, "We're clear, Eagle Eye," then pulled a small electronic box out of his pocket and switched it off.

A man in camouflage fatigues with a sniper rifle stepped out from behind a mausoleum about fifty yards behind Kelly, and a second man dressed the same, with an assault rifle, came out from behind a moss-trimmed family crypt to my right. They headed for the front gate.

"What did you want, Mr. Irving?"

I nodded toward the two men. "Isn't that a little paranoid?"

He turned his head slightly and lifted the hair above his ear. I could see an ugly scar about four inches long. "I pissed off some well-connected drug dealers a few years back. They gave me this. There's still a slug fragment in my head. Word is, they want to give me another one." He let his hair drop. "You were saying."

"You're right about the divorce. The reason I'm here is child custody." He nodded. "I wanted to meet you to get dirt on

Evelyn, but there isn't any." He nodded again, his stone look softening slightly. "Now I'm just looking to understand."

He studied me for a second. "You didn't know?"

I shook my head no.

He dropped the tension from his body and took a softer stance as he thought. After a few moments of silence, he said, "I was a child in the sixties, but I remember watching the Birmingham civil rights march, where black women my mom's age were thrown over cars from the impact of water from the fire hoses. I remember the police dogs attacking children. I remember the Watts Riots, with the burning and looting.

"My dad was a racist. He said they were animals and we should just shoot them. I was young enough to want to believe him and old enough to understand they just wanted what was fair. I understood they were people like me, regardless of skin color."

He looked over at the grave.

"You ever do wrong by your kids, Mr. Irving?"

I had no doubt he already knew the answer.

"Yes."

He looked back at me. "After the riots and segregation ended, most people accepted that skin color didn't define a person. But my dad didn't understand. He couldn't get past his blind hate and the lies he was raised with. He died a racist.

"To him, they were subhuman, and he was too stubborn to hear the truth. I never understood how he could be so blind, until after my son was murdered.

"When Kelly's mother found makeup or girl's clothes in his room, I would make him put them on so that he looked like a boy in a dress, then take him to the mall. I'd follow him around while people laughed and stared. But it didn't stop him. So I burned his things, grounded him, made him work out so he looked more like a man, pinned up Playboy centerfolds in his room, and gave him a crew cut every two weeks."

He looked down for a few seconds in thought, and then back up at me. "It had been a few years since we had found any girl's clothes or makeup. I thought we had cured him. Thought I'd turned him into a man. One day, I responded to a knife fight at his school. I saw him. Miniskirt, fishnet hose, fake boobs, wig, and makeup. He was huddled with a group of girls, playing drama queen. If I hadn't known it was my son, I would have thought he was just another stupid teenage girl, doing all the wrong things to impress stupid boys."

He shook his head and half smiled, his voice taking on a friendly rhythm and tone. "Your wife was taking his things to school for him. He'd dress before school and change back before he came home. He'd been doing it for years right under my nose. The great Detective Bandeau didn't have a clue."

His smile faded to grief. He stared at the ground. "I gave up on Kelly that day. I accepted that I had a gay son and that I was powerless to do anything about it. A month later, he nearly died from illegal progesterone use. I stopped caring and disowned him. The only reason he still lived in my house was because my wife wouldn't let me kick him out … and it would have hurt my promotion possibilities.

"For two years he avoided me and I avoided him. He tried to tell me he wasn't gay, that he was a transsexual, like Eve. I didn't want to hear it. I knew what he was. He was a sick, perverted little queer, and no one on earth was going to tell me different. Especially not him."

He looked over and watched a black SUV drive slowly through the cemetery. His hand slipped inside his coat. I shifted to the side so that if bullets started flying, I would be somewhat out of the line of fire and able to use the car for a shield. After the SUV wound out of sight, he relaxed and turned his attention back to me.

His brows furrowed, old and deep. "And then he was gone. Dead.

"I thought I didn't care, but I was wrong. With him gone, I didn't have anything to prove anymore. No righteous indignation to defend. No more 'I'm right—You're wrong.' No more disappointment because he wasn't the person I wanted him to be.

"I let go of the anger and expectations. I saw him differently—as a real person separate from me—the good and the bad. I also saw myself differently—the good and the bad.

"My dad was a racist. I was a homophobe. Same thing. Blind hate and stubborn refusal to accept reality."

He looked back at the grave. "My son would have been thirty-three at sunrise today. He deserved a better father and the chance to live his life with no apologies for who he was."

His stare hardened and his voice became rigid and monotone. "Is there anything else, Mr. Irving?"

"Why did you tell me all that?"

His stare softened as his eyes moistened. His voice broke a little. "Fair question. At one point, Evelyn's stepfather tried to talk me into letting Kelly be Cinnamon. At the time, I knew with every fiber of my body that they had made a mistake allowing Evelyn to become a girl. I threatened to sue them if they so much as talked to Kelly.

"When I was doing a background on you, I ran one on your wife. She's lived her life making no apologies for who she is. I wished I had listened to her stepdad. Kelly had greatness in him, like your wife."

He pursed his lips and shrugged. "Regrets. The older you get, the more you have." He glanced at his watch then looked at me with his hard, penetrating eyes. "I hear you had a little disagreement with Mr. Jones."

I guess I shouldn't have been surprised he knew. Being understandably paranoid, he probably had someone following me. I shrugged. "We met. He tripped."

His lip curled into a smile. "Yeah. I saw the video of him *tripping*." His smile faded, replaced by hate. "The gun belonged to the senior Mr. Jones and was supposedly lost sixteen years ago. Ballistics say it was the gun that killed my son."

I was both happy to hear it and terrified. If it went to trial, Evelyn would be called as a witness and the papers would out her. He saw my concern. "It won't go to trial, Mr. Irving. Mr. Jones will claim it was part of his father's estate and that he has no knowledge of its use or whereabouts before he inherited it. It will be his word against Evelyn's. We both know where that will go."

He had a look that made me uneasy. "I've always known it was him, but now I really know."

He glanced back at his watch again. "I need to get to work. But before you go, you might want to spend a moment and pay respects to my daughter."

I wasn't sure I had heard him right but I wasn't going to ask for clarification.

"Thank you for meeting with me," I said.

He pulled a DVD out of his pocket and handed it to me. "A souvenir."

It didn't have a label and before I could ask what was on it, he was getting into his car. I slipped it in my jacket pocket and watched him drive off before going out to the grave marker.

"Kelly Cinnamon Bandeau. 1977–1994. Beloved daughter."

Chapter 54
Chowchilla
Sam

Since flying down to L.A., I had been thinking a lot about Clora. Love at first sight in the eighth grade. We broke up once in high school but were back together within forty-eight hours. She had been my world, and I had never questioned that we would grow old together.

Worn down by taking care of two young kids, her friend had offered her something to help. At first, I had no idea where all her energy came from, but the house was spotless and she was a tiger in bed again, so I didn't much care.

Then checks started bouncing and the credit cards maxed out. She claimed she didn't know how, even though she had signed everything. By then, even I knew something was wrong. The house had gone from spotless to a garbage dump, and the kids were always dirty and hungry when I got home. Then she admitted she was hooked on meth. We got professional help but she couldn't stay with the program.

The kids started getting more bruises than usual, and when I asked about them, she would say they fell or ran into a wall. I'd seen them fall and hit walls a lot, just like our friends' toddlers. But these bruises were ... different. Worse.

Looking down, I noticed my hands were turning white from choking the steering wheel and my speed had crept up to eighty-four. I let off on the gas and slowed to a more acceptable ten over the limit, like everyone else.

Hoping it would help take my mind off the pile of shit my life had become, I concentrated on the scenery of California's Central Valley.

Not much help. The haze from field burning shrouded the far-off hills and the valley looked as desolate as my life. Brown everywhere. The flat and rolling earth was brown. The sage and tumbleweeds were brown. Even many of the irrigated fields and orchards were covered in the ash and dust that filled the smoke-laden sky, making them appear brown from a distance.

I had told myself that driving home would give me a chance to think things through, but I knew the real reason: the Central California Women's Facility in Chowchilla.

When they took Clora away after she pleaded no-contest to manufacturing and trafficking, I was done with her. I didn't even know which prison she was sent to until I needed her to sign documents allowing Evelyn to adopt our kids.

I wasn't sure why I wanted to see her. What would I say?

I hit the steering wheel. "Shit, shit, shit. It's not fair. I try so damn hard. I think I have it perfect, and God just kicks me in the balls. Twice.

"I'll never trust a god-damned woman again."

I watched the guard bring Clora out. Except for the scars on her face from picking imaginary shards of glass and bugs from under her skin when she had been on meth, she hadn't changed much. Her hair was cut short, she'd put on some extra weight, and she looked a little older, but I guess I did too.

I hadn't expected to see fear in her eyes.

"Are the kids alright?" she asked.

"Um. Yeah. Of course. Why wouldn't they be?"

I realized why she had asked. Before the journals, the death of one of our children was the only thing in the world that could have dragged me here and she knew it.

She shuddered and relaxed a little. "No reason. So why are you here?"

A strong current of anger ran below her words, but that was to be expected after the way I had cut her off from the kids. She had tried to write, and I had sent her letters back unopened. She got the message.

I shrugged. "Don't know. Just been thinking about you. Was driving by and decided to see how you were doing."

Skeptical anger flared in her eyes. "*Just* driving by?"

As innocently as I could, I said, "Yeah. I was down in L.A., heading home, and thought that since I was close ..."

She nodded, obviously not buying it, since Chowchilla is about as "close" to anything as the moon. She let the anger go. "How are Chris, Angela, and Grace?"

Grace? Her question caught me off guard. I didn't think she knew about Grace, but of course. Her mom talked to the kids on the phone every birthday and holiday. She visited us every Christmas and would have told Clora about Grace long ago.

My eyes teared. "They're all doing great."

Clora leaned back in her chair and studied me, just like she used to. "I haven't seen or heard from you in thirteen years, and you just drop in for a chat? Why are you here, Sam?"

I shook my head and shifted in my chair. "Don't know."

We just watched each other for a minute without a word, each lost in our own thoughts and regrets.

"Do you still love me?" she asked.

Her question surprised me. What surprised me more was that I didn't have an answer. I thought I hated her. I certainly hated the druggy she had been. But seeing the lost hopelessness in what had once been endlessly hopeful eyes stirred something inside. Love? Pity? Compassion? My old reflex of wanting to protect her?

I wanted to roll back time and stop her from taking the first pill. I wanted to have never met Eve. I sat staring at her, unable to answer.

Her mask slipped away, and I saw the Clora I had once loved. "What's wrong, Sam?"

I shook my head and sat up straight. Put my mask on.

"Nothing."

Her eyes hardened, and she shook her head with complete assurance.

"We were soul mates, Sam. If I hadn't messed up so bad ..." She swallowed hard. "You're hurting. Almost as bad as when they led me out of the courtroom and out of your life forever. Are you leaving Evelyn?"

I nodded yes.

She sighed. "Do you still love her?"

Why did everyone keep asking me that stupid question?

"What difference does it make?"

"Mom said Eve is a lot like me. Is she?"

I looked away. I had never thought about it. *Is she? Does it matter?*

"A little, I guess."

An old and distant pain echoed in the shadow of Clora's voice. "Mom said Eve is a great mother. Is she?"

I half smiled, nodded, and avoided eye contact.

"Yes. She is."

Clora's eyes were red and moist.

She whispered, "Good. They deserve better than me."

I didn't know how to respond. They deserved better than a drug-crazed woman, but she had been a good mom before …

She shivered. "If there was any chance of my ever getting out, I would celebrate the prospect of your divorce. I would dream of fixing everything and making you love me again. I would dream of getting my children back. But I know they won't let me go until long after it is too late. After they are lost to me."

"But you'll get out on parole."

Her chuckle was filled with ironic defeat. "No, Sam. I was sleeping off a high in the bedroom when Randy killed the cop in the garage. They had me for an easy manufacturing and trafficking conviction, but Randy was dead and they wanted someone to parade in front of the public. The district attorney wanted to charge me with accessory to murder. The charge was so absurd that the grand jury wouldn't buy it. But the label cop-killer stuck. The system thinks I got off on a technicality. The parole board will be real slow to let me out."

She had hurt our kids and run off with another man, abandoning her family. By the time they arrested her, I had disowned her and filed for divorce. I knew little more about what had happened than what was reported in the papers. The only reason I went to the sentencing hearing was to know she was out of my life for good.

"When you went to trial, you didn't fight the charges. Why not?"

She was looking down and it was hard to understand her. "I got clean enough in jail to realize what I had done to you and the kids. I hated myself for it." She looked up. Her lip trembled and she wrapped her arms around herself for warmth. She looked me straight in the eyes. "Still do." The infinite pain in her words and the self-hate in her eyes chilled me.

She continued. "With a no-contest deal, they dropped the other two dozen BS charges. A cop was dead. If I fought it, the trial would have been a media circus and I would have been convicted anyway. No trial, no circus. I had put you and our children through too much already."

When she went to jail, the press had made her sound like a murderous drug lord, when in reality she had been a lost soul, shacking up with a man to feed her addiction.

I knew that she had been a great person, but the drugs had screwed her up. I knew that if she had gone into rehab and had been able to stick with it, she could have been a great person again.

But I hadn't cared when the media turned her into a bad stereotype, stripped of her humanity. She had become a face to hate and loathe. All the wonderful things she had been and could have been again, with a little help, had been trampled beneath the ink and pixels that run our lives.

I wasn't sure I agreed with her decision not to fight it, but it was a little late to debate it. I didn't know what else to say so I told her about Chris's diving, Grace's involvement in children's theater, and Angela's poetry.

Our time was almost up.

"Sam. I don't know why you want to divorce Evelyn and it certainly isn't my business. But they lost one mother already. Do you want them to lose a second one?"

It wasn't her business. "It's not that simple."

She took a long deep breath and studied me.

"I know. My no-contest wasn't simple. It had far-reaching implications that I didn't realize. Do our—" she choked and tears filled her eyes. She sniffled. "Do *your* children a favor Sam. Take your time. Make sure you know what this will do to them before you walk out the door like I did.

"I know you would give your life for your children. So what is a little of your time?"

I could see Evelyn's van in the driveway and pulled to the curb down the street from our house. It was almost eleven p.m. When she was in Bodega, she had threatened to make my life hell and I knew she was more than capable. I also knew she had more than enough reason to hate me after my "Adam" comments, and after me telling her to pack up and leave. I hoped that she would have cooled off by now and be more understanding than I had been.

I still didn't see any way to save the relationship, but I needed time to think things through and see how reasonable she would be about custody. I called the home phone. Evelyn picked up on the first ring.

"I'm down the street. Should I find a hotel or come home?"

A chill filled the silence. After a few moments, she said, "Did you prove I killed Cinnamon and Zach? Or was the trip to prove

I'm some type of pervert and unfit to be a mother."

"I'm sorry."

Her tone was flippant. "Sorry you went or sorry you didn't find anything?"

"Neither. I'll find a hotel."

"Wait, wait. What do you mean *neither*?"

I wasn't sure what I meant or how to put it into words. I wasn't sorry I had gone. I had found a wonderful extended family who loved her and had spent the last sixteen years praying for her safety. I had found why she woke screaming at night. I had found why she panicked and nearly beat me senseless when I tried to throw her in the ocean. I had found why she loved mermaids and dolphins.

"Don't know. Guess I'm glad I found a lot of things I wasn't looking for."

What I didn't find was a reason for her not to tell me. Maybe not on the first date, but certainly after I had proposed. I couldn't say whether I would or wouldn't have married her. I was never given that chance. But I had a right to know.

I could hear hope. "Then everything is alright?"

"No."

Her slow exhale was filled with sadness, and I could hear the tears in her heart.

"The kids miss you. We need to be civil in front of them. If you can do that, come home. If not …"

"I'll sleep on the couch."

Her voice was shaking. "Is that necessary?"

"I'm sorry."

Chapter 55
A House Divided
Evelyn

I lay awake in the bedroom listening to Sam's light snoring while staring at the clock. Sam had been civil last night when he got home, and the hostility I had seen in his eyes at my dad's house had burned down to smoldering embers of resentment. At least he was home. At least we could talk.

The kids weren't expecting Sam for two more days and would be thrilled he was home. I knew I would be the bad guy because he had left. But that was alright. We were a whole family again—at least for a while.

I could hear Chris in his room playing on his computer. Both the girls were probably still asleep. I forced myself out from under the warmth of Mom's comforter, like I had every morning since Sam had read the journals. The edge of Angela's bed sagged as I sat. She peeked up, glared, and then rolled over. I leaned down and kissed her cheek. She pulled her blanket up to cover her face.

I whispered, "I need you to do me a favor, sweetheart." She didn't move. "I need you to very, very quietly go get Grace up, then go get Chris, and then go say good morning to your father."

Her blanket slapped my face as she threw it off and great hope shined in her eyes.

"For real?"

I smiled and nodded. "For real."

She muffled her squeal, jumped out of bed, and scurried to her sister's room. I went to the kitchen, where I could start the coffee and watch without being in Sam's space.

In less than a minute, I heard them thunder down the hall to my room. Seconds later, they stampeded into the family room. Sam had always been a heavy sleeper and didn't see—or hear—

them coming. Grace landed squarely on his chest. He jerked awake, his attempt to sit up thwarted by her. She gave him a big hug and kiss.

Angela dropped down beside the couch and hugged her dad and Grace. Chris hovered over them. I could see the little boy who wanted to express his joy with complete abandon, wrestling with the young man who was yielding to society's expectation of emotional restraint. Sam reached up and pulled Chris down into a group hug.

By the time breakfast was finished, the friction between Sam and me had evaporated the kids' initial joy at their dad being home. Angela had become moody. Chris was banging everything around. And Grace had withdrawn completely again.

Angela and Grace had been scheduled to spend the day working on a Girl Scout quilting project and hanging with friends. Since their dad was home, I had expected them to cancel.

"But Mom," Angela said. "If we don't go, we won't get our quilting badges."

I knew they had already qualified for their badges and that they were trying to escape the arctic winter that had descended on our house. I wished I could join them.

"Okay. Get your things."

While we were getting into the van, Chris came out and asked to be dropped at Bobby's so they could practice pitching.

When I got back, Sam was standing in the middle of the garage looking around.

I asked, "What are you doing?"

"Nothing," he said, turning to go back into the house. I realized he had been figuring out what he would take and what he would leave.

"We need to talk," I said.

"Yes. We do." His words were cold and ominous.

I followed him into the family room, and we sat on opposite sides.

Sam said, "I want out, but the kids …"

I had told myself he would come around, would adjust. That I could deal with it if he decided he wanted a divorce, but time stopped.

He wants out? He doesn't love me?

My shattered heart hardened against him. He didn't want me

because I had been born wrong. I could make excuses for the ignorant and stupid, but not Sam. He had been my husband for ten years. He knew me better than anyone. He was well-educated in the realities of being transgendered. He knew I was a woman and always had been.

I needed to hear him say it and mean it. I asked, "Don't you love me?"

He looked away. "No."

"Oh." I knew it was a lie, but he wanted to believe it. I shuddered to shake off the hurt.

His voice was pained but resigned. "We need to figure out what to do with the kids."

I had been going to tell him about the kids finding the journals, but it wasn't important anymore. I slowly nodded as I stared blankly at a stain on the rug and struggled to listen to him.

"Angela and Grace probably need to be with you for now," he continued. "Chris is old enough to be with me. I'll try to find someplace close so they can visit each other after school and on weekends if they want."

It sounded reasonable, if you could call one of your worst nightmares reasonable. I looked up at him. His mouth tightened at the sight of my tears.

"I'm sorry, Sam. I didn't mean to lie. You have to know that by now."

He trembled, tried to say something, and then looked away. After a few seconds, he said, "It doesn't matter. It's over. We need to do what is best for the kids."

"But why? Why is it over? Couples work through far worse than—"

His glare stopped me in mid-sentence. I didn't want to cry in front of him, so I hurried to my room and slammed the door behind me.

Chapter 56
The DVD
Evelyn

I was glad it was Monday. It had been a cold weekend in the Irving home. Sam had spent most of it cleaning the garage and doing yard work, so he could avoid me. To escape the subzero chill and vastness that separated Sam and me, the kids had hung out at friends' houses or had hidden in their rooms.

I saw no point in telling Sam about the visit to the hospital, and the kids wisely didn't mention what had happened either. Since I paid the bills, Sam would never see the medical statements.

I started laundry after Sam had left for work and the kids were at school. I dumped Sam's bag into the basket and headed for the laundry room. On the way through the family room, I grabbed Sam's jacket and the bedding he had been using.

With three children and a husband who didn't always empty their pockets, I always took time to go through the clothes. Sometimes I got lucky and came up with money, which went into a college fund jar. But most of the time, the pockets contained used tissue, old homework, store receipts, and to-do lists.

I pulled a DVD out of Sam's jacket. No label. He'd taken his laptop, but he always kept the disks in the computer bag. I was curious, so once I got the white load going, I headed for the office.

The DVD's directory listed a single movie; I clicked on it. I stared at the monitor, my mind momentarily unable to make sense of what I saw. Sam and Brandon were standing in the aisle of a church. "You went to high school with Evelyn. Do you remember her?"

Brandon kept referring to me as a boy. He said I was possessed, that I had seduced and lied to Sam, and that Sam wanted out because he wasn't gay.

"It's *her* Brandon. Feminine pronoun. And yes, I married her."

How did Sam get this? Why does he have it?

I laughed when Brandon said Sam needed to give his heart to Jesus and be cured of his homosexuality.

I was surprised that Sam was so versed in the Adams, Wright, and Lohr study. He must have been paying more attention to my ramblings than I'd thought.

When Sam said, "With that hard-on you have for homosexuals, I wonder if you aren't another anti-gay preacher with a boyfriend in the wings," I cheered, but my joy was short-lived. Brandon tried to hit Sam and then pulled a gun. I saw a muzzle flash and my heart stopped. Before I knew what had happened, Brandon was on the ground with Sam standing over him, rubbing his elbow.

I replayed it two more times, then in slow motion, then regular speed again, then frame by frame, then regular speed again.

Why didn't Sam tell me?

The phone rang. Caller ID said it was Dad. I was still mad at him, but trying to act like an adult, so I answered it.

"Hi, Eve. How is everything?"

I couldn't help myself. "If it was anyone but you, I'd say fine. But since it's your fault, lousy."

"I'm sorry, Eve. If I could fix it, I would. I expected Sam to be more reasonable when he got back, especially after—"

He stopped talking, like he had said something he shouldn't have. My voice was cold and demanding. "After what?"

His voice was hesitant. "After he found out why you kept it a secret."

I frowned in puzzlement. "Dad. Lies have brought me nothing but pain. Please don't start lying to me."

"I'm sorry, Eve. There was a little run-in down in L.A. Nothing serious."

Dad knew about Brandon. My voice was colder than an ice bath in an igloo. "You wouldn't be talking about the little-run-in-that's-nothing-serious when Brandon tried to kill Sam like he killed Cinnamon and Zack?"

Dad was so quiet, I thought the call had dropped for a second. I heard him barely breathing, so I waited for him to say something.

"Sam told you?"

"No." I wasn't going to tell him how I found out. I wanted him to sweat.

"Who did?"

My voice was sharp and angry. "No one."

He knew I was being difficult. When I was a teen, he would send me to my room when I was this unreasonable and intractable. He couldn't do that now. *Ha ha.*

He sighed. "I'm sorry, Eve. I really am. You already have too much going on. Sam's fine and Brandon took the worst of it. I didn't want to worry you."

I appreciated his concern. My guilt at being the south end of a northbound mule was beginning to nag at my conscience.

"Sorry, Dad. Sam had a DVD in his jacket when he came back. It had video footage showing the whole thing."

"Really?"

"Yeah. Really," I said, with the sarcasm and maturity of a fourteen-year-old prima donna.

"Sorry. I wasn't questioning you. I was just surprised. How'd he get it?"

I pulled in my claws. "Don't have a clue."

I stared at the screen. I had paused it at the point where Sam said, "I married *her*." He had stood up for me. He had called Brandon a hypocrite. He had gone to L.A. and beat up the man who had tried to kill me and taken the lives of two people I loved. He was my prince. Maybe we still had a chance.

"Mind if I come over and see?" Dad asked.

"Sure. And bring that footlocker in your closet. Since I'm out of the closet, it might as well be, too."

Chapter 57
Down Too Long
Evelyn

It had been three weeks since Sam had returned. He was still sleeping on the couch, and no matter how accommodating I was, he remained cold and distant, while refusing to talk.

We had, with detached and logical civility, decided custody and how to split our assets. So far, the lawyer's warning of disappearing bank accounts and a refinance on the house hadn't materialized.

We hadn't made an official announcement to the kids, but they were smart; they knew. Struggling with their fears and the uncertainty, their grades had begun slipping as all their energy went into being clingy and difficult.

To acclimate our kids to the pending division of our family, I was spending more time with the girls and Sam was spending more time with Chris. Early this morning, Sam had taken Chris abalone diving.

It would be Chris's eighth dive and he was now staying down nearly as long as his dad. They had moved to the deeper places, where they always found abalone over eight inches. My dad had been consulting in Eureka and would join them at their dive spot.

While they were abalone diving, the girls and I went to Chinatown in San Francisco to play tourist. We stood at the Dragon Gate, ready to start our day of exploration, when my cell phone rang with Dad's ringtone. They were supposed to be diving and if the dive had been called off, Sam would be calling.

"What's wrong?"

"Everyone's fine," Dad said.

Those dreaded words stopped my breathing. All the city squawking was gone and my attention was solidly on my dad's voice. "Chris blacked out. He started breathing again the second Sam got him to the surface. He was fine, but we called the Coast Guard to be sure. They airlifted him and Sam to Santa Rosa Memorial Hospital. You should head up there. I'm loading the gear and will meet you."

I'm sure he could smell my fear.

He added, "He really is fine, Eve. The airlift was just a precaution."

I said "Thanks" and hung up.

I had expected sharks. I had expected waves smashing them against rocks. I hadn't expected shallow water blackout. Blackout was caused when a diver hyperventilated, causing the normal "breathe, dummy" reflex to be short-circuited. Instead of burning lungs to tell the diver he was out of air, the brain ran out of oxygen and the diver would go to sleep. If he was alone or had an inattentive buddy, he would drown. Even when rescue and resuscitation was immediate, the lack of oxygen to the brain could cause permanent damage in only a few minutes.

I stuffed down the fear and anger. I had to get to my son. He needed me.

I was directed to an exam room, but stopped outside the door when I heard Chris say something about his "mom."

"The answer is no," Sam said.

"It's not fair. Angela and I want to see our mom."

"No. A prison is no place for children."

The anger and frustration was strong in Chris's voice. "We're not children. We've seen videos of Mom's prison on the web. It's not that bad a place."

Sam lowered his voice, which meant he had dug in. "No. If you want to see her, you will need to wait until you're eighteen."

I waited in the hall for another minute. Sam shifted the conversation to Chris's blackout, and they discussed the details of what Chris had experienced. The conversation was scaring me, so I stepped into the room. Chris was wired to a blood oxygen monitor and heart monitor, with a blanket over him for warmth. Sam sat next to him, wearing only his wetsuit pants. The aroma of Chris's hot chocolate, Sam's coffee, and a neoprene dive suit collided, eradicating the antiseptic smell of the hospital.

I threaded my arm through the wires, hugged Chris, and kissed his forehead. "You alright, honey?"

"I'm fine, Mom. It was like I was dreaming, and when I woke up, nothing hurt."

I raised my eyebrows in disbelief. He mumbled. "My chest hurts a little and I do have a little headache, but it's no big deal. Not even as bad as getting sacked in football."

I glared at Sam, but kept my tongue. I let them out of my sight for a few hours and he nearly kills my son. *Like hell he's going to get custody.*

Sam's attitude was dismissive of my concern. "He's fine. He will have a headache and be a little sore and tired for a day or two. The doctor said he could go diving again in three or four days if he wants."

My glare said, "There's no way he is going diving again." Sam's tight mouth and furrowed brow said "Yes, he is."

"It really wasn't a big deal, Mom."

I looked at Chris. He had seen our silent exchange and didn't want to be dry-docked.

"We will talk about it later."

"But, Mom!"

I wanted to lecture him about my responsibility to keep him safe, but lecturing a fifteen-year-old boy about safety is only slightly more effective than lecturing your cellulite about the proper time and place to make its presence known.

With sharp finality, I said, "Later."

After Chris was released, Dad took Sam back up the coast to get his truck while I took the kids home.

Dad's taking him was fine by me because I didn't want to see the scene of the crime, and it would take Sam at least five hours to get home.

For the past three weeks, he had treated me like a disease. He nearly drowned our son. And he was talking to Chris about Clora, after telling me it was a forbidden subject. I wasn't sure I could have remained civil on the drive home.

As I drove through the Novato Narrows, Chris asked if he could go to Bobby's for the rest of the day. Angela and Grace asked me to drop them at the mall early for their shift at the Girl Scouts & Brownies recruiting event. It was obvious all three wanted to be gone when their dad got home. Smart kids.

I gave the girls money for lunch, a movie, and dinner, then dropped them off. Once home, Chris took a quick shower and walked to Bobby's.

I paced the kitchen, waiting for Sam.

Chapter 58
A Poem of Sorrow
Sam

When I got back from the coast, I could tell that Evelyn was ready to cut me into chum and feed me to the sharks. I was still reeling from the panic of seeing Chris floating lifeless in the water. A month ago, Evelyn and I would have been there for each other. Now there was only anger and unsaid accusations.

I made a beeline to the bedroom to take a shower and change before I put away my gear. After my shower, I was headed to the garage when I noticed Angela had left her computer on. I went to turn it off to save a few watts of energy for her grandchildren.

The title on the screen caught my eye. I sat and scrolled down.

What Happened to my Parents
By Angela Irving

What happened to my parents, why do they bicker so,
I hear the words they don't say, and how it pains me so.
For once we were so happy, but now there is no love,
They quarrel with each other, and us they do not love.

Once we were a family, now only pain and lies,
Desperate whispered anger, that pride will not let die.
The anger pain and sadness, within me slowly grows,
Prayers and hope for family, are seed that will not grow.

My parents speak in whispers, and we they imitate,

No longer are we happy, with fear we contemplate.
Perhaps they would be happy, so says my sister Grace,
If we had not come to live, in such a lovely place.

Chris speaks in tearful whispers, a mom we never knew,
Grace talks in lonely whispers, of parents long gone too.
We've come to think that maybe, our mother wants us now,
And that Grace's long gone parents, are close to her somehow.

And as they go on fighting, far out to sea we go,
Like flotsam and the jetsam, thrown hither to and fro.
Like mermaids without water, and divers without air,
Life can seem so lonely, and life is so unfair.

So now we whisper secrets, and try to see what's true,
They said it'd be forever, a love that lovers knew.
But now they are asunder, their love has gone astray,
So will they love us always? Of this I furtive pray.

So will they love me always? Of this I cannot say.

I sat staring at the monitor through blurry eyes. I had been so caught up in Evelyn and me that I had no idea they were hurting this badly. I thought we were being discrete. I thought we were being civil. I knew the kids had been difficult and moody. And my daisy, Grace, hid in her room, barely ate, and no longer chattered endlessly. I knew we were affecting them some, but how could they feel unloved?

Evelyn's voice was cold. "What's wrong?"

I looked to the door. Her arms were crossed, her face was tight, and her eyes sharp. I stood. "You need to read this."

She sat. I went to clean my dive gear.

Chapter 59
Flotsam and Jetsam
Evelyn

Sam took one look at me when he got back from the coast and knew I was ready to keelhaul him. He wisely avoided me by taking a shower.

I had expected him to go straight back out to unload his truck, clean all his dive gear, and putter in the garage until dinner so he wouldn't have to face me. I had planned on cornering him in the garage once he finished putting things away.

After his shower, I heard him go into Angela's room, and then nothing but a couple of mouse clicks. I went to see what was going on.

He was sitting at Angela's computer, his face red and contorted.

"What's wrong?"

He glanced at me, stood, and told me I needed to read something on the computer. As I sat, he walked out.

I read the title, *"What Happened to my Parents,"* then closed my eyes and prayed for the strength and wisdom to deal with this, too.

The poem contained all the things I knew about children and divorce. The fear. The self-blame. Feelings of abandonment. Helplessness. And a frantic search within their limited black-and-white world for some way to make it better.

I dealt with these feelings on a weekly basis, but it was always someone else's child. I knew my children were reacting to us but I thought they were doing better.

Denial: A river in Africa full of crocodiles. That murky fluid thing that sometimes keeps us afloat, but also blinds us to the obvious until it jumps up and bites. I thought I was managing the kids' concerns, but I had been painfully blind.

Sam was still unloading his truck when I went out.

"We need to talk."

Without even looking at me, he said, "Talk," as if he were a king commanding a peasant.

"The kids are hurting."

He ignored me, pulled Chris's kayak out of the bed of his truck, and tossed it on the lawn next to his. I stood there, waiting for a response. He slung his weight belt over his shoulder and turned to me. "Tell me something I don't know."

I stared at the weight belt. He had only one. "Where's Chris's belt."

Indifferent to my concern, Sam said, "Bottom of the ocean," turned, and headed into the garage. I followed.

Shallow water blackout was sudden. Chris wouldn't have been able to drop his belt. "Did he drop it?"

"No. I did. I thought we were talking about the poem."

This wasn't making sense. If you were in trouble, you dropped *your* belt.

"Why Chris's?"

Sam half glared, making it perfectly clear he was annoyed.

"By dropping Chris's weight belt, Chris gets to the surface, with or without me. If I drop mine and then lose my hold on him halfway up, I'm stuck at the surface and he's stuck under the water."

"Oh." In my mind, I saw Chris floating unconscious in the water—not an image I wanted. I shook my head to dislodge the thought and tried to shift back to Angela's poem.

"What are we going to do?"

He set his belt into the garage washtub, pushing his wet suit to the bottom under the soap and water.

"Tell the kids we love them and that nothing in the world could ever change that."

"But they need—"

"They need to know we love them," he said, his voice uncompromising. "No guilt. No games. No shit. No tears. Just an honest, solid, dignified, I love you, and I will always love you."

My eyes filled with tears. When he said "I love you, and I will always love you," it felt like he was saying it to me—but of course, he wasn't. It was time to pick up the girls. I left.

When I got to the mall, Grace and Angela were standing out

front with Daniel and some of the other girls from their troop.

The kids came over to the van.

"Mom? Can we take Daniel home?"

"Sure. Climb in."

Angela and Daniel had been "dating" for almost a year now. Initially, I had expected the normal, short-lived puppy love, followed by an ocean of tears and vows never to love again. Instead, their relationship had evolved into what looked like a true friendship based on mutual like and respect.

I had watched Daniel maturing into an honorable, dignified, responsible, and caring young man. The more he was around, the more he reminded me of Sam—the old Sam.

Angela and Daniel sat in the back and cuddled together while Grace took the front seat next to me. Mystified, I watched them in the rear view mirror. They seemed to have a deep connection that I only saw in couples who had been together many decades. They moved fluidly together, each instinctively responding in perfect harmony with the other—knowing the other's thoughts and needs before a word was spoken or a gesture given. They still had the sparkle of youth and innocence, but there was also a dignity and antiquity to their presence together. They seemed like old souls who had been together in a hundred other lifetimes.

I wondered if they would be the exception, the rare puppy love that matured, endured, and blossomed into a lifetime together.

I would hope and pray.

After dinner, Sam and Chris disappeared back into the garage. I was tired of Sam being a mule's behind. I was angry about Chris's near-drowning. I knew Sam still loved me, but he was hell bent on a divorce. He was acting transphobic. I was tired of his childishness. I was tired of him.

He had launched a tidal wave that would destroy our family and I didn't see any way to stop it. If I had ever had a chance to win him back, I blew it at my dad's house when I had screamed that being a girl wasn't a choice. I had hoped for a miracle, but he had dug in, and it was time to face the reality that sometimes love's just not enough.

After the kids were in bed, I went out to the garage, closed the door behind me, and sat on the step. Sam ignored me. I watched him finish adjusting the chain on Angela's bicycle.

Without looking at me, Sam said, "I thought we could take the kids to Angel Island tomorrow and bike around."

"Why are you doing this, Sam?"

"Doing what?"

I didn't answer. He knew what I meant and I wasn't going to play his game.

"He's fine. We talked. He knows what he did wrong and will be more careful in the future."

That wasn't what I was talking about but it needed addressing, too. "He got lucky today—"

"No!" Sam turned toward me. "It wasn't *luck*. It was safe diving practice. It was a good buddy system. Not luck. Nick was Safety at the surface and had seen Chris black out. If I hadn't gotten to him, Nick would have."

I wanted to scream the words, but tightly said, "He almost drowned."

Sam shook his head no. "You're scared shitless of the water, Eve. I understand that now. I also understand that you once loved the water as much as Chris and I do—probably more. I wish you could get past your past and see the joy I see when he finds some new marvel at the bottom of the ocean. A new fish or plant or crab.

"The diving isn't just about the abalone. It's also about the miracle of life under the sea, the unbelievable diversity. The exploration, adventure, and personal challenge every boy needs."

His eyes narrowed. "Life has no guarantees. You should have died when you were nine. You should have died when you fell into the flood control channel with Cinnamon. You didn't.

"The buddy system worked like it was supposed to. Chris didn't drown. Just because you can't make peace with your friends' deaths, you *will not* use today as an excuse to take diving away from him, or him away from me."

My protective mother instincts wanted to argue with him, but I knew he was right. I had told many smother-love parents that they needed to let their adolescent children safely expand their boundaries and explore the world. Chris was a young man. He needed to be free to discover the world under his father's watchful eyes. He had a fair amount of Sam's stubbornness and would eventually dive without my knowledge if I stopped him now. Diving with his dad would be far safer, and by the time he was on his own, good habits and learned wisdom would protect him.

It hurt, but I nodded in agreement. "You're right."

He blinked as if the last thing on earth he expected was for me to agree. The corner of his mouth curled up.

I didn't give him time to bask in his victory.

"Why do you want a divorce, Sam?"

His body tightened, and his breathing became shallow. "You lied."

I shook my head no. "Try again, Sam. You can come up with a better *lie* than that."

His eyes narrowed. "And what does the great *Doctor* think?"

At some level, I knew he was baiting me but I didn't care. I met his sarcasm head-on.

"The great doctor thinks she made two mistakes. One was not telling you. The second was believing you were more open-minded than you are. Believing you weren't transphobic."

He flinched, his whole body rippling with anger.

I knew I should stop, but my anger kicked me into the fray. "You think that because I was born male that I am a man in a dress, which is ironic, since in action, word, and condescending attitude, you treat me like a woman."

He crossed his arms and leaned against his workbench with an amused smirk.

My intuition screamed for me to stop, but my anger flared and I charged blindly forward. "Everything about your child custody and property division proposals were classic: 'You're the woman so you get our girls and the house.' 'I'm the man, so I get our son and will pay child support and alimony.'"

He sneered. "And since you're a man, you refused the alimony."

I was closer to hating him than I believed possible. I burned with anger and screamed, "I declined the alimony because I earn more than you. I'm trying to be fair. If you don't want me to be fair, I'll take the alimony *and* the children."

His whole body shook like he had been slammed against a cliff by a crashing wave. The reverberations shook the garage. I froze, my flames of anger and self-pity extinguished by his wave of fear and grief. I *could* take the kids, and we both knew it.

But he loved our kids more than life, and taking them would be the cruelest thing I could do to him and our children. I closed my eyes and tried to steady the storm of swirling emotions within me.

"I'm sorry. That was wrong," I said. I looked at him. He was barely containing the fear that was overwhelming him. "I would never take our children away from you, even if I could. They need both of us as much as we need them, and they could never, ever find a better father."

He nodded, turned away, and fumbled with some adjustment on the bike. Several minutes of silence passed before he turned to face me again.

Sam calmly said, "I think it would be best if I moved out. When do we want to tell the kids?"

I shivered. "We can't tell the kids. They're at puberty. Trying to find their sexual identity. Telling them now could confuse them."

He scowled, mouth half open. His jaw tightened, his brow furrowed, and I could see the annoyed anger. "I'm not—" He stopped himself from whatever he was going to say. "I'm talking about the divorce … though it's not like they haven't figured it out."

I looked down, feeling foolish. "I don't know."

"Tomorrow?"

I was tired. I was beginning to want out, too. But I was still praying for a miracle for the sake of our children.

I looked back up. "After Bodega?"

He shook his head no. "It's not for two months."

"It will go by quickly and the kids will have one last good memory of us as a family."

He stared through me for a moment—his thoughts far from us. He nodded and mumbled, "What is a little of my time?"

An ocean, frozen in mid-tempest, stood between us. He looked as defeated as I felt.

"Good night, Sam."

Chapter 60
Losing Grace
Evelyn

The kids were home before me, like usual. Setting my purse down, I did my traditional call, "Mom's home."

Chris and Angela called back with an annoyed, "Hi, Mom," as was becoming the norm, but Grace was silent.

I went by Angela's room and poked my nose in. She was engrossed in a poetry book and didn't even look up. Grace had her door shut like usual, since it was easier to fish for a whale with a bent bobby pin than to get her to close her window.

I knocked and opened the door to cool air and the scent of honeysuckle drifting in. Grace was sitting cross-legged in the middle of her bed with her favorite treasures spread around her. There was the rhinestone hair clip that belonged to her mother. A wristwatch that belonged to her father. A picture of her and her parents when she was a baby. A Care Bear that Sam and I had given her. A small statue of a unicorn that Grandma Rose had given her. Family photos of Angela, Chris, Sam, her, and me. A Christmas photo of her and her Grandma Louise.

"What are you doing, sweetie?"

She shrugged, got up, and started moving her treasures to the top of her dresser.

"You look a little sad. Are you alright?"

Sounding hurt and annoyed, she answered, "Yeah. I'm fine."

Grace mirrored the growing distance between Sam and me by sinking deeper and deeper into herself. Helplessly, I had watched her pull into her own sad world of self-imposed isolation. She had even begun to shun Angela.

"Have you heard any good stories lately?"

She shook her head. "No."

"Do you want to talk?"

"No." She picked up the script for her next play and opened

it. "I need to memorize my lines."

"Would you like me to help?"

"No. I'm fine," she said, with tired sadness.

I was deeply worried about her. She hadn't been eating and only tried to memorize the lines to her next play when I wanted to talk to her. Last week, she had started seeing Dr. Chen, a brilliant child psychologist I sometimes consulted with. Next week, Chris and Angela would start going, too.

Logically, I understood that only a fool tries to shrink their own kids. As their mom, I was part of the family dynamics—part of the problem. But it was still embarrassing to be a child psychologist and need to send my kids to see a shrink.

I watched her, lonely and hurting, and wondered if it wouldn't be better if Sam did move out now instead of waiting until after Bodega.

"Love you, sweetie."

In a lost whisper, she said, "Love you too, Mom."

I shivered from the cool air, stepped into the warmer hall, and closed the door.

Chapter 61
The Truth
Evelyn

Sam went to the family room to read and the kids disappeared into their bedrooms while I cleaned the kitchen. When I punched the button to start the dishwasher, I heard a noise behind me. I turned and saw the kids standing in the doorway. Chris was a half-step ahead of Angela, trying to stand tall and confident, but his back and shoulders were slightly hunched and his eyes held uncertainty. Angela's body and eyes held uncertainty, too. She glanced rapidly between me and the floor and shifted restlessly. Grace peeked around Angela, with the wonder and curiosity of a child who had just seen her first water park mermaid.

"Mom. We need to have a family meeting," Chris said.

We had regular family meetings, where conflicts and concerns could be openly discussed and solutions found. Before the journals, they were usually short. After Sam had become a mule's behind, the kids had called meetings and asked some serious and fair questions, but we had been vague or evasive. I had the impression that the day of reckoning had come.

I tried to be more upbeat than their mood warranted. I smiled. "What for?"

I could see his dad in him. Chris wanted to do whatever they were doing on his terms and in his way. "We have to show you, and then we need to talk."

The scent of doom threatened me. I shivered instinctively to chase it away and said a quick, silent prayer.

I was sure they were going to demand a yes or no on the divorce. I knew the answer was yes. They knew the answer was yes. But saying it would make it too real.

I followed them to the family room, where Sam was sitting in his recliner, reading the rental section of the newspaper. They repeated their request. He looked at me and I shrugged.

Chris went to the entertainment center and turned on the television and DVD player. I took the couch. Angela and Grace sat on the love seat.

Chris held up a CD. "I found a DVD."

I couldn't breathe. My eyes shot to Sam. He didn't seem concerned. Chris continued, while the kid's glances flashed back and forth between Sam and me—mostly on me.

Chris said, "We didn't understand at first, but now we do."

Sam interrupted. "What DVD?"

Chris looked puzzled. "The one of you beating up the preacher who tried to shoot you."

Sam turned white and looked over at me. I grimaced, shrugged, and said, "It was in your jacket. I forgot about it."

I knew I should have destroyed the disk. But I had been so proud of what Sam had done, and it showed me that somewhere deep inside his heart, he still loved me.

I also knew that if I had told him about it, he would have snapped it in half, so I had written, "Research Backup" and dated it, intending to take it to work, but forgot. The kids must have spent a long time going through my home office to find it.

Sam looked back at Chris, his color returning. Chris hit play on the remote, and the DVD started.

I watched Sam watching the video. It began with him and Brandon standing in the aisle. Sam asked Brandon if he remembered me from high school.

I saw a rumble of anger pass through Sam's eyes when Brandon said I was possessed of the devil.

I closed my eyes and prayed while Brandon laid out my history for my children, but when Sam said "It's *her*, Brandon. Feminine pronoun. And yes, I married *her*," I had to open my eyes through the pain to admire *my* Sam, but instead of pride or modesty, I saw despair swallow him.

When the video ended, Grace said, "Is that why you don't love Mom anymore? Cause she was a boy?"

I couldn't help smiling. My children knew and they were alright with it. They still loved me.

Sam looked at me and I saw his anger. It didn't belong on me. He was the one who chose to run away instead of trying to understand. We would all have to deal with the consequences of that choice.

Chris glared at Sam and demanded to know. "Is it?"

The testosterone was pumping. Sam and Chris tried to stare each other down.

"It's not that simple," Sam said.

Chris yelled, "I'm not a child. I understand." He was shaking with anger and frustration. "I see kids at school treat the gay kids like dirt—like you treat Mom."

Grace scurried over to me and climbed onto my lap. The girls and I instinctively made ourselves small.

Sam yelled back, "It's not that simple."

I had expected Chris to back down, but he stood, fists clenched, shoulders hunched, jaw locked, breathing heavy.

Sam shifted forward in his chair, feet firmly planted, and returned the glare. They remained locked in the primitive male posturing for alpha position, with neither flinching for a minute ... then two. Chris's glare slowly filled with sadness, and his jaw loosened and trembled.

Low and hard, Chris said, "You tell us that they are no different than us, and then you hate Mom for being one." Chris shook his head and Sam looked lost. "You were my hero, but it was all a lie."

Chris's eyes filled with tears and he rushed out of the room, with Angela right behind him. Sam sat back in his chair and stared at the floor. I could see a storm of emotions ripping him apart, like coastal rocks ripping apart a careless ship in a blinding storm.

I kissed Grace on the forehead. "You okay, sweetie?" She nodded yes. "You alright going to Angela so I can talk with your dad?" She shot an angry glare at Sam, nodded yes, and slipped off my lap.

When she was safely out of earshot, I said, "I'm sorry, Sam. I really didn't expect them to find it. But it's done."

He glared at me, his expression blaming me for everything.

I was literally a microsecond from saying "Screw you, too" and walking out. But Chris needed his father. I shifted on the couch and leaned closer. "You have about five minutes to go to Chris and be completely honest with him. If it means admitting to him you are transphobic, you need to do it. He will respect you for being honest even if he doesn't agree. If you don't go, there will forever be a wall between you and him."

Sam growled, "I'm not transphobic. You lied."

He had earned the alienation of his family, but the kids needed their father. I sat back and took slow, deep breaths to calm myself. I studied him.

Despite the hurt of the last month, I still loved him, though it was faltering under the constant barrage of anger and rejection. I was still hoping for a miracle, but I wasn't blind. For all the wonderful things he was and did, he was still human, still had failings. My lie had been his Achilles' heel.

"I had my lie, Sam. I believed with all my heart that it didn't matter that I was born a boy. I lived that lie and it has cost me dearly.

"You say you're not transphobic, that you can't live with the fact that I lied to you, and you believe it as much as I believed my lie. My lie may have cost me the man I love. I can't imagine the pain I would feel if it had cost me my children."

He continued staring at the floor. "You've won. They hate me. Leave me alone."

I shivered. "We've all lost, Sam, and they don't hate you. But if you continue to lie to yourself and to them, they will lose their respect for you. The clock is ticking."

I stood and looked at Sam as he wallowed in his self-pity. He wasn't the Sam I had known and loved. He had changed so much in the last month—but we all had.

I was tired of being *nice*. I was tired of being a doormat. Softly I said, "Sam," and waited for him to look up. "The day you read the journal and found out I had been born Adam, I believed my life was over and that I had lost everything. I went to my dad's, wallowing in self-pity and despair. Your mom was there. She said she never took me for a quitter.

"I never took you for a quitter, either, Sam. Or am I more of a man than you?"

Angela and Grace were huddled on Angela's bed, whispering. "May I come in?"

They looked over and nodded yes as they made a space for me to sit between them. "How are my girls doing?"

Her voice unsure, Angela asked, "Were you really a boy?"

"I was born male, but I was never a *boy*."

Grace frowned. "Did it hurt?"

"Did what hurt?"

"Being a boy. Turning into a girl."

"Not too much. Like *The Little Mermaid*, it was worth it to be a princess."

Angela hugged me. "I'm glad you're a girl."

"Me, too," I said.

Grace was still frowning. I smoothed her hair and caressed her cheek. "What's wrong, sweetie?"

"Nothing."

I put on a mock pout, leaned down, and gently bumped foreheads. "Nothing, my eye."

Tears filled Grace's eyes. "Dad doesn't love you."

"He's mad because I didn't tell him I was born a boy."

"He's stupid," Angela said.

I scowled at her. "He's your father and a good man. He deserves more respect than that."

She half glared at me. "Alright. He's acting like an ignoramus."

I tried not to smile. "He does love me. He's just having a hard time feeling it right now."

"Will he stop loving me, too?" Grace asked.

I hugged her. "No, sweetie. He will never stop loving you. Any of you."

She was limp in my embrace, feeling more like a load of laundry than my precious baby girl. I slowly released her, leaned down so I could see her pretty brown eyes, and asked, "What's wrong?"

Her voice was lost and sad. "He doesn't love you."

The meaning of the words went far beyond their literal interpretation. Her pain flooded my heart, causing tears to well up in my eyes. She was saying that if he lied about always loving me, how could she know that he would always love her. In her child's world of absolutes, love is love is love—all or nothing. If he stopped loving me, he might stop loving her.

I pulled Grace back to me. "Oh, baby. I know it's hard to understand, but he does love you and always will." She remained oddly limp, and I could feel her tears.

Angela's lips trembled. "That's what he always said about you."

I pulled Angela to me. "I know it's hard, but love between a husband and wife isn't like the love we have for our children. He does love all of you, and he always will."

I heard Sam knock on Chris's door. I said a prayer for all of us.

Chapter 62
Gone Fishing
Sam

There had only been a couple of times in my life that I had done something that truly shamed me. I'm the father. I'm a mature adult. I'm supposed to set a good example for my children. I didn't know the man who had tried to reason with Chris in his room about that damned DVD, only to sink into a childish yelling contest.

After my infantile display, I had retreated to my garage, not coming out until everyone was asleep.

Not wanting to face Evelyn or the kids, I had gotten up early this morning, left a note telling Evelyn I was diving with Nick, and took off.

I stopped at Duncan's Point because it was close and it gave a good view of the ocean. We never dove there because the surf and currents were notorious killers—dangerous and unpredictable.

Whether it was because of the early hour or because of the cold wind, the point was all mine. I parked myself on one of the picnic benches, with my thermos of coffee and my binoculars. It was the end of whale-watching season, and with the wind beating the water into a frenzy of high breakers, froth, spray, chop, and foam, there was no way in hell I'd see a whale, but I could pretend. After about a minute, I considered retreating to my truck for shelter but didn't have the energy or will to move.

Besides, no one was going to bother me here, and maybe the wind would beat some sense into me.

Chris didn't understand and I didn't know how to make him. He was too young, and you just can't explain some things. It wasn't because she was trans, it was because …

"Damn it. Why? Why do I feel this way? I should be alright with it, but shit. She … Shit."

I sipped on the bitter convenience store coffee and checked out a fishing boat that was dumb enough or desperate enough to be out. I heard a car pull in but I didn't look back. Tourists cruising the scenic Pacific coast were constantly stopping at pullouts, stepping out of their car for two or three minutes to take pictures and then going on their way. I sometimes wondered how many of them spent more time looking at their photos than they spent looking at the ocean. If their memories were of frozen waves on a glossy piece of photo paper, or if in their minds, they could see the crashing surf and white foam in its never-ending assault on the sand and rocks. If they could still hear the rumble of the waves and the piercing, plaintive cry of the seagulls. If they could still smell the salty ozone-filled air and feel the life-affirming wind rippling through their hair.

A minute later, someone sat on the other end of the picnic bench. I glanced over; it was Nick. I wasn't happy to see him. If he hadn't given me the damn journals, I'd still be a blissfully ignorant fool, married to a woman I had loved more than life itself, and would still have a son who loved me.

"What the hell are you doing here?" I asked.

"Eve couldn't get your cell, so she called me. Wanted to remind you to be back by four. Chris has a game."

I frowned at him. "So you told her we weren't diving?"

"She offered enough for me to know you needed some down time, and I didn't volunteer. Thought it was a good day for a drive and happened to see your truck."

I snorted and looked back out to sea. We didn't say a word. Ten minutes passed.

Nick said, "If you don't mind me prying, Eve wasn't real clear, but it sounded like something happened between you and Chris?"

I thought about his question for a minute. "I mind."

We watched the waves for another ten minutes.

I said, "Chris is as bull-headed as me."

In my peripheral vision, I could see Nick's amused silent chuckle but he didn't say anything.

Another car pulled in behind us. A minute later, a kid in his early twenties walked past us with a Wal-Mart newbie fresh-water fishing pole and tackle box. He was headed for the west edge of the point, where a low-tide land bridge allowed people to go out and climb onto a jagged barren rock just beyond the point. The rock went by the well-deserved name of Death Rock.

Even on calm, sunny days, ocean surges and sleeper waves would unexpectedly wash over the top of the rock, grinding the ignorant and foolish into pulp on the malicious outcropping, and then drag them offshore in a strong rip current to feed the fish. Going out on the rock on a day like today was suicide.

Nick called out, "Excuse me?"

The kid stopped, turned, and looked at us like we were an annoyance.

Nick gestured toward the rocks. "Were you going out there?"

The kid said, "Yeah," with a slight sneer, his attitude saying, "What's it to you?"

"They call it Death Rock. Waves break over it. Kills people. It's suicide to go out there."

He rolled his eyes, turned, and tramped over the steep edge. I looked at Nick. He shook his head and said, "That kid's going to get himself killed."

For a second, I thought about suiting up so I could go get him after he was sucked out, but the seas were too rough and the winds were too strong. I'd just get myself killed, too.

I once saw a diver break his collarbone when he was slammed against the rocks by a wave. After that, I put the Coast Guard and Sonoma County Sheriff's numbers in my cell phone, just in case.

"Sonoma County Sheriffs. How can I help you?"

"A young man is fishing on Death Rock off Duncan's Point on Highway One."

The "Oh, shit. Not another one" screamed out of the silence on the phone. Sounding professional and perturbed, he said, "We'll send someone out, but it may take a while."

We watched the young man pick his way up the side of Death Rock and then work his way across the wet and slippery mass to the west side, where he baited and cast his hook.

"Do you think I'm transphobic?"

Nick shook his head no. "Not in what I consider to be the common definition of the word. I've never known you to exhibit antipathy, contempt, aversion, or an irrational fear of the gay or transgendered. By that definition, I would have to say no, you're not."

By that definition? I stared at my coffee, thinking about his double speak. "By what definition would I be?"

His frown deepened. "I don't think that label belongs on you."

I sneered at no one in particular. "That's what Evelyn and Chris say."

He nodded thoughtfully. "Eve is hurting, and Chris is scared. People don't see clearly and they say things they don't mean when they're hurting or scared. How many things have you said since reading the journals that you didn't mean?"

His barb hurt. I had said way too many stupid things and I didn't like him inferring I was scared and hurting—even if it was true. I took a sip of lukewarm coffee, then continued watching the kid with the death wish.

A wave surged up the face of Death Rock, soaking the fisherman with spray. I thought he would wise up and move on, but he checked his hook and threw it back out.

"So what *is* my problem?" I asked.

He shrugged. "Don't know."

Like hell he didn't.

My need to get away from Evelyn didn't make sense to me. I should be alright with who she is—or was—or … But I just …

"You want to talk about Chris?"

I looked away from him, and dug my fingernails into the palm of my hand. After the surging tide of emotions receded, I looked back.

"I had a little run-in with Bra—. You probably heard, since Dave was there." He nodded yes and I continued. "I met Cinnamon's dad after my little run-in. He's a police detective and gave me a DVD. I didn't know what was on it. I put it in my pocket and forgot about it. Evelyn found it and didn't tell me.

"Chris had been snooping around trying to find the journals or something to tell him why I was … angry." I sighed. "He found the DVD and put everything together.

"She lied to me and now I'm the bad guy."

Nick hadn't blinked or flinched. He knew about all of it. I looked pointedly at him. "You've seen the DVD, haven't you?"

His embarrassed grin said it all. "I called Eve when she was watching it. I was curious. You did good. Real good."

I appreciated the pat on the back, but hated the fact that I was a step or two behind everyone else—again—or was it still?

I shook my head. "I feel like everyone has everything all figured out and I'm the only one stupid enough to still be playing the game."

Nick shook his head no. "Everyone involved is trying to figure it out. The family dynamics changed drastically after you read the journals. Your relationship with everyone shifted, forcing everyone to question their relationships with each other.

"We all have rules we live by, Sam, and you changed the rules. It upsets people when the rules change.

"One of your rules is that you will never do something that you would be ashamed to tell your son. That is a highly commendable rule.

"Many people live by the rule that they will not tolerate a cheating spouse. Others choose to tolerate it; even embrace it. Who's wrong?"

We both knew it depended on the personalities involved and the circumstances. He paused, waiting for the obvious answer.

"Duh."

Nick grinned and nodded. "If you can't accept Eve's past, that doesn't make you transphobic or a bad person. It just means that your internal rules make your relationship with Eve unworkable. That's all.

"Many of those rules are formed when we are very young and are buried deep in our subconscious. We don't know where they come from or why. We just react to them without understanding the rules, their impact on us, or their impact on those we love.

"The journals triggered one of those rules for you. A rule which made your relationship with Eve insufferable. I'm still hoping you can come to some kind of understanding or compromise with that rule and work things out.

"You need to figure out what you really want, Sam. What is stronger inside of you? Your love for Eve, or the rule?"

What did I want? Out. But why? Why was it so awful? I shivered. The moronic phrase "A man's got to do what a man's got to do" tromped through my brain. Since becoming a mature adult, I had written that saying off to testosterone-induced stupidity, but damn, it was the only thing that halfway made sense. Leaving her was just something I needed to do.

Intellectually and emotionally, I accepted that she was a woman—because she was. I still wanted to believe my irritation was because she had lied, but the reality was, I was in a blind panic to get away from her. I didn't understand. I wasn't sure I ever would. If it wasn't for the kids, I wouldn't care. I'd just run.

A sleeper wave rose up an easy eight feet above Death Rock. When it receded, the stupid kid was gone.

I pulled out my phone and Nick took my binoculars. We hurried to the edge of the point. As the phone connected, we looked down and watched the water receding, hoping he had miraculously been able to hold onto something and that he hadn't been ground into fish bait on the rocks.

"Sonoma County Sheriffs."

"Sam Irving. I called earlier. The guy fishing off Death Rock was just washed off. We don't see him." Nick nudged me and pointed. "He surfaced about fifty yards out. He's swimming against the rip current."

"Okay. Stay on the line to give us his location. Help is on the way."

"I think he's injured, too," Nick said.

"Think he knows to swim at right angles to the rip current until he's clear before trying to swim to shore?"

Watching the kid, Nick said, "Obviously not."

Even if he was uninjured, it wouldn't be long before the cold North Pacific waters dropped his body temperature enough to induce hypothermia, leading to unconsciousness.

His attempt to swim against a rip current was as foolish as going out onto Death Rock. Rip currents flow as fast as five-and-a-half miles per hour—faster than the Olympic record for a sprint in a heated pool, without fifteen-foot swells.

An average swimmer in good condition, in calm warm water, might manage half that speed, while giving up endurance.

The kid in the water had a long swim ahead of him and needed all the endurance he could get. He was burning up his chance of survival by trying to swim straight back instead of at a right angle, or even diagonally toward shore, so he could escape the current.

We watched him drifting out for about ten minutes, by which time he was too far out for me to see for sure in the chop and spray. Nick began losing sight of him between swells.

I heard the rescue helicopter coming from the south. Nick said, "He's about a half mile out and a quarter mile south of our point." I relayed the information to the dispatcher.

The helicopter was a bright orange Coast Guard HH-65 Dolphin. It circled for a minute, seeming to look, and then dropped down closer to the water. The dispatcher said they located him and thanked us for our help.

We stood watching the helicopter pull the stupid kid from the water and whisk him away.

"That kid got lucky," Nick said.

"Huh?" I looked over at him, trying to figure out how arrogant stupidity and nearly getting himself killed had been lucky.

"If you hadn't had problems at home and come here to think, you wouldn't have been here to call the Coast Guard. The police would have found his car and assumed he had drowned, but his family would have always wondered. Always been searching faces in crowds, looking for him. You being here was lucky for him and his family." He forced a grin. "Everything happens for a reason, Sam."

I looked out to sea and shook my head. Now I knew where Evelyn got that crap.

The kid had gambled with his life and got lucky. Goody for him.

The destruction of my family wasn't some divine plan to save some moron. It was those damn journals—my Death Rock. If Nick was right, my subconscious rules and irrational reaction had been the sleeper wave that had swept me into a sea, where I was drowning. *How do you swim at right angles to a belief or emotion until you can escape it?* I was treading water, and land was getting further away.

I was tired of running from myself. "I should get home," I said.

Nick's smile was tight and concerned. He nodded.

"You're a good man, Sam. You'll figure it out and do the right thing. Take care and good luck."

I needed more than luck.

Chapter 63
Grace is Missing
Sam

It had been a week since the kids had found the DVD. I still hadn't figured out a way to reason with them or how to explain something that I couldn't understand myself.

I elbowed the couch cushion, trying to smooth a lump, then rolled over—again. I still wasn't used to Evelyn not sleeping next to me. I heard Angela cough. When they were little, I liked the way the sound traveled from their rooms into the family room because we could easily tell if they were going to sleep or playing. Now it woke me constantly.

I had barely gotten to sleep when I thought I heard one of the kids. I listened, but there wasn't the flush of the toilet, restless turning, or muffled cries from a bad dream. I crammed the blanket under my chin and slipped into troubled sleep.

I woke at four, chilled by a cool draft wallowing about the family room. Our house wasn't drafty unless Grace's window or the chimney flu were left open. I checked the chimney and then went to check Grace's room. My toes felt the icy air seeping from under Grace's door. I quietly went in. The room was cold, the window open—and she wasn't in her bed.

It took several seconds for the neurons to connect. I instantly bolted for the light switch and then ran to the window. The screen was in place and intact. I turned and looked around the bedroom, fighting images of Chris floating unconscious in the water. A letter lay in the middle of her desk.

Dear mom and dad,

I'm sorry I made you sad and not love mom anymore. I'm going away so you can be happy.

Love Grace

My body tensed from a surge of adrenaline, and the fog of sleep was instantly gone.

How could she think that?

I called out, "Grace. Where are you? Come out, right now."

I dropped down and looked under her bed. "Grace. This isn't funny." I opened her closet and pushed her clothes and junk aside to see if she was hiding underneath. Evelyn stepped into the doorway.

"What's going on? Where's Grace?"

I stood, pointed to the letter, grunted "there," and pushed past her. I was scared, but tried to sound angry. "Grace. Where are you? Come out, right now."

Evelyn called out behind me, "Grace, sweetie. You're scaring Mommy. Where are you hiding?"

Chris's door rattled open. Leaning half asleep against the jam, he said through a yawn, "What's going on?"

"Grace is missing," Evelyn said, the shadows of her voice trembling with fear.

He stood bolt upright, with his eyes huge and mouth hanging open. I headed to the living room to check behind furniture and in the coat closet. I heard Evelyn tell Chris to wake Angela and help us look for Grace.

Angela, Chris, and I worked our way through the house, while Evelyn called Grace's friends and grandparents. When I got to the garage, I found the side door deadbolt unlocked and Grace's bicycle missing.

The panic threatened to overwhelm me but I stuffed it down and retreated back into the house to call the police.

Evelyn was talking to the mom of one of Grace's friends. We exchanged scared looks and she shook her head no.

"Her bike's gone."

She stared at me as disbelief, panic, and fear flooded her eyes. She turned slightly pale, hung up without saying good bye, and dialed 9-1-1. Chris and Angela were standing in the kitchen, watching us.

"My daughter's missing." ... "Ten."

I told the kids to go get dressed.

The emergency dispatcher was loud enough that I could hear her. "Hold, please."

I watched the second hand on the clock. It took her twenty-three seconds to get back to Evelyn, but it seemed like an eternity. I couldn't understand how Grace thought running away could make us happy. The dispatcher confirmed our address and said a police car was on the way.

Evelyn glared at me, and I knew she blamed me.

"I'm going to go look for her."

She grabbed my sleeve to keep me from going. "When did you last see her?" Eve asked.

"At bedtime," I said. "I think I might have heard her a little before eleven when I was going to sleep, but I'm not sure."

She relayed the information to the dispatcher.

The dispatcher said, "Can you give me a description?"

"Brown hair, brown eyes, four feet one, and fifty-seven pounds. She has bangs, her hair falls to mid-back, and she usually wears it in a ponytail."

"Does she have a cell phone or wireless internet device?"

I saw my "oh shit" mirrored in Eve's face. With a cell phone, they could use the GPS in it to locate her.

Softly, Eve said, "No."

"What was she wearing?"

Eve stiffened and closed her eyes. Her tone was, How-the-hell-am-I-supposed-to-know? "I don't know. She went missing in the middle of the night."

The dispatcher remained calm. "Did she have a favorite outfit?"

"Yes. Her angel T-shirt. If I go through her clothes, I can probably figure it out. Should I go check?"

"A police officer is in front of your house," the dispatcher said. "She'll take the rest of the information."

I let the officer in and took over calling Grace's friends. By eight, it was clear that the police search had failed and she wasn't with a friend or relative. I had heard that if the child isn't found within a few hours, the chances of finding them plummeted. If the noise I had heard at eleven had been Grace, she would have been missing for nine hours now.

My parents and Nick were at our house by the time six officers had set up shop in our living room. Two more were in Grace's room. One was doing forensics on her computer, looking for on-line chats, contacts, personal pages, social networks, notes, letters, stories, and anything else that might tell him where she went or who she might have been in contact with. The other sifted through Grace's things, looking for notes, maps, and letters.

I hated sitting around and feeling useless. "I need to clear my head. I'm going for a run."

Evelyn wanted me to stay, and Chris wanted to go with me, but something was nagging at me. I needed to get out by myself and run off some of the frustration and helplessness so I could think clearly.

My usual jogging route took me to Camino Alto, where I always turned east. Inexplicably, I turned north and time slipped away. The sun rose higher in the sky, the pungent odor of eucalyptus filled the warming air, and my mind overflowed with thoughts of Grace. I had done so many things wrong. I should have listened more to her chatter. I should have spent more time playing games and helping her with her plays. I should have talked to her more about what she liked and dreamed of becoming.

After the kids had found the DVD, she would lash out in anger, then dissolve into tears. I should have been there for her. I should have told her I loved her more.

But I was completely at a loss on how to talk with a little girl who couldn't be rational or logical—that was her mother's job. I loved her, but I had no idea what to say or do to fix things. Everything was so muddled and broken and I didn't know how to put it back together.

I was exhausted but unable to stop running from the fear that threatened to devour me. My phone rang with Evelyn's ringtone.

I was hoping for good news. Panting, I leaned against a street sign and answered.

"Yes?"

"They haven't found her but they have been getting tips. Nothing for sure. It's noon. Felicity and Barbara are here. Where are you?"

Barbara? Like that nut case is going to help?

I looked around. "Looks like the north side of San Rafael."

"What are you doing there? Do you need someone to pick you up?"

They haven't found her. All they've got are worthless tips. My run had been fruitless. No insights. The fear of what might have happened to her sucked me dry of hope and strength.

I was about to say yes to Eve's offer to come and get me when the *something* I had been searching for rose from the dark muck that had become my life. *Angela's poem.* "Grace talks in lonely whispers, of parents long gone too ... And that Grace's long gone parents are close to her somehow."

I mumbled, "She's close to them."

"What, Sam? Who's close to whom?"

It would take someone twenty minutes to get to me. I was less than a mile away from her ... if I was right. My aimless run had taken me where I needed to go.

"I'll call you back."

The exhaustion was gone and I ran with a purpose. Five minutes later, I crested a hill at Mount Olivet and looked down at the valley oaks. Grace's purple bike and backpack stood in the shelter of an old majestic oak. Another seven feet down the hill, I could see her laying on the grass next to her parents' grave markers, looking up at the sky. She was absentmindedly picking the pedals off a dandelion and smiling at a small flock of circling seagulls calling out greetings above her.

My legs folded and I fell to my knees, my face inches from the dry soil. The fear I had carried spewed from every pore of my body, releasing the bloated nightmares that had tormented me from the moment I realized Grace was gone. I looked up and sat back on my heels as tears cleansed my soul and I found peace. I had a second chance to do right by her.

I whispered, "Thank you, God," and wiped my tears.

She was oblivious to me as I descended the hill and plopped down next to her.

"How about a hug?"

She scrambled up and threw her arms around me. I clung to her, wanting always to remember the joy of this moment, as the call of the seagulls became a heavenly choir.

"We love you, Grace. It's not your fault. Running away only makes things worse."

"I love you, too, Dad."

"No matter what, your mom and I will always love you."

I hugged her and looked at Peter and Gwynn's markers. *Thank you for watching over her.* I looked up. *You too, Louise.*

When I finally let go of her, she frowned. "Am I grounded?"

"Yeah. You can count on that, young lady," I said, blinking back tears and nodding.

I handed her my cell phone.

"Call your mom and let her know you're okay. She's worried sick."

Chapter 64
Barbara and Barry
Evelyn

Grace's running away yesterday had shaken Sam and me. At first, I had thought her leaving might wake him up, but despite being more attentive to the kids, he was still distant with me.

The thought of how shamelessly I had thrown myself at him last night flashed through my mind, making me cringe. I had always understood on an intellectual level why women abandoned their self-respect and accosted unresponsive partners. Now I understood on an emotional level the blinding desperation and need for security that drives us there.

Maybe if he had taken me up on my offer and realized that I was still the same woman he loved and wanted before he read the journals, it would have been okay. But fudge. I felt like an idiot and a fool—cheap and dirty.

I sat in my car, watching reflections in the mirrored windows of my office. Ten minutes passed while I tried to force myself to go in and start my day. I only had one client—a difficult one—and then about forty hours of treatment plans and insurance forms to work on. But I just sat there, thinking about Grace, Sam, and how stupid I had been.

I was trained in fixing broken families and had helped couples reconcile over far worse, but I had no idea how to get through to Sam. It was clear he didn't want me so I didn't have much hope.

Someone tapped on my window, making me jump and nearly spill my coffee. I looked over to see Barbara standing by my door with a look of concern. I rolled down my window.

"Sorry I scared you. What's wrong?" Barbara asked.

I forced a smile and shook my head. "Just trying to cope with Sam being Sam and Grace's running away."

"Well I thought it was pretty cool how he figured out where

she went. I never would have put two and two together." She frowned. "Or would it be A plus B if C equals D?"

I had to chuckle. "Yeah. It was pretty special. What are you doing here?"

"I have an appointment with that bitch you sent me to. You know what she said last week?"

"Hmmm. No. I don't."

"She said I was more fucked up than she thought."

Innocently, I said, "Oh?"

"She said I shouldn't be shagging guys I don't know." Her eyes got wide and she waved her hands in the air like she was trying to get my attention. "Hello! The guys that know me think I'm crazy and won't shag me, so what else am I supposed to do? If I had to depend on a vibrator, I'd have to sell my Rolls to pay the power bill. Stupid bitch."

I couldn't help laughing. Barbara grinned impishly and said, "I love you, too."

"Thank you. I do feel better. I hate to laugh and run, but I have a client in ten."

Barbara was suddenly serious. "What time do you get off today?"

Sometimes Barbara could be emotionally demanding, and I sensed this could be one of those times. I was tempted to say "Late," but she had been more supportive than I thought possible yesterday after Grace had run away.

Like me, she was a mom with a young daughter. We shared the same fears so she had been able to sense and soothe my anxiety in ways I never would have thought her capable of.

"My paperwork can wait. After my next client," I said.

"Could we go somewhere and talk after? I have something I need to get your opinion on."

"Alright."

Barbara wanted to go to a bar but I redirected her to a small cafe with great tea and desserts.

She was somber for more than five seconds, which was a bad sign. "I ran into Barry."

In our normal banter, I would have replied "Did it hurt?" but this was obviously very serious.

"Your first husband?"

She nodded yes and stared at her tea. "I really need something stronger."

"You have something stronger. Your love for your daughter."

Her eyes moistened and she nodded yes. After a moment of thought, Barbara said, "His wife died last year. Cancer."

I had seen it in the paper. I nodded yes.

"We stood in the store talking for nearly half-an-hour. It was like the last fifteen years never happened. Like we were back before I left."

"Did you talk to Dr. Sharma about him?"

She shook her head no. "We were talking about Madonna today and I didn't want to waste our time on me. Maybe next week."

I smiled and nodded. She sat staring at her tea for several minutes. Still staring down, she said, "He gave me his number. Said he'd like to meet Madonna."

Habits wanted to pull me into therapist mode and say, "How do you feel about that?" but she was my friend. "Why not?"

She blushed and looked up, obviously embarrassed. "I fucked him—and I don't mean in a good way."

"If he was still holding it against you, he wouldn't have given you his number, would he?"

She smiled. "But the doctor said I needed to be human before I could get serious."

I touched her hand. "You made the first big step in being human when you placed Madonna ahead of your wants. You've read two—"

"Three," Barbara beamed, sitting up straighter.

"That's wonderful. Three books on raising children and you are becoming a great mom. Madonna is blossoming." I hesitated. Thoughts stirred in my mind.

"What?" Barbara asked, concern shading her eyes.

"One of the interesting things about raising children in a healthy way, and studying books on the subject, is that we learn a lot about ourselves in the process. When we care and really pay attention, we grow with our children and become better people in the process."

She chuckled. "So I'm growing up, too?"

I smiled. "Something like that."

She nodded thoughtfully. "But it's too soon. I'll just screw it up."

"You and Barry are different people than you were back then—"

She threw her head back and raised her hands skyward.

"God, ain't that the truth. Thank heavens." She hesitated as everyone looked at us. She composed herself and said, "At least me. Barry was always wonderful to me. Truth be told, he was the best husband I ever had." Her face saddened and her eyes teared. "I think he's the only one I ever really felt anything for."

"Go ahead and see him, and if it doesn't work, at least you tried." I said. "And you won't have a wife walk in while you're half naked."

She blushed, leaned close, and whispered, "Actually, we were butt naked and I was cowgirl on top when she walked in. Half-naked just sounded less bad."

Chapter 65
Our Real Mom
Evelyn

I was the last parent in the loading zone in front of the school when Angela finally showed up. "Where's Chris?"

"Don't know." She climbed in and sat at the window seat behind me, where I couldn't see her, instead of sitting in the front seat like usual. Her tone had been curt and a quarter-octave too high—she was lying. I figured Chris and Katelyn were testing their boundaries and went to the mall, an arcade, or some fast food place, and she was covering for him.

I pulled out my phone and hit Chris's cell number. Nothing. My phone was dead. I plugged it into the cigarette lighter and noticed Sam had called a few minutes before. I tried Chris again but the call went straight to voicemail.

"I can't leave without knowing where Chris is. Shall I go in and have the school look for him and call the police when they don't find him, or are you going to tell me?"

Her pained plea scared me. "He's alright, Mom. Please. Let's just go home. Bobby will drop him off later."

Bobby and Chris had been close friends since third grade. A couple of months ago, Bobby had turned sixteen and had gotten his learner's permit, so I figured Bobby was showing off his driving skills for Chris.

"Alright. I'll call Bobby's mom—"

"NO!" The volume and panic in her voice made me jump.

I twisted around to look at her. Her skin was flush, her eyes filled with fear, and she was trying to avoid looking at me. Her chin was trembling. I knew that whatever they had gotten themselves into was far beyond anything they had ever done before.

"Where is he?" My tone said tell-me-and-tell-me-now.

She waffled and then whispered, "He went to Chowchilla."

I shivered as a chill shot through me. I still hadn't recovered from Grace running away less than a week ago, and now this. I was being kicked while I was still down.

"Bobby drove?"

She nodded yes.

"When did they leave?"

She was starting to cry. "Right after you dropped us off. I'm sorry."

At best, Chowchilla was a three-hour drive each way. Even if they would let an unescorted minor into the prison, seven hours wasn't enough time for him to get there, visit, and get back. Chances were he was in the East Bay, but the fact his cell phone was off troubled me.

I called Bobby's mom. "Hi, Vivian. Are Bobby and Chris there?"

"The police didn't call you?"

My heart stopped. "What happened?"

"Oh. Sorry. They're fine, at least until they get home. They were stopped for speeding on the 205 near Tracy this morning. Since a learner's permit requires an adult in the car, they were detained. My husband and Bobby's grandfather went down to get Bobby and the car. I thought they would have called you, too."

"My phone was dead. They probably called Sam. Thanks. Bye."

Sam picked up on the third ring. Without formalities and with what had become his usual, grumpy tone, he said, "I have Chris. He's fine. We'll be home in an hour."

I assumed the missed call from Sam was to tell me he had Chris, but he should have called me at work when he found out this morning. "Why didn't you call—?" The accident rates when using cell phones while driving were about equal to drunk driving, so I dropped it. "I'll see you two at home."

I sat there, thinking about all the mean things I wanted to say to Sam, but knew I wouldn't. Angela's soft voice was trembling. "What happened, Mom?"

Their behavior was completely unacceptable. I stuffed down my anger. "Move over." I moved to the back next to her. "Why did Chris go to Chowchilla?" She looked down. "Look me in the eye."

She looked back up, her eyes filled with tears.

"We want our real mom."

The words seared through my already raw heart with savage ferocity. I knew they had imprinted on Clora when they were infants, and she would always hold a special place in their hearts. I knew Angela didn't mean to diminish my role in their lives. But when she said "our real mom," it hurt almost as bad as when my mom had died.

They were my children. I was their mother. My love was real. I was real. Their wanting Clora was validating Sam's claim that I wasn't a real woman, and by extension, a real mother.

After they had found the DVD and stood up for me, I didn't think I had to worry about them and me, but they were being battered by uncertainty, too. As accepting as they had been, my past had to bring up questions for them about who I was, who they were, and what we meant to each other.

I was losing Sam. I couldn't lose my kids, too.

I tried to pull myself out of myself so I could be there for Angela.

"What's going on, sweetheart?"

Her chin quivered as she glared at me. "You and Dad don't love us anymore."

The pain in the voice of my woman-child spoke sonnets of grief and fear. A family asunder. Future uncertain. Precarious love. And a core wound of mother lost.

Before the journals and the DVD, she could pretend I had always been her mother. But now? She knew I was born wrong and could never have birthed her. She knew her world was falling apart and feared she might lose me. In her pain, I had become a pretender who was not of her blood. A foreigner that her clan leader wanted to exile from her world forever.

Whether it was spirit or chromosomes, I couldn't say. But I had seen it too often to deny the existence of blood bonds. Somewhere deep inside us, we crave to know the face of those who gave us life. I had known this day would come, but why such lousy timing?

"We do love you with all our—"

"Then why are you and Dad getting divorced?"

I wanted to deny the divorce. I wanted to point out her false logic of 'you love all or you love none.' I wanted to tell her we would talk later. I wanted to pretend God would answer my prayers and make everything right. But she was smart. She knew. And God had his reasons for ignoring my prayers.

"Your dad and I are still trying to work it out, but even if we do end up separating, we will both always love you and Chris and Grace. That will never change."

I could see the doubt and turmoil as she wrestled with the demons of divorce.

I continued. "You love Daniel, don't you?"

She nodded yes.

"Does loving him make you love me or your father any less?"

She slowly shook her head no.

"And if someday you should marry Daniel and go away, will that mean you don't love us anymore?"

She sniffled and a doleful "No" whispered from her lips.

"If your father and I separate, it won't change the way we feel about you. You are our children, we love you, and that will never change."

The anger in Angela's eyes settled into concern. "What happened to Chris?"

"Bobby was stopped for speeding. Chris and your dad are on their way back."

She nodded and looked downward in a fixed stare.

"No. He didn't see your other mother. I'll talk to your dad about you two visiting, if that is what you want."

Her eyes snapped onto me with a jumble of emotions: fear, hope, anxiety, joy, and regret. I offered a hug. She wrapped her arms around me and hugged me harder and longer than she had since her Grandmother had died.

"I love you, Mom."

"I love you, too, sweetheart."

Chapter 66
More Half-Truths and Lies
Sam

A parent never wants to get a call from the police saying they have your kid. I had received the call about ten-thirty and knew Evelyn would blame me. Maybe I was to blame, but I was tired of her accusations and didn't need the hassle.

I had hoped to get back before school was out, but there had been an accident that slowed traffic to a stop-and-go, and then the police had taken forever to release Chris to me. It was late, and by now, Evelyn was at the school and waiting for Chris. I called her cell phone but it went straight to voicemail.

Chris and I were silent until I hit the freeway. "Where were you going?" I asked.

"To see my mom."

I tensed and shoved down my anger.

"Why?"

"Because you won't take me."

"We've talked about this before."

He was silent. I wanted to use my old worn-out excuses about his mother, but they were half-truths, like the ones Evelyn had told me. I had told him that Clora wouldn't be out until long after he was grown—the inference being that she was as good as dead. I had told him that she had given him up—the inference being that she didn't love or want him. If he felt anything for his mother, I had wanted it to be the same righteous indignation and anger I had felt for her.

At the time, I had believed the kids were better off without Clora, but now I knew life wasn't that simple. When she gave them up, I knew it was because she loved them ... but I hadn't wanted him to know that.

I needed to undo what I had done, but wasn't sure how. So much was broken, and I couldn't fix any of it.

"Grandma Suzy said she loves us," Chris said, with obstinate defiance.

I gripped the steering wheel harder. I had made it clear to Clora's mom that she could see Chris and Angela *only* if she never, ever talked about Clora.

"What else did Grandma Suzy say?"

He was digging in, becoming defiant. "That my mother made a mistake and was sorry. That she would go back and undo it if she could. That she loves us."

"What else?"

"Nothing."

His "nothing" was filled with bitter anger and stubborn refusal.

Shit. Why does he have to be so much like me?

"What else?" I asked.

Chris folded his arms and stared out the passenger window. When he was younger, there would be a hint of apprehension in his stubbornness, but lately, that had vanished. It had been replaced by a determined willfulness.

But below the stubbornness I could see an old hurt, want, need. I had thought that Eve and I would be enough. We weren't.

Forcing more tolerance into my tone, I said, "Did Angela know you were going?"

His "No" was sharp and defensive. He was assuming all responsibility and consequences for trying to see Clora. I was proud of his willingness to stand by what he believed and accept responsibility for his actions. I was also proud of his loyalty to, and protectiveness of, his sister. But as close as they were, I knew Angela and Chris had to have planned it together.

I shook my head, knowing that Angela would also accept all blame and hold Chris faultless—say it was her idea. I loved how close they were.

My stomach lurched. I realized that if I got Chris and Evelyn got Angela, it could destroy that bond.

I pushed the thought from my head. "What did you want to see your mother for?"

His voice was hesitant and filled with confusion. "Don't know. Just do."

He had run off. I couldn't let it go with just a talk. But how could I punish him for wanting to see his mother? All of us were being battered by the raging seas of half-truths. Our ship was taking on water and I didn't see a way to pump fast enough to keep us afloat.

We were sinking.

Chapter 67
Never Let Go
Sam

When Chris and I arrived home, Eve tried to hug him, but he dodged her and went to his room. She turned to me, the heat of her glare scorching my eyebrows, then marched past me to the living room. The unsaid understanding was that I could follow her or I could leave and not bother coming back.

"Why did you wait so long to call me?" she demanded.

I didn't have a good answer. Anything I said would lay me out for her to fillet.

"We need to talk about the kids, not us."

She pursed her lips and trembled with anger. For a second I thought she was going to scream at me. She had only become unhinged five times in the last ten years—most of it recent. In the heat of the arguments, I had felt justified and believed her outbursts to be female hysterics—but now? I had no right to call her Adam or to call her a man. I had no right to tell her to walk away from her kids. I had attacked her integrity and womanhood. I had been wrong but I hadn't been able to stop myself. And I sure as hell couldn't apologize.

This insanity was forcing me to see myself in a way I never had. I didn't like what I saw. I wasn't the man of reason and integrity I had believed myself to be. I had been cruel to my wife. I had lied to my children. I was the one acting irrational ... even hysterical.

Eve had every right to hate me, but she was still trying. Still loved me.

God! Why can't I just accept?

I sat in the overstuffed chair across from Eve. She stood by the sofa, glaring at me, with her arms folded.

"What did Angela say?" I asked.

The tempest boiling in Eve slowed to a mild thunderstorm.

She sounded tired. "Angela said Chris went to see Clora."

"Why didn't she go, too?"

The corner of Eve's lip rose in a slight smile. "Chris wouldn't let her. Told her it wasn't a place for women and children."

I shook my head. "Did Angela say why?"

I saw her spirit flinch. She took a deep breath. "She said that since we were getting a divorce, I didn't love them anymore. They were looking to Clora."

"They know you love them."

She looked at me with some puzzlement. "Yes. I know."

Her eyes drifted down in deep thought. Her energy shifted from hurt and angry to a peaceful resolve. I had seen that resolve before. She had decided something, and nothing on earth, in heaven, or in the deep blue seas would stop her. What she had just set her mind to do would happen.

She stared straight into my eyes. "I promised Angela that she and Chris could go see their mother."

"NO!"

Her eyes narrowed and she scarcely shook her head no. To her it was a fact as unalterable as the rising of the sun.

I knew I had been wrong to keep them from Clora. I knew I would have to say yes. But it needed to be when *I* was ready. They needed to have *me* take them—not her. She was using Clora to buy favor with my kids.

I was on my feet. "You will *not* take my children into a prison."

She stared at me for a few seconds and with calm assurance said, "Yes. They are your children. And they are my children. And they are Clora's children. And Grandma Rose's, and Grandpa Rich's, and Grandpa Nick's, and Grandma Suzy's.

"As their father, you have certain rights and responsibilities, but they are people, not property. They are old enough that what *they* want matters ... a lot."

She stepped closer to me and continued. "I never agreed with your cutting them off from Clora, but you were the father and my husband so I acquiesced to your wishes. You've decided you don't want to be my husband anymore so I have to stand up for what I feel is best for our children. I hate the idea of taking them into a prison as much as you, but they need to see her. As today proved, they can be as willful as their father and *will* see their mother, with or without our approval."

I heard a sound in the hall and my stomach churned. Eve

looked toward the hall, too, so I knew it wasn't just me.

"Get in here, NOW!" I called.

Chris led, with Angela and Grace lagging behind him.

"How long have you been there?" I demanded to know.

They ignored me. Chris and Angela looked to their mom with hope filling their eyes.

"When can we go?" Chris asked.

Mutiny. She had played me and I had walked right into it.

Eve said, "If you are going to be running away and spying on your father and me, it will be after you're eighteen."

I slumped back into my chair. Grace came over, crawled into my lap, and curled up in my arms. Her sad eyes held confusion and hope. "Why don't you love Mom?" Grace asked. "She *is* a girl."

Everyone was looking at me, and I wondered how we got back on *that*. My mind tumbled over itself, searching for an elusive answer. It seemed like no matter what I did or said, I was the bad guy.

"Grace, sweetie," Evelyn said. "It's not that simple. It's grown-up stuff you can't understand."

Angela glared at me. "We understand."

I almost jumped on her for being disrespectful but Evelyn spoke before I could pull my thoughts together.

"I know you think you understand," Eve said. "But it's more complicated than my being born wrong. I know it's hard, but it's between your—"

"He doesn't want you," Angela said, "like he doesn't want our other mom. Does he love someone else?"

I stared in disbelief. *How could she think that?*

The darkness consumed me as my fragmented thoughts stole my logic. Behind my shocked mask, my frustration screamed like an injured child. The accusations and demands lacerated my thoughts and my hopes.

Eve shook her head no. "No. It's not anything like that."

"Why, Dad?" Grace demanded, staring up at me.

I grabbed the only coherent thought in my head. "It's between your mom and me. I'm sorry it can't be different."

Chris looked straight at me with hot anger.

"You hate our real mom because she made a mistake. You hate our mom because Grandma Louise's diaries said she's different. Are you going to hate us if we make a mistake or are different?"

I had forgotten about the journals and was surprised he had made that connection, but Eve was always saying they understand far more than we give them credit for.

"No. I don't hate your mom … or anyone," I said. I sat there, stumbling over wrong words and wading through scattered thoughts, sounding like an idiot while the kids glared at me.

"This is between your father and me," Eve interjected. "When we decide things, we will let you know. And that includes when you will visit Clora."

Grace trembled and curled up tighter against me. I wished I had never seen the damn journals.

Chris glared at me. "We aren't children."

"No, you're not," Eve said. "Because you are *usually* mature teens, your wish to see your mother is being very seriously considered. I would hope that you are mature enough to respect your father's and my privacy. Allow us to work out our differences however we need to."

Angela had been bravely holding back her tears, but she began to tremble and the sorrow spilled out. Eve pulled Angela to her on the couch, taking her in a hug and holding her as if she would never let go. And I knew that, like me, she never would let any of them go.

Chris trembled with rage and stared into my soul. "I'll be in my room when you've decided what you want to do with us." He turned and stomped away.

Eve's pained look said, "What do you want to do?"

My look said, "Let him go. We'll pick up the pieces later." *If it's possible.*

Chapter 68
Burning the Journals
Sam

Evelyn looked exhausted, standing in the doorway to the family room in her pink satin pajamas.

"They're all asleep," she said. "I'm going to bed. See you in the morning."

I didn't know if she was making an effort to look more sexy since she had begged me to make love to her, or if her offer had spiked my interest.

We had one more issue to address this evening before bed.

"Where are the journals?"

She stiffened. "I have them locked in the garden shed."

"What?"

She blushed a little. "They smelled like lighter fluid. I was concerned about a fire."

I nodded.

"Could you bring them in here?"

Her eyes narrowed. "Why?"

The last week had been hell. Grace had run away, Chris had gone on his little joyride, and all the kids were acting like ... kids. I was emotionally and physically drained. I didn't want to play question and answer. I didn't want to discuss it because I was afraid I would change my mind and regret it later.

"Just get the damn books."

When I returned from the garage with a fresh can of lighter fluid, a trash bag full of books hung over the arm of my recliner in the family room. Evelyn was nowhere in sight. I found her in our bedroom, sitting on the edge of the bed, staring at her feet.

"I need you."

She looked up and I knew she had misunderstood.

"No. In the family room."

Evelyn did a double take when she saw the trash bag sitting

on the hearth with a new can of lighter fluid.

"The kids already know too much," I said. "They can't read these."

She nodded, her eyes fixed on the bag.

"Should I do it or do you want to?" I asked.

Her body shifted toward the fireplace but her feet remained planted in her pink bunny slippers. Her eyes were fixed on the journals.

"You do it," she said softly.

"Are there any you want to keep?"

She shook her head no, her ghostly stare fixed on the journals.

When I opened the bag, the solvent smell assaulted me. I dumped them into the fireplace.

"I'm glad you put them in the garden shed. They stink badly enough they could have blown up the house or gassed someone."

I heard a pained, grief-filled "Mm," behind me and looked back. Her face was red and she looked like she was ready to cry.

Shit. I don't need that, too.

I went back to stacking the journals so the air would circulate between them, ensuring they would burn completely. The can wheezed and spat, with the last of the fluid sploshing onto them.

I looked back at Eve. The threat of tears had subsided and her eyes held mine for a moment. She nodded yes. I watched the match burn in my fingers and knew it was wrong. I blew it out and stood.

I handed Eve the matchbox. She looked puzzled and worried.

"They were your mom's. It's not my place to burn them."

I ached with the pain that tormented her and wished I could make it go away. On reflex, I kissed her forehead. She frowned, her eyes asking me why. I turned away and went to the kitchen to find a beer. I had expected to hear the roar of flames seconds after handing her the matches, but ten minutes later, I heard only the sounds of a sleeping house.

Leaning against the doorframe, I watched her from behind. She was still standing where I had left her, staring at the fireplace. Her faint soft whispers floated to me on solvent fumes; she was talking with her mom. Except for Eve's prayer, the room was still and silent.

Watching her, it was undeniable that she was a woman. Since the initial shock and anger had subsided, I had begun to see things through rational eyes. I understood why she had lied about being born male and I could have forgiven that—wanted to forgive it. But she still should have told me. She had deliberately deceived me, just like Clora had. I couldn't live with someone I couldn't trust.

And then there was the sex thing. They say that ninety percent of a good sexual relationship is between the ears. I had thought it was bull, but now I got it. If I had known, I never could have had sex with Eve. Ten years of blissful love and desire, extinguished by a few words. It was so different now, and the only thing that had changed was my perception of her.

The physical hadn't changed. She was as soft and beautiful and sweet-smelling as before. I knew her lips would still taste like sweet love.

Guilt gnawed at me. I knew I was wrong for feeling the way I did, because I understood that it was our mind and our spirit that determined who we were, not our bodies. But I just couldn't. Not with her.

Maybe they were right. Maybe I was transphobic, but I didn't want to think about it anymore.

I watched Eve whisper prayers and sniffle for another ten minutes.

She moved. The raspy strike and the hiss of the match flooded the silence. Even with the lighter fluid smell thick in the room, the sharp scent of the flame made its way to me. She bent down and tossed the burning match.

The flash was blinding, and a ball of flame rolled out at Eve. She stumbled backwards and tripped. I rushed forward and caught her.

"You okay?" I asked.

She regained her footing and tilted her head back to look up at me. Her hair was singed and face red but not burned. Her eyes were filled with so many emotions that I had to look away.

In a troubled whisper, she said, "Yes. I'm fine," then looked to the fireplace and watched the journals burn while I held her.

The flames were mesmerizing, and I didn't realize I had wrapped my arms around her and pulled her tight against me. It was such an old habit. So natural.

After several minutes, I realized and pulled away.

"Sorry."

She stood nearly motionless, only shifting her weight so she could stand without my support. No words or recognition. I went to the kitchen for a glass of water.

When I returned, she was sitting on the couch, whispering a prayer while she watched the burning journals. Without taking her eyes from the blaze, she patted the cushion next to her. I sat.

In a lost, imploring voice, Eve said, "Hold me. Please."

I got comfortable against some pillows, then Eve curled up next to me, snuggled in my arms, and laid her head on my chest. We watched in silence as the yellow, orange, and blue flames danced on the journals. Dense black smoke billowed off the leather bindings. Pages curled, flared, and died. We witnessed the blaze consuming the secrets Eve had tried so hard to hide, as they became secrets once again.

With the flames long dead, the last of the glowing red embers twinkled into dull gray, leaving behind a pile of ashen ghost pages and curled burnt leather.

I watched Eve sleeping. In the past, I would have woken her and watched her stumble half-asleep to bed as I followed. I stared back at the ash and wished it were that easy to make the past go away, to burn up memories we didn't want, and hold tight to those we cherished.

Eve shifted gently against me in her sleep and sighed.

If only we could turn back time. I closed my eyes and let troubled sleep take me.

Chapter 69
The Visitors List
Evelyn

When I woke at three a.m. on the family room couch with Sam, I had hoped he had come back to me. Instead, he returned to being the angry man I didn't know—and avoided me even more than usual. I guessed it was because he didn't want to face taking the kids to see Clora.

In the four days since I had promised Chris and Angela that we would go to see Clora, they had asked, "When are we going, Mom?" at least a thousand times. I wanted to talk to Sam first, but he wouldn't talk. I got tired of trying to corner him and did some web research on what was involved.

The prison system required Clora to sign and send a questionnaire to us. After we filled out the form and submitted it to the state, they would do a background check before allowing us to visit.

It was doubtful they would dig any deeper than verifying that I was who I said I was, and that I didn't have a police record. Nevertheless, I hated the idea that they could dig into my childhood when it had no bearing on anything. If their records search turned up my name connected with the murders, they might dig into my past. I was beginning to regret telling the kids they could go.

The questionnaire gave me some breathing room. It took up to thirty days for the government to put you on the approved visitor list, provided there weren't any complications or further questions. I had a reprieve from the kids.

I called Sam. I knew he would argue with me, so I was cold, firm, and got straight to the point. "I'm going to write to Clora and ask her to send me Form-106 so I can take the kids to visit. Do you want me to have her send you one?"

His voice was tense. "No."

"You aren't going?"

He hesitated. "I'm already on the list," he said, his voice rumbling with anger.

"What?" He hated her. He wanted nothing to do with her.

He was defensive and curt. "I'm on the list. We can talk later. I need to get back to work. Bye."

He hung up. I stared at the phone as if it had answers.

"He's on the friggin' list?"

The thought flashed through my mind that some prisons allowed conjugal visits. I checked the web and found that in an effort to keep families together, California allowed them but you needed to be married. The guilt for not trusting him was tempered by the fact that I didn't know him anymore.

Tonight felt almost normal, with Sam and the kids engaged in pleasant dinner conversation as everyone shared their day.

"Have you heard anything yet, Mom?" Angela asked.

I knew she was talking about Clora. It had been three weeks since I had submitted the applications. Sam's look was thoughtful and lacked the chill I had expected.

"No," I said.

"May we be excused?" Chris asked.

Before I could say, "Yes," Sam handed Chris and Angela envelopes that were over a quarter-inch thick. The kids looked confused as they read the return address.

"They're from Clora," Sam said. "You can write her back at the address on the envelope."

Four weeks ago, he had wanted nothing to do with Clora and now he was handing them letters? Angela, Chris, and I stared at him in disbelief. Grace looked around, trying to figure out what was going on. Sam forced a smile and added, "She'd like to hear from you."

Nervously fingering the envelopes, Angela and Chris sat staring at Sam for a few seconds. They looked at me, and I hugged the air. They scrambled over to their dad, hugged him, thanked him, and started asking questions.

"It looked like it would be a while until we could go see Clora," he said, interrupting their bombardment. "I asked her to write you and you probably want to write to her. We'll talk about the other things later."

They scurried off to Chris's room to share their letters, while Grace sat watching Sam and me, unsure of what was going on.

I smiled at Grace. "Would you like to help me clean up the kitchen or would you like to go join the other two?"

She scampered off.

I knew how much Sam had wanted to pretend that Clora didn't exist. He could have dug in and made it very difficult for the kids and me, but he hadn't. I was proud of him for being able to move past his anger for the good of his children. I hoped that his newfound maturity would extend to me.

"So ... How did you get the letters?"

He shrugged, and a storm engulfed his face.

"The mail."

He was back to being a mule's behind. I half sneered and started picking up plates to clear the table.

"Sorry," he said. "I skipped a day of work last week and ran down. Asked Clora to write the kids while you got on the visitor list. I had her send them to my work so the kids didn't get blindsided by them suddenly showing up in the mail."

I wanted to ask him why he hadn't told me, but I doubted he knew. Since we were on the subject of Clora and visits, I wanted an answer. I didn't mean for the question to sound accusatory, but it did.

"Why are you on Clora's visitor list?"

His glare said "Up yours" but he didn't say it. His voice was rigid, bordering on belligerent.

"When you adopted the kids, I thought I would need to talk with her and get her to sign papers. I did the questionnaire."

I subdued my anger. "I thought it was all handled by the lawyer."

The storm passed and he settled into indifference.

"Most of it. But it was going to cost a grand for him to take the papers down for her to sign. I was going to do it, but Clora's mom offered so I let her."

After Sam had announced our engagement, I had expected Grandma Suzy to view me as her daughter's replacement and be antagonistic. But from the start, she had been supportive, friendly, and helpful. If she lived closer, she would have been involved in our kids' lives as much as Grandma Louise and Grandma Rose.

"That was eight years ago. You need to re-apply every few years."

He nodded and stared at the empty biscuit basket on the table.

"Because of the problems we had before she went away, as well as some bureaucratic bungling, it took almost three months of jumping through hoops to get on the visitation list. It's stupid, but I felt like if anything ever happened to one of the kids, I should be the one to tell her so I kept it current."

That was the Sam I loved. "That's not stupid. It's incredibly sweet."

He shrugged. "Whatever."

I was curious more than anything.

"Why didn't you tell me?"

He shook his head and looked off in thought.

"Don't know. Didn't seem important."

"How often do you see her?" I said, trying to hide my suspicion and jealousy.

His eyes narrowed. "Twice in twelve years." His "twice" bordered on a dare to pry deeper. I dropped it.

"That was very thoughtful. I'm glad you went," I said.

He pulled another letter out of his pocket and tossed it across the table to me.

"You're on the list. She's expecting us and the kids a week from Thursday. You need to tell the kids."

I raised my eyebrows. "Me?"

"You're the one who promised," he said, with a slight rumble of anger in his voice.

"Do you object?"

He looked back over his shoulder toward the kids bedrooms in thought. Turning back to me, his eyes filled with sad regret, he shook his head no. "The kids are more important than 'pride that will not die.' She's a good person. They need to know her … and she needs them."

I nodded. "You're the one who needs to tell them. They need to have your blessing."

"Yeah," he said. He smiled to himself and nodded. His eyes drifted to me. For a few moments, we once again shared the love and appreciation that had defined our relationship for so long.

He said, "Thanks," and then it was gone.

Chapter 70
Stepmoms
Evelyn

Felicity had called and said it was "crucial to the survival of the world" that she see me today. Every time we talked on the phone, she was off rafting or mountain climbing with Mark, so I knew she hadn't had time to make a new bronze creation.

She seemed excited, and after going to Chowchilla yesterday, I needed to see her, too.

We had planned on meeting at five at the *Olive Garden* for an early dinner. I was fifteen minutes late and not surprised when she wasn't there yet. I got a table, ordered iced tea, and waited. When she walked in, her joy filled the whole restaurant. I could have been legally blind and still seen the collection of rocks on her finger.

"Oh … my … gawd. You didn't."

She squealed, "Yes," nodded hard enough to dislocate something, and held out her hand. I took it and studied the diamond encrusted gold ring. "It's beautiful. It's got to be a thousand carats."

She pulled her hand back and hugged the ring. She tried to talk, but joyous tears stifled the words. We hugged.

"Congratulations. Have you set a date?"

She shook her head no and sniffled, then pulled away. "He was talking next month, but it's not enough time to plan a wedding."

We sat. "Next month? You've only known him for three months."

Felicity chuckled and dabbed her eyes. "And how long did you know Sam?" she asked, with playful teasing.

It had been a completely irresponsible four months. Sam and I knew better, but we both knew, so I had said yes. "But we waited another nine months."

Felicity beamed. "I know. And I will, too. I want to marry on the anniversary of when we met, which gives us time to plan a huge wedding and time to get to really know each other."

I didn't mean to flinch at the word wedding.

Her glow dimmed. "What's wrong? Sam pull something else?" Her face got long and sad. "Oh, gawd. I'm so sorry, Eve. I completely forgot about yesterday."

"No. It's alright. You were getting engaged. That's more important than—"

"Not more important than you. What happened?"

I shrugged. "I'm not sure. I feel like an outsider with my own family now. We dropped Grace off with Rose and headed down to Chowchilla. On the way, Sam told Chris and Angela stories about when he and Clora were growing up."

Felicity's frown bumped up against her anger. "That was mean."

The waitress came, and I mindlessly fingered my cold iced tea glass while we ordered. After she left, I continued. "He didn't mean to be mean. The kids kept asking questions. He'd say a little, and they wanted more and kept asking until he gave it."

"It still wasn't nice. He could have said they would talk later."

I took a sip of my tea. "It's things he should have told them years ago. They want to know their birth mother. It's normal ... especially now. It gives them something to hold on to. Someone else to love them unconditionally so they know they are important and special."

Felicity sighed. "I guess. It just seems like he could have done it when you weren't there."

I continued fingering the cold tea glass. "I don't know. In a way, I'm glad I was there. It makes me part of the kids new world, too."

"But you said you felt like an outsider."

I stared past her at an old black-and-white picture of an elderly Italian couple sitting at a café drinking wine with a little ragamuffin girl. The picture looked to be from the nineteen forties. The old couple would have passed long ago, leaving behind their loved ones.

Was the girl a granddaughter or great-granddaughter? Or just a beggar who happened upon them? The girl would probably be in her seventies if she was still alive. I wondered if she had married, had children, and grown old with her true love. Or did she die tragically when she was a child or young woman? Maybe she never knew true love or the joys and sorrows of having children. There were so many paths our lives could take.

"Are you alright?" Felicity asked.

I looked back at her and blinked the glassy thought of life's many paths from my eyes.

"Yes. Sorry. You were saying?"

"Outsider," she gently repeated.

I nodded. "At first, Clora was so happy that she couldn't stop crying. It made Sam uncomfortable, so he excused himself to the men's room, leaving me with two nervous kids and Clora."

"Chicken."

I shrugged. "That's just Sam. He never could deal with a woman's tears. Once Clora quieted and started asking Chris about his diving, and Angela about her poetry, I saw something awaken inside all three of them, as naturally and effortlessly as the light from the morning sun awakens the earth. There was something magical, spiritual about it ... and Sam missed it.

"On the way home, Chris and Angela talked about how wonderful their mom was and how great it would be if she got out." I looked down and sighed. "I'm not part of their circle."

Felicity reached over and took my hand.

"I've seen that same magic when they are with you. You share it with them, too. Like you said, it's normal and natural that they would have it with her. They still love you. You will always be their mom and hold a special place in their hearts. And you should know, more than most people, that lots of stepmoms feel left out or feel like an intruder sometimes."

I forced a half smile and nodded. When Clora was out of our lives, I was "Mom," not "Stepmom." I didn't like standing on the sideline watching.

They are MY children, darn it ... or at least they used to be.

"I know." I said. "But Sam doesn't want me. Chris and Angela only talk about Clora. And Grace didn't want me. She ran away. If her parents were alive, I'd just be her aunt."

Felicity looked a little peeved. I knew she thought I was wallowing in self-pity. I knew she was right, but fudge, I didn't want to share my kids. Grace was the only one who halfway wanted me and that was because she didn't have anyone else. The waitress came up and asked if we needed more breadsticks.

Felicity smiled at her.

"Do you have worms?"

The waitress frowned. "Um. Worms?"

"Yeah. Worms. Usually pink or red. Look like spaghetti. Wiggle around a lot. You find them in gardens … and this is an *olive* garden. You use them for catching fish. Worms."

"Sorry, Ma'am. We don't have worms."

"Stop it already," I said. I looked at the poor waitress. "We're fine. Thank you."

I wanted to be mad at Felicity, but she was right. I was acting like a child.

She grinned and in a hushed tone sang, "Nobody likes me. Everybody hates me. I think I'll go and eat a—"

"I got it already." Tears threatened my eyes. "You're right and I know better, but it hurts. They were all mine, and now I have to share."

Her concerned mom look was back. "I'm sorry, Eve, but it doesn't mean you're losing them. Their loving Clora won't diminish the love they feel for you or the honored place you hold in their hearts.

"And Grace worships you. I hate to think of what losing you would do to her."

Her smile slipped into a snicker. "At some point, they'll probably pull the 'I want my real mom' crap, like I did with my stepmom." The snicker faded, replaced by loving concern. "But it won't change how they feel about you in their hearts. You will still be their *mom*, just like my stepmom is, and always will be, *my* mom."

Felicity pursed her lips, frowned, and looked down.

"Note to self. Call Mom and tell her I'm sorry."

I bit my lip. "Thank you."

Her eyes sparkled. "You're welcome."

She looked up at the waitress, who was bringing us our food. The waitress seemed a little wary. After she served us and put extra cheese on our dinners, she hesitantly said to me— deliberately ignoring Felicity, "Would you like anything else?"

Felicity smiled at her. "No. We won't need the worms after all. We're fine. Thank you."

The waitress tried to smile before leaving us to our food.

"So what was she like?" Felicity asked.

"You and me. If they had given her a second chance, she'd probably be clean, sober, obeying the law, and supporting herself instead of costing the taxpayers fifty grand a year."

"That's almost enough to hire a teacher," Felicity said.

"Yeah."

"Do you know when she'll get out?"

"Sam said she had another seven or eight on her sentence, but she's never been trouble. Maybe she'll get out early."

The sparkle from her ring threatened to blind me.

"Enough about me. Tell me about you and Mark."

Her eyes moistened, with the gleam of a joyous dream come true, but she slumped a little. "Another time. With Sam and everything, it feels like I would be rubbing salt in your wounds."

I feigned insult. "Another time? You're engaged to a wonderful man and you don't want to tell your best friend about it? No way. I want to hear everything."

"Everything?" she said.

I nodded with ardent interest. "Yes. Absolutely everything."

She glowed like a princess in a fairytale.

"He's just perfect. Sometimes I think I'm going to wake up and it will have been a dream. It's incredible living a dream. He's so smart. Makes me laugh. He's good with people and unbelievably patient, even when customers are being morons or acting like three-year-old brats. I just love him so much. I never thought it was possible to feel this completely, insanely, in love."

Her smile quivered. "I thought you were foolish when you told me you were marrying Sam. You hardly knew him. But now I understand. I really, really understand. It's incredible to know someone's your soul mate. That you are destined for each other."

Yes ... It was.

Chapter 71
One Last Vacation
Evelyn

I wiggled my toes deep into the soft sands of Doran Beach and watched the kids swimming. The warm summer air caressed my skin and carried the alluring scent of salt spray to me. I knew I should just let go of the inevitable and bask in the beauty of the moment, but this was our last family vacation.

Georgette stopped beside me and looked out at Patrick and Chris trying to body surf the small waves of the sheltered cove. "The ocean smells wonderful, doesn't it?" she asked.

She looked good—more relaxed than I had seen her in years. Since last summer, we had kept in touch by phone and email. Patrick had had his transplant and was doing very well and Georgette was now officially a single mom.

I said, "Yes. It does. Patrick is looking good. You wouldn't even know."

Her smile was filled with loving contentment.

"Yeah. He's doing wonderful. He's been so strong and positive through the whole thing. When he saw me worrying, he'd say, 'Mom. Don't worry. Everything will be fine. My angel told me.'"

I smiled, nodded, and looked back out at the kids.

"You've raised a great son."

"I know. The best. But the credit belongs to who he is, not me."

We stood there for a minute before she spoke again. "Missed you when we were setting up base camp. You've been here every year since you married Sam."

"Almost. Missed the year Grace had strep throat."

"That's right. Forgot."

We stood there for a couple more minutes. I knew she had been wanting to ask me something all week. I also knew the gossip mill was running hot and heavy with the news of Sam and me. Rose was the only one who knew why.

Georgette looked at me with concern. "Rose said you and Sam are divorcing."

I looked down at the little mists of sand blowing across my feet.

"Yep."

"Sorry. That really sucks."

"That's the truth."

"So, is this a mutual thing?"

I shook my head and looked back up. I sighed. "His choice."

"He find someone else?"

I looked down again and sneered. "No." That was such a normal assumption. I almost wished …

I caught her wide eyes out of the corner of my eye. "You didn't?"

I scoffed. "Sorry. No." I looked at her caring eyes.

I couldn't tell her why Sam didn't love me anymore, and I couldn't let her just hang. "Sometimes things just don't work out."

She winced. "Was it because you beat the bejesus out of him when he tried to throw you in the ocean last year?"

I was getting annoyed with her well-intentioned prying. My "No," was sharper than I had intended.

"But he worshiped—" She looked down. "Sorry. It's none of my business. If anyone should know that, it's me. I got sick of people wanting to know why Henry was divorcing me. Thank God he had the decency to not tell everyone and still treats Patrick like his."

"Patrick *is* his," I said. "It's not genetics that make us family. It's love."

She put her arm over my shoulder and pulled me to her. "He's a fool for leaving you, Eve."

I had run out of the greaseless sun block and resorted to the oily kind which attracted sand like the Great Pyramid of Giza and was impossible to get off my hands.

"There you go, sweetie," I said, to Grace. "You're good for another four hours."

"Thanks, Mom." She was off in a cloud of sand, running back out to be with her cousins.

Rose pushed her straw hat up off her face and put her

sunglasses back on. She watched Grace racing for the water.

"I shouldn't say it about my son, but Sam's a damn fool."

"No. He's not a fool. He's a mule's behind," I said.

She laughed and then, with finality in her tone, said, "He's being pig-headed. He could never hope to find a better wife and mother. He's breaking his children's hearts over nothing. That makes him a fool."

"It's not nothing."

She looked over at me with an incredulous scowl. "Do you think he's right?"

I blushed and looked away. "No."

She sounded like a hostile attorney cross-examining me. "Then what part of him *not* growing up, *not* accepting that you had a damn good reason to hide it, and being a pig-headed idiot disqualifies him from being a fool?"

He was my husband—at least for a while longer. I needed to stand up for him. I watched the waves crashing on the beach while I looked for some logical defense. I had lied, but even his mom agreed it wasn't worth destroying our family over.

"I wouldn't be so bold as to contradict my husband's mother."

Rose got wide-eyed, laughed, and shook her head. "You ever think of becoming a car salesman? You're slicker than snot when you want to be."

I smiled. "Thought about it once, but Sam would have had to cook dinner every night."

She nodded gravely. "Yeah. He cooks like me. A definite deal breaker."

Tonight would be the final bonfire and my marriage would be over. I had been watching Sam, waiting for one last opportunity to try to talk sense into him. He had slipped away from Doran Beach and headed toward the mouth of the harbor. Rose said she would watch the kids, so I moved up to the road and stood behind a motor home—peeking around the corner every few seconds to see where he was going. He perched on some rocks near the end of the road, facing the ocean.

I walked over. "Is this rock taken?"

He flinched and stiffened but didn't look back. He shook his head no, so I sat.

"Who's watching the kids?" he said. His question carried an undertow of "are you neglecting our children," or was it "*his* children."

"Rose and half your relatives," my undertow saying, "You're a moron and mule's behind for asking."

All it took was two sentences with nine words and we were already drowning. I prayed. *God. Show me some mercy. Throw me an anchor.*

We sat there for several minutes. I hoped our bad start would age well and we could begin again.

"I need to understand."

"You lied." His words were hollow. He didn't even believe them anymore.

"Yes. I did. But I don't understand why it is so bad you need to divorce me and hurt our kids."

His fist tightened and his sunburned knuckles turned pinkish white. He didn't say anything. We sat silently and listened to the seagulls crying, a sailboat sputtering past, and the waves sloshing in lazy, uneven rhythm against the harbor rocks. The retreating tide was pulling past us, mixing the fresh salt air I loved with the pungent rotting vegetation from the mud flats, stagnant harbor water, and rusty fishing boats.

"There is only one reason that makes sense to me, Sam. You know me better than anyone. Do you honestly believe I'm not a real woman?"

The long silence clawed savagely at the air between us.

"You are a woman," he said, his words filled with heartbreak, want, and absolute certainty.

If he had said "No," I would understand. I wanted to say "Then why?" but knew he would emotionally cut and run—that he would say "You lied," and there would be no coming back to this place.

"Thank you," I said. "That means a lot to me."

He shifted, his breathing tense and rattled. We watched a once proud charter boat, weathered to dirty gray with splotches of red rust, chugging from its home in the harbor. It bobbed past, as black and white seagulls circled above, crying for handouts.

I wasn't sure where the question came from.

"Will you remarry?" I asked.

He was motionless except for the pain that crept onto his face. He looked straight at me for the first time since I had sat down. His eyes brimmed with the waters of grief, fear, love, confusion, and want. His heart reached for me, but he pulled it back. He turned away, buried his face in his hands, and sobbed.

After a minute, I moved from my rock with the intention of holding him, comforting him. He heard me and sprang like a bird trying to escape a cat. He leapt from boulder to boulder with the powerful agility I had always admired, until he was far out on the jetty and far out of my reach.

I watched him sit and put his face back into his hands before I slid from the rocks and walked away.

Chapter 72
Wave of Regret
Sam

As an appropriate end to my marriage to Evelyn, an unseasonal squall line moved toward us. As we neared bonfire time at Salmon Creek, the storm line blanketed the sky, stealing our sunset, the full moon, and the bright stars we had expected for our last night.

Monday, I would call the lawyer and tell him to file.

During the traditional last night's marshmallow and s'mores roast, Evelyn and I had always sat together to watch the show and talk about the best parts of our vacation. But tonight, a good half-dozen beach chairs separated us, with no words spoken.

We had expected the clouds to be a weak front that would pass in a few hours, but as the fire died down, the wind began sending loose towels and beach balls skittering across the sand. Under the growing assault of needle-prick stings from the blowing sand, young children, the minimally clothed, and sensitive-skinned family members fled back to the security of the beach house, or headed for the shelter of their motor homes, travel trailers, and tents in the campgrounds. The men and the more sensibly dressed women collected cooking utensils, stray toys, blankets, beach chairs, leftover food, and other comfort items from the sand before returning to what would be an evening of sugar-charged children screaming and laughing while the exhausted adults tried to maintain an acceptable level of chaos.

It would grow quiet within an hour, as most of the boys and half the girls settled down to some form of electronic entertainment, missing the chance to strengthen their ties to cousins, aunts, uncles, and grandparents. It didn't matter. My tie to Evelyn was broken. Maybe it was better never to make those ties in the first place; it would save us from the inevitable lies and pain.

The idea of being cooped up in the beach house with Evelyn and the busybody relatives who had not-so-subtly been sticking their noses into my business made me cringe. I turned north away from the house and wandered along the sandbar, allowing the gusting wind and blowing sand to batter me.

A gnarled log the size of a pickup truck lay half-buried near the mouth of Salmon Creek. It had served as a bench, table, lookout, and fort during the week. I sat on it, with my back to the wind, picking at some soggy fibers in the trunk. Stephen, our family arborist, had said it was a redwood, about four hundred years old. He speculated it had fallen from one of the coastal cliffs during a storm, was battered by the waves, broken by the rocks, and washed ashore here. Its once magnificent trunk now lay mangled and stuck in the sand, only proving that nothing was permanent.

The laughing, animated voices and the children's excited squeals faded as the last of the families retreated. Their joy was replaced by the growing violence of the crashing surf and the staccato rumble of the rising wind intruding on the darkness.

I still couldn't understand why she hadn't told me. Even more, I couldn't find peace inside myself about being married to a … As hard as it would be on Grace, Angela, and Chris, I just couldn't stay with Evelyn. I knew it was me, but …

I watched Evelyn walking toward me, carrying a beach towel and a plastic sandcastle mold one of the children had left behind. I wondered if she would stalk me after we divorced. *No. … She won't.* She could be tenacious when she wanted something, but at some point, she would accept that I was a lost cause and move on.

She stopped about ten feet from me.

"Mind if I sit?"

I shrugged and looked away.

She climbed up and sat down to my left, with three feet between us. I looked to the ocean on my right. The wind was churning dead algae into frothy blankets of foam that grew large in the surf and smothered the sand at the water's edge. In the increasing darkness, the foam appeared gray and dirty.

The savage black tide crept closer as the blowing sand continued to etch away exposed skin. Evelyn had sensitive skin so I expected her to leave, but she sat in silence, ignoring nature's lashing.

I looked at her. "Being a mermaid, you're probably right at home in this weather."

I was instantly ashamed of the meanness in my voice.

Her beautiful, long hair flailed with wild dignity in the gusting wind. In the dim light, I could see that her eyes were kind and calm, but in the shadows behind the calm I saw her pain.

"I'm not a mermaid. I'm a woman. I always have been and always will be," Evelyn said, almost too soft to hear over the rumble of surf and wind.

I knew she was a woman. I wanted to say, "I'm sorry. I do love you," but tentacles, dark and deep, rose up inside me before I could speak.

I shouldn't have called her Adam and tried to take the kids, but she had been just as wrong—more. Like Clora, she had betrayed my trust. I had been right to be angry. She should have told me. I couldn't trust her.

"I love you," she said. "I would have spent my whole life loving you if you could have accepted me for who I am. But you judge and condemn me. You deny me. If that is how it must be, I will mourn *our* loss and move on, because I am stronger than you and all the people who condemn others because God made them different."

I held her stare. "Who is judging and condemning whom, Eve? I could have spent my whole life loving you too, but you deliberately deceived me. I can't trust you. I have every right to be angry."

She started to say something, but closed her eyes and turned her face away. She wasn't arguing. She wasn't justifying. She had surrendered.

In that moment, I fully understood. I wanted to continue blaming her, but I couldn't. She should have told me, but she had good reasons. I might have even done the same thing if I had been in her place.

I was the reason for the divorce. It was me. After talking with Nick, I had hoped to escape my Death Rock, but I couldn't find a way back to safe harbor. Something dark and ugly inside made it impossible for me to love the woman I loved.

We had lost. It was my fault. The battle was over. I stood and trudged up the beach.

After about forty yards, I heard a wave crashing right behind me. I started to turn but was slammed into the sand under a frigid wall of water. *Shit!*

The sleeper wave tumbled me over the sand dune and into Salmon Creek. With the water's course diverted by the dune, its pull was greatly slowed and weakened so I was somehow able to grab one of the few rocks sticking out of the sand and hold on—barely.

When the water's pull became ineffective, I stood and looked back to the log. It—and Eve—were gone. The image of the desolate beach that lay before me collided with the image of Chris floating unconscious in the water. They merged and ripped through my brain like the teeth of a twenty-foot great white.

I ran back toward the surf, scanning the surface, looking for anything in the meager reflections atop the black water and gray foam that might tell me where she was.

I saw something, driftwood or seaweed? *She couldn't have been dragged that far out so quick.* I heard Eve's faint voice carried by the wind. It was her, already a hundred yards out.

She'll drown!

Kelly Bandeau's words flooded through my mind. "I thought I didn't care, but I was wrong. With him gone, I didn't have anything to prove anymore. No righteous indignation to defend. No more, 'I'm right—You're wrong.' No more disappointment because he wasn't the person I wanted him to be."

Like Kelly, my anger and expectations were suddenly gone. I saw Eve with a clarity I didn't know was possible. I saw myself clearly, too. I finally got it.

I don't remember taking off my shoes, the plunge into the surf, or my socks slipping from my feet in the pounding waves. My only thought was to get to Eve. She may have been a strong swimmer once, but she was terrified of the water and no longer physically up to the task of fighting a rip current. I had to get to her.

I knew it was wasted effort, but I prayed anyway. *Please help me, God. I need a miracle.*

When I crested the larger swells, I would look out and correct my course. In the dim light from shore, I could see she hadn't panicked, like when I had tried to throw her into the water. I could also see that she was swimming against the pull of the rip current, instead of parallel to shore.

I was closing the distance between us but she was still over fifty yards away. A large swell lifted me. From my vantage point at its crest, I could see that Eve had stopped swimming and was bobbing in the water—a sign she was exhausted or hypothermic. I had to reach her. If she went under, I would never find her in the watery blackness.

I plowed through the water as the sound of crashing surf faded. Considering the storm, the swells had become relatively smooth. I knew we were in deep water, maybe a half-mile out.

Another swell lifted me and I adjusted my bearings. Eve was only thirty feet from me. I expected joy, but instead saw a sad serenity embrace her. She looked directly at me and love filled her eyes. A bittersweet smile trembled onto her lips and grief shadowed her face. She slipped beneath a wave and was gone. I would have one slim chance.

Chapter 73
For the Greatest Good
Evelyn

The treacherous waters knocked me from the log and swallowed me in their ponderous mass and darkness. I could hear only frantic bubbles, fighting with each other to find the surface amid the turbulence of manic water.

I was pummeled like worthless debris while the violent currents and vicious waters dragged me deeper into the glacial blackness with brutal indifference. I had feared the waters for too long, and now our kinship was lost. The harmony we shared when I was a child was gone. We were strangers. The fairytale mermaid who once moved with grace and ease through the ocean was now only a woman lost.

Blackness possessed the waters. My skin burned from the cold and my arms and legs moved in slow motion. I beat at the water in hopeless hope. I believed myself lost deep below the surface when salt spray and a vengeful frigid wind slapped my face. I gagged on the water-filled air being forced down my throat.

My body writhed with pain, trying to separate the air from the salt water. For a moment, I could breathe again and looked toward shore. Against the faint light from distant homes, I saw Sam standing on the shore, searching the waters. I screamed for help, then was buried by a breaking wave.

I resurfaced and tried to swim out of the rip current, but the waves and eddies turned me until I was swimming straight out to sea. I faced shore once again and saw Sam at the top of a swell coming for me. *Why?* If he just stayed on the beach, I would be gone. Everything would be his: the kids, the house, the cars, the insurance money. Me, my secret, and his reason to hate me would be gone, with no one to blame.

Sam was closer. If I could get to him, I would be safe, but the cold, strong currents had stolen my strength. I was lifted by a swell and could see the house lights on the beach far beyond him. They twinkled in the salt spray like distant, unreachable stars. My heart cried with anguish. We would both drown and our kids would be orphans.

I screamed, "No, Sam! The kids! Go back!" But my plea floundered and drowned in the howl and sting of the malicious wind.

He might get back to shore—to our kids—without me. But if he tried to drag me back through the unrelenting waters, we would both die. He had to know that better than I.

He does love me.

I couldn't leave our children orphaned. He was close enough I could see the love we shared back in his eyes.

Peace came to me as the sea pulled my earthly body to my mermaid grotto. Within the darkness, the waters lifted my woman spirit into the heavens. The circle of my life was complete.

My children and my husband were in God's hands now.

For the greatest good.

Chapter 74
At Death's Door
Sam

I dove, aiming for the uncertain spot where Eve should be, praying that the currents wouldn't pull her from my path. The arctic blackness blotted out the meager surface light, casting a veil of perfect nothingness to conceal her. I dove deep, stretching my arms as wide as I could, desperately sweeping the water. Tide, currents, and darkness quickly stripped me of any reliable sense of depth or direction. By the growing strain in my lungs and the growing pressure on my body, I knew I was too deep and had been down too long, but I pushed deeper, frantic to find her.

Hair brushed my foot. I instantly folded back, plunging deeper into the blackness as my love overrode all of my instincts and experience. Even if I found her, I knew I was well over fifty feet down, and without a weight belt to drop and a wet suit for buoyancy, I had little chance of making it back to the surface alone—and none dragging Eve.

Something big hit my back pushing me deeper. When I instinctively turned to face what I assumed was a great white, my arm wrapped around Eve's limp body. I had found her, but was nearly out of air. I pulled Eve tightly against me, her beautiful soft hair caressing my face, reminding me of her wedding veil. I wanted desperately to see her face one last time. Hear her voice. Tell her that I loved her.

The shark skimmed my back again. Then I heard clicking noises.

Dolphins?

One bumped up against me and paused as if waiting. Tanya's words echoed in my mind. "Was that when the dolphin saved Eve? ... Quite a miracle, wouldn't you say?"

I had prayed for a miracle, but I never expected one. I

hooked one arm over the dolphin's back as I tangled my hand in my belt so that Eve's ragdoll body was bound to me.

The thought "GO" screamed in my mind. As if on command, the dolphin accelerated with such force, I would have lost my grip on it if my arm hadn't lodged in the unseen notch of his dorsal fin. I estimated our depth as the water pressure on my body decreased. *Sixty feet? Fifty? Forty?*

My mind fogged. My lungs were ablaze. I couldn't hold the sour air any longer. It was too late. The last of the air escaped my lungs, my grip on the dolphin loosened, and I began to slip into a dream world. Through the rushing water, I kissed Eve one last time.

When we breached the surface, my head snapped forward with a painful jolt. The dolphin paused. My vision narrowed and I slipped further into unconsciousness.

Eve's hair lashed my face, the sting pulling me from the twilight world that was trying to take me. Half conscious, I coughed out the burning water and shook my head violently to beat back the darkness. My mind began to clear.

I tightened my grip on the dolphin and lifted Eve's lifeless face from the water. My soul cried to God. Eve's angel charged for shore.

The squall line had passed and the full moon lit the white beach. Dozens of people were shining their flashlights out to sea and I could see emergency vehicles on the dunes winding their way onto the beach.

The dolphin didn't slow in the surf. When my legs hit sand, he rolled away and we tumbled. Everyone was racing toward us. I lifted Eve and carried her from the turbulence, laid her on the soft white sand, and began CPR.

Chapter 75
Mom?
Evelyn

I was four, and snuggled in the warmth of my mother as she cradled and rocked me in her arms. It was just her and me, bathed in the joy and love of the moment. The scent of her jasmine perfume filled me with peaceful reassurance. Her eyes sparkled with love and contentment. She was so young and so pretty. I wanted to stay in her loving arms for eternity.

But the image faded, replaced by the soft warmth and chocolate scent of Chris and Angela snuggled against me in bed. I remembered this night. They were four and five. Sam and I had been married less than six months when he went on a business trip, leaving me alone overnight with the kids for the first time. I had been worried they would want their daddy and just fuss and cry. But by the time the hot cocoa was finished, the Goodnight Moon game put away, and the Sesame Street video had ended, our hearts were joined. I was Mommy. They were my kids. We were a real family within our hearts. At that moment, my life was perfect. I didn't want the image to go, but the softness of their snuggles and the scent of chocolate faded.

The yellow glow of the angel nightlight warmed Grace's room as I rocked my just-turned-three baby girl in my arms. She had come to live with us six months earlier and every night she would wake screaming. Sometimes she looked so lost, I would cry for her, and she would ask over and over, "Where are my mommy and daddy?"

Every night, I would hold and rock my poor baby girl in the dim light of her room while softly singing her back to sleep with an old English song. "... Guardian angels God will send thee, All through the night ... In my loving vigil keeping, All through the night ... Breathes a pure and holy feeling, All through the night."

As I snuggled her this night, she fell into a peaceful sleep. After several minutes, she opened her eyes and looked into mine.

"Mommy said you are my new mommy."

In the soft light, the joy in her blessed smile lit her precious little face. She closed her eyes and slipped into peaceful sleep, the wondrous smile still gracing her innocence. I sat rocking her and singing for the rest of the night, my heart unable to part from her angelic presence.

The image faded, but the joy and peace remained. I was lying with Sam's strong arms embracing me, the house was quiet, and perfect contentment filled me. The smell of chocolate emanated from a near-empty box that graced my nightstand. I knew it was our eighth anniversary. The chocolates were horrible, but the kids had given them to us so I had eaten two and made delighted faces. Thankfully, Sam and the kids ate most of the rest.

Everything was so perfect. Everyone was happy. Mom was alive. And my secret was still a secret.

Once again, the image faded, and I stood in a kitchen filled with the scent of chocolate chip cookies and fried chicken. I remembered this place from my childhood. It was an older, two-bedroom apartment—small and tidy. Mom looked up from her journal and smiled at me.

"Come here, Eve."

I didn't remember this image the way I had the others. It was as if I had been sent back in time and was living a new experience. I wore the pink eyelet dress Mom had bought me a week after my father went away—my first one as Eve. I had worn it until there were no more mends or patches that could hold it together. I wouldn't let Mom throw it away, so she magically transformed it into a small accent pillow with silk ribbons and bows. It now sat, tattered and worn, in the top drawer of my dresser.

She was writing in her journal. The page was full, but my eyes settled on the last couple of sentences.

"Today Adam became Evelyn, my daughter. I love Eve and am happy for her, but I grieve for my son who is no more."

I looked up at her through my child's eyes with my adult understanding and saw the pain, love, and joy her heart held for me.

"We cannot understand the mind of God. In His infinite

wisdom, there is a reason for everything. I love you, Eve, and I will always be with you."

I hugged her, and her love filled my essence with peace and a knowing that everything was as it should be—that everything had indeed been for the greatest good.

I asked, "Is this Heaven?"

My body convulsed as if I had been kicked in the chest by a mule. My nerves burned and my frozen skin was impaled by a million needles.

I gagged. Someone rolled me on my side and stuck a plastic-glove-covered finger in my mouth to help dislodge my dinner and half the ocean. The people around me were faceless blurs.

Jasmine? Through the smells of ocean, plastic, antiseptic, and someone who needed a bath, I could still smell my mother's perfume as if she were standing next to me ... she was and always would be. The images of my past and of Mom had filled my heart with a knowing that God's love *is* infinite.

I gasped when they rolled me onto a stretcher, the pain pulling me from my warm memories. My eyes focused and I saw Sam standing over the paramedic. He seemed unaware of the water that slipped from his hair and glimmered as it ran down his face. His worried, love-filled eyes held mine. The blanket draping over his shoulders reminded me of a knight's cape—a fitting adornment for My Prince. My safe harbor. My Sam.

I smiled up at him. His eyes brimmed, and a quivering smile filled his lips. He knelt beside me, gently brushed the hair from my face, and leaned close as our lips and souls caressed. He whispered, "I'm sorry, Eve. You always have been a woman ... will always be *my* woman. I love you."

Our fingers intertwined as our eyes lingered. The Sam I loved had come back to me. In the depths of his soul, I could see the endless love we had always shared. I also saw the regret, the shame ... the fear that he might have lost my love.

As hurtful as he had been, it had been my secrets that had launched the tidal wave. But even as our hearts cried, the core love we shared had stood strong.

I reached up, gently touched his cheek, and whispered, "I love you, too."

Epilogue

Love Reborn
by Angela Irving

A year ago a mermaid drowned, in ocean fierce and deep,
Our father too was down below, their lives were fate's to reap.

We cried and prayed for safe return, while searching from the shore,
But banshee winds and demon waves, mocked us with "no more."

Man and mermaid beneath the sea, did share in one last kiss,
'Til angel came to set them free, from despair and deep abyss.

Three times the water took her, three times God gave her back,
Three times it is perfection, our world's no longer black.

I'm told that life is lessons, peace to the wise revealed,
On the beach, in the cold, through grace and love we healed.

In that painful lesson, I learned how quick we die,
And all that really matters, is the love our hearts untie.

Again a happy family, reunited in our love,
God's plan for us unfinished, absolution from above.

A mermaid in the water, diver and tadpoles too,
We swim and play together, the mermaid no longer blue.

Dad and Mom in harmony, father and son align,
We share, we talk, we laugh and sing, safe harbor so divine.

So now we live in harmony, well, mostly anyway,
For God and love, they opened hearts, I know our love will stay.

For God and love, they open hearts, for this, I always pray.

Autumn Moon Books

Reading Group Guide

Mermaid Drowning

a novel by

Terry Jacobs and Tiffany Jacobs

The Story Idea - From Start to Finish

The story idea for *Mermaid Drowning* originated with the television broadcast of *My Secret Self: A Story of Transgender Children.*

At the time, we were looking for a story that needed to be told; a story that spoke to us. The injustice and discrimination suffered by transgender children spoke loud and clear. These children and their parents want the same things we all want: the right to life, liberty, and the pursuit of happiness; to be safe and accepted; to be treated fairly and with dignity; to have equality under the law. Who doesn't want those things?

We began by researching the causes, manifestations, and life of the transgender child. We were pleased with the understanding and support that many people showed for them. We were deeply troubled by the ignorance and blind hate exhibited by others.

For a story to be real and compelling, it must examine both sides of an issue. With the goal of "equal time," we studied contradicting Christian doctrines and partisan political platforms. We wanted to understand the opinions, myths, and facts that each group used to support its position.

Research showed that unlike the Hollywood and media stereotypes, most transmen and transwomen live normal, productive lives with jobs and families.

Our first story ideas involved a transgender child as the central protagonist. This approach always led to questions of where her journey would ultimately take her – marriage, family, career, and religious faith. A fairytale ending for a child who finds love and acceptance within a closed community would be a lie.

By entering the life of Evelyn as an adult with a family, the reader has an opportunity to see the complex human needs, wants, and dreams we all share, as well as the challenges and discrimination that the transgendered live with.

It took us four years to research and write this novel. When other writers learn that we are a husband and wife writing team, many raise their eyebrows and with a degree of skepticism in their tone say, "And you're still married?"

There are rare times when we have to open the window and let some of the heat out, but mostly we work very well as a team, finding that the weaknesses of one are balanced by the strengths of the other.

Being the better researcher and having more time, Terry wrote the first outline, bloated with facts and short on plot. Tiffany expanded the plot and added complexity. We wrote and rewrote as the extraneous facts were edited out and the characters came to life. New scenes were added and old ones deleted or revised nearly beyond recognition. Characters who were thought critical to the story withered and died, while supposedly minor characters seized center stage.

One would write. The other would rewrite. Together we entered the world of Sam and Evelyn. We cried when Evelyn's mom died. We laughed at Barbara's cluelessness. And we felt deeply for Charley's mom as she tried to hold onto the son she loved, even as Clarissa struggled to become the girl she was inside.

After four years of research and writing, we penned the last words of the novel, "For God and love, they open hearts, for this I always pray."

We hope you enjoyed *Mermaid Drowning*. But more than that, we pray that you find understanding, acceptance, and love for all.

Reader Questions

1. Both Sam and Evelyn have secrets they hide from each other. How do you think this affects their relationship? Should couples have secrets? What kinds?

2. Did Evelyn have a right to hide her past? Why or why not?

3. Should Evelyn have tolerated Sam's lashing out at her, or told him to pack up and leave?

4. How does Sam's desire to never do anything he would be ashamed to tell his children shape his character, his actions, and his world? Do you share that desire?

5. Ashley literally throws herself at Sam as he struggles with his sexual identity and questions the worth of his vision of honor and integrity. Should Sam have had sex with Ashley? How would that have changed him as a person? Would that have changed the outcome of the story? In what ways?

6. Religious faith is a significant part of Eve's life, while Sam's faith is uncommitted. How do you think this affects their relationship? Does faith play a part in your relationships?

7. Is Brandon a villain or a man of deep faith and conviction who is willing to act on his beliefs? What is his motivation? Is he justified?

8. Georgette believes that God punishes us with natural disasters, birth defects, or illness if we stray from religious teachings. Do you agree or disagree? Why or why not?

9. Felicity met Mark the same day she broke up with Dwayne. Was her relationship with Mark a rebound or real love? Do you think it will last? Why or why not?

10. Evelyn is saved by a dolphin—her angel. Does God work miracles through the world around us, or is it just entertaining fiction? Why or why not?

Hard and Controversial Questions

1. *Mermaid Drowning* treats gender dysphoria and transsexuality as natural variations in human psychology, physiology, and expression. Do you agree or disagree? Why?

2. Is our gender identity formed by nature, nurture, or a combination of the two? Why do you believe that?

3. Evelyn kept her past a secret. Many transpeople argue that only by hiding their past can they live a normal life free of prejudice, hate, discrimination, and possibly assault or murder. If the only way for you to live a normal and safe life was to hide a past that many in your society found objectionable, would you? Who would you tell? Who would you not tell?

4. Intersexed infants have ambiguous genitalia—not wholly male or female. They are often surgically assigned a sex at birth and later treated with assigned sex hormones. Many of these children know they are not the gender assigned to their body. Should they live with the gender the doctor and/or their parents chose for them? Why or why not?

5. When a society is sexist, racist, religiously intolerant, or homophobic, to what extent is an individual's acceptance of that majority belief forgivable or excusable?

6. Cinnamon was murdered for being transgendered. Zack was murdered for being her friend. Hate crimes are epidemic in America. Why?

Acknowledgements

We would like to thank Jazz, Riley, Jeremy, and their families for their courage in bringing the subject of gender identity out of the closet and into our homes. Your willingness to invite the public into your lives through the ABC News and Barbara Walters special, *My Secret Self: A Story of Transgender Children*, was an amazing gift. Your stories touched our hearts and gave birth to this novel.

The encouragement of family is always important to success. We would like to thank Matthew, Sandra, Jonathan, Karen, and Lyn for your encouragement and support.

Our thanks to beta readers Gail, Jon, Julie, Karen, Lyn, Mary, and Steph, who waded through the first "finished" manuscript, which was filled with technical flaws, story problems, and scenes in desperate need of editing. The generous gift of your time and your insightful comments were invaluable in making the story the best it could be.

A special thank you to our writers' critique group: Anna, Anne, Jamie, Jesse, Mike, Susan, Tamathy, and Valerie. Your insights and comments helped us improve our writing, as well as ferret out problems with the story and characters.

We would also like to thank Dr. Phillip for his editing, encouragement, and instructive comments.

Lastly, while researching the physical, psychological, and social issues surrounding the subject of gender identity, we came into contact with many knowledgeable transgender individuals and compassionate advocates. They all helped advance our understanding of the subject. They all inspired us with their compassion, hard work, and progress in making the world a better place. We are eternally grateful to them all.

About the Authors

Terry and Tiffany Jacobs are a husband and wife writing team. They spent their childhoods in Southern California's San Fernando Valley, where they met and married. They moved to Northern California to raise their children, a daughter and two sons.

They currently reside in Oregon's Southern Willamette Valley, where they enjoy the lush forests, scenic beaches, and diverse ecology. They are working on their second novel.

Made in the USA
Charleston, SC
16 January 2013